Legend of the Five Rings™

T0023211

The GAME of
100 CANDLES

MARIE BRENNAN

ACONYTE

First published by Aconyte Books in 2023

ISBN 978 1 83908 215 3

Ebook ISBN 978 1 83908 216 0

Cover art by Shen Fei

Rokugan map by Francesca Baerald

Distributed in North America by Simon & Schuster Inc, New York, USA

Printed in the United States of America

9 8 7 6 5 4 3 2 1

ACONYTE BOOKS

An imprint of Asmodee Entertainment Ltd

Mercury House, Shipstones Business Centre

North Gate, Nottingham NG7 7FN, UK

aconytebooks.com // twitter.com/aconytebooks

Dragon Lands

SHELTERED PLAINS CITY

Phoenix Lands

Rokugan

CHAPTER ONE

Tanshu's cool nose touched the side of Sekken's hand a moment before Ameno's voice came through the door. "Little brother, the physician is here."

Surfacing from meditation felt like coming down to earth, like a heavy court robe being draped over Sekken's shoulders. When he meditated, he could forget his body, with all of its demands and betrayals. He could become just a mind – and then not even that. A self that, for brief moments, forgot its own existence, like the Shinseists encouraged.

Until someone interrupted, dragging him back to physical reality. Back to a world where his mother had found yet another physician to examine him, as if this one would have any more success than the half-dozen who came before.

Sighing, Sekken opened his eyes. Tanshu was at his side, alert and prick-eared, and Sekken scratched the dog's jaw. "Thank you." Interruptions were more welcome when they came from his sister, but advance warning made them less jarring.

Tanshu's tail thumped once against the tatami. Then he shifted out of the way as Sekken levered himself carefully to his feet – but not *too* far away, as if the dog could do anything should his master prove unsteady. "You're worse than my childhood nurse," Sekken grumbled, but Tanshu made no reply.

"Brother?"

"Nothing, Ameno. Tell Mother I'll be there shortly."

A soft rustle as his sister departed. Sekken rubbed his eyes and considered changing into something better than his current informal kimono. But no, if his mother had brought another physician to poke at him, they would hardly expect formality. And Sekken wasn't minded to waste energy he might not have, just to look more polished.

He felt solid enough on his feet as he slid the door open and stepped onto the veranda, but the cold air hit like a rebuke. Even with the winter shutters in place, closing away the sight of the gardens and sealing the veranda in dimness, there was a sharp difference between Sekken's brazier-warmed chamber and the atmosphere beyond his door. Tucking his hands inside the sleeves of his quilted robe, he hurried through his family's manor to the room where they greeted visitors.

His mother was there already, seated with the physician while a servant poured tea. "Son, this is Sir Makusa Naotsugu. I sent for him after your… difficulties yesterday."

My collapse, you mean. By now his mother was used to days where Sekken had to take a nap before lunch, then maybe another one after, waking up hardly more refreshed than he'd felt when he lay down. That level of difficulty was frequent enough that it hardly occasioned remark anymore. But yesterday had been one of the bad ones.

"Lord Asako." Naotsugu bowed to him. "I understand that none of the physicians you've seen have been able to offer much assistance, but I may be able to bring a fresh perspective."

"You can try," Sekken said as he knelt, "but forgive me if I don't hold out much hope."

His mother's mouth thinned in reproof, and Sekken grimaced. "Forgive me. I'm afraid my manners suffer alongside my health."

"As is to be expected," Naotsugu said. "Your lady mother gave me the history of your ailment. From the sound of it, your experience serving as a vessel for your honored ancestor Kaimin-nushi badly damaged your elemental strength. Naturally this will be reflected in your inner capacity as well as the outer. If I might examine you–"

Sekken pulled his wrist away when the physician reached for it. "You may not."

"Son!"

He scowled at his mother. "I know you mean well – both of you – but I'm tired of this, and it never produces any results. Some days I'm fine. Other days I'm not. There's no pattern to it, and no predicting whether the day will be a good one or bad. I've taken medicines; I've prayed to the Fortunes; I've practiced sixteen kinds of spiritual techniques. None of them make more than a temporary difference. It seems this is the price of what I did in Seibo Mura, and I simply have to live with that."

The mutinous set of his mother's shoulders said she was

far from ready to accept it. Sekken was her youngest child, and her only son. His whole life he'd been the sheltered one, doted on by his parents, encouraged in his scholarly pursuits. With his sisters' advantageous marriages and good positions, there had never been any need for Sekken to do more than glide through life, the privileged son of a fortunate family.

Until two years ago, when that serenity suddenly cracked. Back then, his family's big worry had been hiding the fact that a dog spirit was haunting him. Sekken had left in pursuit of answers... and he came back broken.

Naotsugu cleared his throat. "By your leave, Lord Asako, Lady Asako, I shall answer your bluntness with my own. I understand that all your previous physicians have looked at your ailment from the perspective of your elemental weakness. I am more concerned with the spirit your lady mother says has attached itself to you."

That startled Sekken out of the familiar rut of his thoughts. "Tanshu?"

At his side, the dog sat up. Unlike Sekken, he'd recovered well from his nadir in Seibo Mura, when the dwindling of the ancient ward he helped maintain had all but drained the life from him. When he chose to exert himself, he could become visible and tangible to other people. But right now, only Sekken could see him.

"The inugami, yes," Naotsugu said. "I know something of how such creatures are made. Through the greatest cruelty, starving a dog until it reaches the point of abject desperation, then cutting off its head–"

Sekken slammed one hand against the floor. "Stop. I've read the same scrolls you have, Sir Naotsugu – but unlike you, I've read a great deal more than that. I have no doubt that *some* heartless individuals have trapped the spirit of a dog in such fashion, forcing it to serve them. But that is not the only way. Like other animals, a dog can become an inugami through attaining great age, and such creatures can agree to serve a human witch. And after that witch, their descendants.

"A moment ago, you referred to my *honored ancestor* Kaimin-nushi. Now you turn around and suggest she was a horrible woman who tortured a dog. Which is it? Make up your mind!"

He fought to get his temper under control. This was, unfortunately, a side effect of being a witch; such people were notoriously unstable in their behavior. He hadn't felt any instability in Kaimin-nushi, on the two occasions when his body served as her vessel… but then, she'd been so great in life that in death, her soul transcended the underworld and became a minor deity. Sekken was just a layabout courtier who'd inherited her dog.

Naotsugu's face had gone rigid, and he bowed low. "Please forgive me, Lord Asako. I meant no slander to your ancestor. Only to suggest that your tie with this creature may be contributing to your recurrent weakness. However it was bound – with whatever good intentions the bond was formed – it may be harming you now."

All the air went out of Sekken. *Tanshu, harming me?*

The dog whined when Sekken looked at him. Certainly *he* was the picture of canine health, his cream and brown fur thick, his eyes bright. Could he possibly be feeding on Sekken's own energy?

No. You know what price you paid, and why. You just assumed you'd be able to recoup your losses afterward... but it doesn't work like that.

He could tell these physicians the full story, all the details he held back. Maybe then he wouldn't have to suffer through their visits anymore.

But that would mean telling his mother the truth.

He'd meant to. When he wrote up his initial report, though, to be carried from where he was recuperating at Ryōdō Temple back to Phoenix Clan lands, it had felt arrogant to put the focus on himself, on his own *noble sacrifice*. And scholar Sekken might be, but he was courtier enough to know how the tale would be spun. Instead of Agasha no Isao Ryōtora protecting Rokugan from the chaos and terror of the Night Parade, it would be all about how a valiant scholar of the Asako family saved Rokugan and Ryōtora alike, at terrible cost to himself.

Ryōtora had saved the Empire. Sekken had only saved Ryōtora.

But he'd told his superiors that Kaimin-nushi had rescued the other man, when Ryōtora attempted to give his life to end the Night Parade. That Sekken himself had merely served as her vessel.

It wasn't entirely false. Like Ryōtora – and unlike Sekken – Kaimin-nushi had been capable of speaking with elemental spirits. Without her assistance, Sekken never could have fed half his strength to Ryōtora, replacing what the other man had sacrificed. And for a time afterward, when the two of them rested at Ryōdō Temple, he'd thought he would recover. He *had* recovered, a little bit;

back then he didn't even have good days. Neither of them did.

Except that every day was good, when Ryōtora was at his side.

His mother leaned forward. "Son? Do you need to lie down again?"

The worry in her eyes cut to the bone. She hated seeing him like this, intermittently weak in body and mind. Even though her son had come home a hero, she would trade all his unexpected glory in a heartbeat if it would restore his health. Sekken couldn't stand the thought of her reaction if she knew the truth. *She would hate Ryōtora. She wouldn't mean to, but she would.*

"I'm fine," he said, and managed a smile. "Truly, I don't think it's Tanshu – but Sir Naotsugu, if you wish to examine him, I'll allow it. Just… not today. Please."

"Not today," his mother echoed firmly. "My son needs his rest."

Sekken remained where he was as his mother escorted the physician out. He wasn't as tired as he had been yesterday; meditation was one of the few activities that seemed to revitalize him at all. Sekken had practiced it dutifully in the past – a samurai child could hardly grow up in Phoenix lands without absorbing the habit – but now he meditated daily, sometimes more than once a day. Still, he wasn't in a hurry to get up.

It meant he was still sitting there when his mother returned. "My apologies," he sighed. "I can't even blame that on weakness, not truly. I've just gotten very tired of trying and getting nowhere."

"I know. But we can't give up." His mother knelt at his side and covered his hand with her own.

He gave her a rueful smile, more honest than the one he'd mustered before. "You've done an admirable job of finding physicians with discretion… but keep summoning new ones to poke at me, and sooner or later, the truth will get out."

Her jaw hardened. "Not if I have anything to say about it."

People already wondered, he knew. Anyone who came back from Dragon territory with such deeds in hand ought to be everywhere at court, toasted and feted and enjoying his newfound prestige. Instead Sekken had spent much of the last year as half a recluse, trying to conceal his weakness. Samurai, even soft-handed courtiers, were not in the habit of admiring men who never knew when they would need to spend all day abed, too exhausted even to read.

He felt his mother's weight shift, preparatory to rising, but then hitching short. Sekken frowned. "What is it?"

Her reluctance was visible. "I don't want to tire you."

"Let me judge what I'm capable of. Tell me."

She let out a slow breath. "The Dragon Clan visitors arrived in town last night. Agasha no Isao Ryōtora is here."

As much as Sekken wanted to bolt straight out the door, he knew better than to try.

For one thing, his quilted kimono was a disgrace, not fit to be seen in public. *Sekken* wasn't fit to be seen in public, not when he hadn't bathed in several days. His manservant Jun helped him with that, then brought cosmetics to disguise the stamp left by yesterday's bout of fatigue. Rice powder helped with the bruised skin beneath his eyes, and a charcoal stick, darkening his eyelashes, drew attention away from the shadows below. Rouge for his lips completed the illusion of health.

And if he was going out, he needed to fortify himself. One of the previous physicians had left instructions, on a scroll longer than Sekken's arm. Nearly everything he ate and drank was dictated by that scroll: ginger when his Fire became weak, vinegar when it was Water that lagged, a prescription for every condition. Since his Earth had failed him the previous day, it was a meal of roasted yams before he could be permitted to go anywhere.

Once upon a time, Sekken had liked roasted yams. But even his favorites palled when he *had* to eat them.

Nor was it only a matter of food. There was a five-herb medicinal tea for him to drink, washing down a rolled-up pellet of delicate paper on which a prayer had been inked. More prayers to recite at the family altars, first to his ancestors – including Kaimin-nushi – then to the Eight Great Fortunes. Meanwhile the servants scurried about, readying enclosed litters for himself and his mother.

At least that last part wasn't a concession to Sekken's ill health. His family had too much wealth and influence to walk through the streets for a political visit, especially when those streets were knee-deep in snow. They would be carried in proper style.

By the time Sekken was ready to leave, it was too late to catch Ryōtora at the Dragon Clan embassy. The servant dispatched to notify the ambassador of their coming returned with the news that she'd already gone with her guest to the governor's palace.

"Then that's where *we'll* go," Sekken said, before his mother could suggest they wait.

Her look said, *I hope you aren't making a mistake.* But they'd had that conversation before, and there was no point in repeating it. She merely nodded and called for servants to carry their litters.

Sekken was glad of the shelter as they headed through the gates of his family's mansion and into the city. The first real snowstorm of the winter had struck the previous day, and although the snow had stopped falling, the air was bitter and sharp. The swaying of the litter unsettled his stomach, but the pan of heated sand on the floorboards kept him warm. Hopefully that would stave off a relapse.

Because above all, Sekken could *not* allow Ryōtora to discover how bad his health still was.

Ryōtora knew perfectly well what Sekken had done, that night in Seibo Mura. And neither of them had been fully recovered when Sekken went back to Phoenix lands, late the previous autumn. Parting had been a sweet ache; during their time at the temple, it had been easy to pretend that neither of them had any obligation to family or clan, that they could simply bask in each other's company and share the little details of their lives that the supernatural chaos of Seibo Mura had given them no time to discuss. When Sekken left, before winter's snows could trap him there, he'd had every confidence of seeing Ryōtora again – though hopefully sooner than this.

But from that autumn until now, over a year later, their only contact had been through intermittent letters. And Sekken had taken great care to omit all mention of his problems from those letters. He remembered all too well how easily the peasant-born Ryōtora could fall into a pit of insecurity, questioning his right to the status of a samurai, much less whether he deserved to have his life saved at such cost… and that was when he thought the cost had been a one-time payment.

Under no circumstances can I collapse in front of him, Sekken thought as the litter stopped and was lowered to the ground. Eventually they'd have to talk about it; he was under no illusions that he could hide this from Ryōtora all winter. But the way to introduce the subject was not by toppling over at their first meeting in more than a year. And that went double when the meeting was at the governor's palace.

The journey there was a short one – hardly any chance for Sekken to risk a chill. When they exited their litters, he found the governor's steward had ordered great braziers to be lit in the front courtyard. The flagstones were already shoveled clean of snow, and between the sunlight and the fires, not even traces of wet remained.

Tucking his hands into his sleeves, Sekken followed his mother to the walkway outside the formal entrance. In the summertime, one could gauge how many people were waiting to speak with the governor by how many pairs of sandals sat in patient ranks. In the winter, however, servants whisked the shoes away to a nearby chamber, where another brazier kept them warm.

In the receiving room he found nearly a dozen samurai, two monks, and one well-connected merchant sitting or conversing in quiet tones. The official start of winter court lay only a few days off, and while the domain of a provincial governor could hardly match the glories of Imperial Winter Court, or even that of the Phoenix Clan Champion – which Sekken had suffered through twice – it was still an occasion for a great deal of political business.

To his great disappointment, though, none of those waiting there were Ryōtora.

Sekken's mother bowed politely to the room, then glided across the tatami to where a familiar woman sat. Kyūkai Province lay close enough to the border with Dragon lands to merit its own permanent envoy, a position Mirumoto Kinmoku had held for as long as Sekken could remember. A swordswoman born male, she was as resilient as good steel; in all that time, the only change he'd seen in her was a little more gray threading through her hair with each passing year. Sekken pitied whoever would eventually be assigned the task of suggesting to her that she might retire.

Normally Sekken liked talking to Kinmoku. The provincial governor, Asako Katahiro, was one of the strictest and most strait-laced men Sekken had ever had the misfortune of dealing with; Kinmoku, prone to earthy bluntness, tended to knock him off his stride. She often apologized for it, blaming her warrior training, but Sekken suspected that was as much performance as truth. Either way, it was entertaining to watch.

And sometimes she wielded it for the benefit of others. No sooner had Sekken and his mother made their greetings than Kinmoku nodded at him. "I hardly imagine you've come here to see me, nor the lord governor. You'll find Isao in the garden."

"Thank you," Sekken said, barely pausing long enough to punctuate his gratitude with a bow before he bolted out the door.

CHAPTER TWO

Phoenix tastes in garden design differed from those in Dragon lands. Although Phoenix territory lay every bit as far north, it wasn't as mountainous, gentling the harsh climate. They relied less on the stark beauties of stone and water, which could survive even the harshest freeze, and attended more to the elegance offered by bare branches and bushes draped in snow.

Ryōtora gazed at them, measuring his breathing. Despite the cold, he'd come outside to gather his wits. All too soon he would have to meet the governor of Kyūkai Province, and he was not ready.

A year wouldn't be enough to prepare him. He'd *had* a year, but everyone had assumed the negotiations over Seibo Mura would be finished long before now. While the village lay close to the Phoenix border, it was still in Dragon Clan lands, and therefore fell under their authority. Yes, a Phoenix had been involved with the problems there, but that wasn't the same as giving them a claim to oversee its future.

Except that, like the Shadowlands to the south, the Night Parade constituted a threat to the entire empire. A threat which had been contained once more... but it remained a matter of imperial concern. And the Phoenix, whose diplomatic position was stronger than that of the reclusive Dragon, considered spiritual affairs everywhere in Rokugan to be their concern. They'd managed to sway some influential ministers, so the official mandate was that the two clans must arrive at a mutually acceptable solution.

And Ryōtora's mandate was to help ensure that solution protected his clan.

When the door slid open behind him, he assumed it was Mirumoto Kinmoku or one of the governor's servants come to fetch him. He turned, an apology on his lips... and found himself facing a man both familiar and strange.

The whole journey to Phoenix Clan lands, he'd imagined his reunion with Sekken. Not one version, but many: would Sekken come to the Dragon Clan's embassy? Would Ryōtora call on him at his house? Even meeting here, at the governor's palace, in half a dozen different ways. Some of their reunions were amusing, others stiff with formality; one or two would have made them an instant scandal of the court.

All of them featured the wrong man.

Ryōtora remembered Sekken as he'd been when they first met, in the headman's house in Seibo Mura. Polished, courtly – at least by the standards of a rural mining village. But that was Sekken on the road, away from the comforts and refinements of home.

The man facing Ryōtora now made the one he'd met a

year ago look like a country bumpkin. His winter kimono was fine silk, pale blue with a snowfall of white embroidery dusting his shoulders and sleeves. His hair, shorn during the troubles, had only grown out to his upper back, and the pin holding part of it in a topknot was white jade, carved into an elegant curlicue. Charcoal and rice powder and rouge transformed his face into a cultured portrait: the face of a wealthy Phoenix courtier, instead of the scholarly enthusiast who'd let his own curiosity draw him into a battle against murderous yōkai.

Ryōtora swallowed hard. It wasn't that he suddenly doubted his memories, or that he believed Sekken had become a different man in the time they'd been apart.

But he'd only ever known part of that man. This beautiful, sophisticated creature was the rest – and Ryōtora didn't know what to say to him.

Sekken seemed equally lost for words. Had Ryōtora himself changed so much? He didn't think so. His clothing was certainly finer, dark green silk instead of practical cotton. But compared to Sekken – compared to everyone who would be at this winter court – he was a boulder, dropped infelicitously in the middle of a well-sculpted garden. As he had always been.

"Ryōtora," Sekken breathed, a smile breaking the porcelain mask of his face. His exhalation plumed in the cold air, and he tapped his chin with the folded fan he held. "No, forgive me. You're Lord Isao now, aren't you? Congratulations on your higher rank. I know I said it in a letter – I think I said it in a letter – but still, better to say it in person."

"It's nothing," Ryōtora said reflexively, bowing. "An empty title, nothing more. My clan has not yet decided where I can best be of use."

"Nor mine." The rueful turn of Sekken's mouth was more familiar, though it carried a shadow Ryōtora couldn't decipher. "I think we made it hard for them. Warriors are easy; when they distinguish themselves on the battlefield, you promote them to command more people. Or you put them in charge of a nicer castle. When courtiers do something politically useful, they get a more senior position in the bureaucracy. But what do you do with a lazy scholar who got himself mixed up with yōkai?"

"Give him somewhere more comfortable to laze about, I would think."

By Ryōtora's standards, that passed for witty banter, but this wasn't at all how he'd expected their first conversation to go. He wished, far too late, that they hadn't met here at the palace.

The shadow flickered back into view before Sekken tipped his face up to the sky. "If you arrived last night, you must have traveled through the worst of that storm."

In hindsight, Ryōtora had made a serious mistake. His eagerness to arrive in Sheltered Plains City meant he ignored the signs of impending bad weather on the final day – after all, weren't the Dragon proud of their ability to endure harsh weather? By the Hour of the Serpent, though, the sky had become a leaden plate, and soon after that the snow began to fall. He should have bowed to the storm and taken shelter somewhere, even if it was a farmhouse rather than an inn. But the road was well-marked, with no cliffs to slip off in the gloom, and so they pressed onward while Ryōtora's hands and feet turned to ice. It had taken him half an hour to thaw out once they finally arrived.

Rather than explain that he only said, "Yes, we did."

Sekken laughed. "Have you offended some great spirit of the sky, that you get dumped on everywhere you go?"

If Sekken had appeared courtly and elegant at their first meeting, Ryōtora had appeared like a sodden puppy. "Not every time. Only when I'm arriving where you are. Perhaps the spirits are doing *your* bidding, Lord Asako."

"Only one, and he doesn't control the weather. Can you see Tanshu still?"

"Tanshu?"

"The dog spirit. That's what I named him. Did I not mention that in one of my letters?" The rice powder made it difficult to tell if Sekken flushed, but the awkward shift in his weight suggested it. "I thought I had. I could have sworn I had."

Diplomatically, Ryōtora said, "Likely you did, and I simply forgot. I'm glad Ta– wait. You named your dog 'Cinnabar'?"

Now the flush was clear. "Yes. Well, sort of. It seemed fitting, since it was the cinnabar from Seibo Mura that let him reach me. But then I thought, no, I want a name for him that will acknowledge the tie to my ancestor. And then I figured out that I could write 'Tanshu' with a different first character, the one that means 'nativity' or 'to be born.'"

Ryōtora stifled a smile as the explanation staggered to a close. "Of course you did." For the first time since the door opened, it felt like he was standing with the Sekken he knew.

A man for whom language was an endlessly fascinating puzzle.

As if a veil had been whisked away, the inugami appeared at Sekken's side. It was a sign of how much stronger Tanshu had become; in Seibo Mura, Ryōtora had needed prayers to be able to see him. When the dog trotted over for a sniff, he realized Tanshu was not just visible, but corporeal. "Does he go everywhere with you?" Ryōtora asked, scratching behind Tanshu's ears.

"Why not? His claws don't scrape the tatami unless he's manifested physically, and he doesn't need to eat or – well, you know – so there's no reason for him not to. And people don't know if he's there or not anyway, unless I tell them."

"But they know about him?"

Sekken's quiet laugh was another cloud in the air. "Oh, yes. Now imagine belonging to a clan and a family renowned for their intellectual curiosity, and you'll have some sense of what my life has been like this past year."

Ryōtora had received glimpses, in the form of the letters they exchanged. The sweep of a brush on a page, though, was irretrievably inadequate for everything they wanted to say. Ryōtora had told Sekken the Agasha family daimyō rewarded his service with an estate in Kinenkan Province; he hadn't said how unqualified he felt to manage any such thing. Such doubts shouldn't be committed to paper, not when a letter had to pass through countless hands on its way to the intended recipient. Samurai were supposed to be honest and trustworthy, but that didn't stop the clans from monitoring communication across their borders.

They'd said nothing of their feelings for one other.

In Ryōdō Temple, it had been easy. The physician-monks there believed in the healing benefits of nature, so the two of them spent long hours lying in various gardens, sleeping to restore their strength, and talking when they weren't asleep. Their mutual weakness kept them from doing anything more than kissing, but it hadn't felt like it mattered. Surely there would be opportunity in the future.

Then they separated. And during that journey from Dragon lands, Ryōtora's escort had briefed him extensively on the political landscape of Sheltered Plains City... including the efforts of Asako Sekken's family to pair him with a spouse suitable to his new prestige.

The silence was stretching out, more awkward with every heartbeat. Then Sekken shook himself and said, "How is Chie?"

"She's well." Ryōtora's tongue stuck to the roof of his mouth. He ought to say that everyone's attention had turned to his younger sister's marriage: since the oversight of mountain shrines was usually passed down within a family, it was important for Chie to have children – assuming she could. The declining fertility of the Dragon Clan as a whole made that more of a question than it should be. But anything touching on marriage felt like a bridge that might collapse if Ryōtora stepped on it. Discussing Chie might lead to discussing Sekken's own marital prospects, and despite days of wrestling with that topic, Ryōtora still didn't know what to say.

"What of your father? Sir Keijun has moved to your new estate?"

Sekken managed the correction so smoothly, no one

overhearing them would have even noticed. It wasn't public knowledge that Dragon samurai had made a widespread practice of shoring up their own numbers by adopting peasant children. Ryōtora's birth father, Masa, remained in Seibo Mura with Chie; his adopted father, Isao Keijun, was the only one Sekken should refer to.

Perhaps he'd known that caution was necessary. The door slid open, and an elegant woman who shared Sekken's pointed chin bowed. "Lord Isao, I presume. I am Asako Fumizuki. Please forgive my rudeness in interrupting you, but the lord governor will be ready to see you shortly. And I fear I must retrieve my son."

"Lady Asako. I am honored to meet you at last." Ryōtora stepped back. The Dragon had sent formal thanks to the Phoenix for Sekken's assistance, but this was Ryōtora's first opportunity to thank Sekken's family directly. They'd nearly lost their son, all for Ryōtora's sake.

But Sekken caught his elbow before he could kneel and lower his face to the floor. "There will be time for proper introductions later. You don't want to keep the lord governor waiting."

Lady Asako was too well-controlled to raise her eyebrows at the presumptuous touch, and Sekken let go a moment later. Ryōtora wanted to argue, but the open door was letting cold air into the palace, and behind Lady Asako he could see Mirumoto Kinmoku waiting.

This wasn't the best opportunity for them to talk, anyway. Ryōtora needed time to absorb the reality of *this* Sekken, elegant and courtly. Time to imagine interactions more suited to the confines of provincial winter court.

"Perhaps you can visit us later," Lady Asako said, stepping aside. "We would be honored to welcome such an esteemed son of the Dragon."

"I would enjoy that," Ryōtora said, and, with a bow to her and Sekken both, went to do something he did not expect to enjoy at all.

"Rise, Lord Isao, Lady Mirumoto."

Ryōtora straightened from his bow. He and Kinmoku knelt in the lower half of the reception room, just in front of the small step up that demarcated the provincial governor's dais. The room glowed, the light of the lanterns reflecting off the gold-painted screens that lined the walls. The transom above the rise in the floor was intricately carved rosewood; so were the edges of the doors that concealed the governor's guards. The elegantly staggered shelves held lacquered boxes, a painted fan, and an agate statuette of one of the Fortunes, while the incense burner below the scroll in the alcove was sculpted jade. Ryōtora could only assume the calligraphy on the scroll was exquisite; he was hardly qualified to judge.

The entire setup could not have made him feel more out of place had it been designed expressly for that purpose.

He'd been in the formal reception room of the Agasha daimyō precisely twice: first when he came of age and passed the final examinations for his training, and a second time after the events in Seibo Mura. But as with gardens, Dragon tastes in decoration leaned toward the austere. Asako Katahiro was only a provincial governor, not even the daimyō of his family, and yet the sheer wealth on display here dizzied Ryōtora.

As did Katahiro's conversation, gliding through the opening pleasantries with sufficient ease that Ryōtora hardly had to do anything other than say "yes" and "no, not at all" and bow at the appropriate points. Sometimes Ryōtora managed these kinds of encounters just fine; other times he found himself tangle-tongued and bereft of words just when he needed them most. It didn't help that he knew courtiers did that on purpose, spinning the unwary around until they hardly knew where the earth was.

But Kinmoku had warned him about Katahiro's favorite trick. Thanks to her, Ryōtora caught the moment when the rhythm of the conversation wanted to push a "yes, of course" from his mouth.

"Forgive me, lord governor," he said instead. "I know there will be plenty of time later to discuss Seibo Mura. But the shrine there already has adequate oversight."

Katahiro's expression didn't falter. It was neither friendly nor stern, just a pleasant, noncommittal serenity. According to Kinmoku, he looked like that almost all the time. It took a great deal to push him over into open anger or sadness, and as for joy or amusement… "I'm not sure I've ever seen him laugh for real," she'd said. "I don't mean he lies; he just never lets go. Between you and me, I don't think he likes being governor very much. He's very, very good at it, though, so don't let pity lead you into carelessness."

Ryōtora couldn't tell if he'd phrased his objection gracefully enough, but he knew it hardly mattered either way. Katahiro said, "A matter as important as the imprisonment of the Night Parade can't be trusted to an unlettered peasant girl."

"Of course not," Ryōtora agreed. "Which is why my clan arranged for her to be educated by a teacher from the Mountain Song Temple."

"A monk!" Katahiro scoffed. "It took a priestess to create the ward, and a priest to restore it. A ward that draws on all five Elements – and no one has a greater understanding of such matters than an ishiken trained by the Isawa."

This was the main point on which the agreement had stalled for the last year. Bad enough that the Phoenix wanted to be involved in Seibo Mura; they wanted to send an *Isawa*. That family's knowledge and skill were surpassed only by their pride, their steadfast belief that no one in the Empire could handle spiritual threats as well as they could.

And although the Dragon and the Phoenix were generally on cordial terms, there were still points of friction. An Isawa overseer would be dropped into a village of Perfect Land adherents, followers of a religious tradition the Phoenix had outlawed as heresy in their own territory. An Isawa overseer would be in a position to note just how badly the Dragon had declined – something Ryōtora's clan was doing its very best to keep concealed.

Even without those complications, an Isawa overseer would still be an outsider. Someone from another clan, coming to do what they believed the Dragon incapable of handling on their own.

Ryōtora was grateful for Kinmoku's coaching. "He'll try to lure you into agreeing," she'd said as they prepared that morning. "He knows you're unused to the maneuvering of court, and you're the hero of Seibo Mura besides. If he can get *you* to bend, even by accident, then we'll have to follow.

But you can't offend him with your refusal, either – that's *also* a lever he can use against us."

A path along a narrow ridge, with a steep fall to either side. Ryōtora clenched his hands, then relaxed them, hoping his sleeves hid the calming gesture. Courtiers, he feared, saw everything. "No one questions the wisdom of the Isawa, lord governor. I hope they do not question the wisdom of the Agasha, either."

Katahiro paused just long enough to make Kinmoku inhale audibly. Then he smiled: a courtier's smile, broad and no deeper than the surface. "Of course not, Lord Isao. I meant only to welcome you to my city. Let us forget these matters for now; I'm sure winter court will give us ample time to discuss our clans' respective traditions."

All too much time. The path Ryōtora had to walk wasn't merely narrow; it was littered with traps. He could only pray for the wit and agility to avoid them.

CHAPTER THREE

It didn't take Sekken long to realize that, however out of place he'd felt in Seibo Mura, Ryōtora had it twice as bad in the city. At least in a rural village, Sekken could take refuge in the comforts and protections afforded by his higher status. Though Ryōtora's new rank elevated him over many of those at winter court, there were plenty more who yet stood above him ... and at heart, he remained a plain-spoken man from a vassal family, more accustomed to tramping about the countryside in observance of his duty than enjoying the pleasures of courtly life.

But Ryōtora couldn't serve his clan by hiding in the Dragon embassy. At winter court especially, he needed to meet other people, to socialize and engage in seemingly frivolous pursuits in order to win goodwill. Since he had precisely zero experience with that, Sekken felt it was his bound duty to help.

The problem was, he had to stop his own family from helping, too.

He couldn't avoid introducing Ryōtora to them. His mother, of course, lived in the city, and two of his sisters,

Ginshō and Ameno, were there for the season; he was lucky it was only the three of them. His father, his sisters' husbands, and his other two sisters with *their* husbands were all scattered across Phoenix lands right now, attending winter courts elsewhere. Naturally, those who were around wanted to meet the man who'd been part of such a momentous event in Sekken's life – and report to the others on what they found.

Under normal circumstances, the three of them would have been his allies. He could make introductions, then leave Ryōtora in someone else's safekeeping when he himself wasn't available.

Normal circumstances, though, didn't involve the risk that Ryōtora would say "your son gave me half his life, and that is a debt I can never repay."

While Sekken had managed to head that off at the palace, he knew better than to assume Ryōtora would give up. And he couldn't ask the other man not to say anything, not without explaining why – an explanation he hadn't yet mustered the strength to give. So Sekken had to keep the man entertained, *and* away from awkward conversations… all while maintaining the unpredictable balance of his own health.

Given the constraints, theater seemed like an ideal diversion. It was indoors, sedentary, and didn't involve talking much to other people, while providing fodder for later conversations. Unfortunately, Ryōtora seemed to have no interest in performances of any kind, whether the formal dramas of nō or the comic hilarity of kyōgen. Nor did he want to attend wrestling matches – an art that the Phoenix admittedly weren't renowned for, but then again, neither were the Dragon. Sekken even unbent enough to suggest perusing the wares in the city's main market, vulgar though that was, but met with an unyielding refusal.

"Incense?" Sekken offered, desperately scraping for an activity Ryōtora might enjoy. "They put the scents into boxes, and then you see if you can identify which boxes hold the same scent or guess at the components that went into it. Or there's, um, comparison parties–"

Ryōtora's brows knit together in confusion. "Comparison parties?"

"Yes, where people bring in things like seashells or roots. They write poems to go with them, and then the judges compare the specimens. You know, evaluating them for length and thickness and so forth – and yes, depending on who's judging and how drunk they are, it gets *exactly* as suggestive as that sounds. 'Oooh, I've never seen one this large and well-shaped before.'" Sekken waggled his eyebrows, then sighed. "But root comparisons happen during the Iris Festival, and that's months away."

He shouldn't have mentioned iris roots. It was too flirtatious, and the conversation got awkward every time it drifted in that direction. They had no opportunity to be private. Such limitations didn't necessarily stop people from having trysts – it was a good third of what winter court was *for* – but those worked better when...

When the people involved weren't Ryōtora and Sekken.

In Sekken's imagination a year before, it had seemed so simple. He would undertake to regularly inspect Seibo Mura, affording himself and Ryōtora plenty of opportunities to enjoy one another's company. But the village was a bone two dogs were fighting over, and with Sekken's health so unreliable, regular trips *anywhere* were impossible. Meanwhile, his family were doing their utmost to set him up with a politically advantageous spouse – a fact which Ryōtora almost certainly knew.

Neither of them had said anything yet. They'd never promised one another marriage during those precious, golden days when they could consider what they wanted for themselves. They both knew the obstacles in the way of that: while peasants might marry for love, lords rarely could. And now, under the scrutiny of winter court rather than free in the wilds of the Dragon mountains, nothing was simple at all.

"What *do* you do with your spare time?" Sekken asked, scrambling to keep the conversation from tripping over that cliff. "It can't be nothing but duty from morning to night." Surely it couldn't. Not even for Ryōtora.

The cut planes of Ryōtora's face had sharpened even more in the last year; he'd lost weight, and never had much to spare to begin with. But Sekken recognized their hardening as defensive embarrassment, not anger. "It isn't. I do like to read."

Memory swam up from the depths like a lost koi: Ryōtora perusing the library at Ryōdō Temple, then falling asleep with a scroll spread across his lap. A little too heartily, Sekken said, "You're in the right part of Rokugan for that! What do you like to read? I already know you'll read medical texts if there's nothing else on offer, but I doubt that's your first choice."

"I find the writings of Akodo no Atsuto Noriaya very thought-provoking."

Of course Ryōtora read moral philosophy for fun. Some of Sekken's despair must have shown through, despite his best efforts, because Ryōtora added hastily, "I also practice the way of tea? My father is a devotee, though his collection of utensils is not at all noteworthy."

Sekken couldn't blame his slow arrival at understanding on any weakness in his Air or Fire. He knew himself; he would have made the same mistake even before Seibo Mura. *Ryōtora isn't wealthy, you fool.*

Of course he didn't want to attend the theater or peruse the market stalls for trinkets to take home. Of course he lacked familiarity with different blends of incense, whose components could be very expensive indeed. While samurai were supposed to be above the petty concerns of money, that mostly meant that too many of them spent what they didn't have, chasing the pleasures and luxuries the world had to offer.

Not Ryōtora, of course. He of all people would know the limits of his purse, and keep stringently within them. Yes, he had an estate now... but given the state of the Dragon Clan, what did that mean? Was it a prosperous farm – or in their lands, more likely to be a productive mine – or a decaying manor outside a depopulated village? Even if the estate produced actual income, Ryōtora would be cautious about spending it.

Saying that out loud would only shame the man further. Offering to pay for things would be even worse. Sekken floundered for a moment. Then he said, "I have an idea. Come with me."

• • •

Sekken's plan did, unfortunately, involve extended proximity with his eldest sister. On the other hand, he defied even Ryōtora to have a meaningful conversation while playing kickball.

As he'd suspected, a game was in progress in the palace's western courtyard when he, Ryōtora, and Tanshu arrived. There often was at this time of day; with many samurai closeted in meetings, their bodyguards and escorts were left at loose ends. The sterner ones – and the lazier ones – sat cross-legged in readiness near their charges, but usually at least a few entertained themselves with a game.

"Ha!" The previous kick had lofted the ball off on a wide arc, but Ginshō lunged and managed to send it back with her toe. Sekken, watching, suspected Shiba Tanezane of having deliberately sent it wild. Kemari was supposed to be a cooperative game rather than a competitive one, the players working together to keep the ball aloft, but those two would find a way to compete over *breathing* if they could. They'd been rivals ever since their school days.

Spotting the new arrivals, Ginshō bowed herself out of the game and came trotting over. "Little brother! Did you need me for something? I hope you aren't planning on joining us." To Ryōtora she confided, "Whatever intelligence the Fortunes saw fit to give him, none of it wound up in his feet."

She couldn't have provided Sekken with a more innocuous excuse to bow out if he'd coached her beforehand. "It's true," he said mournfully to Ryōtora. "But you play kemari, right? I seem to remember a story about that when we were at Ryōdō Temple."

"You remember because the story ended with me in a fishpond," Ryōtora said wryly.

"No fishponds to worry about here!" Ginshō said, gesturing at the courtyard. "Come, show us what you can do."

It was a simple activity, friendly – since Ryōtora had no school rivals here – and absolutely free. Sekken even knew he enjoyed it. Why, then, did Ryōtora hesitate?

"I'll watch from over here," Sekken said, perching himself on the sunlit veranda with Tanshu at his side. Not coincidentally, it took him out of range of any objection Ryōtora might make. The man hesitated a moment longer, but Ginshō was hard to resist; within a few moments, she had him out on the flagstones, body poised to strike the ball.

Sekken breathed a sigh of relief. Social connections achieved, without him having to risk an expenditure of energy that might leave him flat on the ground. *Maybe I'll encourage Ryōtora to play kemari all winter. I wouldn't mind watching.*

Of course, watching called up pleasantly bothersome thoughts. The air might be cold, but soon the exertion would have Ryōtora sweating. Sekken had seen the other man in the bath, and his imagination conjured very vivid images of droplets sliding over that smooth–

"Lord Asako."

Sekken managed not to jump as a shadow fell over him. The newcomer knelt so he wouldn't be staring up toward the sun, and he swallowed a curse. "Lady Isawa."

Isawa Chikayū arranged herself so they were both looking at the kemari game, where Ginshō had just lobbed an easy shot toward Ryōtora. She was one of his mother's contemporaries, but no hints of age showed in her oval face, her perfectly coiffed hair. "It has been difficult to find you not in the immediate company of your Dragon friend."

"Is there some reason you're reluctant to speak in his presence?"

"Only that what I say touches on his mission here."

Chikayū wasn't the priestess the Phoenix wanted to send to supervise the village, but she was one of the most influential Isawa at this court. "I'm afraid the Dragon are rather immovable on that point," Sekken replied, keeping his tone light. "There's a proverb you may have heard, about mountains not stepping aside..."

"You misunderstand me. I am saying I might be able to help him."

Sekken didn't turn his head; he didn't want anyone thinking this conversation was anything other than idle chatter. His gaze remained on the swirling garments of the kemari players. "You don't support the idea of an Isawa overseer?"

A soft breath took the place of a laugh. "I think it would be a good idea, but I also doubt things in Seibo Mura will go wrong so rapidly that we cannot dispatch assistance if the need arises. The recent problems only occurred because we had no records of what Kaimin-nushi had done there so many centuries ago, and so the destruction of the old shrine passed without comment. That will no longer be a problem."

Assuming Mirumoto Kinmoku was doing anything like a good job, she'd probably made the same arguments. Sekken himself would make them, if there were any way for him to support the Dragon side of the debate without sounding unfaithful to his own clan.

For Chikayū to voice them now, she must have found some more valuable prize the Phoenix might attain. "Your trust in the Dragon honors them. What might they do to repay it?"

"Not them, Lord Asako. You."

The bright swirls of fabric abruptly tipped and swam. Sekken's fingers dug into his knees, and he didn't care if Chikayū would see and think it a reaction to what she'd said. *No. Not now.*

But his body didn't care what else might be going on. For days now his health had been cautiously good, tempting him to think that maybe it would stay that way. It had happened before… and every time, his body had eventually betrayed him. A hollow feeling grew inside, as if someone were scooping out the core of Sekken, leaving behind a frail husk.

He had to go home and rest. But he couldn't simply walk away mid-conversation.

At least his wits hadn't failed – not yet. He knew what Chikayū wanted; she'd first proposed it months ago. "You consider me enough of a prize to buy your support for the Dragon?"

"You cannot be certain any of your sisters' children will inherit your Tanshu after you are gone. And from what you reported, it seems as if Kaimin-nushi's line has entirely died out among the Dragon. If we are to keep that heritage alive, the surest way of doing it is for you to have descendants." Chikayū sighed, in an uncharacteristic show of softness. Her next words relaxed slightly from their formal diction.

"If there were any invocation to the spirits that could let you bear children, I'd offer you my son instead of my daughter. Unfortunately, there isn't. But I know you were involved with Chūkan Natsuko some years ago; you aren't *entirely* without interest in women."

Yes, he and Natsuko had indulged in a brief fling. What it had taught Sekken was that, while he could enjoy himself with women, they didn't engage his heart. He respected Natsuko, nothing more. Just like he respected Chikayū's daughter Miyuki.

Respect ought to be enough. It was more than some samurai got, when politics drove them into marriage for the sake of familial or clan alliance.

But Sekken had tasted more. In heart, if not in body.

That, as much as his health, was why he'd dragged his heels on the topic of a possible spouse. No, he and Ryōtora had never promised one another marriage. And Sekken couldn't fathom the idea of shackling the other man to himself as he was now, a constant reminder of the price paid for Ryōtora's life. But to go into a political match after finding out what true passion could be…

He could hardly remember what that felt like now. Everything had gone dull and flat, as if all hope of passion had burned out. Weariness was dragging at his shoulders, and experience told him that soon the drag would become a leaden weight. He ought to weigh Chikayū's offer, ought to calculate how likely the Dragon were to escape interference without her support, and whether he could resign himself to a perfectly unobjectionable marriage in order to get her on their side.

He ought to say yes, right now, and share the wedding cup with Isawa Miyuki before Chikayū discovered just what a broken-down nag she'd purchased.

Sekken couldn't face it. He forced himself to his feet, hoped his bow didn't look as unsteady as it felt. "I will consider your generous offer, Lady Isawa. If you will pardon me, I have just realized I forgot… something."

As excuses went, that one wasn't even transparent. Sekken, retreating from the courtyard, knew she would think his sudden flight was because he had feelings for someone else. And she wouldn't be wrong–

Damn it! He'd left without saying anything to Ryōtora. But turning back would take energy he couldn't spare, and he might as well strap a banner to his back saying "Here find what's left of Asako Sekken." Ryōtora would know. And dealing with his reaction was *another* thing Sekken couldn't spare the energy for.

A familiar litter waited in the front court. Sekken had walked to the palace with Ryōtora, from the Dragon embassy; in hindsight, he was a damned idiot for exerting himself like that. But his mother would understand if she came out and found her litter gone.

She would understand – and worry.

More things he couldn't face. Not right now. As his family's servants hurried up, Sekken poured himself into the padded box. He had just enough left in him to say, "Take me home."

CHAPTER FOUR

Sekken's family mansion was less imposing than the governor's palace, but not by much.

Ryōtora should have visited sooner. Although he'd been introduced to Sekken's mother and the two sisters who were in town, all of those encounters had been brief. The exception was the previous day's kickball game with the eldest sister, Ginshō.

Eldest sister. The phrase felt strange, in his mind and on his tongue. So few Dragon families had more than two children, maybe three. Sekken had no less than four sisters: an unimaginable blessing, not so very far west of here.

Ryōtora didn't know what had pulled Sekken away so abruptly; caught up in the game, he hadn't noticed the other man's departure. He'd merely turned and found the veranda empty. When he tried to excuse himself to go in search, Ginshō had made a laughing comment about courtiers and their busy lives, then dragged Ryōtora out to her favorite teahouse before he could find any reason to beg off. Sekken's eldest sister bore no small resemblance to a very friendly avalanche.

This mansion, though, presented a much less approachable face. Ryōtora's fine clothing and recognized name were enough to get him through the front gate; beyond it he found himself in a courtyard that, while much smaller than that of the governor's palace, featured a beautifully shaped natural boulder with a quote from the Tao of Shinsei inscribed along one of its curves. A few moments later, one of the doors slid open and a familiar man appeared.

"Welcome, Lord Isao," Jun said, bowing low. He had accompanied Sekken to Seibo Mura the previous year, although the Dragon had politely detached the servant before sending the two samurai to Ryōdō Temple. "It is an honor to have you here in Phoenix lands. Please, come inside; it is very cold out."

The weather was not as sharp as it had been, but Ryōtora was still grateful to step up into the brazier-warmed interior. "I asked at the palace this morning, and they said Lord Asako Sekken was at home today."

Jun bowed even lower. "Please forgive my rudeness in contradicting you, Lord Isao. I am afraid our young lord is not here."

"Did he go to the palace after all?" Ryōtora asked, wondering if he'd passed Sekken's litter on the street. "I can look for him there."

"No, our young lord had private business elsewhere. But please, warm yourself before you go. I would be delighted to bring tea."

Ryōtora had little experience of court, but he recognized

a polite dismissal when he saw one. Was Jun covering for something? The man was a commoner; it was considered acceptable, even laudable, for him to lie on behalf of his master. Was there really any "private business"? And did Sekken's absence now have something to do with why he'd vanished so abruptly the previous day?

Either way, Ryōtora would gain nothing by asking. Jun had been imperturbable in Seibo Mura; he would hardly be more easily rattled here, on home ground. Suppressing a frown, Ryōtora was about to decline tea when the door slid open again.

But it wasn't Sekken. Instead, Lady Asako Fumizuki came inside, while her maid shut the door behind her.

"Lord Isao," she said, with a gracious bow. "Please forgive our lack of hospitality, having no one here to greet you when you arrived. I only just returned, myself."

"Forgive my rudeness in showing up unannounced. I came in search of your son."

Her smile was that of a courtier, lips elegantly closed. "Of course. How regrettable that he is not here today. I myself have only a moment before I must be elsewhere; winter court is a very busy time."

And that, too, was a dismissal. Ryōtora inclined his head. "Please let your son know, if he asks, that I will be…" Where would he be? His only real choices were the Dragon embassy or the governor's palace. Mirumoto Kinmoku wanted him to try and make connections at court, using the prestige of his achievements to win support for the Dragon, but Ryōtora feared he was all too likely to damage their standing rather than enhance it.

Lady Asako touched her fan to her cheek. "It occurs to me – Lord Isao, I believe you have not yet had the pleasure of visiting our Kanjiro Library."

She would know, being the library's steward. Its reputation reached beyond Phoenix borders, but one needed an invitation to enter. While that might not be where Kinmoku most wanted Ryōtora, right now, it sounded gloriously safe. "I would welcome an opportunity to see its wonders."

A low desk sat in a corner of the room, with the accoutrements of writing laid neatly on its surface. Lady Asako crossed to it with a gliding stride and knelt gracefully, holding back her lavender sleeve as she wetted the ink stone and rubbed a stick of ink against it. Once that was mixed to her satisfaction, she wrote out a brief note.

"Here," she said, presenting it to Ryōtora. Her hand-writing was, he noted with interest, more efficient than elegant, but its blunt simplicity appealed to him. If it was true that one's calligraphy reflected one's spirit, perhaps he had more in common with Lady Asako than appearances would suggest.

"Thank you," he replied. "Will there be someone at the library to guide me? From what I have heard, the holdings are extensive, and I would hate to wander anywhere I should not."

Another close-lipped smile. "No part of the Kanjiro Library is closed to visitors, Lord Isao. We are different from the Isawa in that respect. Some scrolls reside in locked cases, due to their rarity or fragile condition, and those need permission for access, but you need not fear trespassing into forbidden areas. Still, there will be an archivist there who can guide you. In fact, I recommend telling him you want to visit the fifth floor."

Puzzled, Ryōtora said, "Why that floor particularly?"

For the first time since she came in, a touch of real pleasure lightened Lady Asako's serene countenance. "Because it holds our kaidan collection. I heard a whisper at court that the lord governor intends to hold a Game of a Hundred Candles in a few days' time. Do you have that tradition in your lands?"

Memory coalesced slowly. A courtly party his old lover Kitsuki Hokumei had mentioned, one he attended during his own schooling. "I believe so, though we call it a Gathering of One Hundred Supernatural Tales instead. A storytelling event, with lamps being extinguished as each tale is told?"

"Yes, that's it! We have a very good collection of supernatural stories in our library, should you wish to refresh your memory on any before the gathering. But there are many other things to read as well, should your interests incline in other directions."

Somehow Lady Asako had made Ryōtora drift toward the door as she spoke, without him even realizing. He wanted to stop and say what he should have said before, the day they met at the governor's palace, or during any of their brief encounters since then – but it would be inexcusably awkward now, when the conversation was on other matters entirely. And then she was bowing him out the door, bidding him enjoy himself at the library, and Ryōtora was outside the mansion's retaining wall before he could protest.

As the gate closed behind him, he couldn't help but wonder if Lady Asako had done that deliberately. As if she wanted him gone.

The Kanjiro Library wasn't too far from the mansion, but Ryōtora walked slowly all the same. While he'd been lucky of late – neither the snowstorm nor that game of kemari had flattened him afterward, leaving him unable to rise from his futon – he knew better than to trust that luck would hold. He ought to have refused the game, but by the time he realized what Sekken had in mind, it was too late for him to escape without giving offense.

He'd enjoyed playing. And that made it all the worse, that reminder of what he used to be able to do without fear of his body's betrayal.

And without fear of hurting Sekken. If the other man knew how weak Ryōtora remained... *He gave up half of himself for me,* Ryōtora thought, as he had a thousand times before. *He must never be made to feel it wasn't enough.* That Ryōtora was alive at all was a gift; to wish for more was unforgivable.

But could he make it through the entirety of this visit without giving away the truth? While still doing what the Dragon needed of him?

His clan had taken a risk, sending him all the way here. They knew his limitations, and it wouldn't do their political position any good for him to collapse publicly. If he was the hero of Seibo Mura, then he represented their ability to manage the place as they should. But the weight of his fame might be necessary for them to win concessions from the

Phoenix, and so Ryōtora owed it to them to do his best – however inadequate that might be.

The Kanjiro Library was difficult to miss. The low hill the governor's palace sat on lifted it above the rest of the city, but the library towered nearly as tall, a five-tiered structure that blended the features of pagoda and castle keep. Beautiful gardens ringed it, one for each season; buried amid the words Lady Asako had used to hurry him out the door were instructions for him to enter the grounds through the winter gate. Evergreen trees and stark rocks made Ryōtora feel briefly like he was home again, while actual snow blanketed mounds of white gravel meant to evoke snowbanks during warmer seasons.

The archivist inside accepted Lady Asako's note with a deep bow. "Would the visiting lord like a tour of the library, or does he have a particular collection in mind?"

Ryōtora ought to peruse the kaidan scrolls. Though he did know some supernatural tales, they tended to be the most common ones, stories everyone would have heard before. Granted, with the Asako being the most scholarly family in a scholarly clan, even more obscure tales might be well-known here – but still, he could *try* not to be utterly pedestrian in his choices.

On the other hand, how often would he get to visit a library of this grandeur? "A tour, if it isn't too much trouble."

The archivist was only too glad to show off the city's pride and joy. The ground floor held offices and rooms where authorized visitors could make copies of scrolls from the library's holdings, while the other four were dedicated to those holdings. The levels were named after the elements, as if the building were a five-ring stupa, and the scrolls held on each floor were themed to the element in question.

Which explained why the kaidan were held on the fifth floor. The Void was the realm of the unknowable: a suitable place for supernatural tales.

The Dragon were not without their own libraries, but even so, the massed ranks of shelves that rose around Ryōtora were impressive. The archivist claimed the library held over fifty thousand scrolls – more, Ryōtora imagined, than any person could read in a lifetime. Even Sekken.

The thought brought a smile and sadness both. Standing at the top floor after the archivist was gone, Ryōtora curled his hands into fists, then released them, trying to release the sadness at the same time. How many pleasant hours had Sekken spent in this library, on this very floor? These were the scrolls from which he'd acquired his encyclopedic knowledge of yōkai. Knowledge without which Ryōtora would likely have died in Seibo Mura, meeting an end from which no self-sacrifice could rescue him.

Those thoughts weren't helping, and neither was his usual calming trick with his hands. Tightening his jaw, Ryōtora headed for the section where the archivist had pointed out the kaidan scrolls.

Coming out from between the shelves, he almost ran straight into a petite woman. "Forgive me," Ryōtora said reflexively, stepping back and bowing.

"No, forgive me," the woman said. "I should be more careful."

As they both straightened from their bows, he saw why care was necessary. A strip of silk covered her left eye, and it didn't have the look of a bandage for a fresh wound. In fact, someone had embroidered the delicate outline of a butterfly where it crossed the socket.

"I am Kaikoga Hanemi," the woman said, inclining her head in introduction.

It wasn't just Ryōtora's body that periodically failed him; his memory sometimes went, too. "Forgive me; I am of the Dragon Clan, and I cannot recall which Phoenix family the Kaikoga are vassal to."

"You cannot recall because the answer is 'none.' I am not a Phoenix, but a visitor from the Moth Clan."

Horrified embarrassment bent Ryōtora back over in a new bow. "I should have realized! My sincere apologies, Lady Kaikoga."

"No apologies are needed. Even for a minor clan, our numbers are small. Most samurai go their lives without ever meeting a Moth. May I have the honor of knowing your name?"

Clumsier and clumsier. If he stumbled this badly at court, the Dragon's cause was doomed. "This foolish one is Isao Ryōtora. Agasha no Isao Ryōtora, that is." In his own lands, the clarification was unnecessary; that was why he'd assumed Kaikoga Hanemi had left the senior family off her own name.

She pressed her hands together in delight. "You are the one from Seibo Mura! The priest who saved it, I mean; not that you are from the village itself."

If anything in her manner had suggested she was knowingly implying the truth, Ryōtora might have prayed to the elemental spirits to let him sink straight through the floor. Fortunately, it seemed Hanemi had merely blundered, and now pink marked her cheeks. It eased some of Ryōtora's own embarrassment. "I was in Seibo Mura, yes."

"Lady Mirumoto Kinmoku told me about you," Hanemi confided. "In fact, I'm here as a guest of your clan's ambassador. She's the one who negotiated with the lord governor to gain me access to this library."

Ryōtora's brain was finally supplying him with information. That image embroidered on the silk over her eye wasn't a butterfly, it was a moth, and it marked her as one of the clan's dreamwalkers. They often covered one eye as a kind of sacrifice to aid their explorations of the Realm of Dreams, that liminal, spiritual place the spirit went to in sleep. Or some said they put the eye out entirely, though sacrifice of that kind verged on blood magic.

Standing on the floor dedicated to the Void, it wasn't hard to guess her purpose. "I take it the Kanjiro Library has a noteworthy collection of writings on the Realm of Dreams?"

"Not a large one," Hanemi said, adding with a touch of pride, "My clan's collection is the largest. But this place has the personal diaries of an Isawa who passed away about ten years ago, a man who conducted his own studies of that realm. I've been given permission to read them, and I'm hoping the lord governor will allow me to make copies for my clan."

Then a gleam entered her uncovered eye. "Might I prevail upon you, Lord Isao, to answer some questions? When you can spare the time. Your experiences with the leader of the Night Parade should also go into our library, if you are willing."

Startled, Ryōtora said, "Why? He was a yōkai, not something in the Realm of Dreams."

"What is a yōkai but a creature that slips free of our ordinary categories?" Hanemi asked, sounding very much like Sekken. "And consider: to the best of anyone's knowledge, the leader of the Night Parade is a unique creature, yes? You may find kappa in many rivers, kitsune in many forests, but nowhere is there anything else like that one."

She had the courtesy and the caution not to use Nurarihyon's name, even though it likely posed no danger. "True," Ryōtora said.

Hanemi nodded, as if he'd confirmed her point. "This is only a theory, mind you. But the Realm of Dreams is inhabited by creatures called baku – you know of them, yes?"

"I've seen them carved into temple pillars for good luck," Ryōtora said. Baku were usually depicted as strange, chimerical amalgamations of bear and rhinoceros, ox and tiger, and the long, curving snout of an elephant. "They're holy creatures, eating the nightmares of sleeping humans."

The twitch of her hand called that statement into question. "Some are good, and some are bad ... and sometimes, good or bad, they escape into this world. The founder of my clan theorized that some unique yōkai may actually be baku who took physical form here in the mortal realm. Or perhaps even that such is the fundamental origin of *all* yōkai."

"What about the animals that awaken as yōkai after

living for long enough?" Ryōtora asked, thinking of the cat spirit he and Sekken had encountered in Seibo Mura. He wondered if Sayashi would have found it flattering or insulting to have her nature as a bakeneko attributed to a dream. Then he laughed and rubbed his neck ruefully. "That's a debate better left to Asako Sekken. As are your questions, given that he's the one who actually looked at and spoke to the leader of the Night Parade."

"I would love an introduction," Hanemi said eagerly. "I've tried approaching his family, but it seems Lord Asako has been something of a recluse since returning home."

Ryōtora hoped his sudden twinge of unease didn't show. Sekken, a recluse? It was true that he didn't fit the usual model of a courtier, preferring to wake early and spend his time reading rather than indulging in social frivolities, but ordinarily he would leap at the chance to talk with a fellow scholar. Why would he or his family keep Hanemi away?

Maybe because she wasn't a suitable marriage candidate. No more than Ryōtora was, with the ink decreeing his elevated status hardly dry. But Ryōtora knew better than to dream of that, not when it would mean subjecting Sekken to daily reminders of how his sacrifice wasn't enough.

He didn't know if the maudlin wrench of his thoughts was the first sign of his inner elements unbalancing again, but either way, he didn't want to be in conversation with Hanemi while dealing with it. Bowing, he said, "I will look for an opportunity to introduce you. But I have kept you from your own purpose here long enough."

"As I have with you," Hanemi said, sounding guilty. "Please forgive my presumption in asking after your experiences."

"Not at all," Ryōtora assured her. "I would be happy to speak with you later – perhaps tomorrow." *Assuming I feel well enough.*

He escaped to the kaidan scrolls and sat with one open across a low desk for a long time, but he didn't read a single word.

CHAPTER FIVE

Asako Katahiro's palace contained many elegant places for gatherings: sumptuously decorated chambers, verandas overlooking sculpted gardens, the gardens themselves. But for the Game of a Hundred Candles, he needed something more atmospheric.

So it was that, as the short day drew to a close, Sekken followed his mother across the grounds to the dark-timbered mass of the Komoriyome Pavilion. Disused for years, ever since the death of the governor's grandmother, it stood secluded among trees to the northwest of the main palace.

Inside, he found many of the guests already there. This was intended to be a true gathering, with a full hundred tales told, but to include a hundred people would have lost the intimate feeling it was meant to evoke. Instead, there were twenty-five in total, each of whom would tell four tales. An inauspicious number... but for something like this, that was perversely appropriate.

Sekken might have wished the gathering to be just a little bit smaller. Then perhaps Isawa Chikayū would not have been among the guests.

She was too diplomatic to approach him directly, though he felt her cool gaze on him from across the room. He'd given her a weak excuse for his rapid departure the other day, once he'd recovered enough to write a letter, but his total absence from court would not have passed without comment. How much had she guessed?

"Lord Asako!"

Speaking of people who might have guessed... yet for all that, Sekken couldn't bring himself to be anything other than glad to see Ryōtora. The woman at his side was a stranger, but the band covering one eye identified her even before Ryōtora said, "May I introduce Lady Kaikoga Hanemi? She's a scholar of the Realm of Dreams, as you likely know."

"Yes!" Sekken said, brightening. "Lady Kaikoga, I'd heard you were in the city. I'm sorry we haven't had a chance to meet before now. I understand you're reading Isawa Minokichi's diaries?"

Her enthusiasm loomed larger than her physical stature. "Yes! Are you familiar with his work, Lord Asako? I'd love someone to discuss it with; the governor is far too busy for such things."

"I only know it second-hand, alas. I believe he had a somewhat scandalous reputation – something about indulging one's desires in dreams?"

The tilt of Hanemi's head politely disagreed. "An oversimplification, if you will forgive me correcting you.

He believed that dreams serve an important function, allowing us to say and do things that would be unacceptable in daily life. Rather like unburdening oneself to a geisha or a courtesan, but with the opportunity to act out those impulses in full. In his words, the Realm of Dreams is like the roof hole that permits smoke to escape, allowing the fire to burn more brightly."

It was still an outrageous philosophy. Moralists and Shinseists alike would argue that one should seek to transcend the Three Sins of desire, fear, and regret, not vent them – even in imagination. Rumor claimed Minokichi had eventually retreated entirely into dreams, preferring his life there to the burdens of reality.

"Son." Sekken's mother appeared at his elbow, interrupting before he could fall too deeply into the conversation. "Please forgive me," she said to Hanemi and Ryōtora, "but I believe the governor is about ready to begin."

Translucent paper screens divided the pavilion's main hall, separating it into two rooms. Katahiro gathered them all at one end, where cushions waited for the guests. For some of his entertainments there had been courtesans present to pour tea and play music, but their ostentatious kimono and flirtatious ways would have been out of place tonight; instead, he'd hired two geisha, one male and one female. They sat quietly in their elegant, subdued clothing as the samurai entered and Katahiro stood, spreading his arms.

"My honored guests," he said. "Tonight, we gather to acknowledge the fact that our world is far stranger and more mysterious than we can ever fully comprehend. Soon my servants will light one hundred lanterns and carry them to the room behind the screens. Each of us will tell a story of unsettling, even frightening events. When your tale is done, you will rise and go to the other room, where you will blow out one of the lanterns, then look into the mirror at the center of the room, before returning to us… if you can.

"For as the night continues and the light grows dimmer, they say the boundary between the mortal world and the realm of spirits thins. It takes courage to continue – but courage, after all, is one of the great virtues of the samurai. We will test that virtue tonight!"

At a clap of his hands, servants entered, carrying lanterns covered with blue paper. The female geisha bowed to the floor, then stood up.

"This humble one is Teishi," she said, "and my companion is Dan'ei, of the House of Infinite Petals. As the noble guests begin their journey into wonder, we present the tale of Youth and Age."

Dan'ei lifted his shamisen to his lap and struck a chord, while Teishi swept her sleeves in a graceful arc to assume her opening pose. As the servants lit the lanterns and carried them past the screens to the back room, she began to dance, switching deftly between the roles of the samurai lord riding in his carriage toward a distant town and the youth to whom he offered a ride, sheltered from the rain and the cold. At first their body language was distinct – one strong and stern, the other young and pliable – but over time, the latter became like the former, then passed into stiffness and palsy as the young man aged before the horrified samurai's very eyes.

Sekken didn't even realize the servants had begun dousing the lights in the main room until Teishi concluded her dance, now lit only by the eerie blue glow coming through the screens. He suppressed a shiver. It wasn't the tale that unsettled him; he'd heard it many times before. But to watch the geisha perform the weak, unsteady gestures of the now elderly passenger… *Will I, too, age before my time?*

She bowed herself back to her seat, and Katahiro said, "I will begin our journey into the night."

Sekken had never heard the governor formally tell a story before. He was too duty-bound to favor entertainments like this, where the nature of the stories told inevitably carried a whiff of the forbidden. As exemplified by his first tale, the well-known tragedy of the Peony Lantern Lovers: a young man who, even after being warned that his lover was a ghost, chose to stay with her instead of warding her off and saving his life. Katahiro told it competently, though not inspiringly. It was for his political acumen, not his oratorical skills, that he had risen to his current rank.

When he was done, he rose to his feet, and the two geisha began to play quietly upon their shamisen, plucking with their fingertips instead of a plectrum to give it a softer sound. Their music provided the guests with a diversion as Katahiro vanished behind the screens, the light dimmed infinitesimally, and he returned.

"Lady Isawa." He inclined his head toward Chikayū. "Will you favor us with the next tale?"

Ryōtora received the honor of going third. He, too, was no trained storyteller, but his deep, resonant voice made up for it, and the story he'd chosen suited his relatively monotone delivery. It concerned a figure who nightly stepped out of the scroll on which he was painted and traveled around the walls of the house, until a friend of the scroll's owner set up a trap. She re-rolled the scroll one night, imprisoning him in the wall, where he slowly faded from view.

Sekken hid a smile. Though the wording wasn't verbatim, he recognized which text Ryōtora had gotten the story from. A collection of original tales invented by Asahina Jiyun, not well known outside Crane lands. *Thank you, Mother, for letting him visit the library.*

For his own part, Sekken made a point of never telling the same stories twice at these gatherings. After all, what was the use of a lifetime spent reading if he couldn't draw on it to impress people? His first story was about a monk who went to learn from a famed and supposedly immortal hermit in the Spine of the World, only to discover that in her isolation she had become a kobukaiba. Sekken *had* practiced his storytelling skills, and he took some pride in making a few of the guests jump slightly when the hermit revealed her murderous yōkai nature.

Tale finished, he rose to his feet and headed for the gap at one end of the screens, walking in smooth time to the shamisen melody behind. Coming around the corner, he found himself in the lamp room.

The blue paper over the lanterns gave the room a chill look, despite the fire-warmed air. Some of the lanterns sat on the floor, others on stands; a few dangled from the ceiling, though never too high for a person to easily reach. Sekken chose one of the latter and blew it out, then crossed to where the mirror sat.

His own powdered face looked back at him, as it should. *No yōkai yet,* Sekken thought. There never had been at any performances of the Game of a Hundred Candles he'd attended before. But what had seemed like a harmless diversion in the past felt far more real now, in the wake of his experiences in Seibo Mura.

The others were waiting. Turning his back on the mirror, Sekken returned to the main room.

Tale by tale, the night wore on. Kaidan tended to be brief, but even so, a hundred stories made for a long event. Behind her mask of serenity, Sekken's mother was nervous; neither of them knew if he would be able to make it through the entire gathering. She'd insisted ahead of time that if he began to falter, he should signal her with a touch of his fan. *She* would be the one to feign sudden illness, accepting the shame of having to leave early – escorted, of course, by her son – in order to shelter him from public suspicion. But so far, at least, Sekken felt fine.

They were in the third round of stories when he noticed Ryōtora stiffening. Kaikoga Hanemi was telling another tale Sekken recognized, about a woman who sickened and died because the willow tree of which she was the spirit was killed. By the minute tightening of Ryōtora's mouth, Sekken could guess what was wrong. *He was going to tell that one himself.* To repeat it now would be gauche, an embarrassment for the Dragon.

Sekken cast about for a way to help, but nothing came to mind. He couldn't take Ryōtora aside and summarize a new tale for him. He should have warned the other man to prepare a few extra, just in case this happened. But when

Ryōtora came calling the other day, Sekken had been at Sir Naotsugu's house letting the physician poke and prod at Tanshu, with no conclusive result.

By the time Katahiro called for Ryōtora to speak again, it seemed he'd found an answer. "One day a great battle took place near a rural village," Ryōtora said, choosing his words slowly. "A peasant woman lost sight of her daughter in the chaos, and she feared the girl was lost. After the battle, though, the daughter came home... but she was changed. She no longer remembered anything – not her mother, not her brother, not anyone in her village."

Aoi, Sekken thought, recognizing where Ryōtora aimed. This wasn't out of any scroll; this was their own experiences, carefully rendered anonymous. Sure enough, Ryōtora continued on, with a monk revealing the daughter had been replaced by a bakeneko, a supernatural cat wearing an illusion of the dead girl.

A monk, not a priest. Nothing in the story marked it as having to do with Ryōtora or Seibo Mura. But looking at Ryōtora's solemn expression, Sekken thought, *he means this as a tribute. A way for Fūyō and her daughter to be remembered.*

How many of the stories told tonight had such origins, in the suffering and death of real people?

One by one the lamps were extinguished; bit by bit, the light grew dimmer. Only a few remained when Sekken's fourth story came due, but by their faint illumination, he saw Teishi, the female geisha, lean toward Katahiro and whisper in his ear, one hand coyly covering her mouth. Sekken already didn't like the smile that spread across Katahiro's face, even before the governor spoke.

"Lord Asako Sekken," he said. "Of all those gathered here tonight, only you have journeyed into a Spirit Realm. Tell us that story – the tale of the creature you vanquished there."

Sekken bowed to hide his gritted teeth. "My lord governor, it is not the right sort of tale for tonight."

"Does it not concern a monstrous yōkai?"

"Yes, but the mood is wrong. Tonight is for tales of the unsettling, the unresolved. That matter, I devoutly hope, is quite done with."

He knew even as he protested that it would do no good. Sure enough, Katahiro brushed away the objections with a flick of his fan. "Nonsense. We all crave something new, and this is the newest of all."

One did not lightly refuse the provincial governor. Marshaling his thoughts, Sekken ran over the events, quickly editing them into something like a reasonable narrative. A girl kidnapped away by yōkai and stashed in the cave of an ōmukade, a centipede large enough to wrap itself around a mountain. A decidedly unheroic man who made a mannequin of himself, dressed in his own clothing, with his own hair on its head. The head itself a hollowed-out turnip filled with spit, the only known weakness an ōmukade possessed.

He ended with the man and the girl fleeing, trying to give it something of the open-ended feeling many kaidan had – though obviously his own presence at the gathering gave the lie to that. As he traversed the passage that led to the lamp room, he wondered why Teishi had spoken to Katahiro just then. Was this request her idea? Or had the governor arranged it in advance, instructing her to make it look like her suggestion? Sekken had thought about it earlier, the fact that Katahiro didn't favor this sort of entertainment. The governor must have called the gathering for a reason. And what better reason than to show off his two most famous guests, men who had lived through their own terrible kaidan?

Only three lanterns remained lit. Sekken knelt to blow out one, then stood and forced himself to the mirror. His hair swung forward over his shoulder, still much shorter than it used to be: his sacrifice to kill the ōmukade. Assuming he'd even killed it.

In the chill blue light, his eyes looked like sunken pits. "I still look better than the turnip," he muttered softly, defiantly, and went back out.

Two people had not yet told their fourth tale: Ryōtora and Katahiro. And maybe Ryōtora had followed the same trail of thought Sekken had, because he didn't so much as twitch when Katahiro said, "Lord Isao. You, too, have had an experience unequaled by any at my court."

With most of the lanterns out, a chill had crept into the building. Sekken's hands were very cold. *If he tells that story – he'll tell the whole thing, the parts I left out, and everyone will know–*

Sekken couldn't interrupt the governor, though. He could only sit, stiff with dread, as Katahiro said, "Share your story with us. Tell us how you defeated Nura–"

"*Lord governor.*" Ryōtora's voice cut straight across Katahiro's, politeness be damned. He bowed low, but nothing about his posture was yielding. "It is not wise to speak his name – not at any time, and certainly not tonight."

"Are you afraid, Lord Isao?"

Ryōtora straightened, and Sekken recognized the set of his shoulders. It would not give way for anything. "My concern is for the safety of your city, your province, and your people. Courage is a virtue of the samurai; foolhardiness is not. I will tell a story, because that is the purpose of this gathering... but I will not tell that one."

One did not lightly refuse the provincial governor. But Ryōtora did nothing lightly.

This would do the Dragon no favors at court. Sekken wholeheartedly supported Ryōtora's decision, though, and for better reasons than covering his own tracks. To the people here, the depredations of the Night Parade were a fascinating novelty, an artistic trope come to unexpected life. They hadn't seen the fear, the pain, of the people it targeted. They hadn't seen the wreckage left behind.

The risk of calling that destruction forth again, not the risk of having his omissions revealed, should have been Sekken's main concern.

Katahiro scowled. Sekken was more interested, though, to see a flash of annoyance pass across Teishi's face. *It was her idea. Or at least she has an interest in making Ryōtora tell that story.* Why? Did she want to compose a song about it? Others had already done so, albeit without hearing the tale first-hand.

"Get on with it, then," Katahiro snapped, gesturing with his fan.

Ryōtora did, telling the story of the Resentful Bell, an artifact awakened by the curse of one of those involved in its making. It was a pedestrian choice, but by then, Sekken didn't care. He was ready for this gathering to be done.

Katahiro dragged it out, though. His fourth story was a long one, about a blind musician who went night after night to perform for a gathering of ghosts. When it was finally done, he rose and paced behind the screens. By then, with only one candle remaining, there was almost no light at all. Only the hours spent in the growing dimness let Sekken make out the governor's silhouette against the screens.

And then he couldn't even see that.

By tradition, the last candle was not supposed to be blown out. To do so was to invite the Spirit Realms in. And with the Night Parade having been mentioned – even if Ryōtora stopped the governor from naming Nurarihyon–

Sekken half rose, not knowing what he was about to do.

The doors banged open without warning, and light flooded the room. There was a sudden cacophony of noise, bangs and crackles and shouting, and Sekken was on his feet before he realized the shouts were cheers, coming from Katahiro's servants, standing outside the pavilion. They were the ones who'd flung the doors open, and the light was fireworks bursting outside, celebrating the end of the gathering. Katahiro, laughing, came out from behind the screens.

Sekken didn't feel like laughing. *A fine joke at everyone else's expense,* he thought grimly, seeing Kaikoga Hanemi lower her hand from where she'd clapped it over her mouth.

Ryōtora was at his side, having moved there in the dark. By the unforgiving set of his jaw, he was no more amused than Sekken. "Foolish games," he murmured, his lips barely moving.

"Yes," Sekken agreed, bringing his fan up to cover his mouth. "Welcome, alas, to the world of court."

CHAPTER SIX

Kinmoku was livid, as Ryōtora had known she would be.

"How can you insult the governor like that?" she demanded. "And not just insult him, but on the topic of Seibo Mura in particular. If you'd told your story as requested, you might have won us a degree of sympathy in the negotiations. From people like Isawa Chikayū, if not from Katahiro himself. But you couldn't even find a graceful way to refuse!"

She hadn't said anything the previous night after they left the Komoriyome Pavilion, and Ryōtora had foolishly allowed himself to think that perhaps it meant the incident would pass without comment. But Kinmoku, having slept on it, apparently woke as angry as she'd been when she lay down.

"I have no excuse," he said, not for the first time that morning. "But I will find a way to make it right. I- I will write to the lord governor. Offer to tell him the story privately, perhaps."

"After shaming him publicly?" Kinmoku said, scathing.

"It wasn't the story he cared about; it was the story in the context of an event he'd organized. It was the chance to call upon you, in front of others, and have you oblige him."

She was right, Ryōtora knew... and yet. "Lady Mirumoto," he said. The thought that had been nagging at him since the previous evening might only anger her more – but if he was right, it might also be an important detail. "Did it seem to you that the geisha prompted the lord governor to ask for those stories? Not only from me, but from Lord Asako Sekken. I am not certain it was his idea."

Kinmoku huffed. "You're still missing the point. Whether the idea was Katahiro's or not is irrelevant. It became his, the moment he made the request. The whims of a geisha don't matter."

Of course they didn't. Geisha might be artists, but entertaining for money put them into the lowest rank of society. While their trade didn't leave them spiritually impure like butchers, torturers, and executioners, it also didn't give them any rights in relation to samurai – especially not high-ranking ones like Asako Katahiro. Teishi could only whisper suggestions in the governor's ear and hope they caught his fancy.

But Ryōtora was sure she'd done exactly that. The question was, why?

He wasn't the only one asking that question. An hour after Kinmoku brushed him off, her chief clerk, Sankan Yoichi, found Ryōtora as he struggled with his sixth attempt at an apology letter to the governor. "Lord Isao, Lord Asako Sekken has come to speak with you."

Ryōtora abandoned the letter with more haste than was

quite seemly and went out to the receiving chamber where Sekken was pacing. "Lord Asako," Ryōtora said, bowing. "What brings you here?"

It was, unfortunately, too much to hope that he'd come to offer advice in smoothing over the rift with the governor. But Sekken looked excited – excited, and a little peeved. "Look at this," he said, thrusting a slip of paper at Ryōtora.

Mystified, Ryōtora unfolded it. Two large characters were inked on it, with a syllabic gloss marked above them.

A gloss he recognized from the night before.

"You and I," Sekken said, "need to pay a visit to the House of Infinite Petals."

Ryōtora hoped Sekken couldn't tell this was his first time visiting the licensed quarter of a city.

It wasn't that he found them objectionable. Licensed quarters housed not only prostitutes and their more highbrow cousins, the courtesans, but many kinds of entertainers, including actors, musicians, dancers, and geisha. All of those, however, were luxuries for the wealthy, be they samurai or merchants. Ryōtora had never had the means to enjoy such pleasures on his own, nor the kinds of friendships and connections that would see him invited there at someone else's expense.

For a whole host of reasons, he was glad Sekken had arranged litters for them both. The wind today was ice-edged; the litter sheltered him from both that and the risk of tiring himself by going on foot. The tiny window in the box's side also let Ryōtora peep out at the licensed quarter, indulging his gaping stares while no one else could see.

Gaudy boards leaned out from the eaves of the theaters, advertising the performances and performers offered there, while tempting smells and equally tempting warmth wafted from the noodle stalls and hot pot restaurants. Winter court brought a great many samurai to the city, and even more merchants to siphon money from their purses.

The geisha house, however, lay down a quiet and unassuming side street. Cool, refined elegance was the style of their trade; not for them the ostentatious signs and clothing so abundant elsewhere in the quarter. The gate was dark-stained cypress – and closed.

Climbing out of his litter, Ryōtora said to Sekken, "Won't we have trouble getting in? I, ah… I understand one needs an introduction to gain access to this sort of place."

Sekken was kind enough not to call attention to the tacit admission of inexperience. "One does, but don't worry; my family have hired geisha from this house before. In fact, that's why I asked my mother about Teishi. I don't remember her from before I went to Seibo Mura, but my mother says she's been a favorite of the governor's since she began appearing at events last winter."

If there was cause for suspicion in that, Ryōtora couldn't see it. At his frown, Sekken said, "*No one* had heard of Teishi before last winter. Not here, and not at any of the other houses, either – not that they would accept anyone who abandoned her first loyalty. Which made me ask: who goes from nowhere to a full geisha without any visible apprenticeship?"

The question was rhetorical; he rang the bell before Ryōtora could respond. After a moment, the gate opened to reveal a stocky woman with two hafted truncheons thrust through her belt. The door guard bowed perfunctorily and said, "The day is too young, my lords. If you come back at the Hour of the Monkey, we will be glad to receive you."

"We're not here for entertainment," Sekken said. "I am Asako Sekken, and I need to speak with Teishi."

Another bow, no more heartfelt than the first. "Please forgive this mere guard, but unless your lordship has a prior arrangement with the mother of the house, you have come too early."

Sekken made an inarticulate noise and leaned forward. "I'm not here for a performance, you fool. I only want to talk to Teishi. And not because I'm besotted with her or anything like that, either. Do you have any idea what your house is harboring?"

His voice was rising, enough to catch a curious glance from a water-carrier passing by the mouth of the lane. Intervening hastily, Ryōtora said, "Please, may we speak with the mother of the house instead? It is presumptuous, I know, but we would not be here were our business less urgent."

That suggestion brought Sekken back from the edge he'd been approaching. "Yes, the mother of the house," he agreed, one hand dipping into his sleeve. "And your cooperation in not telling Teishi that we're here."

Ryōtora stiffened when Sekken's hand made a discreet movement toward the door guard. Atsuto Noriaya's writings had touched on this, questioning whether the practice of samurai giving gifts to clerks and lords was, in truth, anything more than a veneer over base bribery. But it was Ryōtora's first time encountering the base form quite so baldly.

"Thank you," Sekken said to him after the gate closed. "I… that was badly done." He passed one hand over his face, sighing. "I have no desire to separate myself from Tanshu, but I fear it's true that witches of my sort aren't as well-controlled as other people. It's making me a liability at court."

"No more so than I am," Ryōtora muttered.

Sekken grimaced in sympathy. "Katahiro offended the Isawa a few years ago when he supported his niece leaving her husband. The husband richly deserved it, but the Isawa still lost face, and they've been making Katahiro regret his decision ever since. For the sake of his family and his province, he needs to make amends somehow, and Seibo Mura gives him a way to do that. So he's striking hard at you in particular."

Because he knew Ryōtora was vulnerable – if not quite how badly so. Ryōtora couldn't ask Sekken for help, though, not against his own clan. That was already more information than he should have offered, though Kinmoku presumably knew it, if only Ryōtora had thought to discuss it with her. Court was like a scroll someone had overwritten a dozen times, leaving a tangle of words he couldn't begin to read. And yet, without that history, how was he supposed to manage?

That wasn't a question Sekken could answer for him, not in the few minutes they had here. The two men stood in silence until the door guard returned and bowed them inside.

She guided them to what Ryōtora suspected was a small administrative building, separate from the rest of the complex. Inside, a gray-haired woman who still carried herself with a geisha's practiced grace waited with tea. "My lords, I apologize for making you wait. Rest assured, I will chastise my guard for her impertinence to you, Lord Asako. Your family are valued patrons of this house."

Valued patrons could not be treated like merchants come to conduct business. Ryōtora sat through a round of tea and light conversation before the woman who ran the House of Infinite Petals said, "I understand you have a problem with one of the geisha under my roof?"

"I fear *you* may be the one with the problem," Sekken said. "Mistress… how long has Teishi been with you?"

"She made her debut last winter."

"Yes, but what about before that? Was she an apprentice here in your house?"

The woman covered her mouth with a long-fingered hand, politely hiding her delicate laugh. "Such questions, Lord Asako! You know the world of flowers and willows prides itself on discretion."

Sekken's gaze flicked to Ryōtora, who felt a bit like laughing himself. *So, I'm to play the uncouth outsider? I suppose that's one role I can manage.*

"Mistress," he said, "we have reason to suspect that Teishi is, in fact, a bakeneko."

She didn't recoil in shock, nor make any protest at his words. In fact, she laughed again, this time with more honesty and less poise. "Oh, I told her the name would give it away eventually!"

For all his courtly control, Sekken almost gaped. "You *know* about this?"

"It's one of the old stories of the House of Infinite Petals," the mistress said, lowering her hand. "One of the very first geisha here, over two hundred years ago, was a cat spirit. The very same one, in fact. So you see, my lords, that it's difficult to answer the question of how long she has been here; the answer is much longer than one would expect!"

Sekken put down his teacup with an ungracious clink. "Mistress, I'm afraid we must speak with this Teishi. Tell her Asako Sekken and Agasha no Isao Ryōtora are here – though I suspect she already knows."

Ryōtora waited until the door had slid shut, leaving him and Sekken alone with the geisha, before he said, "Hello, Sayashi."

She didn't look like he remembered, but that was because in Seibo Mura, she'd worn the face of a dead girl. Now she was a young woman, perhaps in her early twenties, dressed in a lined winter kimono that, while a sober mist gray in color, was still of fine silk. It was a far cry from the peasant in patched cotton he'd known before.

Her true form was that of an enormous black cat, the size of a snow leopard. Her walk held a hint of that swaying grace as she crossed over to where the mother of the house had sat and dropped to her knees on the mat. "Bother. You weren't supposed to guess."

"If you didn't want us to guess," Sekken said, "you shouldn't have named yourself with the characters for 'lucky paw.' And you shouldn't have made Katahiro ask for our stories."

Sayashi lifted her lip in a delicate sneer entirely out of

place in a geisha's expression. This early in the day, her cosmetics were minimal, and her hair was in a simple knot rather than a formal arrangement. "*You* should have told that story properly."

She directed her words at Ryōtora, who scowled. "If you thought I would share the tale of that battle under such conditions–"

"Not *that* story." Sayashi had a remarkable knack for seeming to thrash her tail even in human form. "The one about that girl, the one whose place I took. Aoi."

Confused, Ryōtora said, "I didn't want anyone to know it was a story from Seibo Mura."

"Why would I care if they know where it came from? I'm talking about the part where you found Aoi's body. Where *I led you* to her body, and even was nice enough to burn it so you wouldn't have to sully yourself."

His irritation faded. *In other words, the part where you provided help.*

Ryōtora could have made several replies to that. Sayashi had done nothing to save Aoi while the girl was alive, and she'd spent days lying to Aoi's family, passing herself off as Fūyō's dead daughter. Although she wasn't as malicious as some yōkai – certainly not as evil as her nekomata mother – she wasn't exactly a paragon of virtue, either.

But perhaps that made the small steps all the more important. While recuperating at the temple, Sekken had told Ryōtora about Sayashi's history. Lucky Paw: she must have chosen the name because she used to be a marushime neko, something akin to the "inviting cats" whose sculptures decorated many homes and businesses, one paw raised. For her good deeds she'd been rewarded with the chance to reincarnate as a human, but seeing that as an insult, she'd refused the offer in disgust. "Perhaps," Sekken had said, "she's working her way back toward that. I hope so, at least."

Now Sekken drew a sudden breath, then bowed low to Sayashi. "I fear I have insulted you as well, master. In telling the story of the ōmukade, I made no mention of how you guided me through the Enchanted Country. It is an unforgivable lapse on my part."

His willingness to honor her as his teacher had been part of the bargain that led to her providing that guidance. Sayashi sniffed, but his unprompted apology seemed to have mollified her. Enough so that Ryōtora ventured to ask, "Why are you here, Sayashi? Why pass yourself off as... as a human?"

Faint though his stumble was, Sayashi heard it. "If you're implying I've taken the place of another dead woman, I haven't."

"I'm glad to hear it. But still, why?"

"And why *here*?" Sekken added.

One shoulder rose in an elegant shrug. "Here is as good as anywhere else. And I've been here before, as I think you've heard. It's interesting to come back and see how things have changed. Or haven't."

Sekken hummed under his breath. "I see. So it has nothing to do with the fact that *I* live here."

"Why should it?"

Her answer came a little too readily, and by the sharpening of Sekken's gaze, he noticed that as well as Ryōtora did. "Only that I remember the conversation you and I had in the Enchanted Country, master. I thought perhaps I might have piqued your curiosity."

Ryōtora knew that Sayashi had once refused reincarnation as a human, but either his memory was failing him again, or that particular conversation was one Sekken hadn't shared with him. By the way Sayashi's mouth thinned, though, she knew exactly what he meant.

Pursuing that opening, Sekken added, "If so, it would make sense that you'd come to where I live, to see the proof of what I spoke about. The pleasures of having a community, family, people to stand at your side."

"Hah!" Sayashi's response was no gracious, refined laugh; it was a snap of derision as much as humor, and punctuated by her hand slapping the mat. "You think I'd want to model myself on you, chase your life for my own? You take such pride in those people at your side, as if you can put all your trust in them – but you haven't even told them the truth about yourself. Have you?"

Sekken stiffened. Sayashi's sly look drifted toward Ryōtora. Bewildered, he said, "If you mean the fact that Lord Asako's family is seeking a good marriage for him, I am well aware. And despite what is between us, I do not begrudge it. We both have our duties, after all."

Sayashi laughed again. "See how the wolf bites at him!" she exclaimed. It sounded random, but the hiss of breath through Sekken's teeth said otherwise. "No, little Dragon, that's not what I meant. It was all over court for a time... how Sekken helped his ancestral spirit give you *her* strength, so *she* could save your life."

Those words made even less sense. Oh, Ryōtora could

follow what she meant – but not *why*. What reason would Sekken have to tell a false story, hiding his own sacrifice?

Before he could ask, Sayashi rose gracefully to her feet and bowed to them both, in a mockery of courtesy. "Thank you for honoring me with your visit, my lords. I expect I will see you again; the lord governor does enjoy my company. Until then, may the Fortunes keep you well."

She shuffled out the door with refined, mincing steps. No sooner had it slid shut behind her than it opened again, this time on the stern silhouette of the door guard. Wordlessly, she escorted Ryōtora and Sekken to the side street where their litters still waited, and closed the gate firmly behind them.

Unclenching his jaw, Ryōtora said, "I need an explanation."

Sekken passed one bony hand over his face. "Yes," he mumbled into his palm, then lowered it with a sigh. "But not here."

Not in the licensed district, where anyone might overhear. "My clan's embassy?" Ryōtora suggested.

"Not nearly private enough," Sekken said. "Come on. I know a suitable place."

CHAPTER SEVEN

Sekken had made more than his share of visits to the city's main temple to the Fortune of Longevity. The second physician his mother had hired was an Asako priest assigned to the temple, and the third was a monk of the same order, in the hopes that their divine patron might be able to do something for him. That was after the treatments offered by their family physician had produced no results, apart from the suggestion that Sekken might have angered the Fortune by preserving Ryōtora's life beyond its destined end. Backward logic, to Sekken's mind; surely in all the Heavens, the Fortune of Longevity would be the most pleased by saving someone's life. But it never hurt to make offerings, and so he'd gone weekly ever since.

It meant he knew the lay assistants there well enough to seek one out after he and Ryōtora purified themselves at the entrance. "Is there a chamber currently unoccupied that Lord Isao and I might make use of?"

She showed them to one of the cells used to house patients overnight. It was no bigger than a tearoom, only four and a half mats, but the rooms to either side were empty, giving them as much privacy as Sekken could reasonably hope for. The lay sister bowed herself out and slid the door shut, closing the two men into a space that suddenly felt awkwardly intimate.

But not in a way that prompted enjoyable thoughts. Not with Ryōtora's face set in the hard lines Sekken remembered all too well from before. The other man had looked like that when it came out that Sekken was haunted by an inugami, that his hunt for a witch in Seibo Mura was more than mere idle suspicion.

Sekken was all too aware of the similarities. Once again, he had kept a secret from Ryōtora.

No – *was keeping* a secret. He suspected Sayashi didn't know the rest of it, or she would have flaunted that, too. Which meant he might get away without telling Ryōtora the rest of the truth.

He shouldn't be thinking about *getting away with* anything at all. But Ryōtora was already under so much strain, dealing with the politics of winter court; Sekken couldn't bear the thought of adding to it. Not when doing so would hit Ryōtora where he was most vulnerable, the part of him that believed he didn't deserve the gifts and opportunities he'd been given.

Besides, Sekken was managing remarkably well today, despite the long hours spent at the Game of a Hundred Candles. If he was careful, he might be able to ease through the rest of winter court without any disasters. Without Ryōtora finding out about his health.

A foolish hope, and he knew it. He'd thought that before, and he'd always been disappointed.

But the coward deep within his heart was willing to grasp at any straw, if it let him put the truth off just a little longer.

He'd let the silence stretch out too long, and now Ryōtora broke it, his deep voice flattened of all its resonance. "Why haven't you told people what you did?"

"I have!" Sekken said. "Mostly. It isn't untrue that Kaimin-nushi saved you; without her, I couldn't have done anything."

That was a weasel's response, squirming away from the truth. Sekken wished Tanshu were there; even if the bond between them made him more impulsive than he ought to be, the dog was still a comfort. But he'd known how Sayashi would react if he showed up with the inugami at his side, and so Tanshu waited at home. He had to answer without that support. Eyes averted, Sekken said, "But… no. I haven't told them what I gave you."

Half my life. And all my heart. Which was why it hurt so much to sit here, just out of arm's reach, and to feel like Ryōtora had never been further away.

Disbelief roughened the other man's reply. "That's the *what*. I don't understand the *why*."

"Because the rest of it is enough! Rescuing Chie, serving as Kaimin-nushi's vessel – I don't need more recognition than that."

"But you did so much more! What I owe you–"

"Is a lever they'll use to pitchfork you straight into a trap you can't walk out of!" Sekken could hear the click of his mother's tongue at his terrible metaphor, but in that moment, he didn't care. "You're already struggling to convince Katahiro that the Dragon should be trusted with sole oversight of Seibo Mura. What do you think he would

do if he knew you owe me your life – not my ancestor
working through me, but *me*, Asako Sekken? What do you
think Mirumoto Kinmoku would do? Would she not feel
honor-bound to make some concession to the Phoenix in
return?"

"Maybe it's a concession we *should* make!" Ryōtora flung
back.

Of course he would think that. Reading moral philosophy
in the mountains, with no experience of court and its
merciless grasping for advantage. "Half my life isn't worth
betraying your clan's secrets. Or do you *want* the Isawa
chasing Perfect Land heretics up and down the province?
Finding out that the Dragon can't even keep up their
numbers, that you're making up for it by–"

He stopped himself before the rest of the words came
out. For all the good it did him.

"By adopting peasants en masse," Ryōtora said, in a
stripped tone. "Like me."

"You deserve it," Sekken said, hoping his eyes could
somehow press his desperate sincerity into Ryōtora's heart.
"You know I believe that. And while I doubt every Dragon
samurai with your background has your noble spirit, the
same is true of many who were born to this rank. But will
the overseer that's assigned to you feel the same way? Will
they protect that secret, or announce it for all the Empire
to hear?"

He drew in what felt like the first deep breath in hours.
It would have been just his luck to feel that cored-out
sensation in his gut, the leaden weakness and creeping fog
that would leave him fit for nothing but meditating flat on

his back. But for once, his body and mind were supporting him when he needed them.

No. He couldn't tell Ryōtora the rest of it – not until the matter of Seibo Mura was settled. Otherwise Ryōtora's morals would push him right into disaster. *See how the wolf bites at him,* Sayashi had said. The wolf was the code of virtue samurai were expected to follow, and Ryōtora's obsession with upholding it. But duty to his clan was part of that way, too, and Sekken had to make sure that remained Ryōtora's foremost concern.

Ryōtora stood abruptly, as if he couldn't bear the serenity of kneeling any longer. "I have to tell Mirumoto Kinmoku, at least. She is our senior representative here. The choice of whether or not to acknowledge this debt should be hers." *Not yours*: the words echoed, unspoken, in the air.

The other man's hands tensed, then released. He added, "You've been blocking me from telling your family. Haven't you?"

"Yes," Sekken admitted.

"The choice of whether to tell them is yours," Ryōtora said. Then he bowed and left, closing the door gently behind him.

That parting comment lodged like a barbed arrow in Sekken's heart – as Ryōtora had no doubt meant it to.

He had plenty of reasons not to share the full tale with his family. All the political reasons he'd given Ryōtora, along with the personal ones of embarrassment and shame. But if he didn't...

Then he would feel the unspoken judgment, every time

Ryōtora encountered them at court. The other man would know he was continuing to lie.

Given a choice between *that* shame and the other, Sekken knew which one he preferred. And he had a thought for how to deal with the politics.

He was in luck. Because there was to be an incense gathering at the palace that evening, his mother was home, standing like an overgrown doll while two maids dressed her. They'd only gotten as far as the under-kimono; the elaborately embroidered outer layer waited on its stand, along with the heavy formal sash, a vibrant design of silver threads and pine-dark green. The maids were draping his mother in the middle layer as Sekken entered with Tanshu at his heels, preparing to tie it in place with cords.

His mother's main duty his entire life had been the Kanjiro Library, but she hadn't achieved her coveted position through random chance. She was good enough at reading people's moods to cast one glance at Sekken and tell her maids, "Leave us for now. There is plenty of time before I must go to the palace."

Once they had departed, she said, "I take it your suspicions about that geisha were correct?"

Sekken had almost forgotten about Sayashi. "No. I mean, yes – she's the bakeneko from Seibo Mura. It doesn't really matter, though. I mean, it does, but that's not why I've come to speak with you."

His scattered reply darkened his mother's gaze. Years of schooling were supposed to endow his tongue with eloquence, but he'd shown precious little of that lately. More proof of what he'd lost the previous year, and now he was about to make it worse. The least he could do was exert himself to speak well, even if he paid for that exertion later.

With courtly movements, Sekken knelt on the tatami and bowed until his forehead hovered just above his hands, placed to form a triangle on the mat. "Mother, I have a confession to make. I have not shared the full truth of what happened to me in Seibo Mura – how it is that I came to be as weakened as I am now."

His mother's indrawn breath was the only sound in the room. That, and the steady pulse of Sekken's heart.

"Although I relied upon the aid of Kaimin-nushi," Sekken said, "our ancestral spirit was not the one who saved Ryōtora. It was my decision... and my own strength that I gave to him."

Now he couldn't even hear his mother's breathing.

"*Your* strength," she whispered at last.

Still bowed, Sekken said, "He gave everything of himself to the elemental spirits, in order to restore the ward. His Earth to the earth, his Water to the water, his Air to the air, his Fire to the fire. And Void, of course, is always one, and nothing at all. His sacrifice was absolute and unhesitating. But I felt that Rokugan needs such people – that it would be a great loss for this one to die, when he might be saved. So, with the aid of Kaimin-nushi, I gave him half my Earth, half my Water, half my Air, half my Fire."

Another pause, longer than before. Then his mother said, "Sit up."

The maids had applied rice powder to her face before beginning to dress her, but Sekken thought his mother would have been pale even without it. "So it was not the spirit's presence that did this to you," she said. Her courtly training stood her in good stead; her voice did not so much as waver. "It was that Dragon."

"Ryōtora did *nothing* to me," Sekken said, as firm as the earth itself. "He was prepared to die. What I did was entirely my choice." For once he didn't feel weak… and part of him, thinking of the strength Ryōtora drew from his moral convictions, wondered if this would turn out to be the key. If his elemental strengths had been so out of balance because of his deceit, and by telling the truth, he might put them right at last.

You would have to tell more truths than this one to achieve that goal.

He pushed that thought aside.

With absent-minded grace, his mother tucked the front of her under-kimono beneath her knees and sank to the floor, the untied middle layer pooling around her. Sekken knew that look in her eyes; it was the calculating distraction of a courtier. "Then the Dragon owe us a great deal more than they've admitted. Do they know of your sacrifice? If they do and they've been concealing it, so much the worse for them. Once we tell the lord governor–"

"You will tell him *nothing*."

The hard blade of Sekken's declaration slashed through the tether of her thoughts, snapping her back to the present moment. "What?"

"You will tell him nothing," Sekken repeated. "Why do you think I approached you in private, Mother, instead of declaring this in open court? If I wanted to cut the Dragon delegation off at the knees, I could very easily do that myself. I want nothing of the sort."

Her painted mouth thinned. "Son, the oversight of that village constitutes the best opportunity we've had in three generations to investigate the heresies festering in Dragon lands."

"Spoken like an inquisitor."

She recoiled. Inquisitors had caused trouble for the Kanjiro Library more than once, demanding to examine certain texts, on one occasion arresting an archivist for questioning after he showed too much interest in acquiring a scroll that purported to describe the ancient, uncorrupted form of blood magic. She had no love for the inquisitors, and Sekken regretted his riposte... almost. "I will not let what I did be reduced to a political bargaining tool. I told you because you deserve honesty, and I have not been giving it to you. That is my shame. But if you tell Katahiro – if you make *any* attempt to use this against the Dragon – then I swear by the Little Teacher himself that I will shave my head and retire as a monk."

His mother dismissed that with what would have been a fan flick if she were holding one. "Don't be dramatic."

"I'm not," he said steadily. "I am completely serious. I cannot imagine showing my face in court again, knowing my sacrifice was cheapened for such purposes. I would rather withdraw from the world and spend my remaining days in contemplation of the Tao."

It would probably be the best thing for him anyway. Once Sekken explained his condition, a monastery would exempt him from the strenuous labor monks were expected to engage in, and meditation was about the only thing he could reliably do anymore. He should have considered it as soon as he realized he wasn't getting better.

But his family would lose him. Shinseist monks officially died to the world and began new lives when they took the precepts, and while some bent that principle to the breaking point and beyond, Sekken wouldn't. And although his family was moderately pious, he knew his mother couldn't bear the thought of surrendering her only son to such a life.

Her face had gone mask-like. Sekken kept his own expression steady. Now was not the time to let her see doubts – and in truth, he had none. The cynicism of these negotiations sickened him, even though it was nothing more than the politics he'd been trained for. Of course, his clan cared only about quashing Perfect Land heretics and the other doctrinal irregularities the Dragon were notorious for. As Isawa Chikayū had admitted, Seibo Mura itself didn't need constant Isawa oversight. The village and its secret were just a lever for other goals.

"You love him."

It was the first thing his mother had said in what felt like a century, and it caught Sekken off guard, though it shouldn't have. His mother knew his inclinations, and the way he'd been dancing attendance on Ryōtora was probably transparent all on its own. "I would like to say I would have saved him even if I didn't. That would be the nobler response. But I don't know for sure... because yes, I do."

Her eyes closed, intensifying the impression of a mask. "You know you cannot marry him."

Sekken had performed that calculation many times.

The Dragon hardly ever married out anymore, not for generations; what others attributed to their reclusive ways, he knew stemmed from the need to keep what people they had. So, any such marriage would have to involve Sekken leaving his own clan. Politically it would be a gift to the Dragon, at a time when the Phoenix were trying to wring concessions rather than make them. Spiritually, Chikayū wasn't wrong about what would be lost if Sekken had no children. And with his health in such a parlous state, his only real hope for the future was to marry well, into a family that could support a man with his limitations.

He wondered how much his mother knew, and got his answer when she said, "You could achieve many of your goals if you married Chikayū's daughter."

Sekken was all too aware of Tanshu sitting quietly at his side, the pivot on which so much of his life turned. Marrying Isawa Miyuki meant that Chikayū would get the tsukimono-suji inheritance into her bloodline, the Dragon would get her support for independent oversight of Seibo Mura, and Sekken would get a comfortable future.

"Do they know?" he asked. *About me. About what they'd really get.*

"Not in full detail," his mother said. "But Chikayū, I think, has begun to suspect."

Of course she had. It was a miracle his weakness hadn't become common knowledge already. And once it did, the number of families lining up to marry Sekken to their offspring would shrink abruptly.

It really would be better for him to retire to a monastery. But that wouldn't help Ryōtora.

He knew what Atsuto Noriaya's writings would say.

His heart a stone in his chest, Sekken promised his mother, "I will consider it."

CHAPTER EIGHT

Ryōtora knew he ought to climb back inside the litter after leaving the temple and command the bearers to take him to the Dragon embassy. But that enclosed space, which had seemed so sheltering on the way to the House of Infinite Petals, now felt like a trap. A courtly luxury, a reminder of how unready he was for this world.

You're already struggling to convince Katahiro, Sekken had said. He wasn't wrong. Ryōtora was supposed to be the weight that tipped the scales, the hero whose presence shook the Phoenix loose from their demands. Instead, he'd offended the governor and made everything worse. The Dragon were so weak at court, Sekken had to lie just to help them.

Ryōtora had enough awareness to recognize the self-flagellating spiral of his thoughts. But as he waved off the litter-bearers and began walking toward the embassy, hands tucked into his sleeves for warmth, he lacked the will to pull himself out of it. He walked at an old man's pace, creeping along the streets, because he didn't dare risk anything faster. And his mind was an old man's mind: he thought he knew the way, but when he glanced up, he was disoriented, one corner looking too much like the next. Nothing was familiar. The more he tried to remember the routes he'd traveled before, the more the details turned to sand and ran between his fingers. In the end, humiliated, he had to stop at a bookstall and ask for directions. The embassy turned out to be just a block and a half away.

And once he was through the gate, he had to stop again. *I was going to do something. Talk to someone.* Probably Kinmoku. But about what? The governor? Ryōtora was going to apologize to him. Write a letter. Had he done that already? He remembered trying; he couldn't remember if he'd finished.

The sound of his name brought his head up. How long had he been standing in the courtyard? Long enough for him to become chilled, and for Kinmoku to find him. Or someone had sent for her. "I was going to talk to you," he said vaguely, clawing for the reason.

Kinmoku had been warned about his condition. "Get inside before you freeze," she said. Her tone was half irritated, half concerned, which Ryōtora suspected made her sound very much like a mother. He'd never had a mother, not really. He'd left behind his peasant family when he was still an infant, and Keijun's own wife passed away just two years after the adoption.

While his mind swam through that murk of reminiscence, Kinmoku had taken him inside. A brazier gave much-needed respite to his face and hands; he sat cross-legged to warm his toes with his own thighs. He wasn't tired, but his thoughts still felt half frozen. *I should leave winter court,* he thought. *Before I do my clan more harm. Before Sekken realizes what's going on with me.*

Sekken. Court. That was what he'd wanted to talk to Kinmoku about.

He ought to be graceful about it, but grace was in short supply even when he felt his best. What came out of his mouth was, "Do you know what Sekken did?"

"Lord Asako?" Kinmoku's posture drew up, a swordswoman's wary readiness. "Has he given insult? Or disgraced himself?"

"He saved me. Not the story he's been telling everyone..." Ryōtora grasped for the specifics, lost them, and gave up. "He sacrificed half of himself for me. In Seibo Mura. But he's been lying about it."

Kinmoku relaxed. "Oh. That. Yes, I know. It was in the report I received last year."

"But–" It was like adding two columns of numbers that ought to match and didn't. "Why haven't you said?"

Her eyes pressed briefly shut, then opened again. The look she directed toward him was one of pity. "I was wondering why the Phoenix didn't press that advantage. Apparently, we have Lord Asako to thank for it. If they didn't want to use it, though, I was hardly going to remind them. We have enough difficulties as it is."

Her words made Ryōtora feel even more exhausted. Not in body this time, but in heart. "Sekken gave the same justification."

"Don't judge me," Kinmoku said, her voice hardening. "I've served here in Phoenix lands for as long as you've been alive. If I held myself to your pure-hearted ideals, we'd be asking Katahiro's permission before we so much as sneezed along our eastern border. If you try to sabotage us by spreading the truth Lord Asako has not seen fit to share, you'll be confined to this embassy for 'spiritual contemplation' before you can open your mouth."

Ryōtora's shoulders sagged. *The mountains never learned to step aside*: it was a common proverb among the Dragon. But there was no mountain inside him, no firmness he could stand on. As if someone had stolen the ground out from under his feet when he wasn't looking.

"Yes, Lady Mirumoto," he said. It came out flat and dead.

Her expression softened once more to sympathy. "Get some rest. You'll feel better once you have."

Which just went to show how little she understood his condition. But Ryōtora went anyway.

After an hour's meditation, he discovered that he had not in fact finished writing his apology to the governor, at least not in any form worth sending. Pulling together the scraps of energy he'd managed to gather, Ryōtora shamefacedly requested Kinmoku's assistance. With her aid he was able to draft a reasonable missive, then sent it off before crawling into bed.

When a messenger arrived early the next morning, both of them thought it was a reply from the governor. But the man who came in was the archivist Ryōtora had met at the Kanjiro Library, whose bow had the crispness of anger. "Lady Mirumoto. Lord Isao. Please forgive me for bothering you at such an hour, but I regret to say this is a matter your clan must address."

"What matter?" Kinmoku asked, her expression carefully neutral.

"Lady Kaikoga Hanemi," the archivist said. "She came here as a guest of your clan, and it was through your patronage that she gained access to our Kanjiro Library. As such, I'm afraid we must consider you responsible for her behavior."

His words chilled Ryōtora, but the inevitable question had to come from Kinmoku instead. "What has she done?"

The archivist said, "She has broken into the library."

Kaikoga Hanemi was on the fifth floor of the library, where Ryōtora had met her before – and she was sound asleep.

"Nothing wakes her," the archivist said, as Ryōtora reached out to touch Hanemi's shoulder. "We've called her name, made loud noises, shaken her; none of it has any effect. I presume she is engaged in some exploration of the Realm of Dreams. That is her affair. But she broke into the library during the night in order to conduct her explorations, and that is *our* affair."

Despite his words, Ryōtora still had to try, because the sight in front of him defied all sense. He felt like he should be able to wake Hanemi and ask her what she was doing in the library. But she was as unresponsive as a corpse; were it not for her warmth and her slow, even breaths, Ryōtora might have feared she was dead.

Several scrolls were spread out on the low desk in front of Hanemi. Giving up on the sleeping woman for a moment, Ryōtora bent to examine them, only to have the archivist's sleeve interpose itself between him and the texts. "Forgive me," the archivist said, sounding not at all apologetic, "but you have not been given permission to read these."

"Lady Kaikoga seems to have been reading them when she fell asleep," Ryōtora pointed out. "That makes them relevant to the situation."

"That may be so, Lord Isao, but nevertheless." With swift yet careful hands, the archivist gathered the scrolls up.

Sekken's mother had said only a few parts of the library's holdings were held in locked cases, and Hanemi had spoken of gaining access to texts by a certain Isawa, on the Realm of Dreams. Ryōtora would have to apply to the governor for permission to look at them – or perhaps to Lady Asako. Neither prospect pleased him.

As he bent to examine Hanemi more closely, Kinmoku said, "How is it that Lady Kaikoga got in here? I presume the library was locked up for the night. Did she break through the door, or through a window?" She peered out one of the narrow openings, as if Hanemi might have climbed five stories up the outside of a building.

The archivist's hesitation made her turn back. "Well?" she prompted him.

"My apologies, Lady Mirumoto." He bowed deeply, scrolls tucked securely into his arms. "We have not yet determined how she got inside."

"Then no damage was done, it seems."

That was hardly the most important point, but Ryōtora was alert enough now to know it mattered. While the Dragon were still responsible for Hanemi's transgression, no one could accuse them of harm to the library itself. The scrolls had seemed pristine – what Ryōtora could see of them before the archivist rolled them up.

Kinmoku sighed, looking down at Hanemi. Her irritation showed through. "Well, I doubt you want us to just leave her here. Who knows how long it will be before she wakes? Please send to the embassy for a litter; we'll take care of her there."

And grapple with a lot of questions, Ryōtora thought. He did not envy Hanemi when she awoke.

But by the next morning, she still hadn't stirred.

"What's she doing?" Kinmoku asked Ryōtora, staring down at the sleeping Moth woman.

He shook his head helplessly. "I have no idea. I'm afraid I know no more about the Realm of Dreams than what I was taught during my schooling, and that wasn't much." By the standards of other clans, the Agasha tradition was oddly materialistic. They specialized in studying the properties of different substances, both the material and the metaphysical. They didn't ignore the Spirit Realms, but of those, the Realm of Dreams was perhaps the least important. It rarely impinged on the waking world, nor on the souls of the dead, and it sought neither to direct nor to corrupt human society.

"Is it normal to sleep this long?" Kinmoku asked, even though Ryōtora had just admitted ignorance. When he shook his head again, she said, "Is it possible that Kaikoga somehow walked through a dream to get into the library?"

"One can travel through the Enchanted Country and come out in a different place than one entered, so I suppose it's at least possible. But that requires places where the veil between worlds is thin, and those aren't common. I don't know what such a thing would even look like for the Realm of Dreams. I would expect it to need a sleeper, and there shouldn't have been one in the library."

Kinmoku scowled. "No, not until *she* got there. Why break in at all, anyway? I could understand it if the governor had refused her permission to read those scrolls – though she'd be a fool to doze off like that."

"Unless," Ryōtora said, the thought only now occurring to him, "what she was reading weren't the scrolls she'd been given access to."

It brought a brief silence to the room. Lady Sun's thin winter light filtered through paper screens, making the place habitable without a brazier. Hanemi, ensconced under a thick blanket, felt warm enough to Ryōtora's touch.

"If she overstepped her bounds like that," Kinmoku said in a low voice, "I am going to…"

She didn't finish the thought. After a moment, she shook herself back to alertness. "Do you think she's in danger? Can something hurt her while she's asleep?"

"Possibly," Ryōtora said, trying to sound as if he were doing anything more than guessing. "When you or I fall asleep, we're safe enough. Even if you suffer a terrible injury in a nightmare, you wake with your body intact. But Lady Kaikoga is not an ordinary dreamer. We can expect her to have more control there, which is good; it means she's better able to avoid harmful visions. What I don't know is whether that means her spirit is more fully present, perhaps in ways that leave her vulnerable."

He sat back on his heels, looking up at Kinmoku. "It would help if I could read whatever the library has on the Realm of Dreams. Including the scrolls she was given permission to study – whether those were the ones she was reading in secret or not."

"Assuming anyone is willing to do us favors at the moment." Kinmoku brooded again, hands shoved up her sleeves. Ryōtora suspected that under the shrouding cloth, they were bunched into fists.

She didn't lambaste him again for his failures, but Ryōtora felt guilty all the same. He drew a steadying breath and forced his thoughts in more useful directions. "Even if Lady Kaikoga isn't in danger from her dreams, her body can still suffer. She's been asleep for at least a day, maybe longer. We need to get water down her throat, and depending on how long this continues, food may become an issue as well." Waste, too, but Ryōtora left that part unspoken.

"Can she eat like that?" Kinmoku asked.

"I doubt it," Ryōtora said, "but someone could fortify her through prayers to the spirits."

"Do it, then. She's our guest; whatever idiocy she may have committed, we can't let her come to harm."

He'd known the command would come, and what his response must be. Still, it hurt to force the words out. "Lady Mirumoto... if you insist, I will do what I can. But there may be consequences for me."

The Dragon required their warriors and their priests to train for a little while together, so that each group would know something of how the other operated. Kinmoku's brow furrowed. "The work is done by the spirits, isn't it?

Unless you're suggesting what Lord Asako did, pouring your own strength into Kaikoga. Spiritual matters are your affair, of course, but that strikes me as *extremely* foolish."

"That is not what I had in mind," Ryōtora hastened to assure her. "I know I don't have the strength to spare. But communing with the spirits brings the elemental harmony of your own body and soul into resonance with them. I speak to the fire with my own Fire, to the water with my own Water, and so forth."

"And you don't have very much to speak with."

That was both blunt and inaccurate. *Sometimes* Ryōtora felt like he had plenty. Sometimes he felt like he had almost none. But even when he felt strong… "I can manage communion with the spirits. The problem is, entering into that contact can unbalance me, sometimes quite severely."

Kinmoku was too disciplined to sigh, but the harsh exhale through her nose betrayed much the same sentiment. "You're telling me that if you try to help Kaikoga, we might have you flat on the mat next to her."

He, who'd once borne the ancient and powerful spirit of a mountain on his own metaphysical back. Ryōtora wanted to deny it… but that was pride talking, and Kinmoku needed the truth. "The last physician I spoke to advised me to continue making offerings to the spirits, but not to ask more than the smallest favors of them."

Actually, the man had advised Ryōtora to ask for nothing at all – to stop practicing the techniques he had trained for years to master. To behave as if the gift of speaking to the spirits, rare at the best of times and even more precious as the population of the Dragon Clan dwindled, had never been in him at all. Ryōtora couldn't bear to follow that advice, not in full. He held back from most things.

But if he couldn't serve his clan with that gift… then what good did he serve at all?

Kinmoku didn't point out what they both knew: that he was the only priest presently at the embassy. Ordinarily one was stationed there alongside the ambassador, but Agasha Tōemon's mother had died; it was his duty as a son to travel home for her funeral.

So, functionally speaking, they had no priest at all.

The light coming through the screens dimmed, then brightened again. Kinmoku said, "Well, unconscious people can swallow water at least, with help. Get some into her. Who knows, she might wake up later today."

"If she doesn't," Ryōtora said, "would you like me to do what I can?"

"Yes," Kinmoku said, "but not by throwing yourself out of balance. Talk to that Lord Asako of yours, since we know he's partial to you. Ask him for help – discreet help – in finding someone to tend to Lady Kaikoga. Someone who won't try to take advantage of it in court."

Ryōtora wasn't sure any such person existed. That didn't make the suggestion a bad one, though. "I will, Lady Mirumoto."

CHAPTER NINE

The weather was beautiful. Sekken knew it wasn't really possible for Isawa Chikayū to have arranged it – the light dusting of snow overnight, just enough to gild everything with a fresh layer that sparkled like stars in the pure, unclouded light of morning – not for the whole city, at least. And it would be rather noticeable if she persuaded the spirits that controlled the weather to snow only on Sekken's house.

But it meant the gardens were at their winter best as he and Chikayū's daughter Miyuki meandered along the paths, walking with the slow stride that was more a performance of courtly reserve than real movement. A pace Sekken hoped he'd be able to keep up without fear of tiring.

Tanshu had walked at his side for a time, but the sluggish pace bored him; the dog had loped off a while ago, his spectral paws not denting the snow, leaving his master without even that distraction. Sekken and Miyuki had exhausted the subjects of the weather and the details of the garden, and he still hadn't figured out a way to get past the formalities and into something meaningful.

Possibly he wasn't supposed to. Many a samurai had been married without ever exchanging more than pleasantries about the weather with their future spouse. He should count himself lucky that he wasn't being used as a token of barter for a diplomatic agreement with another clan, destined to spend the rest of his life with some Matsu or Hida or Shinjo for the good of the Phoenix. This stroll through the gardens was his choice; this match, should it happen, would be the same.

But Chikayū and his mother had both encouraged this meeting, which suggested they were hoping for more than resigned acceptance out of him. Which, in turn, suggested that they were hoping he and Miyuki would find something other than empty banalities to converse about.

At his side, Miyuki suddenly raised one silk-draped arm to her mouth. He realized, with some startlement, that she was stifling an abrupt giggle.

"Forgive me," she said, when she noticed him looking. The cold had pinked her cheeks even through the rice powder; now they were redder still. "I- I was trying to think of something to say, and all that came to mind was..."

She caught herself short. Sekken exhaled his own laugh in a puff of frost. "Go ahead. It can't be worse than the inanities I've been coming up with."

"I was going to say – well, I wasn't, because it's silly – but all I could think of was, 'You walk very nicely.'"

This time his laugh was more than just ice crystals in the air. "Thank you. I got very good marks from my teacher, back in the day. And no, I'm not making that up; we spent hours walking in circles while he smacked our shoulders and stomachs and chins with a stick, making sure our posture never sagged."

"Ours did the same," Miyuki said, "but during meditation instead."

It was a splendid opening to a conversation about their respective training, courtier and priestess. One in which they would exchange stories about their youthful adventures and misadventures, the friends they'd made, the instructors they'd loathed. A chance for them to acquaint themselves with each other as people, rather than as prospective husband and wife.

But Sekken had already had that conversation. In the summer-warmed gardens of a Dragon temple, with a priest whose reserve gradually melted away, like a deeply sheltered drift of snow.

After a brief hesitation, Miyuki said, "Obviously I didn't receive the kind of training you did, Lord Asako. We are taught a certain amount of courtesy, of course, because we never know where we will end up serving, and it's necessary for us to be able to speak to people as well as spirits. But I'm afraid I'm not very good at being indirect."

Sekken's heart tightened. *You're not the only one I know with that shortcoming.* "I will not take offense, Lady Isawa."

Miyuki nodded her thanks. "I know why we're here. What my mother hopes to gain, for both your family and mine."

Sekken's father had once arranged for a stallion owned by a Shiba lord to cover the mares at their country estate.

The stallion was renowned for his speed, the mares for their endurance; Sekken's father hoped the cross would produce good stock. Right now, Sekken felt rather like that stallion. *My job is to provide stud service.*

Some hint of his reaction must have slipped through to his expression, but Miyuki took the wrong message from it. "I don't mind, truly," she hastened to assure him. "I like children, and I agree with my mother that it would be a shame if what you've received from your ancestor was lost. And really, aren't most marriages made so that people will have children who can inherit their legacy?"

"It's not the only reason they're made."

The reply slipped out before he could stop it, and Miyuki sobered. "I know. And… I will be blunt again, Lord Asako, and I hope you will continue to be understanding. I know you aren't in love with me. I suspect your heart might be given elsewhere."

How many people had guessed? Probably half the city. If the majority of Sekken's dalliances hadn't been with men, his behavior around Ryōtora might have been taken as simple friendship. But with that context, gossip would assume attraction even if there was none. In his experience, gossip attributed romance and scandal to *any* people who showed particular warmth toward one another – or even particular coldness, on the grounds that the latter was a clever ruse to hide the truth.

During the long months of winter, courtiers had a *lot* of time to gossip.

"I wouldn't disgrace you," he promised Miyuki.

"I know you wouldn't. And I wouldn't mind. If your heart

was elsewhere, I mean. I…" She pressed her lips together in a way no courtly student would have ever been permitted to make habit. "I know it's fashionable to want love. All those grand stories about people pining for one another, divided by war or parental disapproval, that sort of thing. They don't really interest me, though. They never have. So, it wouldn't bother me if we never had that. But… it would bother you. Wouldn't it?"

Sekken dipped his head. He knew his mother had too much restraint to poke a hole in one of the screens so she could spy on him and Miyuki, and Chikayū would never do that to the screens in someone else's house, but he still felt the weight of those gazes on him.

Or maybe the gaze he imagined came from someone else.

Ryōtora would be the first to tell you to uphold your duty above your heart. Even if it put your duty above him.

Especially if it put your duty above him.

"Most of those stories end in tragedy," he said softly, feeling the ache of it deep inside. An ember winter's chill couldn't extinguish, yet bereft of the fuel that would let it blaze. "That's the sort I'm living, Lady Isawa. And… you deserve to know why."

Honesty: another virtue samurai were expected to uphold. Before he could go on speaking, though, one of the doors slid open, and Jun came outside.

"Please excuse me," Sekken said, and went to the veranda.

There were only three reasons someone might interrupt him right now. The first was that Chikayū had decided to leave – but if that were the case, she would have come outside herself. The second was that the governor or someone of high rank had summoned him – but if that were the case, Sekken's mother would have come to tell him.

The third was that Sekken had quietly instructed Jun to come straight to him if Ryōtora called at the mansion. He didn't know if his mother would turn the man away at the door, but he wasn't willing to risk it.

Jun knelt, so he wasn't towering over his master on the ground, and bowed. "Lord Isao is here, my lord."

The timing could not have been worse if Ryōtora had prayed to a malevolent spirit to guide him. But Sekken couldn't very well take steps to make sure his mother didn't send Ryōtora away, then do the sending himself.

Inside, his mother would be waiting. Gritting his teeth, Sekken said, "Bring him out here. Avoid my mother if you can."

Jun bowed, and Sekken went back to Miyuki.

"Forgive me," he said. "I'm about to retaliate for your earlier bluntness by being inexcusably rude, myself. Lord Isao has arrived, and–"

"And he is your guest," Miyuki said immediately. "At court, I mean – not precisely, I know, but–"

Sekken nodded, saving her from more verbal flailing. "Yes. And if he's here, I suspect he needs assistance with something." *Given how we parted before.*

"Shall I remove myself?"

That would feel like Sekken was trying to hide something. As he shook his head, Tanshu went galloping past, ignoring the paths, and leaving very clear pawprints in the snow. Sekken had just enough time to realize that meant the dog had decided to manifest when canine head collided with samurai knee, Tanshu offering energetic greetings to Ryōtora as the priest came into the garden.

"Tanshu!" Sekken chided, which accomplished absolutely nothing. Ryōtora rubbed the dog's head, trying to calm him. Sekken couldn't help but feel the dog's enthusiasm was a wordless rebuke – and Tanshu hadn't even been there at the temple, when they had their argument. Even after all this time, Sekken wasn't quite certain what the boundaries were on his spirit companion's intelligence.

Once Tanshu had quieted down enough to permit conversation, Sekken made awkward introductions between Ryōtora and Miyuki. "I met your lady mother, I believe," Ryōtora said. "At court, and again at the Game of a Hundred Candles." If it troubled him to see Sekken out here with Miyuki, enjoying a quiet stroll, no hint of it came through in his expression. What he lacked in political agility, he made up for in unreadability.

"She is inside," Miyuki said. "I can rejoin her, if your business with Lord Asako is private."

Ryōtora hesitated, his gaze flicking to Sekken. This, Sekken could read; Ryōtora deferred to his judgment. Given that Sekken had been on the verge of telling Miyuki the truth about himself, he supposed that meant he trusted her. Blunt-spoken she might be, but that wasn't the same as letting sensitive matters slip – as Ryōtora himself demonstrated.

Sekken's nod encouraged him to speak, but still, Ryōtora's words came out heavy with reluctance. "I am here on behalf of my ambassador to ask a favor. It is not, I think, a large one… but it is the way of court to tally even small favors, and redeem them as obligations later."

"Anything you need," Sekken said, without hesitation. The memory of his sacrifice hung between them like a stone. Of course, Ryōtora would be loath to add any more obligations to his side of the tally. Even if Sekken had done his damnedest to blot that out from their ledger.

A minute twitch in Ryōtora's jaw greeted his offer. "I appreciate your generosity, Lord Asako. Unfortunately, I fear this favor requires the help of the elemental spirits. And your mother may not be pleased to know of our request, as it concerns Lady Kaikoga."

"The Moth samurai?" Sekken twitched in surprise. "Has Mother taken against her for some reason?"

"You haven't heard?" Ryōtora let out a slow breath, a measure of tension draining from his shoulders. "Then she has chosen not to share it at all widely. I… did not expect that."

He looked up to find both Sekken and Miyuki trying very hard not to look inquisitive. Ryōtora explained, "It seems Lady Kaikoga entered the Kanjiro Library when she should not have. The archivists found her asleep there, and she hasn't woken since. That was two days ago."

"I assume you've tried to wake her."

"By every means we can. Now we're concerned about her health, if she continues to remain asleep. I've… been unable to help her."

The guilt behind those words probably wasn't audible to anyone other than Sekken. Of course, Ryōtora would blame himself for the failure; he felt he ought to be equal to any duty his clan asked of him, no matter what it might be.

Sekken was no priest, and neither was his mother. Ginshō, like their father, was a warrior, and his third sister Ameno was a court painter. The only one of his sisters with the gift for speaking to the spirits was Shūkai, and while she would help in a heartbeat, she was currently at the winter court in Nikesake.

But the woman standing at his side was a priestess.

Miyuki bowed low. "I would offer you my help, Lord Isao, but I'm afraid that my talent for healing is very small. If you would like, however, I would be happy to share your concerns with my mother. Perhaps after she finishes her visit here, if the matter is not one of immediate urgency."

"It is not," Ryōtora said. "But your lady mother…"

The shake of Miyuki's head stopped his protest. "She will be glad to help."

Of course she will be. Sekken kept that thought from his expression. No, Chikayū would not try to count this favor against the Dragon.

It would just be another pebble in the basket on Sekken's shoulders. One more bit of weight, driving him inexorably to his knees.

Ryōtora bowed deeply. "I am more grateful than you can know."

Chikayū sang melodically under her breath as she moved her hands across Kaikoga Hanemi's body. Sekken knew enough to identify the places she touched as meridian points, but not enough to know what information she might be gleaning from them.

At her side sat a tray full of little offering bowls, sake and rice and shavings of aromatic wood that blazed up into flame without warning, then died down into ash. Not long after that, Chikayū sat back on her heels, wiping her hands symbolically clean with a white silk cloth.

"Your surmise is correct, Lord Isao," she said. "Lady Kaikoga's spirit does indeed seem to be in the Realm of Dreams. As one would expect, of course, given her expertise and interests, but the particular balance of Air, Water, and Fire is unmistakable."

The four of them bracketed Chikayū, Ryōtora and Mirumoto Kinmoku on one side, Sekken and Miyuki on the other. Kinmoku said, "Can you wake her?"

"I'm not certain I should." A troubled line creased Chikayū's brow. "Lady Kaikoga is more than merely asleep... how do I describe this? The closest comparison I can think of is, imagine she were deep in communion with a powerful spirit. If you pulled her abruptly from that–"

"You might well anger the spirit," Ryōtora said. "What could she be communing with in the Realm of Dreams? I know it's inhabited by baku, but what else?"

Sekken gave him a lopsided smile. "That may not be a meaningful question. The Realm of Dreams is unique among all the Spirit Realms; where the others try to influence everything that comes within their reach, for good or for ill, dreams are instead influenced by those who touch them. Which is a roundabout way of saying, if you encounter something that isn't a dreamer, then who's to say what it might be, underneath the shape it's taken?"

"Lady Kaikoga had speculations along those lines,

concerning baku becoming yōkai. She wanted to talk to you about them." Regret shadowed Ryōtora's eyes. It had plenty of company there; Sekken realized with a twist of his heart that the other man hadn't been looking particularly well lately. The strain of court was clearly getting to him.

Chikayū raised one hand. "I'm not saying she *is* communing with something in the Realm of Dreams. Only that I cannot think of a better comparison for her current state. She is – call it *rapt*. But with what, who can tell? And without knowing, I'm reluctant to disturb her."

Sekken knew Kinmoku well enough to read the frustration in her posture. "How do we find out?"

"Find someone else experienced enough with the Realm of Dreams to go in search of her spirit. Which is not me, I regret to say. But the lord governor has some interest in this area; I can ask if he knows of anyone."

"That won't be necessary." Kinmoku spoke a little too curtly, and Sekken could guess why. The more favors got asked of the more people, the more difficult things would become for the Dragon. "If she isn't in immediate danger…"

"She isn't," Chikayū confirmed. "Though Lord Isao is right that she will need someone to strengthen her periodically. I would be glad to do that now."

"Please do. We will continue to wait for her to wake on her own."

While Chikayū arranged for more offerings to be brought, Sekken drew Ryōtora aside. "I spoke to my mother," he murmured. "She has no intention of telling others about Lady Kaikoga's intrusion."

Ryōtora's eyes pressed closed, lashes lying against his cheek like a bruise. "I appreciate her discretion."

It was a favor to her son: she hadn't said it outright, but Sekken could tell. A tacit apology for their argument the day Sekken had threatened to retire to a monastery. He only wished he could think of some way to offer a similar apology to Ryōtora now.

They taught courtiers many ways to do that kind of thing. But by the time Sekken left, he still hadn't thought of a single one.

CHAPTER TEN

"Lady Asako. Might I have a moment of your time?"

Sekken's mother stopped and raised one elegant eyebrow. Ryōtora wondered if she could tell he'd been lying in wait for her at the governor's palace, and suspected she probably could. In fairness, he wasn't there only for her; the governor had finally replied to Ryōtora's letter of apology, summoning him to an audience at noon. He'd arrived early, though, specifically in the hopes of catching Asako Fumizuki.

The entry room was empty save for the two of them. Courtly entertainments often lasted long into the night, which meant the participants rarely rose early. Ryōtora was glad of the solitude as Lady Asako skirted the brazier and came close enough to bow. "Lord Isao. From your expression, I surmise that Lady Kaikoga has not yet awakened."

"She has not," Ryōtora confirmed. Chikayū's assistance had strengthened Hanemi, but as for how much longer she would remain asleep, none of them could do more than guess. "Thank you for your discretion in not mentioning her trespass at the library."

Lady Asako acknowledged this with a slight incline of her head. "I will still need to speak with her once she wakes up. But to mention it more widely would serve no purpose."

It would serve the purpose of embarrassing the Dragon at court, since Hanemi was their guest. Ryōtora was glad she didn't consider that worth reaching for. "I realize this is presumptuous," he said, knowing he sounded stiff, "but was wondering if I could ask you for a small favor. In order to help Lady Kaikoga."

"You may ask."

Hardly an encouraging reply; still, he had no choice but to forge ahead. "Your archivist would not let us see the scroll Lady Kaikoga was reading when she fell asleep. I do not know if it has any bearing on her condition, but it might. Can you at least confirm whether or not it was the text she came here to study, the diary of Isawa Minokichi?"

"It was not," Lady Asako said.

Ryōtora bit down on a curse. "Then she broke in to study something she was not permitted to view."

To his surprise, a small frown marred the powdered smoothness of Lady Asako's face. "Yes, but not as you mean it. The scroll she had in front of her is one we do not leave out for anyone to read; however, that is only for reasons of age and delicate condition. Had Lady Kaikoga expressed an interest in seeing it, I would not have hesitated to give my permission."

"Then why…" Ryōtora didn't finish the question; Lady Asako wouldn't be able to answer it, anyway. Only Hanemi knew why she'd broken in to see it, and there was no way to ask her. "What was the scroll?"

"One that might be of interest to you, Lord Isao, now that I consider it. She was looking at the script for a third-century play written by Doji Utaemon. One of the earliest surviving references to the Night Parade."

He couldn't draw breath to reply. *The Night Parade.* Sealed away by the ward in Seibo Mura… wasn't it? But Hanemi had shown an interest in the subject. She'd speculated that Nurarihyon originated as a baku from the Realm of Dreams. And now her own spirit was caught there.

What if the threat wasn't as thoroughly contained as he hoped?

"I would like to see it, if I may." The words came out unsteady, but Ryōtora hardly cared. "Also, Isawa Minokichi's writings. That is what I hoped to ask you for, before you said… they may still be relevant."

"I will make arrangements for you to study them." Lady Asako slipped her fan from her sash and tapped it against her hand. "First, however, I must see to some business here. Please excuse my rudeness."

He gave his thanks and farewell – but Lady Asako, heading deeper into the palace, paused at the door. She stood on the threshold for a long, wordless moment; Ryōtora, watching, didn't know if he should speak or not.

Then she turned to face him. "Lord Isao. I wish to be very clear that what I am about to say is not a price extracted for permitting you to see those scrolls. It is something I ask for its own sake – for my son's sake."

Ryōtora's mouth had gone very dry. "Ask."

"Do not interfere with my son's future." Her gaze was steady, unblinking. "He has told me more of what happened in Seibo Mura. I do not know if he has told me all; I do not need to know. What I have heard is enough. I know what you are to him, and I can guess at what he may be to you. But he needs more than that. And I do not think you can give him what he requires."

Wealth. Status. Connections.

Someone who wasn't broken.

She didn't know that part. But she didn't have to. It was enough that Ryōtora knew. He would cherish every moment of Sekken's company, now and forever, but he would not ask for more than either of them could give.

Even though the soft voice in his heart wished he could.

"Lady Asako," he said, with absolute sincerity, "we want the same things for your son. You have no reason to fear what I might do."

For the first time, her serenity cracked. Behind it he saw a mother: loving, fearful, and desperately glad of Ryōtora's cooperation. "Thank you, Lord Isao," she said, bowing deeper than etiquette required.

And then she was gone.

He sat in silent meditation after that, conserving his strength. Ryōtora couldn't call on the elemental spirits to bolster him, not without risking an imbalance that would leave him incapable of meeting with the governor. The best thing for him to do was absolutely nothing at all: to be still and quiet, fixing his thoughts on emptiness, and to wait until one of the governor's servants came to fetch him.

Trying, the whole time, not to think of Sekken.

Not just the man himself, but their entire situation. Three courtiers passed through, gossiping amongst themselves about Asako Shoun apparently being caught in Sodona Aimaku's bedchamber the previous morning. Did they gossip like that about Ryōtora and Sekken? Not that either man had given people such cause, but Ryōtora doubted they needed it. A poor, upstart Dragon pining after the Phoenix scholar intended for another… to people such as these, that was like candy. Yet what was Ryōtora supposed to do? Avoid Sekken entirely?

It wasn't precisely a relief to stand and leave those thoughts behind, not when what lay ahead was all too likely to be some kind of political trap. But one was his heart, and the other was his duty, and Ryōtora was far more accustomed to the weight of the latter than the former. When the servant called him out of his trance, he rose without hesitation. Holding onto what little serenity his meditation had given him, he went to face the governor.

The letter summoning Ryōtora to the palace had named him alone, with no mention of Mirumoto Kinmoku. His heart sank when he entered the reception room and found not only Asako Katahiro seated on the dais, but a double line of his retainers kneeling along the sides of the room. It was the kind of audience that accompanied either commendations or sentences of judgment, and Ryōtora doubted he was about to be given a reward.

"Lord Agasha no Isao Ryōtora," the governor said, his voice more booming than usual. "You have come."

"As you bid, lord governor," Ryōtora said, approaching to

a suitable distance and then kneeling in a full, formal bow.

"I read your letter. It said you wish to apologize to me." Katahiro held an iron fan in one hand, of the sort that military commanders used as a signal and a symbol of authority. He gestured toward Ryōtora with it. "Go ahead, then."

Someone with Katahiro's years of experience didn't make an encounter this awkward without doing it on purpose. Gritting his teeth, Ryōtora lowered his head again. "Lord governor, I have no excuse for my rudeness to you the other night, when I refused to tell the story of the Night Parade. I spoke out of caution, but perhaps caution slipped over the line into shameful fear." He didn't think it had – especially not with what Lady Asako had just told him – but an apology was not the place to prevaricate and offer further defenses. "If you still wish to know more of what happened in Seibo Mura, I would be glad to relate it to you now, or at a place and time of your choosing."

Not during another Game of a Hundred Candles, he prayed silently. That was the one thing he would have to refuse. But Kinmoku thought Katahiro wouldn't be gauche enough to hold a second gathering so soon after the first; he had to trust *her* years of experience to be right.

"Excellent!" Even in so large a room, Katahiro's voice sounded too loud. Ryōtora wondered if there was a bigger audience than the one he saw, other courtiers gathered behind the paper walls to listen as the unmannerly Dragon priest bent to the governor's will. "I would be delighted to hear your story, Lord Agasha no Isao Ryōtora. Tell it now."

Relief melted Ryōtora's bones, until he was glad he was already kneeling. It wasn't impossible that Katahiro might demand it again later on… but here and now, on a bright winter morning, was the safest time to speak of the Night Parade that he could imagine.

He still didn't name Nurarihyon. The name was known, through all the plays and picture scrolls and books of yōkai that had assumed the creature was nothing more than a literary invention; he and Sekken had spoken it themselves, before they were warned of the danger. It likely wasn't perilous outside of the specific confines of Seibo Mura – or, perhaps, a Game of a Hundred Candles. Still, Ryōtora couldn't bring himself to feel sanguine about uttering it. So instead, on Kinmoku's advice, he played up that peril, alongside the chaos and destruction wrought by Nurarihyon's followers.

Only two things did he leave out: the precise means by which Sekken had saved Ryōtora's life, and the possible connection to Kaikoga Hanemi's present condition.

He justified the former to himself on the grounds of duty, despising himself a little for doing it. Kinmoku knew and had chosen not to share; it wasn't Ryōtora's place to contradict her wishes as ambassador. Still, the omission felt like cowardice.

As for the latter… Ryōtora wished he could have spoken to Kinmoku first about Lady Asako's revelation. If some tendril of Nurarihyon's influence had reached all the way out here to Phoenix Lands, then the governor ought to be warned. But Ryōtora might as well sign a treaty handing Seibo Mura over to Isawa control for the next thousand years, because that would be proof the Dragon *hadn't* contained the Night Parade as well as they claimed.

We have no proof of it yet. Only the slim evidence of a scroll and a sleeping woman. That was what Kinmoku would tell him. *Be sure, before you assume we've failed.*

If we have failed, Ryōtora answered her silently, *then maybe we ought to let the Isawa take over. Whatever the cost to ourselves.*

Until he had more evidence, though, he would remain silent.

"Wonderful!" Katahiro boomed when he was done. "An astonishing tale, and you tell it well. Consider your offense forgiven."

"My lord?" Ryōtora said, startled. *Surely it can't be that easy.*

"Why so surprised? It is my prerogative to decide when I am offended, and when you are forgiven. You have come here, before my most trusted vassals, to offer your contrition and provide what you refused before. I see no point in dragging it out further."

If *he* saw no point, even Ryōtora couldn't find a good reason to argue. Perversely, though, the ease with which Katahiro had wiped away the insult left dread pooling in Ryōtora's gut. There was no reason for the governor to act so forgiving and friendly – no reason immediately apparent, at least. Which meant he must be playing some deeper game. Kinmoku would know what it was, or Sekken. But neither of them was here to advise him.

The vassals kneeling to either side were no help. Whether they were surprised or already in the know, the sort of people summoned for these occasions were far too well-disciplined to gape. When the governor spoke again, two of them rose to their feet without hesitation. "Come, Lord Isao. Now that we've dealt with that, I'm minded to walk in the garden."

Ryōtora himself was much slower to rise, as the vassals slid apart two of the luminous gold screens walling the room. "My lord?"

"Don't keep me waiting, Lord Isao. I might get offended again."

He scrambled up, almost stepping on the hem of his court robe. "Of course not, lord governor."

The garden they went to was not the one he'd been studying before their first meeting. This was smaller and fully enclosed by the palace walls, but no less of a gem for its limited size. And, most startlingly, not a speck of snow lay on anything within it: not the trees, nor the bushes, nor the flowers.

Flowers, in the middle of winter.

"Isn't it beautiful?" Katahiro said. He locked his hands behind his back and gazed out over the improbable scene, making no move to step into the sandals that waited at the garden's edge. "A gift from the Isawa. They made offerings to the elemental spirits, and now it's always spring in this place. There's a mulberry tree further back that used to offer fruit year-round, but that required upkeep; it needs a little seasonal change to go through its cycle. The Isawa haven't been willing to assist with it lately."

He spoke idly, like someone merely showing off a prized display, but even Ryōtora could read the meaning between his words. Something about a niece divorcing an Isawa husband, Sekken had said. Now Katahiro needed to win back their favor – and not only so he could have mulberries in midwinter again.

"Lord governor," Ryōtora said, sweating faintly in the unseasonal warmth. "It truly is a wonder, to have such things all year. But there is also beauty in change. In letting things follow their natural course." He wanted to spin that into some kind of metaphor about things growing in their native place, so as to imply something about the Dragon having control of a village in their own lands, without an interloper being transplanted there. He couldn't think of a good way to phrase it, though. *Sekken would have come up with something.*

Katahiro smiled, as if he weren't particularly attached to the point. "Oh, true enough. When you can have anything, then nothing holds particular flavor. Mulberries taste good because you've gone for months without any. Well, and also because they're sweet."

If there was a message hidden in that, Ryōtora couldn't read it. "My lord, about Seibo Mura..."

"Yes, yes. The village off in your lands." An azalea bush had started to grow a little too wild, dangling one branch over the veranda on which they stood. Katahiro fingered it, then broke off a flower. "It isn't exactly mine to decide on, is it?"

He was technically correct. Katahiro's responsibility was to present a suitable arrangement to the imperial court, one his clan and Ryōtora's had both agreed to. "You have more power in this matter than anyone else," Ryōtora said cautiously.

Or maybe this wasn't the time for caution. Katahiro

seemed to be in an oddly good mood; he'd forgiven Ryōtora's insult with unexpected ease, and now they were enjoying a private moment in his personal garden. It was the sort of access courtiers maneuvered for, and took advantage of when they got it. This might end in disaster and Kinmoku might flay Ryōtora for it... but he had to try.

Katahiro hadn't responded. Ryōtora drew a deep breath and said, "Lord governor, I understand that the Phoenix would be showing my clan great trust in allowing us sole oversight of Seibo Mura. If there is some way we could repay that trust – some favor we could do in return – I would be glad to hear it." The way Katahiro was behaving, Ryōtora almost expected him to say *make my mulberry tree bear fruit again.*

Instead Katahiro's eyebrows rose, while his mouth bent down in a thoughtful frown. "I don't know," he said, tossing the flower to the ground. "I'll think about it. Come, Lord Isao, let's walk."

Ryōtora's mind felt perfectly sharp when he returned to the Dragon embassy, but he was still glad of the litter he rode in. On foot, he would have lost his way again – not because of spiritual exhaustion, but because of mundane confusion.

He couldn't make any sense of his encounter with Katahiro. It felt like he was teetering on the precipice of getting exactly the concession he'd come here for... but why? Surely a single tale wasn't enough to tip that balance. What was going on that Ryōtora couldn't see?

In the courtyard, he climbed out of the litter and shook his sleeves straight, intending to go find Kinmoku. Maybe she could make sense of it, once he told her what had happened.

But a voice stopped him before he could take more than two steps toward the building. "Lord Isao!"

A feminine voice, and not one he recognized. Ryōtora knew the face, though, when he turned and saw who stood in the gateway. "Lady Isawa," he said, bowing to Miyuki. "What brings you here today? Is there something I can do for you?"

Her round face had looked pleasant the previous day, but now it was hard with anger. Stalking forward, her wooden pattens clacking against the paving stones, she came right up to him without bowing. "You can tell me what that Moth woman has done to my mother."

It startled him as much as Katahiro had. "Your lady mother? Has something happened to her?"

"Yes," Miyuki snapped. "She won't wake up."

CHAPTER ELEVEN

The morning hadn't started off as a bad one. Sekken didn't wake as early as his habit used to be, but he still got out of bed at a reasonable hour, thinking that he would eat, dress, and perhaps go to a temple to pray for guidance. Of course, people would gossip if they saw him at the shrine to the Fortune of Marriage, but there was more than one of those in the city. He could seek out one not commonly frequented by samurai.

But in between breakfast and getting dressed, it was like a thief crept in and stole his tact. He snorted outright at a letter from Shiba Yamaguwa, saying out loud that the man ought to have realized by now that a match between them was never going to happen. He snapped at Ameno when she mentioned how little he'd been at court lately, even though she was only trying to warn him that others had noticed. He even yelled at Tanshu for getting in his path one time too many – and that was the one that really stopped him in his tracks, as the dog flinched and gave him a mournful, guilt-inducing look.

Sekken dropped to a heap right where he was standing and buried his head in his hands. *I can't go out like this. I'll be challenged to a duel before noon.* He had plenty of energy, but it was all the wrong kind.

Frustration boiled up in his throat until he wanted to scream. There had once been a time when life wasn't like this; he knew there had been, even if that memory seemed as remote as a previous incarnation. It was as if he'd incurred a debt through the pleasant leisure of his early years, and now the time had come to pay it back.

All because he'd done something *worthwhile*, for once in his idle existence.

Self-pity dragged at him like a sodden weight. He'd spent so many days resisting it, trying to fix what was wrong with him, trying to learn to live with it, trying to pretend nothing was wrong. He was tired of all those things. He wanted to just give in, to lie here on the floor and hate his broken, useless life.

And that was the worst part of all. Because that wasn't what a samurai was supposed to *do*. He had a tiny Ryōtora on his shoulder, frowning at him in disappointment, and for a brief flash he hated Ryōtora, too. For making him want to be more, right when he became less.

"Brother." It was Ameno, braving his temper again. "Isawa Miyuki is here to speak with you. I would send her away, but… she's very upset, and she won't tell me why. She insists on talking to you."

Sekken lifted his head to find Tanshu sitting quietly by his side. At that sign of life, the dog nudged his head under Sekken's hand. Sekken couldn't quite muster the enthusiasm to scratch behind Tanshu's ears, but the contact made his breath hitch, because it was forgiveness and comfort alike. *What would I do if I didn't have Tanshu?*

He would still have his family. Who supported him, helped him, and did their best to keep his secrets, even when he was an unconscionable ass at them. But they had their own lives and concerns, and Tanshu was always there.

"Brother?"

Ameno was still waiting. Sekken shook himself to alertness. *Miyuki. Upset.* He would only add to that if he saw her right now. But hadn't he been on the verge of telling her about himself yesterday, right before Ryōtora showed up? Sekken didn't care if this sent any hope of marriage up in flames. He couldn't in good conscience ask Miyuki to shackle herself to him without first letting her know what lay at the other end of that chain.

"I'll talk to her," he said.

His sister cast a glance around his room. It was, Sekken granted, not as tidy as it should be; because putting things away and taking them out again required energy, he'd developed a tendency to leave books, sashes, and other small items scattered about. But that, too, was something Miyuki ought to see. "Yes, here," he said in response to Ameno's unspoken question. "She probably wants privacy anyway."

It was exactly the sort of privacy that would start rumors – but not in this household. Ameno nodded and went away.

Sekken got up, contemplated clearing away at least a little of the mess, and dismissed it. Besides, he didn't have much time; a moment later, Miyuki came through the door.

She bypassed all the usual pleasantries and slew anything Sekken might have said before it could leave his mouth. "I didn't mind doing your Dragon friend a favor when I thought it would just be a few prayers on behalf of his guest. But now my mother won't wake up, and it's his fault – him and that Moth woman."

"What?" Miyuki's fury was so unexpected, Sekken rather thought he would have been caught flat-footed even on a good day. "What do you mean, she won't wake up?"

"Just like Kaikoga Hanemi. She wasn't in her bed this morning; we had no idea where she'd gone. Then a priest showed up and said he found her at his shrine, asleep inside the hall of worship. We can't wake her up. Whatever's wrong with Kaikoga has spread to my mother. She should never have helped your friend!"

Thank all the Fortunes, Sekken managed to bite back his instinctive, snappish defense of Ryōtora. Instead, he squeezed his eyes shut, trying to sort through the tangle of Miyuki's words. "It can't have spread to your mother from Hanemi. Unless Ryōtora's fallen asleep as well?"

"He's fine," Miyuki snapped. "I went to the Dragon before I came here. Mirumoto Kinmoku claims it isn't their doing, or Kaikoga's, but how would she know?"

"I doubt they did it on purpose."

"I don't care if it was on purpose! My mother won't wake up!"

His tardy mind caught up to what she'd said before. "Wait – you found her at a *shrine*? As in, she sneaked out and went there in the middle of the night?"

A cold silence fell. Then Miyuki said, biting off the words,

"I *hope* you are not implying anything about her intent there."

One only visited a shrine late at night for very rare festivals… and to work foul magic. "I'm not," Sekken said hastily, cursing his lack of tact. "I just– Kaikoga sneaked into the Kanjiro Library at night. Now you found your mother at a shrine. Neither one makes any sense. Where exactly did she go?"

"Ah…" Miyuki had been pale with anger; now she flushed. "The Red Cord Shrine."

Despite everything, a laugh hiccupped into Sekken's throat. The very same place he'd been intending to avoid today: the city's grandest shrine to the Fortune of Marriage, customarily patronized by samurai.

He could guess why Chikayū might want to go there. But why at *night*? He didn't think she would stoop to cursing anyone, and even if she would, there was no need. Up until this morning, everything had been going smoothly with Miyuki – as smoothly as it could under the circumstances, anyway. Chikayū's own marriage was congenial, so far as anyone knew; she would hardly curse her husband.

"That isn't the *point*," Miyuki said, her anger gathering speed again, and he realized too late that some of those thoughts had come out of his mouth. "Do you think it's an accident, this happening to her the night after she touched Kaikoga?"

"No," Sekken was forced to admit. "But there has to be more going on. It's one thing for a Moth to fall asleep like this; maybe she decided to go on a dream journey. How could she pull someone else into it, though? And if it's her, why didn't your mother pass out the moment she started to work on Kaikoga? Why hasn't Ryōtora fallen asleep? Why are people showing up in the strangest places? None of this makes sense."

With a visible effort, Miyuki got herself under control. "That's why I came to you. You're a clever man; everyone knows it. You can figure out what's going on. And you're friends with the Dragon. They'll tell you things they won't tell me."

A cold breeze whispered down Sekken's spine. "You want me to spy for you."

Miyuki recoiled. "I–"

"You want me to use my relationship with Ryōtora, against the interests of the Dragon."

Her mouth hardened. He could see the words pushing to get out: *You're a Phoenix, aren't you?* All too often, this was what it came down to. Clan against clan, with no principle more sacred than loyalty to one's own people.

Then Miyuki sagged. Pressing one hand to her brow, she whispered, "I only want to help my mother."

"I know." Sekken hesitated, words dancing on his own tongue, eager to be set free. But the last thing Miyuki would want to hear right now was a litany of his own woes; with an effort, he dragged the confession back. Instead he said, "I'll do what I can to help you. But… I'm not the clever man you think I am. Not anymore. I don't know if I'll be enough."

"Just try." Miyuki straightened, inhaling deeply as if she could draw composure into herself, like drawing water from a well. "That's all I ask."

•••

Caution could not be permitted to hold Sekken back now. Both Miyuki and Ryōtora needed his help, even if only one of them had asked for it.

He knew better than to wait for Ryōtora to ask. The man would find sixteen different reasons why it was his obligation to take care of this matter himself, and not to ask a samurai from another clan for aid.

Kinmoku's clerk, Sankan Yoichi, showed him to where Ryōtora sat; Sekken was unsurprised to be led to the room where Kaikoga Hanemi lay unconscious. His gaze flicked first to the sleeping woman, as if there might be some visible change, but she still lay with her head supported by a small buckwheat pillow. As near as he could tell, she hadn't so much as turned over in her sleep.

Then he looked at Ryōtora, and his breath caught.

He'd thought the previous day that Ryōtora looked tired. It was worse now – or perhaps Ryōtora simply wasn't bothering to put up a pretense of energy, now that there weren't any strangers around. He knelt by Hanemi's side with a slumped posture that would have earned him a whack from the stick of any teacher, his chin sinking toward his chest. He didn't even rouse when Sekken spoke a quiet greeting and knelt across from him, Hanemi stretched out between them.

"I suppose Lady Isawa went to you," Ryōtora said, his voice dull.

"Yes. She asked me to help."

"Probably for the best."

Nothing Sekken could read into that reply sounded good. "I'm *glad* to help. Anything I can give you, it's yours."

Ryōtora stirred faintly, one hand rising from his knees before sinking back down. "You've already given me more than I could possibly ask for."

Through the tightness in his throat, Sekken said, "You never asked for anything. I know you feel like you can't – like you shouldn't. But you and I solved a puzzle together once before, didn't we? And that turned out pretty well. So, let's see what we can do with this one."

"I'm worried it's *him*." Ryōtora put his shoulders back and lifted his gaze to meet Sekken's, but the effort was visible. "Your mother told me the scroll Lady Kaikoga was reading had to do with the Night Parade. Some play script from... I can't remember."

"Doji Utaemon's play?" At Ryōtora's nod, Sekken scratched his neck in puzzlement. "I've read it myself. Both before I went to Seibo Mura, and after. Why would that pose any risk?"

"Lady Kaikoga had a theory that the Night Parade's leader was originally a baku. That perhaps unique yōkai like him originate in the Realm of Dreams, but somehow come through into the mortal world and stay here to haunt us."

Sekken hummed, thinking. "We don't really know *where* he's imprisoned, do we? Just that the ward holds him back. I suppose it *could* be the Realm of Dreams, though I had assumed the Enchanted Country instead." He could just about imagine it: Hanemi, curious about Nurarihyon, sent her spirit out to... what? Search for him? That seemed incredibly foolish. Which didn't make it impossible, but the dreamwalkers of the Moth Clan were supposed to be wise in such matters, not reckless.

He shared those thoughts with Ryōtora, then added, "And it doesn't really explain why the effect would be contagious. In fact, I'm not at all sure it is. Miyuki thinks so, but if it were, then I'd expect to find *you* asleep, too."

The room was quiet enough that he heard the soft rush of Ryōtora's indrawn breath.

"What is it?" Sekken asked. "Did something happen to you?"

"No. I..."

Sekken waited. Finally, his voice even duller than before, Ryōtora said, "I haven't interacted spiritually with Lady Kaikoga. I examined her physically, but–" His strong jaw trembled visibly. "–For... metaphysical reasons... I have to refrain from communing with the spirits."

The admission made no sense. Ryōtora was a priest. The entire purpose of his training was to commune with the spirits. What could prevent him from doing that?

Cheating on his deal with them.

Once, as a boy, Sekken had run out onto the surface of a frozen pond, not realizing the ice was too thin to support his weight. Luckily the pond hadn't been deep enough to put him in serious danger of drowning, but he still remembered the bone-cracking shock of dropping into that frigid water.

He felt that same shock now.

Ryōtora had offered himself to the spirits in order to restore the ward. And he'd *given* everything of himself; what kept him alive was Sekken's own sacrifice. But from the perspective of the spirits... maybe Ryōtora had weaseled out of his side of the bargain.

Maybe if Ryōtora tried to ask anything of them now, they'd attempt to finish extracting their price.

But if that was true…

Sekken was still in the water, slipping farther under the ice. If that was true, then effectively speaking, Ryōtora wasn't a priest anymore.

The most common reason for peasants to be adopted as samurai was that they exhibited the connection which allowed them to speak with the spirits. It wasn't the reason *Ryōtora* had been adopted; Sir Keijun had taken him in well before that gift became apparent. Still, losing that capacity would strike at the heart of Ryōtora's self, calling into question his entire place in his clan.

No wonder he looked so terrible now. Faced with a problem, duty-bound to address it… and unable to do so. Not without risking everything Sekken had done for him.

Thanking every Fortune and spirit that he'd recovered his sense of tact, Sekken made his voice as gentle as he could. "I see. Then it's possible there *is* some kind of contagion. It would be better not to use such measures to bolster Lady Kaikoga, then, nor Isawa Chikayū. Don't worry; I know some excellent physicians. They have techniques for getting sustenance into patients who aren't able to eat normally. We'll find a way to take care of those two, without endangering anyone else."

"I never meant to endanger anyone."

"I know. And so does Isawa Miyuki. In the meanwhile, you and I can work on figuring out what's happened to these two. If it does have something to do with the Night Parade – and I'm not saying it does, though you're right that we should consider the possibility – anyway, who better to handle that than the two of us?"

The gratitude that flickered in Ryōtora's expression was painful to see. Sekken had just enough warning to rise up and reach across Hanemi, catching Ryōtora's shoulder before the other man could bow to the floor. "Oh, *don't*. We're not strangers to each other anymore, Ryōtora. Even if–" His throat tightened again. "Even if our situation isn't what we hoped it would be, I refuse to go back to acting all formal with each other. Propriety might demand that in public, but not when there's no one around to see."

What he really wanted to do was take Ryōtora into his arms, to support that defeated slump with his own body – as if Sekken himself had any ability to act as a bastion of strength and endurance. But like a fool, he'd chosen to sit across from Ryōtora, which meant there was an unconscious woman between them. It made comfort more than a little awkward.

Maybe it was for the best, anyway. If Hanemi weren't there, Sekken wasn't sure he'd stop at a simple embrace. As much as he yearned to kiss away Ryōtora's cares, that might make what he had to do even harder to bear.

Ryōtora smiled wanly and said, "Your lady mother has already agreed to let me see that script, and also Isawa Minokichi's diaries."

"Excellent," Sekken said briskly, letting enthusiasm hide his other thoughts. "Research – my favorite solution to a problem. I can definitely help. The library might have other useful sources, too, texts on the Realm of Dreams and so forth. We'll find something."

The smile became a little less wan. "Imagine how quickly we might have solved our problems in Seibo Mura, if only you'd had access to your books and scrolls."

"Precisely! And if the Kanjiro Library doesn't have what we need, then we'll just have to travel to Moth Clan lands and ransack *their* shelves." A journey to their lands, far to the south near the Shinomen Mori, would normally be out of the question for him. But right now, the thought of leaving behind winter court and all its complex political tangles was appealing, even if Sekken spent the entire trip in a puddle at the bottom of his litter.

So long as he had Ryōtora there beside him.

CHAPTER TWELVE

The Kanjiro Library felt like a very different place when Ryōtora visited it in Sekken's company.

The archivist hadn't been at all pleased with him or Kinmoku the last time they were here, the morning Hanemi had been found sleeping on the fifth floor. The wind that pushed them out the door was no less cold for being metaphorical, and even with Lady Asako Fumizuki's permission to see the restricted texts, Ryōtora doubted his reception today would have been any warmer.

But Sekken preceded him inside, and the archivist didn't quite dare to let the smile fall off his face when he saw who else had arrived. Instead Ryōtora tagged along at Sekken's heels like an unseen ghost, the archivist opting simply to disregard his presence after the bare minimum of courtesy had been delivered.

Fortunately, Sekken had both knowledge of, and privileges in, the library. The archivist was willing to cede responsibility for bringing out the restricted materials to him, leaving Sekken and Ryōtora free to do their work without a supervisor frowning over them.

"Sorry about that," Sekken said, flashing a brief grin as they climbed the stairs. "Gyokuri is... a little protective of this place."

"No need to apologize," Ryōtora said, grateful Sekken was taking the stairs slowly enough that he didn't need to worry about being visibly winded before they reached the third floor. "The staff of temples and shrines are much the same. I know this site isn't sacred as such, but–"

"But we're Phoenix, so it might as well be. That's precisely it."

The smile this time wasn't quite so brief. Even though they both fell quiet after that, the silence was a pleasant one. His first visit here, Ryōtora had imagined the many hours Sekken had spent in this place; now he didn't have to imagine. The other man fit as comfortably here as he did in his own home.

And he looked *happy*. In ways Ryōtora hadn't known were missing until he saw them return. The tension of the past few weeks melted away, leaving behind a man who hardly seemed to have a care in the world. Which wasn't true, of course; Ryōtora had no doubt that Sekken was still worried about Hanemi and Chikayū. But a weight on Sekken's shoulders seemed to have been lifted, if only for a moment.

If only we could stay this way.

On the fifth floor, Sekken led him over to a cabinet tucked into a back corner. Producing a key from the case dangling from his obi – a beautiful little piece, patterned with ginko leaves stamped in gold dust – he unlocked the cabinet, revealing shelves full of boxes. "Let's see," Sekken murmured, running one fingertip along the shelves. "Here. We'll start with the play script."

Together they unrolled it on a nearby table, while Ryōtora failed to avoid being distracted by the warmth of Sekken's shoulder brushing his. Trying to bring himself back down to earth, he glanced at the scroll, then paused. "I… ah."

Sekken grinned at him, from far too close range. "It *is* from the third century. I told you, language has changed over time."

Ryōtora peered at the thin, faded calligraphy, hoping he hadn't flushed. "I can make out some of it. But this–"

"Try not to touch it." Sekken's hand lifted his own away before it could come into contact with the delicate paper. "That's an archaic verb ending for negation. You hear it sometimes in poetry."

Their hands were still touching. Ryōtora knew he ought to pull back, but the feeble protests of his mind were easy for his body to ignore. Then Sekken's other hand was on his jaw, feather-light, turning his head to–

Footsteps made them spring apart like guilty children. It wasn't the archivist, Gyokuri; instead, it was another patron of the library, an elderly woman who bowed politely to them both before selecting a codex from a nearby shelf and departing.

At least Sekken's exhale was as shaky as Ryōtora's own. "Here. Let me read it to you."

His recitation gave them both time to reassemble their composure. The play wasn't like those performed nowadays; back in the third century, Ryōtora supposed, the conventions of theater hadn't yet developed into their current forms. The story concerned a man sneaking out to visit his lover under the midsummer full moon and running afoul of the Night Parade. It seemed a single actor was supposed to portray all the yōkai the man encountered, swapping masks while onstage, and using body language to convey their different natures. The denouement brought the man's lover out to deliver a brief, poetic soliloquy, wondering if he would ever arrive.

"It never says he ran into the leader of the Night Parade," Sekken said, carefully re-furling the scroll. "But there's certainly an implication of the possibility."

Thinking about ancient theater and malevolent yōkai had effectively banished Ryōtora's distraction. "We know Hanemi is interested in the Night Parade. What would she have learned from this play, though – and how, if she's never read the script, would she know there's something in it?"

"Maybe she *didn't* know. Which could mean there's nothing important in it at all – just that she thought there might be."

Ryōtora sighed. "Well, let's look at Minokichi's diaries."

Sekken returned the play script to the cabinet and brought out the larger box containing the multiple bound volumes of the diaries. "You go through these first," he said, placing the box on the table. "I'm going to skim through what else we have here on the Realm of Dreams."

Fortunately, the diaries were more a record of Minokichi's experiments than a pillow book-style recounting of the man's personal life. The farther Ryōtora read into them, though, the more he realized the difference was not as great as he might have hoped.

Minokichi's starting point was an observation of the role the Three Sins played in the Realm of Dreams. While sleepers might imagine themselves in many situations, the most common were ones focused on their fears, their desires, and their regrets. As Sekken and Hanemi had discussed at the Game of a Hundred Candles, Minokichi was interested in the way dreams could serve as an outlet for impulses samurai were supposed to suppress in daily life – especially their unfulfilled desires.

For most people that was an undirected process. Minokichi, however, had learned the art of lucid dreaming, controlling what he experienced in his sleep. From there he began experimenting with desires of all kinds, placing himself in scenarios where he was anything from a member of the Elemental Council to a poet famed the length and breadth of Rokugan. Everything was recorded in meticulous detail – including some fantasies so frankly sexual, Ryōtora dared not look up from the page, lest Sekken notice his flaming cheeks. *A pillow book would have been tamer.*

But a dark undercurrent ran through it all. These varied experiments eventually coalesced into a grand work: the construction of an ongoing dream of Minokichi's idealized life. Ryōtora could see, long before Minokichi acknowledged it on the page, that the life he lived while he was asleep was becoming more real to him than the one he lived while awake. The man even began speculating as to the nature of "reality," and whether the mortal world itself was not simply a grand, persistent dream, perhaps created by the Heavens themselves.

The diaries ended abruptly. Ryōtora remembered Hanemi saying the writer had passed away about ten years ago, and he looked up to where Sekken was lounging against a post, a book propped on his upraised knee. "Sekken, do you know what happened to Isawa Minokichi?"

"Died in his sleep," Sekken replied, closing the book. "Some people said he was killed in one of his dreams, and that's why he died in real life. Others say he decided not to come back to reality – that he sent his soul into the Realm of Dreams forever, rather than letting it descend to the underworld. No one can say for sure. Even if you encountered Minokichi in your sleep, how could you be sure it was *him* and not a disguised baku, or something you dreamed up?"

That sort of question made Ryōtora's head hurt. He liked the pleasure Sekken clearly took in it, though, the speculative glint that came into the other man's eye.

He liked this entire moment. The two of them working together, with no politics to trouble them, and no one's life immediately in danger. He would have happily stayed there for all of winter court – if only there were a manual that could tell him how to deal with Katahiro.

And maybe, after a fashion, there was.

"Sekken," he said, realizing belatedly that he'd addressed the man familiarly, out where someone might overhear. Rather than apologizing, though, he went on, "What is your view of the lord governor? What sort of person is he?"

The faint twitch of Sekken's brow said he wondered at the

change of subject, but he didn't question it. "Hard-working, dutiful, good at the political game. What exactly are you looking for?"

"Nothing that would put you in a bad position with your clan," Ryōtora hastened to assure him. "It's only… you know how I offended him at the Game of a Hundred Candles. He forgave me far more readily than I expected, and I'm trying to figure out why. I doubt it was out of the goodness of his heart."

"Highly unlikely." Sekken tapped the book against his knee. "I don't know. He's been a little distracted lately, and nobody's sure why. Mostly people have been attributing it to–"

He sat upright, abruptly. But not in alarm; a slow smile spread across his face. "Well, there's your answer. Not about the governor, but about how to learn more of him, without asking any Phoenix samurai to share secrets. Not that I really have any on Katahiro – I haven't been at court much lately. But who do samurai traditionally unburden themselves to?"

With Minokichi's diaries fresh in Ryōtora's mind, it wasn't hard to guess what Sekken meant. Because geisha had no status whatsoever, there was no shame in admitting weakness to them.

But the other reason it was safe to talk to such individuals was that samurai held absolute power over them. A geisha who dared to divulge the secrets of the provincial governor would be killed on the spot – if they were lucky. If not, they could expect a slow and agonizing death.

Unless…

"Sayashi?" he said, very quietly.

The smile broke into an open grin. "He's shown *quite* a bit of favor lately to a certain lady from the House of Infinite Petals. That's no guarantee she knows anything useful to you, of course – but what does she have to fear from a samurai's anger?"

She still wouldn't quite be safe. Bakeneko could be killed. If Katahiro didn't know she was a yōkai, though, he wouldn't have any reason to send a meaningful force after her. And besides, Ryōtora doubted the danger would put Sayashi off at all. The more important question was whether it would amuse her to tell him what might be going on in Katahiro's head.

And whether Ryōtora felt it was fair to use such confidences against the man.

As if that thought were written on Ryōtora's face, Sekken groaned and tipped his head back against the post. "For the love of all the Fortunes – you're allowed to gather information, you know! By methods other than asking him directly! Do you think my clan doesn't have spies in your embassy? The same way *your* clan has spies among *us*?"

"Another person's dishonorable actions do not excuse one's own," Ryōtora said, deliberately sententious. He was only able to hold it a moment, though, before Sekken's gape-mouthed stare set the laughter free. "I'm not being serious. I mean, I am – I do believe that's true, that you can't just say 'someone else acted wrongly first.' But I won't be absurd about it. And I will think about asking her. Thank you."

Sekken shook his head, opening the book again. "It was a small thing. As for what I've found, I'm wondering–"

This time the footsteps that interrupted them were not the slow shuffle of an elderly woman, but the thud of someone taking the stairs an indecorous two or three at a time. Ryōtora and Sekken were both on their feet before Kinmoku rounded the corner. *She* was out of breath, which would take more than a few staircases to achieve; had she run all the way to the library from the Dragon embassy?

By the fire in her eyes, she might have. "It's spreading," she said, "but not through Kaikoga. At least, not through contact with her. Two others have been affected."

"Two–" The sudden whiplash of Ryōtora's thoughts and mood left him briefly staggered. "You mean, two others have fallen asleep? Besides Lady Kaikoga and Lady Isawa?"

"Yes. This morning, Chūkan Ujiteru was found in one of the classrooms at Yōbokutei. Same as the others; no one knows how he got there, and he won't wake up. And it turns out that Asako Shoun–"

Sekken made a stifled noise. "The lady caught in Sodona Aimaku's bedchamber?"

"Her family tried to hush it up and failed," Kinmoku said, nodding. "Otherwise we would have known sooner. She wasn't merely caught there; she was found asleep on the floor."

Sekken began counting them off on his fingers. "Sir Ujiteru this past night. Isawa Chikayū the night before that. Asako Shoun the night before *that*… what about three days ago? The day after Kaikoga Hanemi was found here – did anyone else turn up sleeping somewhere odd?"

"Not that we've yet heard. But given that Shoun's family tried to conceal what happened to her, there might be."

Ryōtora's head spun as he tried to encompass this new picture. It wasn't something that afflicted Hanemi, then spread to Chikayū when she tried to help; others were falling under this curse, too.

His mental choice of word chilled him. *If it's a curse... what's causing it?*

"Lady Kaikoga might not even be the first," Sekken said.

As much as Ryōtora wanted to believe that, he had to shake his head. "It's too much of a coincidence. A Moth scholar studying the Realm of Dreams, and then people begin falling asleep? I'd be happy if you were wrong, but it doesn't seem likely."

"Does she even know all these people?"

It was difficult for Ryōtora to say, given that *he* barely knew them. The names were familiar – all of them save Hanemi had been among the briefings he read en route from Dragon Clan lands, due to their influential positions at court – but Chikayū was the only one he'd had real dealings with. He and Sir Ujiteru had been introduced briefly not long after Ryōtora's arrival, but Asako Shoun he'd only met at–

"The Game of a Hundred Candles."

His words were a faint whisper, too low to overtop Kinmoku saying something to Sekken about Isawa Miyuki. Sekken could tell he'd spoken, though, and cut Kinmoku off with a raised hand. "What was that, Ryōtora?"

"The Game of a Hundred Candles," Ryōtora said, hardly any louder than before. "All of them were there. Weren't they?"

"Let's see, Shoun told the story of–" This time it was

himself Sekken cut off. "The stories don't matter. Yes, all four of them were present."

Silence fell as Ryōtora looked at Sekken, at Kinmoku. As they looked at each other.

"We were all there," Kinmoku said.

Twenty-five people had been, not counting the two geisha, or the servants who brought tea and threw open the doors at the end to reveal the fireworks. Twenty-five people had participated, telling supernatural stories in an abandoned pavilion, as the candles went out one by one.

In a controlled voice, Sekken said, "I've been to gatherings like that before, many times. And before you ask: yes, even gatherings where some idiot blew out the last candle. Young, drunk courtiers do all manner of stupid things. Nothing like this has ever happened before."

"Was a Moth dreamwalker ever there before?" Ryōtora asked. "Or a bakeneko? Or–"

Kinmoku said what his dry mouth couldn't. "Or two people who personally faced the Night Parade."

Before the dread of that possibility could settle too heavily on Ryōtora's shoulders, she shook her head and spoke more strongly. "I don't believe the two of you could have caused this simply by being there. *Especially* not when you had the good sense not to tell that story, Isao. It might have to do with Kaikoga. Or even with that bakeneko – one of you should talk to her."

Whatever Ryōtora might think of questioning Sayashi about the provincial governor, this one wasn't even debatable. "We will. If nothing else, she might be able to shed some light on what's happening."

"Before that," Sekken said grimly, "there's something else we have to do. We can't be sure yet that the affliction is spreading only to those who were there that night; four examples is suggestive, but not absolute, especially not with one night currently unaccounted for. It's suggestive enough, though, that we need to warn the people who might be at risk."

If Ryōtora had thought his mouth dry before, it was nothing to how he felt now. "Including the lord governor."

CHAPTER THIRTEEN

Kinmoku had come on foot to the Kanjiro Library, so she jogged alongside the two men's litters as they went to the governor's palace. It made Sekken feel like he had an armed escort, and one from the Dragon Clan, at that.

But if he'd truly been the sort of person who merited an armed escort wherever he went, he would have been able to insist on an audience with the governor right away. As it was, even with Kinmoku's weight as ambassador behind the request, the three of them were shunted into a side room to wait. While Tanshu settled himself alertly by the door, Sekken poured tea and sighed. "Well, at least we can be fairly sure nothing will go wrong before tonight. It only seems to be striking when people are asleep, and samurai fortunately aren't in the habit of taking naps." Most of them weren't, anyway. He kept waiting for exhaustion to descend upon him, but the quiet hours in the library seemed to have bought him the capacity to keep going now.

What would happen the next time he lay down to sleep, though? How could he nod off, knowing he might not wake the next morning? Weariness would slap him down eventually, he knew... but he doubted any of the three of them would sleep easy tonight.

He occupied himself by taking out his portable writing kit and making a list of everyone who'd participated in the Game of a Hundred Candles. Most were Phoenix, of course; provincial winter court didn't draw a large number of visitors from other clans. Apart from the two Dragon guests and the Moth, there had been a Crane pair, a Firefly envoy, and a priestess from the Centipede. Studying the list, he found himself wondering who might benefit from causing this kind of disruption. That still left the question of *how* the disruption could have been caused, of course – but was there anyone who would want to see the Dragon and the Phoenix further at odds?

All too many, he thought sourly. Every clan benefitted from anything that hampered their adversaries, and in a world where they competed over fertile lands and advantage at court, anyone who wasn't an ally was an adversary. It could be the Unicorn, using their strange name magic to ensure the Dragon didn't take the Phoenix side in debates over that same magic. It could be the Scorpion, sowing distrust to reap a profit elsewhere.

It could even be someone from the imperial court. They were the ones who'd told the Dragon and the Phoenix to reach an agreement over Seibo Mura... but the Otomo were as good as the Scorpion at stirring up animosity, to make sure the clans never grew strong enough to challenge the emperor's throne.

While Sekken's thoughts pursued the political angle,

Ryōtora had been thinking about something else. "What's Yōbokutei?"

Sekken blinked back to his surroundings. "It's one of the schools for courtiers. I trained there myself. So did Sir Ujiteru, for that matter."

"Does he continue to have any connection with it?"

"Not really. He's the governor's official chronicler; that's why he was at the gathering. He gets invited to everything of significance, so he can keep a record of it. I never heard that he had any ambition to go back and teach, or anything like that."

Ryōtora spread his hand and laid his fingers against the tatami, one by one. "A school. A shrine. Lady Aimaku's bedchamber. The Kanjiro Library."

"Hmmm, yes. Can we learn anything from where people were found?" Sekken carefully wiped his brush dry and closed up his kit. That list was short enough that even his unreliable memory could probably hold onto it. "I would wonder about a pattern of people going where they shouldn't – the bedchamber; the library with a restricted scroll; the shrine at night – if it weren't for the school. I can't see any kind of forbidden aspect to that."

Kinmoku murmured under her breath, as if a thought had come to her. When Sekken raised an inquisitive brow, she looked faintly embarrassed, but she spoke anyway. "Do you ever have the sort of dream where it's time for your naming ceremony, but you're in a ratty old kimono, and you can't find your obi, and somehow the castle is four times the size it ought to be, and you don't know which room you're supposed to go to?"

By the half-suppressed groan that leaked from Ryōtora, he knew all too well. As did Sekken; he just managed to keep the groan fully inside. "You think Sir Ujiteru was dreaming about his school days. That all of them went to places they were dreaming about."

"It's a theory, at least."

"A good one," Sekken agreed. "As part of the tests for my ceremony, I had to write a critical commentary on Shiba Yasuaki's biography of Isawa Asahina. Most nights I went to sleep thinking about my research, and half the time I dreamt I was in the library, doing whatever work I had planned for the next day. If Lady Kaikoga was thinking about the Night Parade…"

Ryōtora's exhalation was eloquent with relief. "Then this problem might not truly have its roots in the Night Parade itself."

"I can't see its leader being responsible for Asako Shoun's behavior, can you?" Sekken smiled ironically. "Not really his style. But it *is* hers – not the part where she gets caught, of course. She and Sodona Aimaku have been carrying on for years; they're just usually more discreet."

Then he sobered. *How many other secrets will be dragged into the light by this?*

It wasn't as if Shoun's and Aimaku's husbands didn't know about their wives' relationship. They were willing to turn a blind eye so long as neither one brought disgrace upon herself. But there were other kinds of embarrassment, and other people at court whose affairs weren't an open secret. If Sekken fell asleep, would someone find him the next morning in Ryōtora's bedchamber?

If Ryōtora fell asleep, would he show up in Sekken's?

You should be so lucky, Sekken thought bitterly. Most of the dreams he remembered these days were more like what Kinmoku described, except that instead of being late to an important lecture or called upon to recite a poetry assignment he'd forgotten to complete, he was out in public and so exhausted he couldn't even get home. His hands tensed at the vivid sense memory – false though it was – of dragging himself across a floor or down a street, too weak to stand, people watching or turning away, but never helping.

Chikayū had presumably turned up at the Red Cord Shrine because she was dreaming about her daughter's wedding to Sekken. But should that match even happen? He still hadn't told Miyuki the truth.

This problem takes priority, he told himself. It was true... and it still felt like a dodge.

Tanshu huffed quietly, not quite a bark. He hadn't manifested, which meant nobody but Sekken could hear him anyway, but the dog spirit had good manners; he knew how to alert his master without being unnecessarily loud. Tucking away his writing kit, Sekken said, "I think we're about to be summoned."

Sure enough, a tap came at the door. Then it slid open to reveal one of Katahiro's pages, kneeling politely to beckon them all through. "If my lords and my lady will be so kind as to follow me, the governor has returned."

In Kinmoku, Sekken saw a mirror for his own brief confusion. The response they'd been given before had claimed the governor was occupied with another meeting, not that he was out of the palace. Which was it? And why the conflicting answers?

Sekken remembered Ryōtora's query in the library, just before Kinmoku arrived. Yes, Katahiro was probably up to something, but Sekken couldn't begin to fathom what it might be. This wasn't like his usual games at all.

The only way to find out was to talk to him. "Stay," Sekken murmured to Tanshu as they approached the room where Katahiro waited. It had been made very clear to him when he first returned to Phoenix lands that bringing an unseen spirit into the governor's presence would be considered a breach of both security and etiquette.

They found Katahiro red-cheeked and rubbing his hands over a brazier to warm them. "Bracing out there, isn't it?" the governor said as they entered. Although his topknot was lacquered into its usual severe smoothness, a few windblown strands had slipped free around his ears.

"Were you outdoors, my lord?" Sekken asked cautiously. The day was a bitter one, with intermittent spates of freezing rain. Not remotely good weather for outdoor recreation.

"I went for a ride," Katahiro said. "It makes the warmth feel so much better, when you come into it from the cold."

"That's true, my lord." The response came out on reflex, replacing the things Sekken wanted to say and couldn't. Katahiro generally used rides out of the palace as a chance to talk privately with other people, away from prying eyes. Who had he gone with, and who could Sekken persuade to tell him?

Katahiro shook his sleeves out and settled himself on the dais. They'd been brought to a smaller reception room, not the main, formal one; the walls here were painted with scenes of the Realm of Blessed Ancestors. Generations of Asako governors floated on clouds or lounged beneath willows, sipping sake from delicate cups. "I'm told you wanted to see me rather urgently," Katahiro said. "Regarding a sensitive matter?"

Sekken wanted to be the one to answer that, in the hopes that hearing it from a fellow Phoenix and Asako samurai would soften Katahiro's response. But ultimately, the problem still seemed to have its roots in Kaikoga Hanemi, and she was a Dragon guest. Besides, Kinmoku outranked him.

She related what they had learned in the cool, unemotional tone of a soldier reporting on a battle. After the first few words, Sekken pulled his gaze from her and watched Katahiro instead. Unfortunately, the governor's expression gave little away. He didn't seem surprised to hear of Asako Shoun and Sodona Aimaku, nor of Chūkan Ujiteru. Had his underlings informed him of those matters before he went for his ride? Had that news *occasioned* the ride?

This was why Sekken preferred reading to politics. He hated feeling like he was playing a game of go in which he could only see half of his opponent's pieces. Where to defend, where to attack – all of it was little more than guesswork.

"So you think those of us at the Game of a Hundred Candles are at risk?" Katahiro asked when Kinmoku was done.

"Only when you are asleep, lord governor. At this moment, we believe you are safe."

He chuckled and slapped one knee. "Then my defense is easy. I simply won't sleep!"

It was hardly the response this matter needed. "My lord," Sekken said, "while I have perfect confidence in your strength of will and body to remain awake, others who attended the gathering may not be as resilient. With your permission, I would like to warn–"

"Definitely not." This time the slap was harder, decisive instead of amused. "This is *my* court, Asako Sekken, not yours. I will decide when and how people should be warned. Do you want to start a panic? People might turn against this Moth woman… or even against the Dragon."

Sekken went very still. Was that a veiled threat?

He couldn't tell. Not because fog had descended on his thoughts again, but because of that feeling of a game of go with half the pieces invisible. What did the governor want out of all of this?

Seibo Mura, Sekken would have said without hesitation, but the expected press didn't come. The hint that if the Dragon would only bow to Isawa oversight, then Katahiro would make sure whatever Kaikoga Hanemi might or might not have done wouldn't fall on their heads. It was a perfect opening… and Katahiro didn't take it.

Kinmoku nodded in acknowledgment. "We will, of course, defer to you, lord governor. We are, as you say, in your court, and we are grateful for your attention to our safety."

This entire time, Ryōtora had been kneeling silently behind the other two. Even with his new title, everyone in the room outranked him; it wasn't his place to speak unless either Katahiro or Kinmoku called on him to do so. But abruptly, and in contravention of all protocol, he suddenly shifted forward on the mat and bowed low. "Lord governor, with your permission, I would like to do something that might aid in this matter."

Katahiro's mouth tightened in a rare show of suspicion. "Why does it need my permission?"

Still bowed, Ryōtora said, "It is possible that I, as a priest, might be able to learn more of what is going on by calling upon the spirits to help me examine Lady Kaikoga."

The strangled, inarticulate protest that escaped Sekken was drowned out by Kinmoku's snap of, "*Isao!*"

Dread curled its hand tight around Sekken's heart. Surely Ryōtora wouldn't offer this if Sekken's worst fears were correct, if the spirits were likely to claim his life as their belated price. Surely not even *Ryōtora* would do that. Yes, he'd been willing to die once before – but that was when the Empire itself was at risk. Right now, all they had were four people who wouldn't wake up.

Even so. *Metaphysical reasons,* Ryōtora had said. *I have to refrain from communing with the spirits.* There was *some* kind of danger in this offer, and the alarm in Kinmoku's response said she knew it, too.

Ryōtora ignored them both. "I ask for your permission, lord governor, because it is likely that what I have in mind will require me to absent myself from your winter court for some time. Given the delicacy of our negotiations, I would not want you to think that I intend to give insult by my failure to attend."

His phrasing was nicely gracious. Had Ryōtora always

been able to speak like this, or had someone schooled him before sending him east to Phoenix lands? Sekken's own tongue had lost all grace. *Don't do this,* he wanted to say. *Whatever it will do to you isn't worth it. We'll find someone else.*

Who? Chikayū was asleep. Miyuki wasn't likely to assist. The Dragon had no other priest here.

Katahiro grunted thoughtfully. After that, nothing. Ryōtora remained bowed, and Sekken remained frozen. Kinmoku looked like she was holding her breath.

Then Katahiro said, "No."

Ryōtora jerked slightly, almost rising. "Lord governor–"

"You make a good point, Lord Isao. Since it does sound like Kaikoga Hanemi is the origin of this problem, someone should look at her more closely. But the ones falling asleep are my people, aren't they? So I'll have one of my own look at her."

Tension flooded out of Sekken. He heard an echo of his relief in Kinmoku's voice as she said, "That is very generous of you, lord governor. We have Lady Kaikoga at our embassy; we will return there and await your priest."

"No," Katahiro said again, far too bluntly. "I can't leave her there with you. Go back to your embassy, but I'll send some of my guards to collect her and bring her here."

"Lord governor!" All Kinmoku's relief was gone, replaced by barely restrained alarm. "Lady Kaikoga is our guest–"

"And she may be the source of a curse spreading through my court. I could arrest her if I wanted to. Consider yourself lucky, Lady Mirumoto, that I'm not."

This had all the subtlety of a kick to the chest. Friendly

help with one hand; not even veiled threat with the other. What was Katahiro hoping to achieve?

Sekken couldn't tell – but he *could* tell that attempting to pursue the matter would not make anything better. In his peripheral vision he saw Ryōtora drawing breath to speak; he intervened before the other man could. "Once again, my lord, you show your generosity. I would be happy to assist in transporting Lady Kaikoga to your palace, if it pleases you."

"No need," Katahiro said, cutting off that last line of hope. "Thank you for bringing this to my attention. You may leave now."

For a moment Sekken though he might have to break etiquette and physically pull Ryōtora away. But the man bowed one last time, jaw set in a hard line, and followed Sekken and Kinmoku out the door.

Tanshu was waiting outside, on his feet, with the alert posture that said he already knew something was wrong. Sekken beckoned for his dog to follow, and they all walked in silence until they reached the front entrance of the palace. Beyond, another gust of freezing rain was falling.

In weather like this, a folding fan could serve only one purpose. Sekken snapped his open and held it over his mouth as he said, "Go along with it for now. Fighting him will only give him a foothold to do worse."

"I know." Kinmoku didn't bother to hide her mouth, but her gritted teeth served just as well to thwart any attempt to read her lips.

As did the discouraged hang of Ryōtora's head. "If he has her, he could say anything he wants."

Would the governor lie? Ordinarily Sekken would say

no; political creature though he was, Katahiro didn't usually resort to outright falsehood. Right now, though, Sekken didn't trust his own judgment at all.

"I can do one thing, at least," he murmured.

He didn't dare glance down, lest any watcher realize what he was doing. It was normal enough these days for his cold fingers to seek out Tanshu's warm ruff, and the inugami perked up at his touch. "Go with these two, Tanshu," Sekken said. "Then stay with Lady Kaikoga. But be careful; don't let anyone sense your presence or try to banish you."

Would those instructions even work? Sekken didn't know. But Tanshu let out a brief, affirmative-sounding bark, and Ryōtora looked relieved; for now, that was good enough.

CHAPTER FOURTEEN

Ryōtora expected his dreams that night to be uneasy, and they were.

The day hadn't exhausted him like he feared it would. First because Katahiro intervened and took Hanemi into his own custody, and second because by the time that was done, it was too late for him and Sekken to pursue their other avenue of inquiry: talking to Sayashi. "By now she'll be with a client," Sekken said when Ryōtora suggested it.

"We could ask the mother of her house–"

"To tell us where Sayashi is? We'd be lucky if we were only thrown out. The world of flowers and willows maintains discretion; it *has* to, given how their life works." Sekken shook his head. "No, we'll go in the morning."

He didn't add, *assuming we're both awake for it.* But Ryōtora knew they were both thinking that.

So Ryōtora fell into a fitful sleep, sometimes dreaming of visiting the House of Infinite Petals, sometimes dreaming that he was examining Hanemi, with someone – Kinmoku, or Sekken, or Hanemi herself – asking him if that was a good idea. Wondering, even in his sleep, whether that meant someone was going to find him amid the geisha the next morning, or wherever in the governor's palace his people had taken the Moth for examination.

Part of him almost hoped so. If he fell under this curse, maybe he would be able to study it from the other side. He might do more good there than he could out here.

And he'd be removed from the political dance. A tiny, shameful corner of himself would welcome that escape.

But when Ryōtora opened his eyes, he was still in his own room… and Sankan Yoichi, who'd roused him, had news.

News that jolted him fully awake. "Have you found her yet?" Ryōtora asked, scrambling to his feet and reaching for his kimono. "Did anyone see her leave?"

"No one, Lord Isao." Yoichi looked stricken. "I swear the guards were alert last night; we would have noticed–"

"I'm not faulting you. Given where people have been found, I suspect they aren't going there by normal means."

Yoichi swallowed, the knot of his throat bobbing. "Y-yes, Lord Isao. The governor's guards would have had to overlook her as well. Lady Mirumoto was found in the Komoriyome Pavilion."

Despite the cold pebbling his skin, Ryōtora stopped with his kimono half on. "Of course," he murmured. Given their suspicions about the Game of a Hundred Candles, it wasn't surprising that Kinmoku's dreams might have led her back to the building where the gathering took place.

His half-alert mind had been thinking of it the way Sekken would, like an intellectual puzzle. A problem to be solved. Now, though, the weight of it landed on him like a rockfall. *Kinmoku* had been caught by the curse. And that meant–

Yoichi bowed again. "Lord Isao... ordinarily the ambassador's responsibilities would fall to Lord Agasha Tōemon. In his absence, you are the highest-ranking samurai here."

The cold overtaking Ryōtora had nothing to do with the winter air. "Are you saying I'm in charge of the embassy now?"

"Yes, Lord Isao."

"But I–"

Ryōtora stopped his idiotic protest before more than two words escaped. What did it matter that he wasn't prepared for the ambassador's role? Duty did not wait on preparation. And fate cared nothing for the fact that Ryōtora would have gladly volunteered himself to fall under the curse in Kinmoku's place.

He forced himself to pull his kimono the rest of the way on and to reach for his obi. The familiar motions steadied him. "How much of the embassy's work can carry on without my involvement?"

"Most of it, Lord Isao." Yoichi hesitated, then said, "In truth, only the negotiations over Seibo Mura require your direct input."

Of course they did. "Good," Ryōtora said, though nothing about this was good. "Sir Yoichi, I'll ask your assistance in helping our routine affairs to continue. Notify me if anything needs my approval or attention, but my focus must be on dealing with this problem. The sooner we get Lady Mirumoto back, the better."

•••

When Sekken arrived a little while later, one look at the man's face told Ryōtora he'd already heard the news. "The governor has kept her in custody as well," Ryōtora said, bypassing any niceties of greeting. "I'm trying to decide if it's worth demanding her back here or not."

Sekken's mouth twitched, hinting at a grimace restrained. "She did trespass in the governor's palace, whether she meant to or not. I wonder if he instructed his guards to search the pavilion this morning. Normally I don't think they'd bother. Do you think you could learn much by examining Lady Mirumoto, the way you meant to do with Lady Kaikoga?"

Examining Hanemi had been a long shot, anyway. Isawa Chikayū hadn't found anything in her own study, though she hadn't delved all that deeply. Ryōtora had offered mostly out of an impulse to do *something*… but if he was going to risk collapse, it ought to be for the root of the problem, not one of its branches. "Probably not," he admitted.

"Then I'd leave her there for now. At least until we've talked to Sayashi."

Ryōtora held out one hand when Sekken turned to leave. "I know I said I would go with you, but…" The extended hand turned into a gesture around him, as if to take in the whole embassy. "With Mirumoto Kinmoku asleep, her duties fall to me."

He wasn't sure if some of his dread had seeped into his voice, or if Sekken could simply guess at it, but either way, the other man's lips pressed together in sympathy. "I understand."

Then Sekken hesitated, peering at him. "Are you well,

Ryōtora? I mean, obviously you've had a great deal on your mind, even before this. But you look..."

How did Ryōtora look? He hadn't paused to examine himself in a mirror this morning. Still, he could guess: although he faithfully took his medications and meditated when he could, winter court had placed many demands on the fragile structure of his health. Naturally Sekken would notice.

"I'm fine," Ryōtora said. He had to be fine. There was no alternative.

Another hesitation, though Sekken was too well-trained to let his thoughts show on his powdered face. Then he said, "We should talk after I return from the House of Infinite Petals. I can deal with Sayashi myself; your clan needs you more."

Ryōtora let his bow conceal the stab of guilt he felt as Sekken departed. *I didn't lie*, he told himself, straightening. *What I said was true.*

It just wasn't his real reason for begging off their trip to the licensed quarter.

He did have things to take care of at the embassy first, mostly involving Yoichi briefing him on various trade arrangements and other matters, in case something came up that would indeed require his attention. When that was done, Ryōtora curled his hands tight, holding them as fists for longer than usual before releasing. "Sir Yoichi, I may need your assistance. But there is some risk involved, and I want you to consider carefully before agreeing. This is a request, not an order from your temporary ambassador."

"My lord?"

"What I intend to do may result in my collapse," Ryōtora said. "If that happens, it would be beneficial if I had someone to help me back to the embassy... before the guards find me."

Yoichi's expression was wary, but not reluctant. "Whose guards, my lord?"

Ryōtora drew a deep breath. "The provincial governor's."

He knew perfectly well that what he was doing was not honorable.

Unfortunately, he didn't see that he had much choice. They'd already told Katahiro that the affliction seemed to be striking those who had participated in the Game of a Hundred Candles, but the implication so far was that the problem originated with Kaikoga Hanemi. If Ryōtora asked for permission to inspect the Komoriyome Pavilion, he would be shifting the focus from the dreamwalker to the gathering itself – suggesting that the Phoenix governor, not his Moth guest, might somehow be at fault for what had happened.

The possibility hadn't even occurred to Ryōtora until Yoichi said that Kinmoku had been found there. Had the same thought come to her? Did her sleeping mind conjure the idea of investigating there, and her body followed?

If Ryōtora asked to visit the pavilion, he had a strong suspicion that Katahiro would refuse, offering instead to send his own people. And that, in turn, was an offer Ryōtora wouldn't be able to refuse – not without implying that he distrusted either the competence or the honesty of the priest in Katahiro's service.

The delicate cut-and-thrust of the whole situation made his head hurt. But he knew the lesson every person learned in childhood: sometimes it was easier to ask forgiveness than permission, on the grounds that he hadn't *known* he was doing something wrong.

The governor's message about Kinmoku had not said outright that she trespassed somewhere forbidden. His delicacy was Ryōtora's opportunity... even if Ryōtora felt guilty for exploiting it.

Yoichi followed quietly at his heels as he climbed out of his litter in the front courtyard of the palace. The embassy clerk had showed no hesitation in agreeing to come, which added to the guilt, but also brought a great deal of relief. If they were caught, Yoichi risked being sent back to Dragon lands in disgrace, depending on how angry Katahiro chose to be. With his strong arm to help, though, Ryōtora stood an actual chance of making it back to someplace he was allowed to be. It might still end in Ryōtora's weakness being exposed to the world, but that was a risk he was prepared to take.

First, though, they had to get to the pavilion.

Ryōtora skirted the front building rather than entering, as many people did when they knew where to go. This wasn't the path Kinmoku had led him along when they came for the gathering, but he remembered that the Komoriyome Pavilion was on the northwestern side of the complex. As long as he didn't attempt to enter the governor's inner palace, no one should object to him wandering the gardens – or so he hoped.

The weather worked in his favor, reducing the number of

courtiers strolling the paths. Ryōtora huddled his shoulders beneath his quilted kimono and hoped the cold wouldn't drain him too badly. He didn't dare hurry, though; he and Yoichi walked sedately, as if they were conversing. Yoichi's eyes darted from side to side as they went, but he had enough restraint not to touch the swords at his hip.

"How long will you need, my lord?" Yoichi murmured.

"I don't know. It depends on what I find – and how long my own strength holds out." This wasn't a type of investigation Ryōtora had ever been trained for, nor did he know any formal invocations that could assure him of getting a useful answer from the spirits. He would simply have to make offerings, pray, and hope.

The Komoriyome Pavilion was a sullen mass against the gray sky. Or was that simply Ryōtora's own dread, infusing the place with the weight of his worries? It seemed to be deserted. As Sekken had said, the guards had little reason to be concerned with a pavilion that had not been inhabited in years.

Sekken, Ryōtora thought. The other man would not be pleased to know he'd slipped off to do this on his own. But Ryōtora could not in good conscience ask Sekken to go creeping around behind the back of his own clan. If trouble came of this, let it fall on the heads of the Dragon only.

The ground all around the pavilion was open, with no cover. Casting his gaze across it, Ryōtora saw where the guards' steps had marred the surface of the snow. Had Kinmoku left footprints? Had anyone bothered to look for that, before trampling either evidence or its lack?

He could ask later – perhaps. "Follow the path they

walked," he murmured to Yoichi, as if someone might be close enough to overhear. "We don't want to leave any more trace of ourselves than we must."

As if they were a pair of shinobi. He swallowed down a fresh wave of guilt and hurried across the snow.

Gaining the shelter of the building brought little relief. Wooden shutters had been slid across the outer walls to protect the paper from the weather; pushing those aside to admit more light would be as good as waving a banner that someone was in the pavilion. Yoichi left one of them open just a crack, and the two men stood quietly in the darkness until their eyes adjusted.

Not that there was much to see. The pavilion had long since been cleared of all the cushions and screens used during the gathering, leaving an empty, echoing space little warmer than the air outside. Even the gold leaf and etched brackets decorating the panels of the ceiling above seemed wan and cold. Ryōtora shoved his hands deeper into his sleeves, seeking comfort that was nowhere to be had.

"Did they say where exactly Lady Mirumoto was found?" he asked Yoichi. The other man shook his head.

It hardly mattered. The question was a delaying tactic, a flimsy reason for Ryōtora not to move toward the far end of the now-open room, to where the candles and the mirror had stood. If anything supernatural had happened during the gathering, whatever traces might remain would be there.

He feared that less than he feared what he might be about to do to himself.

Fear is one of the Three Sins. He forced himself forward.

Ryōtora had brought offerings for the spirits. Sake, rice,

incense, and a piece of soft paper folded into a shape like a butterfly, made by one of the servants at the embassy. Ryōtora lacked the skill of a street magician, who could make that paper dance above a wafting fan as if it were alive. But of all the elemental spirits, air had the most sense of humor; he hoped they would be amused by his fumbling efforts to keep the butterfly aloft.

Though the sharp crack made him wince, he clapped his hands to attract the attention of the spirits – and hopefully *only* the spirits. Then he bowed and began to pray, laying out the offerings and lighting the incense before tossing the butterfly into the air.

He was braced for the vertiginous rush that overtook him. The same thing happened every time he attempted to commune, as if the boundaries between the elements that made him up and those that surrounded him had been badly eroded. He'd given his own strength in offering, a year and a half ago; now communion made him feel as if a part of himself were elsewhere. But this time he didn't let the unsteadiness dissuade him. Curling his fingers against the cold mat, he breathed out his question in a cloud of cold frost.

What happened here?

The dizziness intensified. Sometimes when Ryōtora was exceptionally exhausted, even closing his eyes left him feeling as if he were spinning and floating like that paper butterfly, too disoriented to relax into sleep. The same was true now – but not because he'd already tipped over into a state of collapse. *Everything* was sliding, unstable, unreal. The spirits of the air giggled, and the traces of water that lingered in the wood and the matting murmured as if he'd disturbed their rest. The earth groaned luxuriantly and stretched, like a cat preparing to curl up in a new and more comfortable position. Ryōtora felt the urge to curl up along with it.

No. He fought to maintain a hold on his flesh. He could feel it now, like a seductive whirlpool, drawing his spirit downward… or sideways. Out of the mortal realm, and into the Realm of Dreams.

After all, wouldn't it be nice to rest? To just let his eyes stay closed, let himself slump to the floor. The spirits were dreaming. He could dream alongside them, retreating to someplace warm, someplace without responsibility. Without a body that persistently betrayed him. In dreams, he could be himself again – or even something better.

Fighting his way up from that felt like climbing a mountain with a lead weight on his back. Tears seeped from beneath his eyelids, hot against his cold cheeks. Yes, he wanted that. He wanted it so badly he could *taste* it.

But other things were more important than his desires. His clan needed him. If he let himself stay here, he would be abandoning everything he valued.

Ryōtora reached for the strength that so often escaped him, and *demanded* that it answer.

"Lord Isao!"

Yoichi's urgent hiss snapped his eyes open. The clerk was at the crack in the shutters, peering outward. Then he hurried across to Ryōtora, dropping to one knee. "Guards are coming this way. I will go out to meet them; you leave by the back."

Everything seemed preternaturally sharp, not fogged by exhaustion as Ryōtora expected. "Sir Yoichi–"

"You are the ambassador now, my lord. You cannot be caught here. I will buy you time. *Go!*"

There was no arguing with his urgency, nor with his logic. As Yoichi hurried back to the open shutter, Ryōtora turned to the far wall and slid it open. An unbroken expanse of snow stretched before him, ready to receive the damning evidence of his footprints.

With a fluent ease Ryōtora didn't know he possessed, he muttered an extemporaneous poem under his breath.

*Lighter than the wind
are the footfalls of a man
carried by duty*

The spirits of the air danced in delight at his offering. This *was* an invocation Ryōtora knew; it was taught to all Agasha priests who traveled through the mountains, enabling them to walk lightly on surfaces that might otherwise give way beneath their feet.

When he stepped out into the snow, whispering prayers under his breath, he left no mark.

As an angry voice called out from the far side of the hall, Ryōtora slid the shutter closed behind him and ran.

CHAPTER FIFTEEN

Doubts plagued Sekken all the way to the House of Infinite Petals. The look Ryōtora had, so drained and empty... he'd said he was fine, but of course Ryōtora would say that. Anything else would be an admission of personal weakness. Even though he ought to know he could admit such things to Sekken, with no loss of dignity.

Except this was Ryōtora. He might think the exact opposite: that Sekken was the last person in all the world to whom he could show anything other than perfect health.

Sekken knew all too well what that felt like.

It was long past time for them to talk – but not until Sekken's business was done at the House of Infinite Petals. For once, he understood Ryōtora's mentality; personal weakness couldn't be allowed to get in the way of pursuing the matter at hand, not even if he paid a price for it later.

Sekken just wished he could be doing more to help Ryōtora than merely talking to Sayashi. First, though, he had to think of something more he *could* do to help. Even at his best, Sekken wouldn't have been the most adroit ally in court; he simply didn't spend enough time there, accumulating the sorts of connections and favors that would help get things done. In his current condition, he was of dubious utility at all.

Yet he had a better footing at court than Ryōtora did. Especially with the other man suddenly thrust into the role of ambassador.

Except that you aren't a member of Ryōtora's clan. It isn't your place to help him.

Some might even say it would be disloyal for him to do so.

Sekken smacked an angry hand against the wall of his litter. From outside came one of the bearer's voices: "My lord?"

"Never mind," he called back, annoyance seeping through into his response. Not with the bearer; with himself. With everything. With the stupid demands of his status as a samurai, which placed loyalty to his clan above…

Not above everything. That thought came in Ryōtora's voice.

Yes, a samurai was supposed to be loyal to his lord and his clan. But their code had seven tenets, and that was only one of them. Honesty demanded that Sekken not allow the Dragon to be blamed for something that might not be their fault. Compassion demanded that he help a man in need. Righteousness demanded that he seek justice in this situation, not whatever benefited his own clan the most.

Samurai had committed suicide in protest rather than carry out unjust orders, their last service to their lords the irrevocable rebuke of their deaths. Compared to that, Sekken's dilemma here was *easy*.

And he even had some thoughts for how to go about helping, now that he'd resolved to do so. While Sekken himself might not be the most adept at court, his mother and Ameno were a different matter. Even Ginshō had her own angle on political affairs, from the perspective of a swordswoman serving courtiers. They might have some insight into what new game Katahiro was playing. It was something Sekken ought to ask about, regardless of his reason.

No. He couldn't claim he was reaching for honesty with one hand, while hiding the truth behind his back with the other. He would tell them why he was asking.

Might share a few more truths with a few more people while you're at it.

But not at this moment, because he'd arrived at the House of Infinite Petals.

Sekken climbed out of the litter, rapped on the gate, and gave the stocky guard a winning smile. "Hello again. Yes, I know I'm early again. I need to speak with Teishi on a matter of some urgency – unrelated to any attachment on either of our parts, I assure you. Or if I must jump over some obstacles first, then please inform the mother of the house that I'm here."

One discreet bribe later, he was seated again in the room he and Ryōtora had been escorted to before. Sekken wasn't surprised to see the mistress arrive soon after; even if *she* didn't feel the need to force her samurai guest through some preliminary steps, Sayashi might well insist on it.

But after she'd knelt and poured tea for him, the conversation took an unexpected turn. "I would gladly give you the opportunity to speak with Teishi," the mistress said, "but I regret to inform my noble guest that she is not here."

At this hour of the morning, she couldn't possibly mean that Sayashi had already left to attend a client. "Did she vanish four days ago?" Sekken asked, leaning forward eagerly. He didn't know if a bakeneko could be struck down by this affliction, but they still hadn't turned up a victim for the night after Hanemi fell asleep.

"She has not vanished at all," the mistress said, defensiveness and surprise ruffling her serenity. "Much less four days ago! No, I mean only that she has not yet returned from her engagement last night."

That put Sekken back on his heels. The law forbade geisha from sleeping with their clients; they could be drummed out of their houses for doing so. Not that an overnight stay necessarily meant anything illicit had taken place, of course – but ordinarily these houses maintained strict control over their people.

Of course, most of their people owed an enormous debt to their house for years of training, the clothes and makeup they wore, the instruments they played, and so forth. Sekken doubted that Sayashi owed any such debt. "Is that normal?" he asked. "Did you expect her to stay out all night?"

Before the mistress could answer, he held up one hand. "I know you must be discreet, but given Teishi's... unusual nature, I have a strong need to speak with her. I assume that rumors have reached you about the recent problems?"

"My lord, I would not presume to–"

"In other words, yes, they have. I'm investigating that matter, and Teishi may be able to help. Was her client last night the provincial governor?"

The air of unflappable serenity was back, but the pause

before the woman answered betrayed the struggle within. Then she said, "Yes."

"As I suspected. Mistress, she may not return for some time." First Kaikoga Hanemi, then Mirumoto Kinmoku; Sekken wouldn't be surprised to find that Chūkan Ujiteru and Asako Shoun had been brought to the palace as well. "Does the governor know about Teishi's true nature?"

"If he does," the mistress said, "then she has not shared that fact with me."

Sekken hoped he didn't – that he'd only kept Sayashi at the palace because she'd been present for the Game of a Hundred Candles. Otherwise, the bakeneko might find herself in very dire straits. Even if none of this was Sayashi's fault, blaming her would save face for all the samurai involved.

He tucked his feet under him and stood. "I will make inquiries at the palace. If Teishi returns here, will you send word to me?"

"Yes, my lord." The mistress bowed gracefully. "I am most grateful for my lord's concern."

Sekken had a plan for what to do when he got to the palace – and it utterly failed to account for something he should have seen coming.

I presume that rumors have reached you about the recent problems, he'd said to the mother of the geisha house… but of course if rumors had spread that far, they would be all throughout the court by now. Sekken no sooner set foot inside the palace than the maelstrom of gossip began to swirl around him.

"I heard the Dragon ambassador was the most recent one caught," a Shiba lord whose name he'd forgotten murmured to him. The man's fan was raised just far enough to make a pretense of discretion, not far enough to actually achieve it. "And now that Isao Ryōtora fellow is ambassador in her place. Do you think he has something to do with this? None of this began until he arrived, after all."

"*Weeks* after he arrived," Sekken snapped. Mitsusada; that was the man's name. "Didn't you come late to winter court, Lord Shiba? As I recall, none of these problems cropped up until after *you* arrived."

Mitsusada drew himself up like an offended peacock. "I was delayed by the snowstorm, Lord Asako."

It had been a stab in the dark on Sekken's part; he had no idea when most of the attendees had reached the city, except that the storm had delayed more than a few. Smiling as if he'd known all along, he said, "I would not be in a hurry to fling accusations, Lord Shiba. After all, the answer is likely to have less to do with timing and more to do with motivation. Who would benefit from seeing the Dragon blamed?"

That part wasn't a blind thrust. Memory was coming back: his sister Ameno had mentioned Shiba Mitsusada complaining about the Dragon refusing to provide him with a copy of a rare sixth-century commentary on the Sutra of the Seasons. It was hardly the sort of dispute that would provoke this kind of disruption – but Sekken's question had the desired effect, which was to make Mitsusada scowl and walk away after the most perfunctory of bows.

Unfortunately, Mitsusada was far from the last. Everyone

was talking about the sleeping victims, and those who weren't gossiping about how Kaikoga or the Dragon might be to blame were speculating as to who would be next. Gambling might be a disgraceful pastime for samurai, but that didn't prevent it from being popular, and Sekken rather suspected more than a few people were laying discreet wagers.

Then a different thread caught his ear. "Forgive me, Sir Hiroie," he said, breaking into a conversation with a good deal less grace than he should have. "I could not help but overhear. Did you say something about Doji Suemaru?"

Koganshi Hiroie and those he was speaking with were all low-ranking enough that they couldn't snub Sekken for his rudeness. Hiroie bowed. "I am sure it is nothing, Lord Asako. Merely that Lord Doji has not been seen in a few days. His deputy ambassador says he is unwell, and we have no reason to question that explanation."

No reason except that Doji Suemaru, as the Crane Clan ambassador, had been present for the Game of a Hundred Candles. "I hope he recovers soon," Sekken said, with perfect sincerity; it was true whether Suemaru was a victim of this curse or not. "How long has he been ill?"

"Four days, my lord."

Hiroie was adept enough to let that statement of fact speak for itself. By now everyone knew the sequence, and that there was a hole in it. But if Doji Suemaru was the second one to fall asleep, why would the Crane not admit that, now that everyone knew about the problem? Where had their ambassador been found?

If he *was* the missing victim, that changed the political

calculus. Should the Crane turn against the Dragon, things would become much worse for Ryōtora and his clan.

Which made it all the more urgent that Sekken extricate himself from the mire of gossip and find some useful information.

He escaped by the inelegant expedient of implying that he needed to relieve himself, and slipped away from the main chambers where court attendees gathered. But a privy was too defiled a place to attempt anything remotely spiritual, so he had to brave the sharp chill outside to find the solitude he needed.

Then – leaning against one of the pillars that supported the covered walkway between buildings, in case he fell over – Sekken closed his eyes and reached for Tanshu.

This was the sort of experiment Isawa Chikayū had been urging him to undertake ever since he returned with an inugami bound to him. For his ancestor Kaimin-nushi, no doubt Tanshu had been an important supernatural ally; for Sekken, a courtier with no more spiritual potential than a reasonably attractive rock, the inugami was little more than a pet. But the magical practices of tsukimono-suji did not require one to commune with the elements, and there were presumably things Sekken could learn to do, if only he exerted himself.

Exertion, of course, was exactly the problem. But he'd sent Tanshu off, hoping the dog would understand his orders, to keep an eye on Kaikoga Hanemi; now he had no better way to call Tanshu back than to hope the bond between them could be plucked like the string of a biwa.

It couldn't, at least not the way he'd imagined. Sekken

had been spending a good deal more time in meditation this last year and a half, though, and he'd learned that when he settled his mind to contemplate the present moment in all its fine detail, he did indeed have a vague sense of *dogness* that was both part and not part of himself. Usually that sense was fairly immediate, because Tanshu stuck to his side like a burr. Now, however, it felt more distant.

Come, he thought, as if he were recalling Tanshu from the garden. The dog understood spoken commands; would that carry through whatever bound them now? He tried visualizing instead, Tanshu getting up from wherever he was and trotting across the palace to where Sekken stood.

Then he had a dizzying sense of exactly that, and he had to sit down very abruptly. He scrambled to his feet a moment later, lest anyone find him splayed out on the walkway, but he thought – he hoped – that Tanshu was coming.

It didn't take long for the dog to arrive. *He* had no need to walk at a courtier's dignified pace, and Sekken often suspected, though he'd never gotten around to proving it, that Tanshu could walk through walls. The inugami trotted up, looking very pleased with himself, and plunked his rear down in front of Sekken like a courtier kneeling to receive his lord's accolades.

Sekken himself knelt, a more dignified posture than his previous one, and devoted both hands to scratching behind Tanshu's ears. "You did it, didn't you?" he whispered, feeling unutterably proud. "You understood what I said, and you've been watching over Kaikoga this entire time. Without being caught!"

Tanshu leaned forward as if to nudge him, but instead he

pressed himself into Sekken's forehead and stayed that way. Following a suspicion, Sekken closed his eyes and stilled his thoughts again.

It wasn't precisely a vision. Everything was blurry, the colors muted – though a riot of sensations went through Sekken's mind that he thought might be scents, if scents were fully illustrated scrolls written by fifty different hands. He wasn't quite watching a scene play out, as if performed by actors on a stage; it was more like a summary of a play, noting that first one thing happened and then another, but glossing over many of the details along the way.

By the time Sekken drew back, dizzy in a way that had nothing to do with weakness, he had a sense of what Tanshu meant to convey. Yes, he'd been watching over Kaikoga Hanemi. But whereas Sekken had feared that Katahiro's priest would come to examine or treat her, and in so doing, notice Tanshu... he saw no evidence that any priest had come at all.

"You're sure?" he asked, the way he would have said to a human. "No priest? No one like Ryōtora, or your old mistress Kaimin-nushi?" As if communing with the spirits imparted a particular scent a dog's nose might pick up. Though for all Sekken knew, it did.

Tanshu huffed quietly, as if to say, *yes, I'm sure.*

Sekken sat back on his heels, fighting the urge to swear. Hadn't Katahiro said he'd take care of that? His exact phrasing had slipped from Sekken's memory, but it hardly mattered. The question wasn't whether Katahiro had lied; honesty might be a virtue, but no one survived as a provincial governor without embracing the need for the occasional politic lie.

The question was why he wouldn't take such an obvious step to address this problem. Why not examine the first victim? Why not try to wake Kaikoga Hanemi? Katahiro stood to gain a great deal if he could claim his own people lifted this curse. And he didn't seem to be gaining anything more valuable by letting it spread. What was he waiting for?

None of those were questions Tanshu could answer. But the dog might be able to help with something else.

"I have a new mission for you," Sekken murmured, burying his cold fingers in the dog's ruff. "Do you remember the bakeneko from Seibo Mura?"

A low growl answered him.

"Don't hurt her," Sekken cautioned. "But I need to find her. She supposedly came here last night; I need to know if that's true, and if so, whether she's still here. Do you think you can search for her scent?"

Ordinarily a dog would need something to take the scent from: a known trail, a garment worn by the quarry, anything to say *this is what you have to find*. Sekken doubted even a highly intelligent inugami could recall a scent last encountered a year and a half ago, and he hadn't thought to ask the mother of the House of Infinite Petals for something of Teishi's. But whether priests had a distinctive smell or not, Sekken rather suspected that bakeneko *did*.

The huff was a little less quiet this time. Yes, Tanshu could do it – or at least he was willing to try.

"Come find me when you're done," Sekken said, rising once more to his feet. "Either in there, or at my house." He jerked his chin at the main building of the palace.

It turned out to be a mistake.

Only a quick grab at the post kept him from toppling off the walkway to the ground. The exhaustion hit like an avalanche of snow, faster and harder than it ever had before, blanketing him, cutting off all air. Sekken couldn't keep his grip on the post. He collapsed, and only after a warm, furry body had cushioned his fall did he realize Tanshu had manifested physically, keeping him from striking the boards with his head.

No. Not now. Not here. As if there was ever a good time and place for his elemental strength to betray him.

He'd been right not to conduct the experiments Chikayū wanted. And he should have been smart enough not to conduct this one in the middle of the governor's palace.

Sekken crawled off Tanshu, murmuring a pointless apology, and dragged himself first to a sitting position, then – with the help of the post – to standing. Even that much movement, however, proved to him that he didn't stand a chance of getting out of here on his own. Tanshu, manifested or not, wouldn't be enough. He needed help.

"Go find someone," he mumbled to the inugami. "My mother, or…" Who would be here today? Potentially all of his family. "Ginshō. Ameno. Someone I can trust. Find them and bring them here."

Tanshu didn't even bark this time. He shot off like an arrow from a bow.

Sekken sagged against the post, feeling like a paper-thin husk of himself, his mind not much stronger. Meditation helped, sometimes. Should he sit? If he propped his back against the post, he might be able to manage sitting. But the walkway looked a very long way down.

Then voices, from the other building across the garden. Coming around the corner of the veranda. Tanshu had brought *Isawa Miyuki*?

No, he hadn't. The dog was nowhere in sight, and Miyuki was talking to someone Sekken ought to recognize but couldn't. She hadn't seen him yet.

She couldn't see him. Not like this. Sekken lurched into motion, knowing he looked ridiculous, not caring, just so long as he could get around another corner before Miyuki noticed the apparent drunk disgracing himself at court. He made it without hearing his name, so at least she hadn't identified the drunk. Where was he? Sekken couldn't remember which side of the palace he'd gone out in order to find privacy. Would Tanshu be able to find him, if he collapsed somewhere else?

There. Up ahead, an archway he remembered. It led to the court where the kemari game had taken place. No one would be playing in weather like this, but the warriors might still be there–

He had to cling to the archway, but the Fortunes were with him. Ginshō, diligent to a fault, was practicing her daily thousand strikes with a few other swordsmen.

She spotted him immediately. Sekken ducked behind the wall before anyone else could see him, which ended with him slumped at its base, wishing pathetically that the world would stop spinning. Then Ginshō was there, anchoring reality.

Her face was red with exertion and white with horror. "Brother–"

"It's bad," he managed. "Have to get out of here. Where's Tanshu?"

"I haven't seen him." Ginshō cast a swift glance around, then slung one of his arms over her shoulders. "Can you walk?"

"Yes. Maybe." His body tried to give the lie to his first answer as soon as she hauled him to his feet.

Ginshō said grimly, "We'll have to try. If I carry you out of here, someone *will* notice."

"Tanshu," Sekken said, stupidly. Where had the dog gone? If Ginshō was this close by, why hadn't he gone for her first?

His sister ignored him. With one muscled arm tight around his waist, she was doing her best to unobtrusively manhandle him down a path that felt twelve miles long. If someone found them, maybe Sekken could claim he'd sprained his ankle – assuming he could get the words out without slurring.

Someone did find them.

Tanshu came racing through a gate up ahead, with a figure hard at his heels. A man Sekken would have recognized through any exhaustion, through any mental fog, through the veil of death itself.

The last person he wanted to see.

Ryōtora.

CHAPTER SIXTEEN

Ryōtora had barely made it back to a part of the palace grounds where he felt safe when Tanshu raced into view, snow flying from his paws.

His first thought was that the dog was trying to warn him of pursuers, and he looked frantically around for a place to hide. But Tanshu had come from the other direction, and Ryōtora didn't think there was any way the guards at the pavilion could have alerted someone in the palace proper to intercept him.

Tanshu skidded to a halt and barked once. Then he pivoted to go back the way he'd come, looking over his shoulder, and barked again. When Ryōtora still stood, mute and uncomprehending, the dog resorted to grabbing a sleeve-end in his teeth and dragging.

He wants me to follow him. Ryōtora didn't know why, but he trusted Tanshu, and so he went.

Across a bridge spanning a frozen pond, through an open gate in a garden wall – and then Ryōtora stopped again, because now he knew why Tanshu had come for him.

At sufficient distance, Sekken's behavior might have been

mistaken for normal: one arm slung over his sister in a display of brotherly camaraderie. From behind, the extent to which she was holding him up might have been mistaken for assistance offered to a man with an injured foot. But seeing Sekken's face, gray with exhaustion, Ryōtora knew it was nothing of the sort.

Ginshō's step hitched at the sight of Ryōtora, unbalancing Sekken enough that the man began to slip. Ryōtora leapt forward to help catch him, taking Sekken's other arm over his own shoulders. "What happened? Did he fall asleep? Where did you find him?"

She cursed with all the earthy inventiveness of a soldier, trying to reclaim her brother's weight entirely for herself. "It's not that; it's just one of his usual–"

The words cut off, but not soon enough. The warmth brought on by Ryōtora's flight from the pavilion deserted him. "One of his usual *what*?"

He heard voices in the distance. So did Ginshō, and she cursed again. "Help me get him out of here and back to our mansion. We can talk after that."

Ryōtora himself was better off leaving the palace, and he understood her urgency, if not its cause. He clamped his mouth shut, hitched Sekken's arm to a better position, and began to move.

They got Sekken into a litter without being spotted, though Ryōtora had to walk alongside Ginshō all the way back to their family mansion. She refused to say anything while they were in the streets, but she didn't have to; a suspicion was already forming in Ryōtora's gut.

One of his usual– What word would have finished that sentence? Fits? Collapses? There were plenty of options... all of which Ryōtora had used to describe himself.

That drained, enervated look on Sekken's face, and his inability to even protest while Ryōtora and Ginshō dragged him across the grounds and stuffed him into a litter. Ryōtora wasn't sure he'd been fully conscious by then. It was a state he recognized all too well, though in his own experience it was rarely quite so bad.

He'd been a fool to think he was the only one to suffer consequences. He'd assumed that Sekken, having given away half his own strength, had recovered it with time and effort, just as a child grew stronger and brighter with maturity and education. That only Ryōtora, living on borrowed vitality, was subject to such lapses.

But it seemed one could not make such a sacrifice and hope to recover in full.

At the mansion, servants burst into action with a speed and agility that told Ryōtora this was not the first time they'd had to do it. Before he could protest, Sekken was bundled away from him, into a back part of the house, with someone calling for a specific broth to be made at once. Ryōtora dared not follow; he remained, standing and mute, on the veranda. Eventually a servant ushered him inside – less out of conscious hospitality, Ryōtora thought, and more out of the reflexive assumption that any samurai at the manor should not be left in the cold.

The cold came with him, carried deep inside. *All this time. Both of us are broken.*

When Ginshō came into the room, the brief stillness in

her body said she'd forgotten he might still be there. Then she moved again, coming to kneel across from him, the curling smoke of the brazier between them not enough to veil the hard set of her jaw.

"You need not explain," Ryōtora said softly, looking at the burning coals rather than at her. "I believe I understand. He has been like this since his return?"

She lacked a courtier's subtlety and finesse. "Yes."

Ryōtora shifted back so he could bow to the floor – the bow he'd been wanting to give since his arrival in the city, but Sekken had persistently blocked him. "It is my fault. Had I known before now, I would have…"

Would have what?

It took him a moment to realize those words hadn't merely been in his head; someone else had said them as well. Ryōtora didn't need to rise from his bow to know Asako Fumizuki's voice; she had come silently into the room.

"Would have tried to help," he said.

"We have consulted many physicians," Lady Asako said. "To the best of my understanding, Lord Isao, you are no kind of physician at all. What could you possibly do for him that they cannot?"

Ryōtora could imagine all too well what Sekken had been through, because the Dragon had done the same for him. Medicines. Acupuncture. Meditative exercises. Attempts to rebuild his Earth, his Water, his Air, his Fire, any gain too soon fading away, like sake poured into a jar with a hole at the bottom, and no one could find the hole to plug it. A problem with no solution.

He couldn't tell Lady Asako that. The last thing she

would want to hear right now was that her son had ruined his health for so little result – that in place of one healthy man and one dead, they had two living half-lives. Now was not the time to ask for her sympathy.

Now was the time to offer what little he could. Ryōtora said, "I can be the person who caused his weakness. The one to whom he gave the strength he now lacks."

Ginshō's indrawn breath was audible. Lady Asako's was not. It seemed Sekken had told his mother the truth, but not his whole family. Ryōtora remained low, his face poised over his carefully placed hands. Running from the pavilion and then making the journey here had, for once, not sapped him; his posture was steady.

Lady Asako said, "Lord Isao, for such a matter as this, I must lay aside polite discretion and ask directly what you mean. Because I know this much: my son would not want you to harm yourself in order to help him."

Ryōtora's heart tightened painfully. No, Sekken would not want that. And however much a part of Ryōtora felt like he ought to – like he *owed* Sekken whatever he could do, no matter the cost – that part was drowned out by the rest. Not just the voice that spoke of his duty to his clan, but the one that said he had to respect Sekken's wishes.

"I understand," he said. "But it is possible that anything I can do for him will have a greater effect than the same action coming from another. It is, after all, Lord Asako's own strength I will be using to help him."

He heard Ginshō shift on the mat. "I say let him try. We've attempted much stupider solutions."

The soft brush of cloth against tatami was Lady Asako

coming toward Ryōtora. Shibori-dyed silk in a pattern like snowflakes entered his peripheral vision, and then was eclipsed by a slender hand. Ryōtora did not resist as she lifted his chin and studied his gaze, with disconcerting directness.

"Please," she said, releasing him. "Help my son. If you can."

Lady Asako herself led Ryōtora deeper into the house. Ginshō didn't follow, but the third daughter, Ameno, was in Sekken's bedchamber, watching over her sleeping brother with a half-touched bowl of broth at her knee. Seeing that, Ryōtora remembered Sekken saying he knew many excellent physicians, with techniques for feeding patients unable to swallow on their own.

This was why he was familiar with such things.

Ameno's eyes widened as the two of them came in, and she rose to her feet. Lady Asako gestured for Ryōtora to kneel where her daughter had been. "Tell us what you need, Lord Isao."

"Offerings," he said, paying more attention to tucking his kimono under his knees than it required. "Whatever you have will be suitable." This would be no grand prayer, a huge ritual to summon the attention of a powerful spirit; he was working with the smallest kind, the ones that made up the mind and body of a human being.

Ameno went out. While he waited for her to return, Ryōtora cast about for something to say to Lady Asako, and came up with nothing. He could not look away from Sekken.

It was like the morning Ryōtora had awoken in the ruins of Seibo Mura to find Sekken asleep next to him – *asleep*, when the other man habitually woke with the dawn. His hair wasn't cropped short anymore, but he had the same fragile, translucent look to him, like a soap bubble that might break at the slightest touch. His bony, long-fingered hands were limp against the futon; with Lady Asako there, Ryōtora didn't dare take one into his own.

I did this to him.

No, another part of him answered. *Sekken chose this, for your sake.*

He didn't know what he was choosing.

Do you think that would have changed his mind?

He was painfully glad when Ameno returned with a tray of simple offerings. Doing this so soon after his investigation at the Komoriyome Pavilion was a significant risk... but still, Ryōtora clapped his hands, bowed, and began to pray.

It wasn't a difficult communion. Some spirits resisted outside intrusion, especially if the offering was insufficient, but with Sekken it was like one drop of water melding into another. Of course: Ryōtora's Water had originally been Sekken's. This was less about one spirit contacting another; it was more like an island briefly separating a channel off from the river, only for the two to rejoin at the far end.

The island could be removed. In Earth terms rather than Water, Ryōtora was like a stone that had been lifted into the air. The weight of the world *wanted* to drag the stone back down. His Air wanted to escape the silken bag into which it had been blown; his Fire wanted to burn through the barrier that separated the two men. That would be the natural course to follow.

But Sekken wouldn't want that. Ryōtora took a deep breath, and held firm.

Apart from returning what he'd been given, what could he do?

If he'd needed confirmation that Sekken's collapse had nothing to do with the sleep afflicting the others, he had it now. Ryōtora felt none of the dreaming lassitude that had tried to pull him under at the pavilion, only the echoing emptiness of a well, drawn nearly dry. It was a sensation he knew intimately, though he'd never had the chance to observe it from the outside. His own experience told him that he couldn't simply refill the well – at least, not with elemental spirits drawn from outside. They would only drain right back out again, through unseen cracks in the container of the soul.

Thinking in terms of a container gave him pause. One of the common metaphors used to discuss the role of the Void in the cosmos was a bowl or a jar: the empty space within, though nothing in its own right, was what defined the bowl and gave it purpose. Ryōtora's own physicians had speculated that the problem might be less some lack in his Earth or his Fire than an overreach by his Void, creating emptiness where there should be substance. But apart from some tattooed monks – whose strange abilities often applied only to themselves – the Dragon had no one who could work with the Void directly.

Without opening his eyes, Ryōtora asked, "Has Sekken been treated at any point by an ishiken?"

"No," Lady Asako said. "I have considered it, but…"

But those who could interact with the Void were rare even among the Phoenix. And given that Sekken's family had clearly been trying to keep his condition secret – was that why Hanemi had mentioned him being reclusive? – they could not simply ask for an ishiken's help.

Ryōtora wondered if that was part of the deal with Isawa Miyuki's family. After all, her mother Chikayū was involved in the negotiations seeking to send an ishiken to Seibo Mura.

Neither politics nor his own relationship with Sekken were useful thoughts to indulge in right now. Ryōtora explained his thinking, and Lady Asako said, "My son has tried numerous meditative techniques, which I would hope could address any such imbalance of Void. But I will admit we have not considered it consciously in those terms before now. Perhaps…" She fell silent for a moment, then said, "It is worth trying."

Even if it was worth trying, it did nothing for Sekken *now*. Ryōtora hesitated, then drew a deep breath. So far, his communion had gone well; he could risk trying just a bit more.

He restricted his prayers to little more than the movement of his lips and tongue, hoping Lady Asako and her daughter were still behind him, where they could not see. *One drop from the stream,* he said to the spirits of Water; to the Air, *one breath from the silk.* One spark from the Fire, and the smallest increment of descent from the Earth suspended overhead. *Two must not become one, as they were before. Just a gift, from one to the other.*

The spirits balked at such restraint. Why should they hold back, when generosity was much easier?

Because, Ryōtora said to them, if you give yourselves in full, the one who receives you will not be grateful. But if you hold back, I will make new offerings in thanks.

It was a peculiar sort of bargain, promising greater rewards if the spirits helped *less*. But it worked: he felt a tiny portion of his strength flow away, not enough to weaken him, just enough – he hoped – to aid Sekken.

When he ended the communion and opened his eyes, he wasn't sure if his imagination put a little more color into the man's face, a little more ease into his breathing. The soft sound that escaped Lady Asako reassured him: a tiny, choked-off sob of relief.

Ryōtora was cautious in rising and turning around, lest the room spin and put him right back on the mat. It also gave Lady Asako a moment to secure her composure; by the time he faced her, she was serene once more. "Thank you, Lord Isao."

"I cannot be sure it will last," he warned her. "If this truly is an imbalance of Void, what I have done may fade."

"We'll make sure he rests," Ameno said.

Resting wouldn't do much, if Sekken's condition was indeed the same as Ryōtora's own. He couldn't say that, though, without giving away what he wanted to keep secret. He only bowed and said, "I have troubled you for long enough."

"You are a welcome guest here," Lady Asako said, more warmly than he'd ever heard from her. "But you have already taken much time away from your own duties."

Less his duties than his crimes. In the shock of dealing with Sekken, Ryōtora had allowed the events at the Komoriyome Pavilion to be driven from his mind. His absence might help reinforce his innocence, if anyone from the governor's palace had come looking for him, but it was long past time for Ryōtora to return to the embassy.

And whatever waited for him there. "Please inform me if he wakes, or if his circumstances change," Ryōtora said, and bowed himself out.

He sagged with relief when he reached the embassy and found Yoichi waiting for him inside.

It wasn't the same as escaping consequences entirely, of course. "I'm forbidden to return to the palace," Yoichi said, discouraged. "Which means I can no longer serve this embassy effectively. I will report this back to our lands; no doubt they will send a replacement for me."

"You can still serve *very* well," Ryōtora said, "by helping me. Sir Yoichi, I will be utterly lost without your assistance and guidance. And we can hope that once this matter is settled, the governor will forgive you." He wasn't sure how; that kind of lenience was a favor, just like everything else at court, and favors never came without a price. The Dragon's political treasury was perilously bare these days.

But he meant what he said, and Yoichi nodded his thanks. "What did you discover in the pavilion?"

Ryōtora described the odd behavior of the spirits there, ending with, "It certainly seems like the gathering disrupted the spiritual atmosphere, creating a thin spot through which the Realm of Dreams can influence the waking world."

Yoichi grimaced. "Which might still have something to do with Lady Kaikoga… but you must realize what else you're implying."

"Yes," Ryōtora said. "That the governor may also bear some responsibility for what's happening. Whether he realized it or not, his gathering created the circumstances that led to this affliction."

He'd known it was possible before they went to the pavilion. He wouldn't have taken the risk of going, otherwise.

Ryōtora wished he had found a different answer.

"What are you going to do?" Yoichi asked.

Ryōtora sighed. "I made a promise to some spirits," he said. "Those of the elements within *me*. They did what I asked, and so I owe them offerings. I am going to have a bath, and a good meal, and I will ask Atsumaru Otane to play the flute for me. Once that is done… we will see."

CHAPTER SEVENTEEN

Even before he opened his eyes, Sekken knew what had happened. No blissful period of ignorance cushioned his waking; the ache in his body reminded him of the terrible collapse that had preceded the darkness. The collapse, and Ginshō…

…and Ryōtora.

Lying there with his eyes closed as if he were still asleep was a coward's response and wouldn't solve anything. He was a grown man, and not *that* much of a coward: he forced himself to open his eyes.

He wasn't surprised to find Tanshu curled up on his futon and Ginshō kneeling a little distance away. By now his family was accustomed to the ups and downs of his health, but the severity of the most recent downswing would have alarmed them. She knelt with her own eyes shut, but it was a warrior's readiness rather than a meditative trance; she came alert even faster than Tanshu did, moving to Sekken's side as soon as he drew breath to speak. "Don't sit up."

"I didn't plan on trying to," Sekken said. It came out a rasp, and she supported his head enough for him to drink from a cup. Which herbs had they decided he needed the most right now? Judging by the taste, all of them. But he was used to unpleasant flavors these days, and he swallowed without protest.

With his head returned to its pillow, he tried speech again. "Ryōtora?"

"Yes," Ginshō said. Although she was the eldest of his sisters, separated from him by nearly a decade of age, she knew him well enough to read the question packed into that single word. "I know you didn't want him to know, but I needed his help to get you away from the palace. And besides, he'd already seen."

Sekken's memories of that moment swam with exhaustion, but he remembered. "Better him than all of court, I guess."

Was that truly better, though? Court would only mock and pity him. Ryōtora… Ryōtora would feel guilt. It was too much to hope that he hadn't guessed the story behind Sekken's collapse.

"He treated you," Ginshō said. "I don't know exactly what he did. Mother told him not to harm himself for your sake. I think she likes him."

That was news to Sekken. His mother thought well of Ryōtora? Oh, he knew she admired what the man had done in Seibo Mura; still, that was a far cry from caring about Ryōtora's own health, when Sekken's was so badly damaged. *I underestimated her,* Sekken thought. After a year and a half of his mother moving the heavens themselves to heal him – without success – he'd come to believe she would do anything to restore his strength. Well, anything short of blood magic. Apparently, he should add "hurting Ryōtora" to that list.

The fact that he could think through that at all was a sign that whatever Ryōtora had done had helped. Normally Sekken would expect his skull to be stuffed with bean curd, after a collapse like that.

He attempted to sit up, to test how far that went, and got flattened by a glare from Ginshō. She was an iaijutsu master with those looks, whipping them out faster than thought.

"I can't stay here forever," Sekken said, once more flat on his back. Tanshu rose and resettled himself, head across Sekken's belly as if to pin him down. "I have to talk to Ryōtora." Though he was still working on scraping back together the things he had wanted to say.

"And you think we're going to stuff you into a litter to visit the Dragon embassy? If you need to talk to him, he can come here."

"He's the ambassador now, with Lady Mirumoto asleep; he can't just–"

"He can and he will. And you know it."

Sekken did. Feeling like a resentful child, and resenting that feeling, he muttered, "Can I at least have something to eat?"

He got broth, and when that went all right, he got a little solid food. An elementally balanced meal, as if a tray of snacks could make up for everything he lacked. Ameno brought it in and sat with him and Ginshō as he ate, both of them watching like he might topple over mid-bite. "I'm doing better," Sekken said in the wake of a swallow. "Truly I am. I know it isn't the same as doing *well*, but I'm not incapacitated."

Ginshō and Ameno exchanged looks. "Lord Isao had a theory," Ameno said, and shared with Sekken Ryōtora's speculations about an overreach of Void.

It was plausible, and it induced a flicker Sekken took a moment to identify. Something he hadn't felt in quite some time: hope. "If that's true," he said, putting the bowl down and sinking his fingers into Tanshu's ruff, "then how do I fix it?"

"With the help of an ishiken."

He'd been so caught up in his thoughts, he hadn't heard his mother slide the door open. She didn't shut it behind her; instead, she remained standing in the doorway. "Son, Isawa Miyuki is here, asking to see you."

"She can't come in," Ameno said immediately. "If she sees—"

Sekken held up one hand. The fact that his mother had come to tell him at all, rather than turning Miyuki away, said she was thinking along the same lines as he was. "She has to," he said to Ameno. "I'm not marrying anyone who doesn't know the truth. It would be dishonest and cruel."

He heard the rest of what his mother hadn't said, too. Miyuki wasn't an ishiken, and nor was her mother. But they were Isawa, and influential enough to arrange for him to consult with one of those rare, Void-touched priests. They could help him.

If they wanted to.

He reached inside himself, gauging how much strength

he had. It would be enough – he hoped. "I will speak with her," Sekken said. "If you all will give us some privacy."

Miyuki's self-discipline was not strong enough for her to fully control her expression when she came in, and Sekken wondered just how bad he looked.

She neither recoiled nor commented, though, as she bowed and then knelt alongside his futon. "Lord Asako. I came looking for you yesterday; your mother recommended I come back today. I- I thought I saw you at the palace–"

"You did," Sekken said. "At least, if what you saw was somebody frantically stumbling away like a drunken invalid. The drunken part is untrue, but as for the invalid..."

He drew a deep breath, fighting the urge to touch Tanshu for comfort, and then he explained.

Miyuki sat silent, eyes wide and mouth pressed flat, as he told the story. The *whole* story, starting all the way back in Seibo Mura. Ryōtora's sacrifice, and Sekken's desperate move to save him. The recuperation in Dragon lands, and why Sekken had elided some of the truth in his report to his clan. The months that had followed. One physician after another. Never any success.

"So..." Miyuki said hesitantly when he was done. "In order to manage, you need a great deal of rest and medication?"

"No," Sekken replied, his voice heavy. "I take a great deal of rest and medication, and *still* sometimes I can't manage. I think they help, but they aren't enough. Our current theory – new as of today – is that my Void is overpowering everything else, negating everything I do to try and restore myself. My mother wants the two of us to marry because she knows your family can afford to take care of me even if I'm useless, and because now she's hoping you can introduce me to an ishiken who might pull a miracle out of the Void. It's all quite mercenary."

Miyuki's mouth flattened again. "Well, *my* mother wants us to marry so a grandchild of hers might inherit your inugami. So we're being mercenary, too."

"What do *you* want?" Sekken asked quietly. "I give you my word I won't be offended by the truth. In your place, I wouldn't consider me a very attractive proposition."

She'd taken the whole thing better than he feared. Or better than he wanted? If Miyuki refused him over this, Sekken would feel no guilt at all; he'd meant what he said about owing her honesty. But he owed too many things to too many people, and there wasn't enough of him to pay them all.

Miyuki's gaze softened, sinking to her knees. "I... I don't know. I want to help you if I can, whether we marry or not – I think it's wrong that you've had to hide this, especially when that makes it harder for you to get the help you need. But... it's difficult to think that far ahead, when right now all my worries are for my mother."

"Of course," Sekken said immediately. "I – augh. I hadn't told you about my condition sooner because I knew you were preoccupied with your mother. As you should be! Did the governor bring her to the palace as well?"

Miyuki nodded. "Along with Asako Shoun and Chūkan Ujiteru. And today it's Shiba Tōhachi."

Sekken didn't bother asking where the newest victim had been found. The answer might be embarrassing, and the

important part was that the curse was continuing. Would
keep continuing, until everyone at the Game of a Hundred
Candles had fallen asleep. And then...

Then what? Something new, and worse? Or would they
all just sleep forever?

He told Miyuki what they'd guessed at so far: that the
victims had all attended the gathering, and that they
were found wherever their dreams had led them. As he
finished, Tanshu laid his head on Sekken's knee, as if in
polite reminder. "I haven't forgotten you," he said fondly,
scratching the dog's ears.

Miyuki's gaze flicked downward. "Tanshu?"

"Yes." The brief amusement faded. "I had him watching
over Kaikoga Hanemi. This may have changed since
yesterday, though I doubt it... the governor hasn't had
anyone examine her. He claimed he was going to look into
the matter, but I'm not sure he is. And I have no idea *why*."

Her look of confusion matched his own. "Doesn't he
want to fix this?"

"There's something else, too," Sekken said. "I, ah...
normally I would do this myself, but I'm under orders not
to leave my futon. Would you be willing to ask if anyone has
come here from the House of Infinite Petals?"

Miyuki returned a few minutes later, shaking her head.
Sekken grimaced. "Then that probably means Teishi still
hasn't returned."

"The geisha? What does she have to do with this?"

"She's actually a bakeneko," Sekken said. "Her real name's
Sayashi; Ryōtora and I met her in Seibo Mura. I don't think
she's responsible for what's happening – at least, not on

purpose – but she went to the governor's palace two nights ago, and she hasn't come back. Under the circumstances, it seems ominous."

Miyuki folded herself back onto the mat, looking thoughtful and excited. "Two nights ago? Lady Nene was complaining that she heard a terrible yowling at the palace. Like an angry cat."

Sekken's eyes popped wide. "Angry – or *hurt*?"

"She said angry, but it could be the other. I can try to find out."

"Please do," Sekken said fervently. "I was going to send Tanshu to look for her, but… you know those tests your mother was interested in having me conduct? I tried one of them – that's how I know a priest hasn't been to see Lady Kaikoga – but, well. It's possible that's what touched off this most recent collapse."

Alarmed, Miyuki said, "Then don't do that."

A muted whuff from Tanshu drew her gaze, and Sekken realized the dog had manifested. Tanshu climbed to his feet and crossed the short distance to stand at Miyuki's side, looking back at Sekken. He whuffed again.

"I think he wants to go with you," Sekken said.

Miyuki looked astonished – and honored. "You would send him off like that? Away from you?"

Sekken smiled. "I think he's capable of far more than I've yet discovered. And he's certainly smart enough to make his own decisions. Tanshu, go with Lady Isawa; if you can find any sign of a bakeneko, let one of us know."

She hesitantly extended one hand to Tanshu, looking gratified when the inugami's response was to shove his head under it. "I'll go right now," Miyuki said. "You, Lord Asako, should rest."

Sekken did rest, for a while. More precisely, he meditated, trying in his untutored, not-an-ishiken, not-even-a-priest way to sense whether his weakness truly was a matter of the Void. Not of what should be there and wasn't, but what wasn't there to begin with, because the Void was non-being.

What that would even feel like, he didn't know. But by the time he opened his eyes again, he knew he had enough strength in him to risk one more draining conversation.

His sister was right, though; Sekken couldn't just get up and go to the embassy. He had Jun bring him soap and a basin of hot water, enough to scrub himself down a little, and then dressed himself in a new loose robe… and while he was doing that, another servant went to the Dragon to request Ryōtora's presence.

Sekken didn't know how long it would take to hear back. As it turned out, he had just enough time to clean himself up before Ryōtora arrived.

The silence was awkward, and this time Sekken didn't even have Tanshu to distract himself with. "I'm sorry–" he began.

"Don't be." Ryōtora's gaze was heavy, but not angry. It took in Sekken's disorganized room in one unsurprised sweep. "I… I understand why you didn't tell me."

Because of how it would make Ryōtora feel. "I don't regret *anything*," Sekken said, fiercely. "Even if I never get out of this futon again, I still won't be sorry for what I did. I want you to believe that."

A soft, painful smile touched Ryōtora's lips. "I do. And I never want you to feel that I'm not grateful. Seven lifetimes wouldn't be enough to repay what you did for me."

Sekken snorted, gesturing around himself as if to take in, not the clutter, but the entire city. "I owe you for such a miserable winter court. The mess over Seibo Mura was bad enough, but now you're having to deal with this business of people falling asleep."

Ryōtora's expression darkened, the melancholy shadows hardening to anger. "It may be that the lord governor is at least partially to blame."

Weakened though he was, Sekken couldn't entirely blame that for the curse that escaped him when Ryōtora outlined what he'd found in the Komoriyome Pavilion. "If you go publicly accusing Katahiro…"

"I know. I've been wrestling with that for the last day. I don't see any good way to do it."

"No, you wouldn't. Because there isn't one." Sekken gritted his teeth. Then a thought came to him, and his jaw eased. "Well. The good way to do it is to not have the accusation come from *you*."

"Who else could do it?"

"A Phoenix," Sekken said. "One with reason to be investigating this on her own. It's a little more difficult because Sir Yoichi was already caught at the pavilion, so they may have tightened up the guard… but Isawa Miyuki was here earlier today. She's gone off with Tanshu to try and locate Sayashi. She's a priestess, too. If she visits the pavilion and finds the same thing you did…"

Assuming the governor hadn't sent someone to clean

it up – if that was even possible. And assuming Miyuki was willing to sneak around like that. But Sekken rather suspected she might be.

He explained what Miyuki had said about the yowling cat, along with what he'd learned about Kaikoga Hanemi before his abortive attempt to send Tanshu after Sayashi. "And before you can suggest it," he said wearily, "yes, I'm aware that may have caused my collapse. There's a physician who thinks Tanshu may be the source of my problems, but he hasn't found proof of it yet."

Ryōtora drew breath to respond, but Sekken barreled on before he could. "Don't try to look for a pattern; there isn't one. Some days are good, some are bad, and there's no predicting what it'll be. It doesn't correlate with what I've been doing – though that doesn't stop me from trying to do as little as I can stand, in the hopes that it won't be too much. Was the cold weather too much for me the day you played kemari, or was it my conversation with Isawa Chikayū? Who knows. In the fall I went riding outside the city, even had a bit of a gallop, and I was fine. The day you arrived here for winter court, all I did was sit around the house, and I still fell over. There's no pattern to it at all."

He was breathing hard by the time he finished, and painfully aware he'd just flung that speech out without warning. But he couldn't take one more round of prodding, of theories, of proposals for trying this or that – not even from Ryōtora. Not today.

Into the silence, Ryōtora delivered a single word: "When?"

"What?"

"When in the fall did you go riding?"

It wasn't at all the reply Sekken had expected. "I don't know. I didn't record the date. In the Month of the Crane, I suppose, about–"

"–two-thirds of the way through the month?"

That stopped Sekken short. "Yes. I think so. How did you know?"

Instead of answering, Ryōtora said, "The day you and I argued in the temple. After we met with Sayashi. What did you do after I left?"

"Went home," Sekken replied, slowly. "Argued with my mother. That was the day I told her what I'd done for you. And I told her that if she tried to use it for political advantage, I would shave my head and become a monk."

"Was that strenuous? Not physically, but mentally. Emotionally. Did you feel like you were exerting yourself?"

The memory was vivid. Kneeling on the floor of her room, wincing at his own fumble-tongued words, and pulling himself together so he could make his case with all the cogency and force it deserved.

And another memory came with it. The thoughts Sekken had on his way to the House of Infinite Petals, fallen by the wayside in the chaos that ensued. "Yes, I did. Ryōtora ..."

"I got lost on the way back to the embassy." His resonant voice had thinned to a whisper. "By the time I got there, I could barely put two thoughts in order. In the Month of the Crane, around the twentieth day, I couldn't even rise out of bed. And when *I* played kemari, *you* became exhausted."

Sekken tried to reply, but his voice refused to work.

Ryōtora's eyes pinched shut. "I felt it, when I tried to heal you. The elemental spirits within me *wanted* to flow into you; it was all I could do to hold them back. My strength, my energy – they're yours. They're *still* yours. The two of us are linked."

And when one of them drew too deeply from that pool … the other was left with nothing.

Sickness rose up to overwhelm Sekken. Every time he'd felt well, every time he'd decided to revel in a good day and enjoy himself like he used to … Ryōtora paid the price.

And vice versa. Sekken wasn't the only one who'd been hiding bouts of weakness. No wonder Ryōtora had been so understanding: he could hardly chide Sekken for keeping secrets when he was doing the same.

Ryōtora's hand rose, as if to reach out, then dropped. "Praying to the spirits … I risked it in the pavilion because I had to. And when it nearly dragged me under, I- I *forced* the spirits within me to respond. It wasn't Tanshu that brought you down. It was me."

They were hurting each other, every time one of them stretched too far. Like two men drowning, each shoving the other down in a frantic bid to reach the surface.

Sekken felt like he was drowning now. He couldn't breathe past the knowledge choking him.

This time, Ryōtora didn't cut the gesture short. He reached out, and Sekken took his hand, bowing over it. Not in courtesy; he pressed the backs of Ryōtora's fingers to his own brow. Fighting to hold back the tears that wanted to slip free. *I wish I had died rather than inflict this on him.*

But he knew what Ryōtora would say to that.

As Sekken drew in a shuddering gasp and straightened, it

occurred to him – briefly, absurdly – that perhaps the best thing would be for one of them to fall victim to the curse. Rest might not be as restorative as it ought to be, but they couldn't drain each other nearly so badly if one of them was out cold.

Then it stopped seeming quite so absurd. Not that being afflicted would be good, but– "We can't work on this together. The sleeping curse, I mean."

"What?" Ryōtora stared at him, hand slipping away.

Sekken's voice solidified. The rope he'd found to cling to might be studded with thorns, but it was preferable to falling into an abyss of guilt. "If we're both running around investigating, we'll just drive each other to collapse. Better that one of us act with full effectiveness than both of us at half, or less. And the Dragon need you far more than my clan needs me. I'll stay home and be quiet. Use all the strength you need."

"No!" Ryōtora's eyes had gone wide with horror. "I *can't* do that. Not knowing what it will do to you."

"I gave you my strength before. I'm happy to give it again – and it's the only approach that makes sense. You know it as well as I do."

"I don't want to do this without you!"

The cry was ragged, desperate, and true. Sekken answered it with a gentle, ironic smile. "You won't. I've been with you ever since Seibo Mura."

CHAPTER EIGHTEEN

With every step Ryōtora took, he couldn't help thinking: *what is this costing Sekken?*

It didn't work like that, he knew – not really. The feeling he'd struggled with all this time, that even the most innocuous activity might drain him worse than expected, wasn't true. Their significant collapses and losses of mental acuity seemed to accompany significant exertion on the other one's part; simple actions should inflict minimal drain on Sekken. Hardly anything for the man to even notice, when he was accustomed to so much worse.

Thoughts like that didn't help. Not in the slightest.

He's resting so you can act. Don't squander that.

Thoughts like that weren't much better.

When Ryōtora arrived back at the embassy, Yoichi's welcoming expression rapidly turned to alarm. "Lord Isao, is everything all right?"

"Nothing is all right," Ryōtora snapped. He regretted it an instant later, after Yoichi stiffened. "Forgive me. I– there was no excuse for that." Plenty of reason, but no excuse.

"There is nothing to forgive," Yoichi said. "I spoke

foolishly; until our difficulties are dealt with, everything will not be all right. But you looked as if some new problem was weighing upon you. If there is anything I can do…"

Yoichi could not make two half men whole once more. That was only part of what Ryōtora had discussed with Sekken, though, and with a deep breath, he forced his thoughts toward matters more important than himself. "I have to speak with Isawa Miyuki. Lord Asako suggested that we might recruit *her* to investigate the pavilion and then accuse the governor – that it might be more readily accepted, coming from a Phoenix. But that assumes she's willing to help."

"Shall I send a message to her house, my lord?"

"Yes," Ryōtora said, and then, "No. Wait. She's at the palace, helping Lord Asako with a favor. I'll seek her there."

He hadn't gotten past the entrance room of the embassy, so he turned to head out immediately. A stifled noise from Yoichi stopped him. "Is there a problem?"

"Forgive me, Lord Isao, but yes. If you show your face at the palace… with word out now about this affliction, people have begun to whisper about our clan's involvement. And although you have not yet accused the governor directly, he knows I was caught at the pavilion. There can be no reason for me to have gone there except to investigate a gathering *he* arranged. The accusation is implicit."

Ryōtora's teeth ground together. "He can't arrest me, can he? Not without causing a diplomatic incident between our clans."

"I don't think he'll try to arrest you," Yoichi hastened to assure him. "But there's a great deal of ill will at present, and if you show your face at the palace, you'll give it all a target. Forgive me, my lord, but… when you told me about your own difficulties, you said that sometimes it manifests as a lack of stabilizing Earth, causing you to lose your temper more easily. What if that strikes you today?"

It was a diplomatic way of saying *you'll wind up in a duel.* Which was entirely possible even without a sudden decline in Earth – though in theory, with Sekken resting quietly, Ryōtora didn't have to worry about that.

No, he thought sourly. *If I wind up in a duel, it will be no one's fault but my own.*

Yoichi was right… and yet. "I know I asked you to advise me," Ryōtora said. "Tell me – since you know Lady Mirumoto better than I – do you think she would stay away from the palace?"

The clerk's hesitation betrayed his answer before he spoke. "No, my lord. She… she would say that remaining in the embassy would only shame the Dragon, giving everyone reason to think we have something to hide."

Kinmoku was a swordswoman; she could fight her own duels. Ryōtora was a priest, and could not. "If I do get challenged, who would represent me?"

"I would, my lord. That is – normally I would."

But Yoichi couldn't go to the palace. Ryōtora pinched the bridge of his nose, sighing. "I'll have to risk it. I can always insist the duel take place here at the embassy, or in some neutral location." He could insist so long as the governor didn't countermand it. However forgiving Katahiro had been lately, Ryōtora couldn't trust it, not when the man's motivations and goals were so dangerously unknown.

I could paralyze myself here all day, trying to play every branch to its end. Better to find Miyuki, talk to her, and hopefully end all of this sooner – or at least put Katahiro back on his heels.

This time, Yoichi didn't protest as Ryōtora left. But the clerk's parting words chased him out the door: "May the Fortunes watch over you, Lord Isao."

As soon as Ryōtora entered the palace, he knew Yoichi had been right.

On both counts. Yes, Ryōtora felt the weight of unfriendly gazes on him; he saw others turn their backs with deliberate incivility, shunning him as no longer worthy of their company. But he also heard the whispers of surprise that he would show himself at court. Staying away longer would only have fed those whispers, cementing their suspicion against the Dragon through the sheer absence of rebuttal.

He bowed very deliberately to the whole room, taking a certain sullen pleasure in answering their rudeness with courtesy. "Perhaps someone here would be so kind as to direct me," he said, loud enough for all to hear. "I was told Lady Isawa Miyuki had come to court today. Where might I find her?"

"Why do you seek her?" The question came from a man Ryōtora hadn't even been introduced to, one whose bearing was as proud as the mountains embroidered on his kimono. "Haven't you done enough already to her family, when her mother lies under your curse?"

Clearly the sleeping Kaikoga Hanemi didn't make a

good target; blame had shifted from the Moth to her hosts. Ryōtora said evenly, "Four things are best delivered in person: congratulations, accusations, apologies, and declarations of love. Which do you think I come bearing?" Technically he came for none of those, though he would probably apologize before asking for Miyuki's help. But he'd found that line in one of the stories he read in preparation for the Game of a Hundred Candles, and it sounded suitably courtly.

"Why did you strike down Doji Suemaru?" a woman asked, gliding toward him. "Were you not aware that the Crane support you in the negotiations over Seibo Mura? *Supported*, I should say; they hardly do so now, with Lord Doji missing."

The courtiers were all drifting closer, hemming Ryōtora in. He fought to keep his breathing steady as the man in the mountain kimono sniffed. "You should just concede that your clan isn't fit to oversee that village. It was *your* mistakes that freed the Night Parade in the first place, after all. Now you come here to create more chaos – and then cap it all by sending your clerk to plant evidence that will let you blame the lord governor!"

Ryōtora's teeth clenched so hard his jaw ached, knowing Kinmoku would have issued a challenge on the spot. That level of bald-faced accusation… it *demanded* an answer. But if Ryōtora called him out, the man would be free to insist the duel take place under the governor's supervision, here at the palace. The one place Yoichi could no longer go.

"Shiba Mitsusada," a woman's voice snapped.

The lack of honorifics cut through the room like a knife.

The crowd, turning, opened enough of a gap for Ryōtora to see Isawa Miyuki standing at the far end, her expression winter-cold.

With crisp, cutting diction, she said, "I do not believe you were at the Game of a Hundred Candles, nor were any of your kin. While your zeal does you credit, would you not agree that it is more appropriate for accusations to come from those more directly affected?"

Ryōtora didn't need to consult the embassy's chart of Phoenix nobility to know that Miyuki outranked Mitsusada; it was evident in how the man bowed, murmuring, "Lady Isawa."

The crowd parted for her as she came forward. Miyuki's entrance had disrupted the moment enough that Ryōtora could get away without challenging Mitsusada, at least for now... but her expression hadn't warmed at all, and in hindsight, her words to the Shiba lord were ominous.

"Lord Isao," she said. "Let us talk – in private."

True privacy was hard to come by at the palace. They wound up in a garden that made a stark contrast to the enchanted one the governor had shown Ryōtora, the more delicate bushes swaddled in snow-covered cloth to protect them.

"Lady Isawa," Ryōtora began, when Miyuki finally stopped and turned to face him.

"I don't *care* whose fault it is," she said angrily. "I don't think it's yours – not directly, the way people have begun saying – but I think it's disgusting, how everyone's in more of a rush to assign blame than to deal with the problem. As if this is a game, and the most important thing is who has the most points at the end, rather than whether they've done anything for the people affected."

He stemmed the flow of her words with a bow. "I agree."

Miyuki's lip curled. "And yet your clerk was at the Komoriyome Pavilion–"

"Not because I'm hoping to find reason to blame the governor. Lady Isawa, I don't think we can wake the sleepers until we properly understand what has *happened* to them. We're calling it a curse, an affliction… but those are just words, not explanations." Ryōtora hesitated, then thought, *Sekken trusts her.* He plunged ahead. "Sankan Yoichi was found at the pavilion because he stayed to cover for my escape. I went to see if there was any spiritual trace that might explain why this seems to be affecting only people who were at the gathering."

She inhaled sharply, frustration draining out of her expression. "The governor said he sent… but he also said he would have someone examine the sleepers. And Lord Asako claims no one has."

"Precisely. Even if the governor did have one of his people investigate at the pavilion, would he share with us what I found?"

He hadn't calculated his phrasing as bait, but it worked anyway. Miyuki came forward a half-step. "What did you find?"

"A thin spot," Ryōtora said. "The spirits there are being strongly affected by the Realm of Dreams – specifically in the place where the mirror stood."

Miyuki hadn't been there that night, but either she'd attended other such gatherings before, or she'd made some inquiries afterward. Her lips pressed together. "So even if this *was* ultimately caused by that Moth… the game had something to do with it as well."

Which meant that Katahiro, as host, would bear some of the blame – but Ryōtora understood Miyuki's desire to focus less on blame than on what could be done. "Even if the lord governor were willing to let me try to address this problem, I wouldn't know where to begin. How do you persuade spirits to stop dreaming?"

"I have no idea." She smiled bitterly. "It's the sort of thing Lady Kaikoga would be ideally suited to deal with. There must be others who can help."

"Only if the lord governor allows it," Ryōtora said. "If I bring it up, though…"

"You'll look like you're accusing him. Yes, I see."

The dull gray sky pressed down on them. This deep into winter, night came on early, adding to Ryōtora's feeling that he was running out of time. "Lord Asako suggested that you might be willing to investigate the pavilion yourself. And that if you're able to confirm what I sensed…"

Her gaze fixed on him. "Then *I* could accuse the governor. That's what you're after, isn't it?"

He could try to cushion the matter, but what would be the point? "Yes. Coming from my clan, it will be seen merely as a political gambit. Coming from a Phoenix, from an *Isawa*… people might listen."

Miyuki didn't reply. Ryōtora wished he could tell what she thought of him. Had she guessed the depth of attachment he and Sekken felt for each other? If so, she was taking it remarkably well. Or else she'd laid all thoughts of that aside until the greater threat had been dealt with.

If so, he admired her for it. She was right; far too few people were treating this threat as it deserved. If it weren't for the probability that one or more people were watching, Ryōtora might have knelt right there in the garden. Desperation creeping into his voice, he said, "I know it's absurd for me to ask for your help–"

She dismissed that with a small flick of her fingers. "I'm doing this for my mother, not for you. And for all the other people caught in this mess. No, I was only trying to think *how* to do it. He's put guards around the pavilion, you see."

Ryōtora swallowed a curse. *As I feared.*

But Miyuki was willing to help. That was a step in the right direction.

Out of nowhere, Tanshu appeared and butted his head against Miyuki's leg. She startled and looked down. "Yes, what is it? Oh. Yes." To Ryōtora she said, "Lord Asako asked me– ah–"

"To look for the bakeneko," Ryōtora said, saving her from the uncertainty of whether she ought to share that information or not. "Did you have any luck?"

"Not exactly. It does seem she was here a few nights ago; I told Sekken that Lady Nene was complaining about it. Teishi showed up claiming the governor had sent for her, but he said he hadn't."

Ryōtora frowned. "Why would she do that?"

"I have no idea. He ended up letting her into his chambers anyway, and Lady Nene assumed Teishi left at some point. But she also heard yowling, like a cat, and Tanshu tracked what I assume is her scent to one of the walls around the palace compound." Miyuki shivered and tucked her hands into her sleeves. "I think something went wrong and she fled."

"And no one has seen her since?"

"Not that I've been able to discover. Lady Nene will be glad to see the back of her," Miyuki said, with the long-suffering tone of one who'd had to listen to a tedious litany of complaints. "She was hoping – Lady Nene was, I mean – that the governor had finally cooled on Teishi. He hadn't engaged her for an evening since the gathering, which was a long gap for him. Do you think that's why Teishi showed up the way she did? Would something like her *care* about that?"

"She might," Ryōtora murmured, but his thoughts weren't on Sayashi's feelings. Instead, he was remembering Sekken telling him that Teishi had made her debut and rapidly become a favorite of the governor's. It might be just an infatuation, the sort of thing that happened all too often between geisha and their patrons, but…

Miyuki bent forward to peer at him. "Lord Isao?"

He focused on her, blinking. "What if it's not about personal feelings at all? What if this *does* have to do with Sayashi?"

"You think she caused this?"

"I think I want to know what she's been doing with the governor. Or *to* him."

Miyuki's eyes widened in alarm. "You mean– well, it's true that he's been acting oddly the last few days. Only that's happened when she *wasn't* around. As if he's coming out from under some kind of enchantment?"

"I don't know." Ryōtora made an inarticulate noise of

frustration. "We were fools not to talk to her sooner. The one time we tried, it was before people began falling asleep, and she– she distracted us with other matters." Possibly on purpose. He wouldn't put it past her.

Where would Sayashi have gone when she fled? It sounded like she'd climbed over the wall in cat form, which implied she couldn't just step across to the Enchanted Country whenever she pleased. Because the governor's palace was warded against that, or because she simply couldn't? Humans needed places where the barrier between realms was thin, but powerful yōkai were less constrained. How powerful was Sayashi? In Seibo Mura she and Sekken had waited for twilight, a liminal time that made the transition easier. Did that mean she wasn't especially powerful, or just that it was harder when she had to bring a fellow traveler along?

He had no answers to any of those questions, and they hardly mattered anyway. Days had passed since Sayashi fled the palace. She'd had plenty of time to leave the city entirely, journeying in search of a place that would let her escape to the Enchanted Country. Or just to set up a new life in another part of Rokugan, where no one knew her true nature.

Ryōtora realized his fingernails were digging into his palms, and made his hands relax. *Don't give up before you've tried.* Sayashi *might* be gone beyond reach… or she might not.

He knelt in front of Tanshu and took the dog's head between his hands. Even with Sekken resting, Ryōtora was reluctant to extend himself in communion with the elemental spirits, but it might not be necessary. "Can you track her?" Ryōtora asked. "Can you follow the bakeneko's trail? If she's gone more than a day away, there's no point in pursuing her, but she might be close. Will you search for her?"

"Can he understand that?" Miyuki asked, interested.

"I have no idea," Ryōtora admitted. "Tanshu, do you understand what I'm asking?"

The inugami let out a muffled bark. "I suppose that's a yes," Ryōtora said, wishing he could be sure. If only Sekken had done more to test and develop his bond with the dog… but of course, there were reasons why he hadn't.

Ryōtora stood, brushing off his hands. No sooner had Tanshu been released than he vanished. "We'll have to hope he's gone after Sayashi," Ryōtora said.

"I think he has," Miyuki said. "I'll light incense to the Fortunes for him to succeed."

For all of us to, Ryōtora thought. *We need all the help we can get.*

CHAPTER NINETEEN

It had been difficult enough for Sekken to accept, over the last year or so, that sometimes the only thing he could do with himself was sit quietly, doing nothing.

It only got harder now that he understood why.

His reflexive impulse, ingrained in him before he even began his formal schooling and only reinforced since then, was to try to *solve it*. So what if he couldn't go riding, or walk around town, or do a very bad job of playing kemari? Those were never his favorite activities anyway. Since he had to stay put, surely he could spend his time reading and–

But he couldn't. Reading took energy. *Thinking* took energy. All those times he found himself feeling dull-witted and slow, those were because Ryōtora had to exert his own mind. If Sekken tried to do that now, he might leave the other man flat-footed at a bad moment.

He could only sit. Or lie down. Sleep. Maybe meditate.

He was going out of his skull with frustration before that first day ended.

And his family could tell. Sekken had shared with them what he and Ryōtora had figured out; he couldn't keep it secret, not after they'd poured so much time and effort into trying to fix him. Ginshō had cursed. Ameno had clapped one hand over her mouth in wide-eyed horror. His mother...

His mother had sat quietly, lashes veiling her eyes so he could read nothing from them.

It didn't take any real mental energy to imagine their responses after that. Ginshō would go practice something martial, taking her aggravations out on a dummy or somebody like Shiba Tanezane. She hated being "the stupid one" in their family, even though she wasn't stupid at all; her training simply meant she wasn't as well-read as Sekken or their mother or their fourth sister Esato, as well-connected at court as their mother or Ameno. She didn't have the spiritual gifts of their second sister Shūkai. More than any of them, she was their father's daughter – but Hyōsuke was with Shūkai in Nikesake, too far to offer Ginshō support.

Ameno would weep in private, where no one else could see, and then write a poem. It was her way of corralling her feelings and bringing them to heel, unraveling them to their smallest threads and then picking out the precise words to capture their essence. She never shared those poems publicly, although Sekken thought they were very good; they were for Ameno alone, and sometimes for the Fortunes. She was probably at a shrine even now, offering her words to the Fortune of Longevity or some other suitable spirit, praying for Sekken to recover somehow.

And his mother...

No physicians showed up at the house, but that meant nothing except that Sekken's mother wasn't yet ready to summon one. Right now, she would be ransacking the Kanjiro Library and sending discreet queries to scholars of her acquaintance, equipping herself with the knowledge she would need to solve this problem.

Exactly the way Sekken would be doing, if he didn't know it would hurt Ryōtora.

He might not be able to do anything, but his family could. And that gave him a shred of an idea.

Ryōtora sent no messages, likely because he didn't want to tempt Sekken into effort he wasn't supposed to make. As considerate as that was, the silence still would have infuriated him – except that whatever Ryōtora had done that day left Sekken flattened enough that he invited his family to take their supper in his chamber that night, rather than him leaving to dine with them. While everyone else sat around a brazier sharing a hearty hot pot of eggs, lotus root, and mashed rice dumplings in miso broth, he picked at his elementally balanced tray, wondering how much good it actually did.

And he told them everything he knew about the situation with the sleeping curse, from what Ryōtora had found at the pavilion to the possible involvement of Sayashi. All of them knew bits of it, and his mother more than most, but over the past few days he'd lost track of who'd heard what. Since he didn't want to put mental effort into tracing the answers to that question, it was easier to just tell everyone everything.

Ending his somewhat confused litany with a request. "I

can't help Ryōtora," he said, fighting the urge to stab his chopsticks into his block of tofu simmered with medicinal herbs. Illness was no excuse for shockingly bad manners. "Or rather, the only way I can help him is by doing nothing. But *you* three aren't constrained like that. So, I'm asking you: please do what you can for him. Whether it's research, or support at court, or… anything." He had to force himself not to start thinking about what forms that "anything" might take. *Don't use your mind any more than you have to:* it was the worst trap he could imagine being caught in. His mind was the most useful part of him; without that, what was the *point* of Sekken?

Just like Ryōtora, having to avoid communion with the spirits. A scholar who couldn't think and a priest who couldn't pray; what a pair they made.

Ameno let out a small, conflicted noise. "If the governor thinks we're going against him…"

"Let him," Ginshō said bluntly. "I don't know what game he's playing these days, but if he isn't doing anything to solve this problem, then he deserves to be shamed for it. And so does everybody else who's taking advantage. Did you hear what Shiba Mitsusada said to Lord Isao's face this afternoon? Trying to force him into a duel he *knew* Sir Yoichi wouldn't be able to fight. I can find a reason to thrash Mitsusada. And he'll know why I'm doing it."

Her eagerness warmed Sekken more than that hot pot would have. "Thank you."

Not to be outdone, Ameno said, "Asako Harunaga wants me to paint a new scroll for his tearoom. I was going to turn him down – he's going to be irritatingly fussy about it; you know what he's like – but I can tell him instead that I'm so *very* distracted by my worries over the tensions at court. Enough people there are former students of his; if he starts chastising them all for their behavior, they'll listen."

As one of those former students, Sekken could vouch for that. The mere sound of his name in Harunaga's voice still had the power to drag him into perfect posture and a reflexive bow.

His mother had eaten lightly and was blowing across the remaining liquid in her bowl to cool it. Sekken tried not to hold his breath. *I think she likes him,* Ginshō had said of her mother, referring to Ryōtora – but that was before Sekken discovered the true nature of his weakness. Now Sekken was the one confined to bed, while Ryōtora had free run of his life. How would she have reacted to that?

"The Komoriyome Pavilion is the key," his mother said. "We *must* get Isawa Miyuki or someone else in there to examine it properly."

Sekken bit his tongue to avoid defending Ryōtora's examination of the place. It was true that someone else might be able to do more, and even if they couldn't, Ryōtora still needed a Phoenix to confirm and voice his claims. Releasing his tongue, he said, "Would it work to stage a distraction for the guards? It would need to be convincing, of course, but–"

A single glance from his mother was enough to silence him. "It is not your responsibility to work it out, son. I will see what I can arrange."

The truth of her words burned like acid. His responsibility was to sit here, eat his medicinal tofu, and do nothing. Even while Ryōtora was taunted toward duels and who knew what other dangers.

On cue, his mother put down her bowl and rose gracefully to her feet. "And we are tiring you by sitting here and talking. We will do what we can; you should rest."

He could take some small comfort in having mobilized his family to help Ryōtora. But Sekken wanted to *be* there: to watch Ginshō bait Mitsusada into a duel and then humiliate him with a single strike; to smirk behind his fan as Harunaga chided everyone like they were still twelve year-olds under his tutelage. To contribute to the plan for getting Miyuki to the pavilion.

To be at Ryōtora's side, when the other man needed him most.

But that was exactly where Ryōtora needed him *not* to be.

Sekken stabbed his chopsticks into his half-eaten tofu and left them there until the servants came to clear everything away.

That night, a thought from earlier in the day came back and took up residence at the heart of Sekken's brain. Like a petitioner determined to gain its lord's attention, it knelt in front of him and refused to move.

The best thing would be for one of us to fall victim to the curse.

Could he make that happen?

Sekken didn't know how the affliction was selecting its victims. The effect wasn't going in the order people had told their tales, nor by their location in the city, nor even by the degrees of relationship or social bonds between them; it seemed to be utterly random. Which meant there was no obvious way for him to put himself in its path.

But he could try. And if he succeeded, then Sekken would be saved from staring down a tunnel of absolute boredom, forbidden to exercise even his intellect too strenuously, lest he dull Ryōtora's own thoughts. He might even be able to learn something useful, examining the curse from the inside – though how he would communicate what he learned, Sekken had no idea. Meanwhile, Ryōtora would have the freedom to act as needed.

Sekken *hoped* he would. That, admittedly, was a roll of the dice. He couldn't be sure that his spirit's activities in the Realm of Dreams wouldn't use up some of their shared strength. Or just the simple fact of his spirit being there in the first place.

From everything he'd read, though, he didn't think it would. There was a sense in which the Realm of Dreams wasn't *real*; wasn't that part of Isawa Minokichi's argument for using it as a place to indulge? Others disagreed, but their arguments were moral, not metaphysical. They were concerned with the possibility that giving in to one's desires in sleep might encourage a person to do the same while awake, not with the use of elemental energy as translated across that boundary. Sekken could argue for a connection there, hinging on the role of Earth in stability and self-control, but–

He reined his thoughts in, out of what had already become dreary reflex. *Don't think too hard.*

Except… it was late at night. The Hour of the Rat. Not late by courtly standards, of course, but Sekken rather doubted Ryōtora was enjoying himself at some party that was one-quarter poetry, three-quarters drinking. If the man was still awake – which he might be; that was his natural inclination, in sharp contrast with Sekken – he would be at the Dragon embassy, sitting up in sleepless thought. It might be worth dulling his wits for a little while, if it meant Sekken was able to remove himself from that board entirely.

So, he thought, trying to ignore the pleasure that came with being able to let his mind loose on a problem. *Presume for the moment that you can safely fall under this curse without harming Ryōtora. How do you arrange that?*

Sleeping was easy. He'd become a master of it this past year; lassitude weighted his limbs even now, after a day of Ryōtora probably running hither and yon. All Sekken had to do was lie down, and he'd be out within minutes.

Dreaming was easy, too. Sekken's visions usually slipped away from him moments after waking, but he knew he had them. Everyone entered the Realm of Dreams when they slept – at least, everyone who dreamed did so. Was that true of all creatures? Sekken realized he didn't actually know. Animals seemed to dream; he'd seen dogs and cats twitching in their sleep, as if chasing prey, and sometimes they startled awake the way a human might. He wondered if they, too, had vague dreams of flying, until an abrupt sensation of falling jolted them to alertness. Was there any way to find out?

Focus, he chided himself. His thoughts were wandering, and it was a novel sensation to know why. What Ginshō had said about Ryōtora being insulted at court, under conditions where he couldn't respond... yes, holding his tongue would have taken a great deal of Earth. So, for once, Sekken actually had an explanation for his own scattered mind. Had Ryōtora kept any kind of journal of his own bouts of weakness? Sekken had in the early days, before he gave it up in frustration and–

Focus!

He drummed his hands against his own knees to ground himself and tried again. Sleeping was easy. Dreaming was easy. But could he *stay* in the Realm of Dreams?

In theory, yes. Like the practice of tsukimono-suji, dreamwalking didn't require spiritual gifts. Sekken knew more than a few people who claimed to have mastered lucid dreaming, the ability to control the visions of their own sleeping minds. If they got caught in a nightmare, they could recognize it as such and do something to change it. In cosmological terms, they had gained a small measure of control over the Realm of Dreams.

But only the part of it immediately around themselves. *True* masters, like the Moth dreamwalkers, could do far more than that. They could shape dreams like an artist, banishing things or summoning them into being; they could even control the dreams of others. That was, after all, why people were blaming Kaikoga Hanemi: she had the capacity to trap others with her in that realm.

Sekken, on the other hand, wasn't even a lucid dreamer. He couldn't decide, before going to sleep, that he would dream about a certain thing, and thereby make it happen – at least, he didn't think he could. His lack of ability to remember his visions meant he couldn't be sure... though he suspected that lucid dreamers also had better memories. For now, he had to assume no skill in that regard, much less in true dreamwalking.

Which left him at "pray to the Fortunes and hope for the best."

So he did. The mansion held no shrine to the Fortune of Sleep – it was a minor entity that rarely had establishments of its own; at most it tended to get a small shrine tucked into the corner of temples to the Fortunes of Longevity or Contentment – but he lay down and mentally promised that he would build one in thanks if his prayers came true. In the Realm of Dreams or out of it; both, if he had to. So long as he was the one who fell asleep tonight and didn't wake up.

In a sudden burst of inspiration, he thought, *Take me to Kaikoga Hanemi.* Whether she was the one dragging people under or not, maybe he could find her. If he could coax his mind into dreaming of the Moth… would it be the real Hanemi, or just his vision of her?

That was out of his control. *Kaikoga Hanemi,* he thought, over and over again, the way he'd heard a lucid dreamer recommend. He built the image of her in his mind: small, unassuming, with that band of embroidered cloth over one eye. Should he cover one of *his* eyes? If Sekken had cloth within easy reach, he would have done it, but in a fit of helpfulness Ameno had tidied his room, so the thin sashes he'd been using for his informal robes were all put away in a box on the other side of the room. Lethargy had gripped his body firmly enough that he didn't want to get up to search. Maybe that was a good sign, a hint that his efforts were working. *Kaikoga Hanemi. The Moth dreamwalker. I want to dream of Kaikoga Hanemi.*

Praying, hoping, he slipped away.

When Sekken opened his eyes the next morning, a wave of despair broke over him.

He wasn't in the Realm of Dreams. If he had been, his back wouldn't have been complaining about spending too long in a twisted position, one leg flung sideways across his futon. There wouldn't be a bitter-smelling pot of medicinal tea sitting not far away, promising him another day full of healthful food he didn't want to eat.

Another day of useless sitting. And another day after that, and another, into infinity.

No, not to infinity. Sooner or later Ryōtora would solve the problem of the curse – without Sekken's help – and then he would probably insist on spending at least an equal amount of time utterly immobile, so that Sekken could enjoy the freedom of something like a normal life.

Was that to be their future? Trading off with each other, always knowing that one's pleasure came at the cost of the other's misery?

The impossibility of it all ground Sekken's heart into dust. Their only options were to lurch along the way they had been, taking turns draining each other of life, or make good on Sekken's threat to his mother. They could retire to the same monastery and spend the rest of their lives meditating together.

There had to be another option, something besides mutual suffering or mutual stagnation. But Sekken didn't know what it was, and he couldn't afford to try and imagine it. By now Ryōtora would be up and about; he would need his strength. Sekken's strength.

Pushing himself upright, Sekken grimly downed the tea and prepared for another day of meditation.

CHAPTER TWENTY

The first word out of Ryōtora's mouth when he saw Yoichi the next morning was, "Who?"

"Not Lord Asako Sekken," the clerk assured him. "Lady Asako Fumizuki sent a messenger to let us know and requested that I alert her once you were awake."

Ryōtora had slept longer than he expected to, which made him wonder if that had something to do with Sekken. His body wanted to rise late anyway; it didn't take much encouragement for it to lie abed until well after dawn.

But he was awake. So was Sekken. And Lady Asako was taking steps to reassure them both, which was unexpectedly touching.

By the time Ryōtora was dressed and ready to go out, a Phoenix servant had brought the news: the victim this time was a different Asako, a lady named Seifū. "The governor's niece?" Ryōtora said, staring in horror.

The servant bowed low. "Yes, Lord Isao. And the lord governor requires your presence at court this afternoon."

That didn't bode well at all. But what could Ryōtora do, except assure the servant that he would be there?

Yoichi insisted on him changing into his finest kimono, one brocaded with dragons amid clouds. It felt painfully unsubtle to Ryōtora, but he trusted the clerk's judgment. If he had to represent his clan without Kinmoku or even Yoichi at his side, then it was his responsibility to look the part.

As the litter carried him to the palace, Ryōtora tried to persuade himself that the governor's summons meant Katahiro was finally doing something about the sleeping curse. Even in his own mind, though, the words sounded thin and unconvincing.

The palace was busier than he would have expected for the Hour of the Horse, shortly after noon. It was his first, unwelcome clue that the summons was not for a private conversation, but for a public audience. Courtiers had their fans out again, whispering coyly behind them, and Ryōtora braced himself as he realized Shiba Mitsusada was heading straight for him.

To his surprise, though, the Phoenix lord's stiff bow was deeper than mere greeting required. "Lord Isao. Please forgive me for my harsh words yesterday. I spoke in error."

As apologies went, it wasn't very gracious – but any apology at all was unexpected. Habit alone pushed a reply out of Ryōtora's mouth: "There is nothing to forgive, Lord Shiba. I'm sure we're all just concerned for those affected. May the Fortunes bring us an answer soon."

Mitsusada bowed again and left. Under his breath, Ryōtora murmured, "What happened to *him*?"

"My sister happened."

He hadn't meant to be overheard, but he turned to find Sekken's third sister Ameno at his side. "Ginshō found herself in a quarrel with Lord Shiba this morning," she said, her own fan out and not quite covering her face. "I'm afraid he very much got the worst of their duel. We may hope his lesson in manners will last beyond today – though the evidence of history suggests otherwise."

A messenger from Asako Fumizuki, and now this. It was too much for coincidence, and while Ryōtora assumed Sekken's hand lay behind it all, the actual deeds belonged to others. "I am indebted to your family."

Ameno closed her fan. "Nonsense. We can't have you thinking the Phoenix are incapable of basic civility. Do you know what the governor has planned for today?" When Ryōtora shook his head, she sighed, amusement cooling to tension. "Nor I. Normally I would be able to make an educated guess, but…"

One of Katahiro's retainers entered the room and spoke in a strong voice. "Lord Asako Katahiro, governor of Kyūkai Province, will be holding an open audience in the formal receiving chamber shortly. He summons Lord Agasha no Isao Ryōtora to be present."

Ryōtora felt the weight of everyone's gazes on his back as he moved toward the door, and heard the shuffling of their feet on the mats as they followed.

If he'd found the formal receiving room imposing before, it was oppressive now, with so many people flocking to see what the governor would do. The screens farthest from the dais had been removed to expand the space, so that despite the crowd, Ryōtora was still very much exposed as he came forward and knelt in front of the dais step. A few retainers lined the walls, but he knew there would be more behind the closed doors to one side. It was the customary place to put guards, in case an attendee proved troublesome... or in case the governor needed someone taken into custody.

He won't arrest me. Will he? I'm the temporary ambassador; taking me prisoner would spark open conflict between our clans.

Ryōtora wished he could trust that to protect him.

"Asako Seifū," Katahiro said without preamble. "Shiba Tōhachi. Mirumoto Kinmoku. Chūkan Ujiteru. Isawa Chikayū. Asako Shoun. Doji Suemaru. Kaikoga Hanemi. All these people have fallen asleep and cannot be woken."

And what have you done to stop it? Ryōtora was briefly, guiltily grateful that Sekken was sitting quietly at home – that he didn't have to fear his self-control slipping and letting that question out of his mouth. And he wished, quite uselessly, that he could have gotten Miyuki into the pavilion last night.

"I cannot ignore the obvious," Katahiro said. "This sequence of events began with a Moth dreamwalker – someone capable of trapping others in their dreams. Kaikoga Hanemi is in this city as a guest of the Dragon Clan, and so it is only right that I inform the Dragon ambassador of my decision. I hereby find Kaikoga Hanemi guilty of causing this affliction."

Ryōtora jerked. "Lord governor–"

Katahiro spoke over him, with the inexorable force of a storm. "She must be stopped, before others fall under her spell. Before I *myself* fall victim to it. I therefore sentence Kaikoga Hanemi to death."

This time, Ryōtora couldn't even move. *Death. He's going to kill her.*

As if he had not just condemned a woman on the grounds of nothing more than supposition, Katahiro went on, "I recognize that this gives offense to both the Moth and the Dragon Clans. To the Moth I will make reparations directly, but to the Dragon, I grant independent oversight of Seibo Mura. May this restore peace between our clans."

It wouldn't restore *anything*. Ryōtora couldn't get words past the strangling horror. Over and over again he'd been told that Asako Katahiro was a deft politician, that he had years of experience in governing his province. Ryōtora had come to Phoenix lands prepared for layers of courtly traps, all designed to force the Dragon to accept Isawa oversight of Seibo Mura. Instead, he found this: a man who ignored the dispute for which he was supposed to broker a deal, did nothing to help people afflicted by a curse, and then tried to settle both matters at once with a blunt callousness that would shame even a Hida.

Kinmoku would have known how to stop it. *Sekken* would know. But while Ryōtora might have the other man's strength in him, it didn't give him Sekken's training, his eloquence, his ability to call his own governor out on the idiocy of this decision. And Sekken wasn't there.

But someone else was.

A soft shuffling broke the silence of the chamber. Then Asako Fumizuki was at Ryōtora's side, kneeling on the mat in a graceful bow. "Lord governor, I beg your permission to speak."

Warily, Katahiro said, "You have it."

"My lord, our Kanjiro Library holds the wisdom of many ages within its walls. Some of that wisdom concerns the Realm of Dreams, and the arts of those who have mastered its ways... but I fear our knowledge of such matters is dreadfully incomplete. Your zeal to wake the sleepers is admirable, my lord; however, I must caution you that your actions may not have the desired effect.

"There is a chance that executing Kaikoga Hanemi will free the others, yes. But if her actions have trapped them there, then it may be that only her actions can free them – that her death, while they still sleep, will ensure they remain in dreams forever."

"Nonsense," Katahiro scoffed. "That isn't how it works."

Lady Asako lowered her head to the mat. "I beg you to accept my advice, my lord. Though I know you have studied Isawa Minokichi's writings, none of us – you included – are sufficiently knowledgeable concerning the Realm of Dreams to be certain what effect her execution would have. Given the perils, would it not be overly hasty to resort to a measure we cannot take back?"

As Ryōtora bowed to match Sekken's mother, he glimpsed Katahiro's jaw hardening in anger. Ryōtora said, "Lord governor, I have the greatest respect for Lady Asako's wisdom. If she feels this is too dangerous to risk, I join her in begging you to give it further consideration."

He heard someone else move, though he didn't dare lift his head to see who it was. The voice was the reedy tone of an elderly man. "If the words of your old teacher carry any weight with you, lord governor, then hear me now. The Shinseist monk Meipō wrote that to kill in haste is a greater sin than to kill in anger, and Shiba Otondo wrote that many things may be endured for the sake of saving a life. The victims of this affliction only sleep; we may yet find a way to wake them. But if Kaikoga Hanemi is executed, we cannot bring her back from death."

Silence once more. Ryōtora remained motionless, fingers digging into the mat. What would he do if Katahiro refused to reconsider? The governor had Hanemi – not to mention Kinmoku. If Ryōtora attempted anything rash, the ambassador might pay the price.

"Fine," Katahiro ground out at last, without even a semblance of courtesy. "The Moth lives for now. I will find another way to–"

He didn't finish that sentence. And as Ryōtora delivered his thanks in a voice shaking with relief, part of him wondered what the rest of it would have been.

Outside on the veranda, after the audience was ended, Ryōtora bowed deeply to Asako Fumizuki. "Lady Asako, I cannot express my gratitude enough. It was thanks to your words, not mine, that a life was saved today."

"Thank Asako Harunaga," she said dryly. "I think the governor might have dismissed me, but his own master? Quoting Meipō, who was Asako Sōkan – the governor's own ancestor – before he retired to a monastery? I wish I had thought of that."

Footsteps thudded against the boards, and Ryōtora turned to see Isawa Miyuki hurrying toward them. "I just heard what happened," she said breathlessly. "Lord Isao, we *must* do something, and soon." Her gaze flicked to Sekken's mother, and she stumbled over her next words. "Have you – that is – you and I, ah, perhaps we should talk privately."

Lady Asako dismissed this with a flick. "I know what you're planning; my son told me. Come to dinner at my mansion tonight. I think I've found a way to help you."

Before Ryōtora could say anything, she gave him a small bow. "But not you. A matter such as this… you should not be seen anywhere near it."

No, he could not help Miyuki break into the pavilion – however much he wanted to. "Once more, Lady Asako, I am in your debt."

"It has become a question of saving lives," she said grimly. "That, Lord Isao, is not a matter for debts."

Even though Lady Asako's logic was sound, Ryōtora chafed at having to sit idle at the Dragon embassy while others took risks on his behalf.

Not on your behalf, he reminded himself. *On behalf of those struck down by this curse.* And if this made him chafe, how must Sekken feel, unable to do even as much as Ryōtora was?

He hadn't gone to the mansion after leaving the palace, and he couldn't tell whether that was courtesy or cowardice. Would Sekken prefer not to be reminded of all the troubles he was missing? His mother and sisters would probably inform him of the latest developments anyway – or perhaps not, given how protective they were of his health. When Ryōtora found himself writing out a note for one of the embassy servants to deliver to Lady Asako, leaving it to her discretion whether or not to pass his message along to Sekken, he knew it was courtesy and cowardice both.

I don't want to face him right now. Not with the truth of their situation finally clear. Not when they finally knew just how much power they had to hurt each other.

It was one thing to accept that their duties meant they could only hope for brief gifts of each other's company, little pleasures slipped in where opportunity allowed. It was another thing entirely to know they were fighting, however unintentionally, over the scraps of life shared between them. The former brought regret, but the latter left him hollow with shock.

Turning instead to conversation with Yoichi wasn't precisely comforting, but Ryōtora preferred the weight of duty to that of guilt. "Can we involve an imperial observer?" he asked the clerk, thinking of how the Seibo Mura negotiations had been handed off to Katahiro in the first place. "I know there isn't one at winter court, but is there anyone from the imperial families in the city who might be willing to speak up in defense of Lady Kaikoga?"

Yoichi's grimace foreshadowed his answer. "Ordinarily, yes. Miya Nyokan – but she's expecting a child, and so she's retired to an estate out in the country until after the birth. We can try sending a message to her, but..."

"If it won't give offense," Ryōtora began, then cut himself off. "No, if the governor is willing to consider such drastic measures, we have to try everything we can. Help me write the letter, please; you'll know better than I do how to address an imperial lady."

After that one they wrote several more letters, to all the representatives from other clans in the city. The Moth might be a minor clan from distant lands, hardly capable of striking back if the governor murdered one of their own, but Ryōtora hoped the specter of such a bloody and summary excuse for justice would spur others to action. That took much of the day, and he lost the rest to pacing, wondering what Miyuki and Lady Asako were doing, wondering how long it would take the Crane or the Lion to respond to his messages, wondering if there would be any benefit to requesting a private audience with Katahiro.

He knew the answer to that last one. Any such audience was only likely to make things worse.

Around the Hour of the Boar, he finally accepted that no replies would be forthcoming that night, and he made himself lie down. But he slept only fitfully, and then he roused with a jerk, suddenly aware that something was in his room.

The curse– he thought, half-coherent. Was this how it began?

A damp nose nudged his cheek, and he sat bolt upright.

"Tanshu," Ryōtora gasped when he had calmed himself enough to speak. The dog was barely discernible in the faint light from outside, but a soft huff confirmed his guess. Had something happened to Sekken? Why would Tanshu come to Ryōtora?

Then the rest of his wits assembled themselves. "Have you found Sayashi?"

Another huff, and a head nudging his elbow with what felt a great deal like urgency.

Ryōtora scrambled to his feet and grabbed the first kimono he could find in the dark. "Show me."

•••

It occurred to him, as he followed Tanshu into the quiet, frozen streets, that he'd sent an inugami to track a bakeneko. Although he mostly thought of Sekken's companion as a dog, not as a yōkai, it was entirely possible for Tanshu to have followed Sayashi across the border into the Enchanted Country – and he might be taking Ryōtora there now.

This didn't feel like that realm, though. Sekken had talked about how much more *real* everything there seemed; while the cold biting at Ryōtora's face certainly felt real enough, it didn't have that deeper quality, the sense that only now was he experiencing the truth behind the mortal realm's pale representation. And his dislocated sense of time probably had more to do with being awakened in the middle of the night and hurrying through streets that normally teemed with people than with any transition to another kind of reality.

He had no idea where Tanshu was taking him. Not to the palace, nor to the licensed quarter; not to any part of the city Ryōtora knew. All around him were ordinary houses and shops, the realm of commoners instead of samurai. The kind of place where a patrol of constables might stop a man for questioning. Normally they wouldn't dare harass a samurai… but normally a samurai didn't walk alone, without even a servant to carry a lantern for him.

Then Tanshu stopped, head pointed toward a house, and whuffed.

Ryōtora eyed the house, a looming bulk in the night. "Sayashi's in there?" he whispered, trying to imagine how he was supposed to make use of this information. Knock on the door? Ask the confused, half-asleep householders whether they had a bakeneko on the premises? He couldn't imagine that going well.

Tanshu trotted forward a few steps, his head dipping low. He huffed again.

He looked like he didn't want to approach too closely – likely fearing that the scent of him would put Sayashi on guard, or even make her bolt again. Ryōtora eased forward, then saw what he'd overlooked in the shadows. A deeper shadow at the base of the house, in between a stack of barrels and a small hand cart.

The houses of the poor sat directly on the ground, but these people had enough wealth to build some elevated rooms with wooden flooring. Which left a gap beneath sometimes used for storage.

Or for hiding. Ryōtora had crawled into such a gap the day his father told him the truth of his origins, convinced Sir Keijun would not come looking for him there.

Knowing he risked drawing attention from the householders or their neighbors, Ryōtora still ventured a whisper. "Sayashi? Are you there?"

No answer. But Tanshu whined, very softly.

"I'm coming in," Ryōtora whispered, then hesitated. He wasn't a child anymore; the space would be very cramped, and *very* dark. Gritting his teeth against the instincts of the past year, he rubbed his hands together quickly, murmuring a near-soundless prayer. The spirits obliged him with a tiny ball of light, hovering in front of him as he got on his hands and knees, fitting himself between barrels and cart to peer under the house.

He almost overlooked her. Even with the light, she was

a black cat in a black space, without so much as a slitted eye to cast a reflection back at him. But in the quiet of deep night, her breathing led him to her: quick and shallow, with a labored rasp that spoke of pain.

An injured cat's instinct was to seek shelter, hidden away from threats. Why Sayashi had chosen this house, Ryōtora didn't know – but she was hurt.

And tiny. In Seibo Mura she'd been the size of a snow leopard. If Tanshu hadn't pointed him here, Ryōtora would have assumed this was an ordinary house cat.

The sight of her, so small and vulnerable, made his throat tighten. When he whispered her name past that constriction, she didn't stir. Cautiously he put one hand out, touching her back. Her fur rippled in an instinctive flinch.

With all the gentleness and care he could muster, Ryōtora slid his hands under the cat and scooped up her warm, unresisting weight. Sayashi mewled softly, but neither woke nor clawed him. Getting out from under the house with his hands full took more than a little agility, Ryōtora biting down on curses that might wake someone above him, but finally he was in the open air once more.

Tanshu had vanished, and Ryōtora couldn't spare the time to look for him. Hurrying through the streets, trying not to jostle Sayashi any more than he had to, it seemed to take forever to reach the Dragon embassy. The guard at the entrance recognized him and opened the gate. "My lord, is that a–"

"A bakeneko," Ryōtora said, and the man twitched back in surprise. "I need some blankets, some…" What would she need? He'd never kept a cat as a pet, much less treated one that was injured.

She needed the help of the elemental spirits. "Offerings," he said, and the guard leapt to rouse a servant.

The last time he'd healed someone, it had been his birth father Masa, in the battle-torn ruins of Seibo Mura. Now he knelt over the small, limp body of a cat, unsure whether he should be angry at her, whether her injuries were simply the harvest of her own misdeeds or something else entirely. She wasn't bleeding, but the spirits told him her ribs were cracked, the organs inside bruised and swollen. It was impossible not to feel sympathy. Anger, if it was merited, could come later.

His healing skill was small at best, though. Ryōtora sat back on his heels, wiping his brow, and looked up at Yoichi, who stood sleepy-eyed and trying not to yawn in the corner. "I've done what I can," he said. "I can only hope it will be enough."

The clerk didn't ask why he'd shown up in the middle of the night with an injured bakeneko in house cat form. He only said, "Rest, my lord. I will watch over her."

Ryōtora rubbed his eyes and stood. "And protect her. It's possible the governor will come looking."

CHAPTER TWENTY-ONE

Thanks to the malaise that sapped him out of nowhere, Sekken knew even before his mother and sisters returned from the palace that something must have happened. He abruptly felt as fragile as rice paper and dull at heart, and he could only wonder with increasing dread what was happening to Ryōtora.

By the time his family returned, he'd spun out a dozen scenarios, each of them more gruesome and unlikely than the previous. None of them, however, quite lived up to what his mother described.

"But– we're *Phoenix*," Sekken said. He knew he was gaping at her like a child, but he couldn't bring himself to stop. "Other clans *mock* us for being unwilling to kill." Sometimes it was necessary and unavoidable; their hands were by no means pure. Their situation with the curse, though… this wasn't the Five Nights of Shame, when the entire Snake Clan was overtaken by a malevolent spirit and the only way to protect Rokugan was for the Phoenix to annihilate them, down to the last child. It was just some people falling asleep.

Wasn't it?

Sekken couldn't remember the last time he'd seen his mother so angry – or so willing to show that anger. "If I have to write to the Elemental Council, I will. But the time it will take for a messenger to come and go, not to mention the time they'll spend in debate…"

By then, Kaikoga Hanemi might be dead. And who knew what else Katahiro might do? Not only to the Moth, but to the Dragon. "Is Ryōtora–"

"He's fine," Ginshō said. Unlike their mother, she'd gone cold and rigid, concealing her fury behind discipline. "It took him by surprise, of course, but it took *all* of us by surprise. He went back to his embassy, and I hope he'll stay there. I think if the governor can find any reason to take offense at the Dragon, he will."

Ameno intervened before Sekken could respond. "Brother, I know you want to be involved in this, but…"

But his involvement consisted of resting. Of supporting Ryōtora by doing nothing at all.

Or at least by meditating. Sekken's skills in that regard might have improved enormously over the last year, but today it felt like trying to rein in a toddler mid-tantrum. His fury at Katahiro flared up – breathe it down. His fear for Ryōtora – breathe it down. His burning wish to solve this puzzle, to contribute something, *anything* of value – breathe it down. Over and over again, two steps forward, two steps back.

He switched tactics. A monk from the Temple of the Five-Fold Balance had taught him a variety of techniques meant to bolster particular elements; what did Ryōtora need most right now? Earth, to help him maintain patience and resist Katahiro's attempts to knock him off his stride. Air, to perform the delicate dance of courtly politics with grace. Water, flowing around these threats, perceiving the truth behind the deceptions–

All of them. He needed all of them. An ideal samurai, an ideal *person*, balanced the five elements against one another, drawing on the strengths of every one.

So Sekken would give Ryōtora all of them.

The techniques were more than a little unorthodox, and Sekken had stopped practicing them when they seemed to offer no predictable benefit. But by now his family was used to him doing all manner of peculiar things for his health, whether that was meditating on all fours – an Earth technique meant to evoke stability and the spiritual power of animals – or hanging upside down from a rafter like a bat.

Whether it did Ryōtora any good, he didn't know. But by the time he finished one round, Sekken had at least given *himself* an idea. And if he was careful enough in how he went about it, then he might be able to do some good for them both.

He sat down at his desk and wrote out a brief note, not bothering with the usual flowery courtesies. "Stay until he's read it," he told Jun, handing it over for the servant to deliver, "and make sure he understands that I mean what I say about timing."

Jun bowed and left, and Sekken started the cycle again.

He didn't tell his mother or sisters what he was planning, because he didn't want them to argue. His mother was distracted anyway; according to Jun, she had dinner with Isawa Miyuki – who did not come to speak with Sekken – and then the two of them went out. Ameno was visiting Lady Aimaku, and Ginshō went drinking with Shiba Tanezane, so there was no one around to countermand Sekken's order that his guest should be allowed in, despite the late hour.

Makusa Naotsugu visibly stifled a yawn as he bowed in greeting. "Lord Asako. I have made house calls at the Hour of the Boar in the past, but usually for emergencies. It is extremely unusual for a patient to say in advance that he wishes for me to visit so late at night."

"I have my reasons," Sekken said. Then, thinking of Isawa Chikayū being found asleep at a shrine, he hastened to add, "Reasons which have nothing to do with foul magic. I promise, Sir Naotsugu, you'll understand in a moment; I just didn't want to put all of this in a letter. Would you like some tea?"

"I think I might need it," Naotsugu admitted, seating himself on a cushion.

Sekken handed over a cup, then poured a second for himself. "Normally this would be the point at which I'd use my courtly wiles to imply that if you tell anyone what I'm about to divulge to you, then you'll suffer all manner of unpleasant consequences. But phrasing that with suitable elegance and subtlety would require effort I really can't afford to spend right now, so can we just pretend I've done it properly and move on?"

That was bluntness with a vengeance and then some, and Naotsugu visibly recoiled. "I– ah–"

"Excellent," Sekken said, and told him what he and Ryōtora had discovered.

The yawns vanished as if they had never been and the tea cooled in Naotsugu's hand, completely forgotten. At the end of the explanation, Sekken said, "This is why we're meeting so late. I hope Ryōtora – sorry, Lord Isao – oh, never mind, Ryōtora – is asleep by now. If there's a time I can afford to think a little, it's now."

"I wouldn't trust that too far," Naotsugu cautioned him. "Any drain on your shared elemental energy will take time to rebound, and you can't be certain Lord Isao will have recovered by the time he wakes."

"I know. I'm not hoping to solve this problem myself; I'm hoping *you* can solve it. My mother brought you to examine me because you specialize in the study of spiritual bonds. You were wrong about Tanshu being what drains me, but maybe you can make something of this." Sekken hoped the pang that went through him didn't show. He hadn't seen Tanshu in over a day, since he sent the inugami off to help Miyuki. Had Tanshu accompanied her to the mansion tonight? If so, why hadn't he come to greet his master?

Naotsugu frowned into his tea as if he could divine the answers in his own reflection. "Such a connection between people... may I speak freely, Lord Asako?"

"Since I'm more or less incapable of holding my own tongue right now, go right ahead."

The other man drew a deep breath. "Very well. I want to stress, Lord Asako, that I do not in *any* way feel you've done something blasphemous."

Sekken was alert enough to guess what he meant. "You're talking about blood magic."

"I've heard that it can be used to forge coercive bonds between the user and the victim, for a variety of foul purposes. And there is a sense in which the kind of sacrifice Lord Isao made – and the sacrifice you made in return – are akin to the blood sacrifices used to propitiate malevolent spirits."

Similar thoughts had gone through Sekken's head, that terrible night in Seibo Mura when he realized Ryōtora was preparing to give his life to restore the ward that kept Nurarihyon trapped. Blood magic had been common practice in Rokugan before the dawn of the Empire, and not in a defiled way; it was only after the balance of the realms changed that malevolent spirits became drawn to even voluntary blood sacrifices, corrupting those who called on them. But it was still possible for a priest to offer himself up as a living sacrifice to the elemental spirits. Or for a courtier to do much the same, with the aid of his holy ancestor.

He couldn't fault Naotsugu for thinking along those lines, not when he'd done the same himself. Still, Sekken grimaced. "If those are truly the terms we should be thinking in, that will make dealing with this… difficult." It was more weariness than politeness that made him gloss over phrases like *we'll have inquisitors and Kuni witch-hunters clawing at our heels.*

"There is another, less… troublesome way to conceive of it," Naotsugu said. "As a karmic bond – one forged and felt within a lifetime, rather than carried over from one life to the next."

"I thought those usually meant people became lovers or dire enemies in their next incarnations. Not that they were drawing on each other's strength."

"Generally, yes. But there are exceptions, or at least stories of exceptions. Whether they're true or not, who can say." Naotsugu finally sipped the tea, grimacing at its lukewarm bitterness. "One in particular comes to mind. It's a fourth-century tale of twins born with such a strong karmic link, their situation was much like yours."

Like children born with their bodies conjoined, Sekken thought. Some of whom lived fine lives, albeit very peculiar ones, and some of whom suffered not just debilitating but lethal consequences. It put his own difficulties in perspective. "What came of them?"

"It took some time for their parents to discover the twins' condition, as you might expect. It was especially hard on them as they grew; maturation places particular demands on the body and spirit, ones entirely outside the control of the individual. They grew very weak, and their parents feared for their lives. Ultimately, they were brought to Phoenix lands, where an ishiken – supposedly Isawa Yasōji, though that detail may have been added later – attempted to sever the link between them."

"Attempted." Sekken's mouth was very dry, but he didn't trust his hand to lift his tea without spilling it. "Not succeeded?"

Naotsugu shrugged apologetically. "We don't truly know. This was centuries ago, and the tale is not a first-hand report. The text says they lived apart after that, never seeing each other again – but whether that's an effect of their separation, a precaution to avoid a renewal of their bond, or a measure they resorted to because the separation failed, I cannot say."

Never seeing each other again. Now Sekken couldn't have drunk the tea if he wanted to; his throat had closed up.

The other man regarded him with sympathy. "I think you should not make any hasty decisions, Lord Asako. I am happy to discuss this further if you wish, and also with Lord Isao. It may be that if I go looking, I can find more information. The Isawa, in particular, might have other records. But for now, I suspect it's better if you rest. The hour is very late."

"Yes," Sekken whispered, and did not rise to see him out.

You know what you should do.

The answer was in everything from plays to the moral philosophy of Atsuto Noriaya. If this connection to Ryōtora hampered Sekken's ability to serve his family and his clan – and it did, for both of them – then the right thing to do was to renounce it. Samurai were "those who served"; they were not meant to serve themselves. Greater considerations came first, the heart not even a distant second.

You don't know if it will work, the traitorous, selfish part of his mind argued. Sir Naotsugu admitted that himself. There's no benefit in risking an untried solution, with no hope of success.

But what benefit was there in not trying anything at all?

Sekken hadn't been able to motivate himself to get undressed for bed; he'd just laid down on his futon, still fully clothed. There he lay motionless, unsleeping, trapped in the swirl of his own thoughts. What hour was it now?

Rat? Ox? If he didn't sleep, he would only tire Ryōtora out for the next day. But telling himself that hardly made it easier to drift off.

Finally, he sat up. Sir Naotsugu hadn't said it outright, but the message had been there: this wasn't a thing for Sekken to decide on his own. It affected both him and Ryōtora. They had to talk about it – with each other.

It had been years since he slipped out of the house unseen, but he hadn't forgotten how. Who would think to keep watch for him now, when Sekken had spent the last year and then some as a reclusive invalid? There was no feeling of getting away with something deliciously forbidden as he hurried through the dark, quiet streets, hardly feeling the cold. Instead, it was a feeling more like a ball rolling down a hill, gathering momentum as it went. Like it could never do anything but fall.

At the Dragon embassy, they let him in. He was Lord Asako Sekken; he wouldn't call at this hour without good reason. And Ryōtora would want to see him.

Ryōtora was asleep, of course. The small lantern in Sekken's hand shed gentle light over the cut planes of his face as Sekken eased the door shut. For a moment Sekken let himself simply *look*, as he had not permitted himself to do since the day Ryōtora arrived in the city. There had been too many walls between them, the secrets they were both keeping, the need for Sekken to marry someone who could bring children and connections to his family. He couldn't let himself truly see Ryōtora, because then…

Then he would *want*. For himself, not for his family and clan. He would want this noble, admirable, driven man, who made Sekken dream of becoming more. Of living up to what Ryōtora deserved.

The light, falling on Ryōtora's face, made the other man stir. And when he opened his eyes, Sekken knew the truth.

I can never give him up.

He sank to his knees at Ryōtora's side. "Forgive me," he breathed, setting the lantern on the mat. "I shouldn't disturb you like this, but I–"

"It's fine," Ryōtora said, blinking sleep out of his eyes. He looked disoriented, not quite awake – but not upset. "I'm glad to see you."

There were so many other things they should discuss. More important things, like the governor and Kaikoga Hanemi and whether Ryōtora had learned anything they could use to stop the curse. But what came out of Sekken's mouth was, "We have to be together. No matter what that looks like. It's the only way I can survive this – in mind, in heart, if not in body. I- I *need* you. You're what makes all of this worthwhile." A lifetime of weakness, in exchange for Ryōtora. Even if Sekken had known the consequences for what he was doing, that night in Seibo Mura, he would have made the same choice. So long as it meant they could be together.

Ryōtora's gaze softened. "Of course we need each other. All this time, I haven't been able to solve the problem, because I didn't understand its cause. But now that I do... isn't the answer obvious? We're already joined. The solution is to *accept* that, and to never let ourselves be parted again. Only then can we be whole."

Sekken hadn't dared hope the answer could be so simple,

and so *right*. But Ryōtora was a priest; he knew these matters in a way no mere scholar ever could. If he believed this was possible, it must be so.

Politics could go to the underworld, for all Sekken cared, and take duty with them. He had everything he needed, right here.

He cupped Ryōtora's jaw in his palms, the way he'd been wanting to do since that first reunion at the governor's palace, and he kissed him. Gently at first, then deeply, letting the reins of self-control slip from his hands. Passion of any kind had been a danger for so long – but not now. Not with Ryōtora.

Not so long as they were together.

CHAPTER TWENTY-TWO

With Sayashi safely ensconced and a guard standing over her, Ryōtora was finally free to stumble back to bed. After the unreality of the night, he felt like he was walking through a dream.

The moment he opened his door, he knew he was awake – and living in a nightmare.

Sekken lay in Ryōtora's bed, black hair fanning around his head like the silken backing of a scroll. He was in his sleep robe, not properly dressed, and the front panels had fallen open enough to show the rise and fall of his chest. He didn't stir, not even when the light fell directly on his face.

"No," Ryōtora said, unable to lift his voice above a whisper. "Fortunes, no – please. *Not him.*"

But no prayer would change the truth. The sleeping curse had found its next victim: Asako Sekken.

Ryōtora didn't remember crossing the floor, but suddenly he was on his knees alongside the futon. One hand, reaching out, hesitating, finally came to rest on Sekken's shoulder. It was warm, solid, and motionless. The other man breathed on, the soft and regular rhythm of sleep.

"Sekken," Ryōtora said, then again, louder. Knowing it was stupid, but he couldn't stop himself. As if mere wishing could do what nothing else had done, simply because Ryōtora *needed Sekken to wake.*

Only after footsteps pounded toward him on the veranda did Ryōtora realize his voice had risen to a shout. Then Yoichi was there, biting back a curse. "My lord–"

"I found him here," Ryōtora said, helplessly. "When I came in. I– he–"

Words failed him. Yoichi said, "I'll send a messenger to his family. We'll be discreet."

Because otherwise people would hear that Sekken had been found in Ryōtora's bed, just as Asako Shoun was found at *her* lover's house. But what did it matter? Ryōtora would trade his reputation in a heartbeat if it would wake Sekken up.

Yoichi left. Ryōtora stayed, transfixed by the sight of Sekken's gently parted lips, the dark crescent of his lashes against his skin. He looked so *peaceful.* There had been no chance to study any victim of the curse other than Kaikoga Hanemi, and to Ryōtora, she had been nothing more than a puzzle and a source of difficulty. Were they all this peaceful? Did that mean their dreams were pleasant ones, or simply that they were too disconnected from their sleeping bodies to show any pain?

It has to be the former. If the Fortunes have any kindness, they must give me that. They've taken so much already.

The other day, after Sekken's collapse, Ryōtora hadn't

dared take the man's hand in his own. Not with Lady Asako there. Now he gathered the long, bony fingers between his own palms, cradling them as if they might break. The prayers he whispered were no formal phrases taught to him by his Agasha instructors, just half-formed pleas for the blessings that had eluded him so far.

He didn't let go when Yoichi returned, bearing a lantern. Not even when the door opened again, this time to admit Lady Asako.

Her breath hitched at the sight of her son, even though she must have been told what she would find. She sank down at Ryōtora's side, and she reached out – but only to touch the bare skin where Sekken's sleeve had fallen back. Not to take his hand from Ryōtora's.

"I found him here," Ryōtora said again, numbly. He couldn't look at her. Couldn't look away from Sekken. "I was out of the embassy – Tanshu came to me–"

The dog had gone missing. Or had he? Ryōtora forced himself to release Sekken so that he could form his own fingers into a mudra. When he whispered a prayer, his vision refocused. He wasn't at all surprised to see Tanshu on the other side of Sekken, pressed up against the man's body as if to feed him strength through sheer proximity. But the inugami's eyes were open, and wet brown as they gazed at Ryōtora.

"He is there? And awake?" Lady Asako asked.

"Yes."

"Good." She let out a slow, ragged breath. Then another. "It will come for each of us, in time. Everyone who was at the Game of a Hundred Candles. I- I didn't know whether to hope it would strike me first, or him."

Guilt weighted her admission, but Ryōtora understood. As a mother, she would give anything to protect her son. But by that same token, she was better able to defend him. To act when he could not.

Unless action could be taken from the other side. "I wonder if he sought it," Ryōtora said. "He told me it might be better if he fell asleep. For my sake."

This time the breath she drew in was sharper. "I had just returned from the palace when your messenger came. I took Miyuki to the pavilion. She confirmed what you said, and more – she thinks whatever happened there was not simply a consequence of the game. She believes someone set it up deliberately."

Anger gave Ryōtora the spark he needed to drag his gaze away from Sekken. Lady Asako was not her polished, elegant courtly self; with no cosmetics on and her kimono a simple gray, she looked nearly as vulnerable as her son. Ryōtora felt vulnerable himself as he said, "We were *targeted*?"

"Perhaps," Lady Asako said. "Miyuki couldn't tell what the intended purpose was, nor whether it had specific targets; the effect itself is gone, and only the echoes remain. But you understand… if so, that puts you and your clan in more danger."

Even through the grief locking his heart in bands of iron, he felt the spike of fear. Yes, they would be in danger. People would think *they* had arranged this, in order to strike at the governor. Perhaps to remove him from the political board, to be replaced by someone more sympathetic to the Dragon.

For all Ryōtora knew, it could even be true. Kinmoku

wouldn't have done it... but every clan had its dishonorable agents, working from the shadows.

He rubbed his burning eyes. He hadn't been blinking enough. Half of him wanted to lie down next to Sekken, to wrap himself around the other man and wait for the curse to claim him, too. But that wouldn't do Sekken any good. "I found the bakeneko. The geisha. She's injured – I'm waiting for her to wake up. She might have answers."

"Let us hope so," Lady Asako said. "If she does not..."

They both left that sentence unfinished.

Dawn had no sooner cracked the horizon than a pounding came at the gate. Even from inside the embassy, Ryōtora could hear the shout. "Open, in the name of the provincial governor!"

"Stay here," Yoichi said, when Ryōtora would have risen. "I will see what the messenger wants."

He wasn't speaking from an excess of etiquette. After the previous day's audience, none of them trusted what the governor might do next. Even so... "It feels like cowardice to hide," Ryōtora muttered to Lady Asako.

She had stayed to watch over her son and wait for Sayashi to wake. Despite the long, sleepless night, she had somehow assembled her usual courtly mask, in demeanor if not with actual cosmetics. "It is not cowardice," she said. "Courtesy is the wall that shields your duty. An ambassador does not open his own gate; let your clerk deal with this, and thereby purchase time and space with which to consider your next action."

Her words steadied him, even if they were a courtier's

perspective on the virtues of a samurai. And Ryōtora was grateful for it when Yoichi returned, white-faced and clenching his fists.

"By order of Lord Asako Katahiro," he said, his voice stiff with fury and apprehension, "all those who attended the Game of a Hundred Candles at the Komoriyome Pavilion are to relocate immediately to the governor's palace, where he can protect them."

The curse that came from Lady Asako was worthy of her daughter Ginshō. "*Protection*," she spat. "I don't trust that in the slightest."

Ryōtora's heart sat like lead in his chest. "It doesn't matter if we trust it," he said dully. "We have to obey."

"*I* have to obey," she said. "I am a Phoenix, and a resident of this province. You, Lord Isao, are a Dragon and an ambassador. You have no obligation to follow his orders, especially when he has given you reason to doubt your safety."

"But if I refuse... what if he sends his warriors here to take me by force?"

Lady Asako's smile was as sharp as a katana's edge. "*Then* you will go. But not before. Make *him* be the one to push this confrontation to that point; let *him* explain to his family daimyō and the Elemental Council why 'protecting' you required him to storm your embassy and capture you against your will."

Ever since Ryōtora arrived in the city, politics had felt like a treacherous field of ice beneath his feet. Oddly, that vision – Phoenix forces breaking the gate down, or climbing over the walls, coming for Ryōtora with their blades drawn –

gave him secure footing at last. He'd faced the terrors of the Night Parade. Humans with swords did not frighten him.

He bowed to Lady Asako. "Thank you. I will do as you advise."

Yoichi cleared his throat. "Lord Isao, Lady Asako… there is one other problem. The order specifies all who were present, be they waking or sleeping."

Sekken. Of course: having gathered all the other victims into his grasp, Katahiro would not want to let the most recent one slip through.

"No one knows he's here," Yoichi reminded him. "Or rather, very few know, and all but Lady Asako are Dragon."

Ryōtora's jaw tensed. "They'll ask, though. When the others come, and the only ones absent are myself and Sekken…" No, there had been two Crane at the gathering, a Centipede priestess, and one lone man from the Firefly. Doji Suemaru was already asleep, but would his companion refuse to bow? Could the minor clan samurai trust public outrage to protect them against a Phoenix provincial governor?

"I don't want my son in Katahiro's hands," Lady Asako said vehemently. Then her face twisted. "But if you hide him here…"

That *would* give Katahiro justification to storm the place. "The governor will figure out where Sekken is," Ryōtora said. "Our connection is too well known, even if the nature of it is not – and I have to assume that people have guessed."

For some reason, his words smoothed the conflict from Lady Asako's expression. She stood utterly still for a moment, then nodded, crisply, as if an internal debate had ended with a unanimous vote. "My son is only under

Katahiro's authority if he is a member of the Phoenix Clan," she said.

Ryōtora flinched. "You would make him rōnin? Just to protect him from the governor?" Could she even *do* that, without approval from someone of higher status?

"No," Lady Asako said. "I would make him a Dragon."

All the breath went out of Ryōtora.

"You love each other," she went on, without acrimony. "And if you marry him, taking him into your family, then he is no longer a Phoenix. You can even tell Katahiro's messengers, with perfect honesty, that Asako Sekken is not here. Because the man asleep in your embassy will be Isao Sekken instead."

It should have been cause for delight. They could be together at last, as Ryōtora wanted so badly he hadn't even allowed himself to think about it, lest the impossibility of it break him. But...

But not like this. And not even because Katahiro might rightly argue that Sekken needed his lord's permission to wed. Because Ryōtora did not want to buy that future as a political gambit, running roughshod over what Sekken himself might want.

Yes, he loved Sekken. More deeply than he could ever have anticipated, the night he arrived in Seibo Mura and found an unwanted Phoenix visitor already there. Sekken's trust and esteem had healed the wound in Ryōtora's heart, the bone-deep cut of his inferior birth. His presence had given Ryōtora the strength to face the Night Parade, and his sacrifice had saved Ryōtora's life. If by invoking the elemental spirits Ryōtora could have burned to ash everything that threatened Sekken's well-being, he would have done it without hesitation.

But neither the curse nor their shared affliction could be solved that way. And if they bound themselves more closely together, knowing that every move each of them made came at a cost to the other… what would that do to them in the long run? Over time it might poison their affection for each other, until they had nothing left but resentment.

Sekken might be willing to risk it anyway. With the gates of possibility suddenly flung open, Ryōtora knew that *he* was willing.

But that wasn't a choice he could make on Sekken's behalf. Especially not when he'd be doing it merely to save himself some difficulty.

He bowed deeply to Lady Asako. "I am honored that you would trust me and my clan with your son's future. But despite my feelings – despite what I believe Sekken's own feelings to be – I will not put him through a marriage ceremony he is not awake for and cannot agree to. We will protect him as best as we can, regardless. If the governor's messengers ask after him, I will lie and say he is not here."

Lady Asako's eyes widened. "Lord Isao… my son has spoken often of you, and always in praise. According to him, one of your finest qualities is your deep and resolute sense of honor. That you would bend that honor for his sake…" She bowed, even more deeply than Ryōtora had. "My family will be forever in your debt."

"It may be a question of saving lives," Ryōtora said. "That, Lady Asako, is not a matter for debts."

•••

The messenger wasn't happy to receive Ryōtora's refusal, but he didn't press the issue right away. Instead, he departed, and Lady Asako slipped away, so that her presence at the Dragon embassy would not raise questions. Yoichi tried to insist that Ryōtora sleep, but his stomach was too curdled with tension for that. "I'll be with Sekken," he said, turning to go back to his room. There were no practical constraints on him anymore; tired though he was, he still might as well pray to the spirits and see if anything useful came of it. If that meant he collapsed, so be it.

But before he could get more than halfway to his room, a servant ran up, panting. "Lord Isao, the, uh. The cat is awake."

Sayashi. Ryōtora would have sworn he was sapped of energy, but somehow, he managed to run.

Which proved to be a mistake. When he flung the door open, he got only a glimpse of a small black cat licking her paw in the manner of one trying to soothe herself; then the cat levitated off the futon and simultaneously tried to bolt for cover under a table while growing to the size of a snow leopard. The results were… not good.

Ryōtora held up his hands as the table landed on its side, dumping the bowls that held what was left of his offerings. "Sayashi! It's all right. You're safe. No one's going to hurt you."

She had fluffed up, which was incongruous on that large of a body. Then she mewled and sank down, curling onto her less injured side. Ryōtora came forward slowly, not wanting to startle her again. "You're at the Dragon embassy," he said, gentling his voice. "I found you under a house last night. I could tell you were hurt, so I brought you here and did what I could to heal you. But I could only do so much."

Sayashi was panting in pain. Ryōtora wasn't entirely sure she'd heard or understood him – or that she was in any state for human speech – but then she whispered, "The house…"

"Tanshu led me to it," Ryōtora said. "You fled there, I think. After you were attacked at the governor's palace?"

She began licking herself again, miserably. "I was… I needed somewhere safe."

"That house is safe?"

"It's home." She winced, and he couldn't tell whether it was for her injuries or her own choice of words. "I used to live there."

Why would a bakeneko live in a house like that? Then Ryōtora understood. "When you were simply a cat."

It was like seeing Sekken asleep, stripped of all the artifice a courtier learned. Yes, Sayashi was a yōkai, bold and powerful and contemptuous of human frailty. Once upon a time, though, she'd been an ordinary cat in an ordinary house. Perhaps with a family that loved her. That family would be long gone… but when danger threatened, Sayashi's instinct was still to bolt for home.

He knew better than to press for more information. It was a mark of how tired and pained Sayashi was that rather than flinging out a screen of other words, she merely sank back, exhausted. He uncorked the flask that had toppled to the floor and poured some water into one of the empty bowls; she roused enough to lap at it.

The water seemed to fortify her, and Ryōtora sat cross-legged nearby. "I know you're still hurt, so let me tell you what I know, and you can fill in the gaps. Is that acceptable?"

With a trace of her usual manner, Sayashi said, "I'll let you know."

He wasn't likely to get a more cooperative answer – even though he felt he deserved one, after crawling under a house to retrieve her. "Tracing backward, then. You hid under that house because you needed safety, and you needed safety because you had to flee the governor's palace after someone attacked you. Possibly Katahiro himself? Possibly because he discovered you're a bakeneko."

"He's known for ages," Sayashi whispered, closing her eyes.

That was interesting. "He hadn't summoned you," Ryōtora said. "You went to the palace on your own – I don't know why. But he's been acting strangely, which might have something to do with his relationship with you, because his strange behavior started when he *stopped* seeing you. You've been a favorite of his for some time, and at the Game of a Hundred Candles you tried to provoke me and Sekken into telling our stories of the Night Parade. You claimed that was only out of spite, because we'd neglected your role in Seibo Mura, but I'm starting to doubt that."

One eye slitted open enough to glare at him. "It's the truth."

"Then I apologize for questioning it. But I don't think you're an innocent observer of all of this, Sayashi. I think that whatever started at the Game of a Hundred Candles has something to do with *you*. And I think that when you went to the governor, he figured that out, which is why you had to flee."

Her tail lashed. "So much effort, to get so much wrong."

"Oh? Then please, enlighten me." It took great effort to keep his voice under control.

She drew in a deep breath and tried to push herself semi-upright, front paws on the mat. It was an unwise move; Ryōtora had done what he could to knit the cracked ribs, but the muscles were still bruised, and Sayashi dropped abruptly back onto her side. With a hiss of annoyance, she said, "Fine. I'll do this while lying as flat as a nursing mother."

"You think the governor uncovered *my* secret machinations? You think *I* arranged to ensnare all of you in my web of cursed sleep? You're a fool, samurai. I'll admit to some involvement ... but what's going on now was never my idea to begin with."

The room threatened to spin around Ryōtora. "The governor. *He's* doing this? On purpose?"

"After a fashion." Sayashi's fur fluffed, involuntarily. "What you've been talking to since the Game of a Hundred Candles isn't the provincial governor. It's a baku. A spirit from the Realm of Dreams has taken Asako Katahiro's place."

CHAPTER TWENTY-THREE

Sekken rode into the courtyard and swung down from his gelding's saddle amid a gentle shower of cherry blossom petals. Several caught in the horse's mane – and in Sekken's own – but he left them where they were. Sometimes nature's accidents were more beautiful than any courtly artifice.

Lady Sun shed benevolent warmth over the courtyard as he passed the reins to one of the servants. "Is Ryōtora here?" Sekken asked.

"He is with his guests," the servant said, bowing. "They are in the garden."

Sekken had forgotten about Ryōtora's guests. Grinning, he loped around the side of the house, heading for the greenery beyond.

More cherry blossoms snowed down here; Ryōtora had taken the precaution of setting a parasol above the small platform where he knelt. With the spring weather so fine, Sekken wasn't surprised he'd chosen to conduct a more casual tray-style ceremony. Ryōtora's studies with Asako Harunaga had made him a master of several different approaches, including the most formal, multi-hour tea event. But this was no day to be cooped up inside the confines of a tearoom; instead, he'd brought his guests out here, to enjoy themselves amid the burgeoning life of the garden.

Sekken hung back, not wanting to interrupt. By the looks of it, the gathering was almost over; the guests were examining the utensils Ryōtora had used, their comments not quite audible where Sekken stood. He hid a smile as the small iron kettle was passed around. That kettle had been his gift to Ryōtora last year, acquired with great difficulty from an Asahina lord. Sekken himself knew relatively little about what made one tea implement better than another, but the simple fact that the kettle was prized meant it was worth getting for Ryōtora. His husband's delight repaid every bit of the expense.

When the guests rose at last, Sekken drew behind a willow tree, not wanting to be pulled into conversation. Only after they were gone did he advance, moving quietly over the moss-covered ground. Ryōtora's back was to him, an expanse of fine lavender silk subtly brocaded with a pattern like willow branches. Sekken's fingers slid up that silk as he quoted, "*As for today, let us go linger among the springtime hills.*"

He felt the laughter in Ryōtora's chest, and his husband completed the poem: "*If it gets dark, won't shelter beneath the flowers be enough?*"

In that deep, resonant voice, shelter beneath the flowers sounded a great deal like an invitation. Ryōtora turned and kissed him, all the more enticing for its restraint. Neither of them was minded to shock the servants by carrying on out here, in broad daylight.

At least, they weren't minded to do it *again*.

Effervescent joy rose up in Sekken's body at the memory, and not just for the pleasure it had brought. That incident had occurred not long after their wedding, when the two of them were still drunk on the experience of being together at last. Of being *themselves* at last – for, as Ryōtora had promised, their marriage had stabilized the bond created in Seibo Mura. Neither of them had to fear weakness or confusion anymore. They were joined as one, stronger together than they were apart, and the limitations of the past were a fast-fading memory.

"Help me carry these inside," Ryōtora said when they came up for air.

No real help was needed, with everything on one tray, and the brazier left for a servant to move when it finished cooling. Still, Sekken didn't mind. He picked up the tray and said, "I hope Lady Nene was suitably impressed by the teakettle."

Ryōtora laughed. "More than impressed. It turns out she was hoping to get it for herself. But she said that if it could not be hers, then at least it was right that it be mine."

Of course she had. Nene could not deny Ryōtora's skill at the tea ceremony. And he'd established himself easily at court after the wedding, winning admiration for his forthright, upstanding nature. Even jaded courtiers had to acknowledge virtue when it shone so brightly before them, and Ryōtora had done more than a little to reshape the atmosphere of the palace into a more congenial form.

Speaking of the palace… "Are you ready for tonight?" Sekken asked, holding the tray as Ryōtora stowed its contents one by one in their locked cabinet.

By way of answer, Ryōtora drew from his sleeve a small, lacquered box, inlaid with mother-of-pearl shaped into a spray of flowers. "Tell me what you think."

Sekken removed the lid and inhaled deeply. A rich mix of scents greeted him, layered and subtle. "Cypress," he said, "and plum blossom, peony, some kind of citrus rind… mandarin? No, kumquat. Along with lychee and just a touch of dragon's blood resin."

Ryōtora reclaimed the box, shaking his head, but not because Sekken was wrong. "You're always able to guess what's in my incense, no matter how subtle the blend."

"Because I know *you*," Sekken said. "And the blend is beautiful."

They took their time getting dressed for court, with a bit of distraction along the way. But eventually they were both ready, Ryōtora far outshining Sekken in a kimono with a flowing water pattern. They didn't need litters for their health anymore, but formality still mattered; they let themselves be carried to the palace, and to the incense party the governor had organized.

Katahiro greeted them both with a broad smile that suggested he'd already enjoyed some sake. Sekken didn't begrudge him that: Katahiro was a vastly happier man ever since he'd retired from his post as provincial governor, allowing his niece Seifū to take his place. He looked substantially older than he used to, but not nearly as severe. These days he spent his time practicing calligraphy, and recently he'd also picked up the biwa. "Will we hear a song from you tonight?" Ryōtora asked.

"No, I couldn't," Katahiro said, waving off the request. "You'd rather hear *good* music."

"Good music comes from a pure heart; I have no doubt yours will be splendid."

Sekken hid his own smile behind his fan. Yes, Ryōtora had settled in well, devoting himself to learning courtly flattery with the same dedication he showed to everything else in his life. His efforts had been rewarded last month with an appointment to oversee the city's main temple to the Fortune of Wisdom and Mercy.

Asako Shoun and Sodona Aimaku glided past them on the veranda, laughing quietly to each other. Sekken, watching them go, didn't hear Isawa Chikayū until she was right next to him. "Sekken," she said. "I am in *desperate* need of your advice."

"Oh dear," Sekken said, amused. By the sound of it, he could guess what was coming. "Tsuguzoe is causing problems?"

"No end of them!" Chikayū said with feeling. "I'm delighted, of course, that my grandson has inherited his own inugami. But that creature chews on *everything*, just like a real puppy. How can I stop him?"

Sekken couldn't hold back his laugh. "I have no idea. Tanshu came to me as an adult, after all. Have you tried asking *him* to discipline Tsuguzoe?" None of them quite knew if the young inugami was somehow Tanshu's offspring – and if so, who the mother might be – but Sekken's spirit companion was watching over the puppy with as much attention as if he were.

"He can see what's happening as well as I can!" Chikayū exclaimed. Then she softened, as he'd known she would. Even her complaints were born of happiness. "I will try. In truth, it's difficult to be angry with him – or with the boy. You make very attractive sons, Sekken."

"Yes, he does." That came from Ryōtora, who'd parted with Katahiro and come to join them. The look he gave Sekken bid fair to summon a blush from beneath the rice powder on his cheeks. Then Ryōtora added, "But your daughter deserves an equal share of the credit. How is Miyuki?"

The two of them strolled on, chatting, toward the informal chamber where the incense gathering was to be held. Sekken paused, looking out over the palace grounds. In the middle distance he could see Mirumoto Kinmoku walking with someone, her hands moving as if miming some clever bit of swordplay before her head tipped back in a full-bodied laugh; beyond her, Doji Suemaru was knee-deep in a flooded paddy, harvesting rice. The setting sun gilded the entire scene like a painting, and the warmth of the moment filled Sekken's heart.

Perfect. Everything had turned out so perfectly in the end. He could scarcely even remember what used to cause him such worry. Seibo Mura was safely under Dragon control; Isawa Chikayū had the tsukimono-suji heir she wanted. He and Ryōtora were both healthy again, and Ryōtora had become the darling of the provincial court–

For the briefest of moments, it felt like a cloud passed over the sun.

No such thing had happened, of course. Lady Sun shone

on, liquid gold like the clearest honey. Inside the building, Sekken heard Ryōtora speaking, and then someone exclaiming in delight at whatever he'd said. Some clever turn of phrase, or an allusion to a famous poem–

The light shone on, but a chill touched Sekken's heart.

Why should he feel chilled? Winter was well behind them, and he had nothing to trouble him. Everything was exactly as he might hope for.

But...

Against his will, Sekken turned to look toward Ryōtora. His strong, pale profile almost shone in the building's dim interior, the cosmetics of a courtier powdering his skin, darkening his lashes. He was beautiful without those things, of course – not conventionally beautiful, perhaps, his features stronger than aristocratic tastes tended to admire, but he'd learned how to soften his appearance–

Why would he do that?

Sekken's hand tightened around his fan. What kind of question was that? Ryōtora had adapted to court, that was all. Far better than Sekken might have expected, for a vassal samurai born to a peasant family. But he'd shaped himself into what he needed to be, first for his adopted father, Sir Keijun, and then a second time for...

For Sekken.

Because Sekken wanted him to fit in at court.

The golden light mocked the tension now twisting inside Sekken. *Of course I wanted this. Why shouldn't I? We're married; Ryōtora is a Phoenix now. He's become part of my life, and I want him to be happy.*

But...

But Ryōtora wouldn't be happy with this.

Parts of it, certainly. He loved Sekken; of that, Sekken had no doubt. He– he practiced the way of tea. Surely he appreciated having the opportunity to study with a master like Asako Harunaga, to present his guests with such fine utensils, not only elegant but famed. To craft incense out of fine ingredients, to– to–

To quote poetry? To display his victory over Lady Nene in the form of a prized teakettle, bought for more money than Sir Keijun had probably seen in his entire life?

Everything around Sekken was still perfect. Everyone was happy. *He* was happy.

It felt like a shell. Like the painted exterior of a lantern, so fragile one could put a finger through it.

"My heart, are you coming in?"

Sekken jumped at the question. Ryōtora was in the doorway, beckoning him to join them. Without thinking, Sekken said, "Not today. I'm minded to…" What did he want to do, if not this?

The answer to that had always been the same, ever since he was a boy. "To go read. Come find me at the library when you're done."

Ryōtora came forward, standing close enough they could have kissed, but holding back. His eyes smiled into Sekken's as he said, "Enjoy yourself."

Sekken entered the grounds of the Kanjiro Library by the autumn gate, passing through an arching tunnel of Phoenix-red maple leaves. He loved the library in all seasons, but this was his favorite, when the vivid colors of the foliage stood out against the piercing blue sky, and just enough chill nipped the air to make him feel awake and alive. Half the time he wound up sitting in a window gazing out over the city, rather than actually reading the book or the scroll in his lap.

He suspected that would happen today. What had he come to the library for? He couldn't quite remember. Maybe just because it was a perfect autumn day, and with Ryōtora happily ensconced at the palace, Sekken was free to occupy himself however he pleased.

A frown sapped the faint smile on his face. Yes, of course Ryōtora was happy. Why wouldn't he be?

The stairs creaked beneath Sekken's feet as he climbed them. If he was mostly going to look out over the city, it made sense to climb to the top floor, but he stopped at the fifth out of sheer habit. A collection of kaidan, maybe? Though they were entirely the wrong mood for a bright, cheerful day like this one. Not that it mattered, if he wasn't likely to read. Still, for some reason the idea of kaidan drew him. Maybe someone would host a Game of a Hundred Candles as the nights grew longer.

Footsteps creaked on the floor above his head, and Sekken paused.

There are only five floors in the Kanjiro Library.

Of course there were only five. One for each element. Why would anyone build the tower with six floors?

But the stairs had continued upward. Hadn't they?

Sekken turned to look. The staircase stopped here at the fifth floor, the way it always had. How distracted must he be, to imagine that changing? He shook his head and turned away–

Another creak. Then a quick rhythm, as someone walked swiftly across a floor Sekken *knew* wasn't there.

There was a small stepladder patrons could use to reach for items on top shelves. Sekken dragged two low desks together, stood the ladder atop them, and, with straining, was just able to rap his knuckles on the boards of the ceiling.

Silence. Sekken waited, hoping the entire rickety arrangement wouldn't topple or splinter apart beneath him.

Then quick steps again, and the unknown person rapped back.

"Hello?" he called, feeling awkward. One of the archivists might hear him and wonder what on earth he was doing. Or another patron – but he hadn't seen or heard any, apart from whoever was on the floor that couldn't exist. The library seemed empty, just the way Sekken liked it.

No response came from above. Sekken tried to reach up to knock again, but the desks creaked ominously; they weren't meant to take this kind of weight. And what good would more knocking do?

He climbed down carefully, holding his breath as if that would make the process any safer. So focused was he on that task, he almost didn't notice what he saw out of the corner of his eye.

The staircase continued upward again, instead of stopping at the fifth floor.

When he turned to face it, though, there was no additional flight. Just the landing, precisely where it ought to be.

As if the way to the impossible floor was only there when he wasn't paying attention.

"Well, that's unhelpful," Sekken muttered. How was he

supposed to investigate something while simultaneously ignoring it?

He tried sidling toward the stairs without really looking at them, with an unsurprising lack of results. Sekken wished Ryōtora were there. Maybe a priest would be able to solve this problem – and at the very least, they could enjoy the intriguing puzzle together.

More intriguing than incense games. A chill rippled down Sekken's back, as if the life he had now with Ryōtora was as impossible as the sixth floor of the Kanjiro Library. The doubts he'd had at the palace returned. They'd fallen from his mind so easily, as ephemeral as the cherry blossoms–

Cherry blossoms? But it was autumn. Wasn't it?

Sekken lunged, and his foot landed on the first riser of the stairs.

He stood, panting, half-expecting the step to vanish from beneath him. Now that he was on the extra flight of stairs, though, they stayed put… for now. He had the unsettling feeling that if he relinquished this victory, they would disappear again. That they *wanted* to disappear.

No. Not the stairs themselves. Whatever spirit was trying to hide them from Sekken.

"Come up here," a voice said from above. "Quickly!"

Every book-trained instinct in Sekken shouted a warning. How many yōkai thrived on luring humans to their doom with the thin wail of lost children or voices crying out for help? Many of them female, or at least approximating femininity, and that was definitely a woman speaking.

But it was an odd way to lure people to their doom, hiding in a place the potential victims couldn't see.

Unless whatever is hiding the stairs is trying to keep this thing imprisoned.

"*Move!*" the woman snapped, strain pulling the word taut. "I don't know how long I can keep the stairs there!"

Sekken had a thousand questions, and a growing sense that a superfluous staircase was the least of the things wrong in his world. But if he retreated to safety, he doubted his curiosity would ever be satisfied.

Gritting his teeth, he flung himself up the stairs.

He arrived at the top, panting and disheveled, in a small, windowless room lit only by a single lantern. It was definitely *not* part of the library. It had the feeling of a prison.

And it held a single occupant: a small woman in a silvery-gray kimono, its monotony thrown into sharp relief by the colorful silk shrouding one eye. A woman Sekken knew, though not well enough to recognize her by voice alone.

"Kaikoga Hanemi," he said, gaping at her. The world swam around him, trying to push itself back into the configuration it had taken before, thwarted by the immovable shape of the woman in front of him. "What are you doing here? Where *is* here?"

She gave him a tired, ironical bow. "Welcome to the Realm of Dreams, Lord Asako."

CHAPTER TWENTY-FOUR

A *baku*.

It isn't Katahiro at all.

Ryōtora understood what Sayashi had said... and he didn't understand anything at all. "How– but–"

The bakeneko's slitted eyes were hazed with pain, but still held a gleam of malicious amusement. "Didn't notice, did you? Well, that's to be expected."

He didn't know whether she meant that baku were subtle or he was obtuse. Knowing her, the ambiguity was deliberate, and she probably meant both. Sayashi began grooming herself once more, speaking in between swipes of her tongue. "Katahiro has known my true nature since the first time I was hired to entertain him. Some Isawa had warded his personal chambers against yōkai, and the alarms went off when I tried to enter. He took the ward down after that. Katahiro, I mean – not the baku. That's how I knew something had happened, when I went to the palace a few days ago. The governor was treating me like an ordinary woman."

"Is he the one that hurt you?"

"Yes. I confronted him once I realized something else had slipped into Katahiro's place." Sayashi's lip twitched in a sneer, apparently directed at herself. "Stupid of me. I should have known better."

"I would have done the same," Ryōtora said.

Her whiskers flicked at him as if to say, *of course you would have.*

Ryōtora refused to be baited. "Why did you go to the palace? You weren't summoned, were you?"

"No," Sayashi said. "But I'd heard about people falling asleep, and I knew Katahiro probably had something to do with that."

"Why him?"

The extensive exploration of one paw was probably more reluctance to speak than a balm for her wounds, but he waited patiently, and Sayashi eventually rewarded him with an answer. "Because we'd been reading those diaries together. The ones written by that man who vanished into his own dreams."

Isawa Minokichi. "I thought those were held in the Kanjiro Library."

"The originals are. Katahiro made copies for his own use."

Memory flickered. Kaikoga Hanemi, meeting Sekken at the gathering, had said something about the governor being too busy to discuss Minokichi's work. Ryōtora hadn't paid any attention to it at the time. Because why would someone like Asako Katahiro, an influential governor, be interested in theories about dreams?

He knew the answer to that. He and Kinmoku had sat

in this very room the night he arrived, discussing the provincial court. Ryōtora had read a dossier on his way to Phoenix lands, but Kinmoku had her own observations to offer. *Between you and me,* she'd said of Katahiro, *I don't think he likes being governor very much.*

A man burdened by his duties, and an Isawa who spoke of escaping them in dreams. Yes, he could see how that might appeal to Katahiro. To many samurai, in fact.

"We experimented with it together," Sayashi said. "It's easy for me to cross over; cats are half creatures of dream anyway. But we're not good at controlling others' dreams; that takes more skill. And baku tend to object to us interfering over there."

Ryōtora almost asked what Katahiro's idealized life looked like, but swallowed the question. That was no business of his. "But why would Katahiro want to be possessed by a baku?"

Sayashi sniffed delicately. "I don't think he did. There was one baku we encountered… it was curious. In dreams, it can do anything it likes, but here in the mortal realm, that isn't so easy. And Katahiro was getting more and more attached to the life he built for himself there. I think they've swapped places: Katahiro is off in a dream, and the baku holds the reins."

It made sense of the governor's odd behavior. Ryōtora had almost forgotten Kinmoku's evaluation of Katahiro because the man seemed to be enjoying his position very much: reveling in the power it gave him, but not especially interested in tiresome matters like the negotiations over Seibo Mura.

But then his behavior had shifted. "He tried to execute Kaikoga Hanemi. And he's been gathering up all the people who fell asleep; as of today, he's started gathering the ones who are still awake, too. How malevolent are baku?"

"How malevolent are dreams?" Sayashi asked dryly. "Some are; some aren't. And one can turn into the other."

Ryōtora's hands tensed. Quietly, he said, "And one person has been falling asleep every night since the game. Since the baku presumably crossed over. What happens when it runs out of victims?"

Her tail twitched. "I don't recommend waiting to find out."

Ryōtora had no intention of waiting – but that didn't tell him what to *do*.

Sekken was asleep. Kinmoku was asleep. Tanshu seemed singularly uninclined to leave his sleeping master's side. Sayashi was injured, and unreliable at the best of times. Even Asako Fumizuki was gone, swept into the baku's control. Ryōtora prayed all the sleepers were safe, but Sayashi hadn't been able to do more than speculate as to why they were falling to that curse in the first place. "I tried to ask the baku," she'd said when he pressed her. "You've seen the result."

Sayashi attacked, and badly injured. But the baku didn't seem to be hurting the sleepers. Ryōtora went to his bedchamber, took Sekken's unresisting hand in his own, and prayed to the spirits, hoping he could somehow commune with Sekken himself. All he got was the same impression Chikayū had described when she examined Hanemi, days ago: the sense that Sekken was utterly rapt, caught up in a vision Ryōtora couldn't see. No overtone of fear or darkness, though.

He tried to reassure himself with logic. One sleeper dragged under per night; there must be a reason for that. And even though the baku had threatened to kill Hanemi, it had changed its mind. That suggested it *needed* the sleepers. Therefore, it was unlikely the baku would harm any of those already under the effect, or the attendees from the gathering who were now held prisoner at the palace… at least, not until the curse had caught them all in its net.

Logic wasn't as reassuring as he would have liked.

Ryōtora made himself stop and breathe, working his hands in a steady pattern of clench and release, like a form of meditation. What did he have to work with? The elemental spirits, since it seemed he could commune without fear so long as Sekken was idle or sleeping. Yoichi and the other staff of the embassy.

Isawa Miyuki.

That was his answer, if only he could figure out the right question. Miyuki had seen the pavilion for herself; she would believe him about the baku. But what then? Ryōtora had been thinking in terms of publicly shaming the governor, turning responsibility back onto him. Katahiro, however, was in the Realm of Dreams. A baku was unlikely to care about shame.

Miyuki first, he told himself. Doing anything without help wouldn't get him very far.

But when he told Yoichi his intentions, the clerk immediately frowned. "My lord, you cannot leave the embassy."

"If I go out quietly—"

"Can you be sure the governor – or rather, this baku creature – has not set people to watch? Or that no one will recognize you in the streets? It's possible they are even keeping watch on Lady Isawa's house. Her mother is in custody, and she is known to be connected with Lord Asako Sekken and the rest of his family. They may anticipate that you would go there." Yoichi bowed in apology. "No, my lord. I cannot permit it."

In theory Ryōtora outranked him, as the temporary ambassador. In practice, he knew better than to think that would matter. It was a samurai's obligation to disobey his lord's orders, if it was for his lord's own good.

And Yoichi was right. The Dragon could justifiably resist the governor's demands while inside their own embassy. If Ryōtora were caught outside, though, any resistance would lead to a fight. Then *he* would be at fault for the resulting conflict, not Katahiro – or rather, the baku wearing Katahiro's face.

"A messenger, then," he said, wondering if it would be better to send a written note, or only something verbal. Would the governor's people put his messenger to the question?

Before he could finish weighing that dilemma, someone else solved it for him. One of the guards from the embassy gate entered and announced, "My lord, Lady Isawa Miyuki has arrived."

"Thank the Fortunes," Ryōtora said, and hurried outside.

Miyuki, out in the courtyard, looked like she'd hardly slept any more than he had. Her anxious hand-wringing stopped at the sight of him. "Lord Isao! They're saying

Asako Fumizuki has been arrested. If she's in trouble because she helped me–"

"It isn't your fault," Ryōtora reassured her. "And it isn't arrest – not exactly. The governor is insisting that all samurai who attended the Game of a Hundred Candles come to his palace. He claims it's for our protection, but…"

She sagged in relief. "Then he doesn't know what I did last night?"

"We can hope not," Ryōtora began, and then someone started pounding on the embassy gate, demanding that they open it in the name of the provincial governor.

Miyuki darted out of sight. Ryōtora exchanged glances with Yoichi. "What do I do?" Ryōtora murmured.

"Your decision," Yoichi whispered back. "If they try to force entry, we'll do what we can to block them, but…"

But they might break through. If Ryōtora was in the courtyard when that happened, it would be easy for them to grab him.

He wasn't accustomed to thinking of himself as someone important enough to protect.

He also wasn't accustomed to hiding. "If they take me," he said, "you have to tell Lady Isawa what I've learned. Do you understand?"

Yoichi nodded, and Ryōtora gestured for the guards to open the gate.

No one tried to push through, but the single messenger of earlier now had a quartet of guards at his back. "I apologize for the difficulty I am giving you," Ryōtora said, taking refuge in the stiff phrasings of formal speech, "but my answer remains unchanged. While I am grateful for the concern the lord governor shows for my safety, I have faith in the ability of my people to protect me as much as anyone can."

The messenger brushed this off. "I understand, Lord Isao, and I am not here for you. All others have been brought to the palace, except for you ... and Asako Sekken. It is for him that we have come."

Ryōtora's heart thumped against his ribs. *Just like Lady Asako predicted.* Only it had come even faster than he feared.

"He is not at his family's mansion," the messenger continued, "nor at the Kanjiro Library. His association with you is well known. If you have him here, awake or asleep, the governor requires you to surrender him at once."

I could have avoided this. A hasty wedding ritual, bringing Sekken into the Dragon, would have given Ryōtora the minimal justification necessary to say *Asako Sekken is not here* and call it the truth.

A legalistic solution. That would still have been dishonest, and it would have trampled on Sekken's consent. All to give Ryōtora a flimsy shield against the discomfort of lying.

There was a saying among the Dragon: *If you must drink poison, then lick the cup dry.*

"I would gladly assist if I could," Ryōtora said, "but Lord Asako Sekken is not here. I have not seen him since the day before yesterday."

The messenger scowled. "You are certain?"

"Completely. If you cannot find him, then it is likely he has fallen victim to the curse, and his dreams have taken him somewhere unexpected. Much like Lord Doji Suemaru, perhaps – has he been found yet?"

By the messenger's deepening scowl, the answer was *no*. But he didn't press further. Instead, he announced, "I will leave these guards outside, in case Asako Sekken comes here. If you hear anything of where he may be, the lord governor requires you to inform him at once. *You* may not be his vassal, but Asako is."

"Of course." Ryōtora bowed with deep courtesy, letting the movement hide his face. The guards would not only be there to catch would-be visitors, but to keep Ryōtora and the other Dragon penned in. He wondered if there was any secret way out of the embassy, and cursed the fact that none of his priestly training had included methods of hiding himself from watchful eyes.

Even after the gate closed, he remained where he was, hands clenched tight into fists. Miyuki hurried back out. "If Sekken isn't here, then where–"

Ryōtora said, "Follow me."

"So he *is* here," Miyuki said when the door slid open to reveal Sekken. "But– I thought–"

"That I would not lie?" Ryōtora smiled without humor. "Yes. That is why the messenger believed me."

He expected to feel sick to his stomach. So many years of his life striving to live with perfect virtue, to embody all the ideals of the samurai class to which he'd been elevated. Even his smallest missteps had been cause for self-recrimination, making him feel like he'd failed Sir Keijun.

But virtue was not a game of shogi, to be won by memorizing a set of rules and leveraging them for advantage. It was a map of the mountains, offering guidance on how to reach the peak of right action. The map's holder had to choose what path he took to that destination.

Surrendering a helpless man to an inhuman spirit's control was not the right action. If preventing that required Ryōtora to lie, then so be it.

Miyuki was kind enough not to draw further attention to his behavior. She merely bowed her gratitude, then said, "What now?"

"Now," Ryōtora said, "I tell you what I've learned. Someone in the Phoenix needs to know this – especially if I am taken prisoner."

Sayashi looked displeased to be woken up, but for the discussion that followed, Ryōtora wanted her advice. "If we are going to act," he said, "then it would be best if we do so before tonight. I can't stay awake forever, and there's a chance that if I go to sleep, I'll be caught in the Realm of Dreams myself. A very *high* chance, if the baku can target me specifically."

"How should I know what it can do?" Sayashi muttered, tucking her paws resentfully beneath herself. "If I were it, I would absolutely try to target you."

Miyuki was staring at the enormous cat with an expression that suggested she was torn between wanting to back away to safety, and wanting to stroke Sayashi's plush black fur. "You– you really were the geisha? Teishi?"

Sayashi's whiskers lifted with pride. "I would show you, but I'm injured."

Yoichi set down the tray he was carrying and poured Ryōtora a cup of tea. It was brewed strong enough to shrivel his tongue, but Ryōtora didn't complain; he'd hardly slept the night before, and weariness pressed down on him more with every passing hour. "Forgive me if this is a foolish question," Yoichi said to Sayashi, "but would Lord Isao be able to do something useful from the far side? If the governor – Asako Katahiro, I mean – if he is in the Realm of Dreams, could Lord Isao find him there and persuade him to return to his body?"

"I have no skill at navigating that realm," Ryōtora said. "More likely I'd be trapped in some vision of my own. I might not even realize it *was* a dream."

"An exorcism, then," Miyuki suggested. "Only... I don't know how to conduct one."

Sayashi's golden eyes flicked to Ryōtora, clearly remembering the time he'd tried to banish *her* from the mortal realm. "I do," he told Miyuki, then addressed the bakeneko. "Do you think that would work? There's no ward this time to keep spirits contained, as there was in Seibo Mura."

Grudgingly, she said, "It might. It depends on how strong you are, and how strong the baku is. At the very least you might disrupt its hold on the governor's body. That could weaken it."

And possibly lend credence to accusations that the person in front of them wasn't Asako Katahiro at all. Hope flared briefly in Ryōtora's heart, then he thought it through, and the flame guttered. "Unfortunately, the method I know requires making a prayer strip and then touching it to the target. There's no chance I could get close enough to the governor; his guards would cut me down before I came within arm's reach."

"I could try?" Miyuki sounded less than certain. "I stand a better chance than you would, at least. If he doesn't know that I went to the pavilion, I could try playing for his sympathy. Its sympathy, I mean. Talking up how worried I am about my mother." By the tremor in her voice, that wouldn't be a lie. Finding out about the baku had shaken Miyuki badly.

As plans went, it was thin, but they lacked a better one. "We can work together to make the prayer strip," Ryōtora said. "When you apply it, all you have to do is command the spirit to return to its own realm."

Creating such things was best done in a sacred space, but they had what they needed on the embassy grounds. The gardens in the back included both a tearoom and a small shrine, the two buildings sharing a single fountain for purification. Ryōtora and Miyuki used the dippers there to cleanse their hands and mouths, then went into the shrine to pray and present offerings. Such preparations weren't always necessary – Ryōtora had occasionally been forced to make do with a more slapdash approach – but Sayashi's words about strength had stuck with him. A prayer strip made with proper reverence would be more effective than one thrown together in haste.

And the preparations helped bring the two of them into harmony, too. They'd studiously avoided the topic of their personal lives, the tangle of affection and obligation that made such a snarl of Sekken's future and, by extension, theirs as well. Both of them knew that was a question for later, irrelevant if they couldn't solve their more pressing difficulties first.

Some people would have brought it up anyway. Ryōtora liked that Miyuki hadn't. He liked *her*; she seemed good-hearted and sensible, and he bore her no ill will for accusing the Dragon in the aftermath of her mother falling asleep. He knew firsthand the devastation of seeing a loved one unconscious and unresponsive like that. If Sekken had to marry a woman who could bear children to continue his tsukimono-suji lineage, then Miyuki was a good choice. Ryōtora didn't resent her for that.

He only resented the situation that trapped all three of them, leaving them with no choices that didn't hurt.

But the purifications helped clear his mind of that tension. And if Miyuki harbored any ill feelings toward him, there was no sign of it as he began his invocation. Ryōtora made two wards, one for each of them, though he and Miyuki couldn't precisely work together. The various priestly traditions had different ways of invoking the spirits; her Isawa training would not be the same as what Ryōtora had learned from his Agasha instructors.

She added her prayers to his own, though, and being present as Ryōtora infused the paper wards with the energy of the spirits gave her a better understanding of what they would do. "Place this on his head if you can," Ryōtora said, giving her one of the pair, "or his chest or back. It can potentially work from any contact, but those will be the most powerful."

She accepted it with both hands, formally. "What will you do now?"

"See if there is a way for Yoichi to get you out of the embassy without being seen," Ryōtora said. "After that... I don't know."

But Yoichi came onto the veranda as they crossed the wintry garden, looking pale and tense. "Another messenger?" Ryōtora asked, resigned.

"No," Yoichi said. "The governor himself has come."

The embassy was not built as a castle, with watchtowers and other such features. It had an enclosing wall, though, and while Ryōtora and Miyuki worked on the wards, the embassy staff had built small platforms that allowed their guards to see over that wall, so they wouldn't have to open the gate.

The governor's voice, coming from outside, sounded reasonable rather than angry. "Lord Isao, let us keep this civilized. I have no desire to shout my words through the boards of this gate for all the neighborhood to hear."

Ryōtora doubted many people were loitering nearby to listen. Commoners knew better than to remain when a score of samurai, armed and armored, moved through the streets. "Forgive me, lord governor, but if I step outside the gate, I doubt I will have the opportunity to step back in. If you would be willing to enter, though, I would be happy to receive you and discuss the situation in private."

Would the real Katahiro have laughed like that– a short, amused bark? "Without my guards, I presume? No, Lord Isao, I'm not that much of a fool."

"A compromise, then," Ryōtora said. "Let us both give our word that neither we nor our followers will attack, and then open the gate. You remain outside; I remain inside. We will converse face to face across the threshold."

Yoichi stiffened. What was a baku's promise worth? But

Ryōtora had his prayer strip inside his sleeve. If this gamble gave him the opportunity he needed...

"Very well," the governor said after a long pause. "You have my word."

The gate creaked open. The massed forces of the Dragon embassy stood behind Ryōtora, ready to defend him; the ranks of the Phoenix stood behind their leader, ready to defend *him*.

And the baku stood, posture loose but eyes sharp, smiling at Ryōtora.

It felt like it should have been obvious. The creature didn't carry itself with Katahiro's stiff correctness, didn't have his air of weighing everything for merit and benefit before he spoke. But it seemed aware enough of the governor's situation, his duties, not fumbling in ignorance at unfamiliar things... and truly, what reason should Ryōtora have had to suspect that a spirit had taken Katahiro's place?

He held his ground, not attempting to lunge forward. The distance between them was still too great; someone would put a spear through Ryōtora before he could get anything like close enough. "Lord governor," he said, with a polite bow.

No bow answered him in return. "I know you have Asako Sekken in there, asleep. Hand him over and surrender yourself as well. This is your last opportunity to do so without trouble. If I have to ask again, I will do so with the edge of a sword."

"Then you will start a war," Ryōtora said, his voice steady. "My clan knows I am not responsible for the affliction that has plagued your court."

"If war is the outcome, then so be it."

The smile that accompanied those words was unnerving. It was the same smile the baku had worn when it spoke of mulberries tasting sweeter because they were only available for part of the year. *To a creature like that, this is no different,* Ryōtora thought, chilled to the bone. *War, ripe fruit – they're both just experiences. Ones that taste sweeter because they're real. Because the decisions this creature makes have meaning, here in the mortal realm.*

"But you don't want that," the baku said quietly, gently. "War is so very tiring. You're tired, Lord Isao, aren't you? I know your health is not good. And court has never been your milieu. You aren't supposed to be the ambassador. So many burdens placed on your shoulders. You must dream of laying them down."

The voice was smooth, soothing. Soporific. Despite the tea he'd drunk, Ryōtora's eyelids sagged.

He'd worried about what would happen when he lay down tonight. He'd never considered that the baku might be able to drag him down before then.

"You can rest, Lord Isao. I will keep you safe. I will make things better. Easier. You'll be happy."

Happiness is not the purpose of a samurai's life. But it was so very, very tempting.

A soft weight was settling over him, like a warm blanket in winter. He wanted to close his eyes. Just for a moment. Slip into dreams, like the spirits in the pavilion had offered.

From behind him came a shriek. "My lord, help me!"

It pierced the fog enough to bring Ryōtora around, in time to see Miyuki dart through the ranks of the Dragon. One of the guards tried reflexively to grab her arm, but she'd taken them by surprise; she dragged herself free, ripping the seam of her sleeve. Ryōtora reached out, letting weariness slow him enough to miss. "They've been holding me prisoner," Miyuki wailed as she hurtled through the gate, straight at the governor.

A Phoenix guard stepped up, too late. Ryōtora was the threat, or the Dragon behind him. Not a crying, escaped captive from their own clan. Miyuki flung herself into the governor's arms–

–and slapped her prayer strip directly into his forehead.

"Return from whence you came," Ryōtora mumbled, underneath Miyuki shouting her own command.

The world swam, like it did in his most exhausted moments. A shimmering blue light burst across Ryōtora's vision.

Then his eyes drifted shut. He sagged against the boards of the gate, slid down them to the ground, and gave himself up to sleep.

CHAPTER TWENTY-FIVE

"I'm asleep?" Sekken asked. Then he pressed the heel of his hand to his forehead. "Of course I am. I guess the curse caught me at last."

Hanemi's uncovered eye gleamed with interest. "Curse? Is that how you've been referring to it?"

"What else should we call it?"

Instead of answering, she rose and circled him, like a prospective buyer examining a horse. "You're more alert than most of them. Tell me, Lord Asako, have you practiced lucid dreaming?"

His fruitless attempt to get himself caught – or had it simply borne delayed fruit? – didn't count. "Not really. Why do you ask?"

"Because the others kept drifting back into their pleasant dreams, even when I tried to pull them out. You noticed me here, and you're *continuing* to notice me. It suggests you have some skill."

Sekken remembered the serene, gilded atmosphere of

the palace, and the way he'd managed to forget his doubts en route to the library. Yes, it would have been all too easy to slip back in. But… "No skill involved," he said, ducking his chin. "The truth is that my dreams, however gratifying, are too false for me to believe in."

Not just their health, implausibly restored by the simple expedient of marriage. The real sticking point was Ryōtora as a happy Phoenix courtier. Whatever else might or might not be possible, their future would not look like *that*.

Hanemi didn't press. For Sekken to do so was rude, but he had to ask. Gesturing at the windowless walls, he said, "I somehow doubt this is *your* most pleasant dream, Lady Kaikoga."

She snorted. "No. This is where you get put when you cause too much trouble for the baku responsible for all of this."

Then she eyed him, tilting her head like a bird. "Why did you just laugh?"

"Because sticking me in the library would have been a far better trap than the one I escaped. Here, Sekken! Have an intellectual mystery to chase! Though I suppose it wouldn't want me looking too closely at the situation, would it?" Joking was easier than examining the question of who had crafted that vision of courtly life with Ryōtora: the baku, or Sekken's own heart. "Everyone's been blaming *you* for people falling asleep. It's been one per night since the Game of a Hundred Candles; I appear to be the most recent."

The Moth woman hummed deep in her throat. "One per night, you say? That makes sense."

"Then do share, because I'm still *very* puzzled." Sekken shook out his sleeves and settled onto the floor. For the first time, he noticed that compared to Ryōtora, his clothing was very drab, stained here and there with blots of ink. Had it changed when he came to the library, or had it been like that the whole time? He rather suspected the latter.

Noticing him examining his clothing, Hanemi said, "It's your image of yourself, Lord Asako."

He remembered now, from the reading he'd done the day he and Ryōtora came to the library. An individual's appearance here reflected their inner sense of self and could not generally be changed. *So this is me, in my own head? Dull and stained with ink.* He could hardly deny it. Sekken didn't mind dressing finely – it was fun to peacock every now and then – but left to his own devices, he would just throw on a ratty old kimono and settle down with a book.

Though it was a little embarrassing to be seen that way. One of many hazards in the Realm of Dreams: samurai society expected its members to maintain an outward appearance of serenity and restraint, but here, one's inner feelings were put on display.

Hanemi knelt beside him. "Everything around you – this prison included – has been created by a particular baku, a very powerful one. It managed to snare *me* for a time in a vision of my ideal life."

Sekken wasn't about to ask what that had been. Both out of politeness, and because he was reeling at the thought of anything successfully trapping a Moth dreamwalker. "But you escaped?"

"Partially." Her mouth pinched with annoyance. "I've

been unable to wake myself up. Or, for that matter, to escape the sphere of the baku's control. If I could contact my clan ... we have what you might call holdings here in the Realm of Dreams, akin to our holdings in the mortal realm. A persistent dream structure under our control. The other Moth there would be able to help, if only I could reach them."

She sighed, looking up at the low ceiling of the room. "So then I started trying to rouse the others. When I'd made too much of a nuisance of myself, the baku trapped me here."

The staircase up to the room had vanished. Sekken had the unpleasant feeling that *me* had become *us*. "I suppose that was its fallback, after my mother convinced it not to kill you. Well, I'm awake now – no, wrong word. Aware that I'm dreaming. Can the two of us ... I don't know, attack the baku?" He ignored the part of his mind that immediately questioned what he could attack the creature *with*. Hanemi might be able to dream a sword into existence for him, but Sekken would barely know what to do with it.

Hanemi said dryly, "Even if it were here, I wouldn't recommend that. But it isn't."

"Then where is it?"

"That's the peculiar part. You said people have been falling asleep every night since the Game of a Hundred Candles?" When Sekken nodded, she made that thoughtful, humming sound again. "Sometimes a baku manages to enter the mortal realm. My clan keeps records of such events. Usually it's bad when that happens, because the ones that cross over tend to be of a malevolent sort."

"Eaters of dreams," Sekken said. "Instead of eating

people's nightmares, protecting them in their sleep, those baku eat the good dreams."

Hanemi nodded. "In this instance, though, I don't think the baku has fully made the transition. It's still controlling things here, which suggests it is somehow only *partially* in the mortal realm. And…" She gazed around the room again. "I know this will sound odd, under the circumstances. But I'm not convinced this one is a dream-eater."

Because the visions entrapping people were, from what Sekken had seen, pleasant ones. Chikayū had her tsukimono-suji heir; Shoun and Aimaku were together. Doji Suemaru…

The Crane lord had been knee-deep in mud, harvesting rice. But he'd seemed happy, too.

And they were only sleeping. Not dead.

"Malevolent or not," he said, "this can't go on. There has to be some way to–"

Before he could finish that sentence, the world began to shake.

Sekken had been in earthquakes before. The Great Wall of the North was prone to them; only two years ago, an earthquake had destroyed the shrine in Seibo Mura, beginning the process of freeing the Night Parade. He instinctively braced himself, thinking, *I should get outside* – but how could he do that, when there was no exit from the room?

And it wasn't just the ground shaking. It was *everything*.

The walls. The ceiling. The air itself, vibrating against Sekken's skin. *Sekken* shook, as if the bits that made him up were trying to slide apart.

Hanemi shot to her feet. She alone remained firm, even when nothing around her was. With a calm gesture, she touched the wall – and then it slid aside, as if it had been a door all along.

They were on the sixth floor of a building with only five floors. Yet somehow, outside was something that almost, but not quite, resembled the grounds of the governor's palace.

"It's gone," Hanemi said, her conversational tone at odds with the fierce smile on her face. "Something broke the baku's hold here."

Only after she walked outside could Sekken convince himself to trust that door. He shot through not a moment too soon; the room behind him faded even as he left it. Or maybe it faded *because* he left it. "We can wake up, then?"

"I can." Hanemi pressed her lips together, looking around. "But the rest of you …"

They were all there, the people trapped by the baku. Shiba Tōhachi and Asako Shoun; Mirumoto Kinmoku and Asako Seifū; Chūkan Ujiteru, holding the jade feather netsuke awarded to the top student each year at the Yōbokutei. Doji Suemaru, mud-spattered and starting to look embarrassed. Isawa Chikayū, her brows drawing together in a hard line as she gazed around, taking in the destabilizing world.

The others hadn't all vanished, though – the people born of their dreams, rather than pulled into them. Sodona Aimaku still clung to Shoun's arm, laughing as if the garden around them weren't flickering into a rice paddy one moment, a scholarly teaching hall the next. Katahiro gripped his biwa and shrank back behind his niece Seifū. Ryōtora...

Two Ryōtoras stood a little distance away.

One was the picture of courtly elegance, with brocade on his shoulders and rice powder on his face. The other wore the kind of sturdy cotton kimono found among both rural samurai and the peasants they ruled over... and somehow, incongruously, he was shorter than everyone else, his own double included.

With the baku's hold broken, there was no benevolent confusion for Sekken to hide behind. He knew immediately that the second Ryōtora was the real one, manifesting as he saw himself. Smaller, more easily overshadowed, rather than the personification of the immovable mountains that Sekken knew him to be. The sight made Sekken's heart ache.

But worse was having them side by side. The real Ryōtora stared at the false one, and he undoubtedly knew enough about the Realm of Dreams to understand what its polished appearance meant. That what Sekken wanted wasn't *him*, as he really was.

Two Ryōtoras – but only for an instant. Then the false one vanished as if it had never been.

Yes, that had been a pleasant dream. The sort of life Sekken used to vaguely imagine for himself, when he bothered to think about his future at all. A life he would never have. Not only had his ruined health seen to that, but Sekken himself had changed too much to want it. Idleness and entertainment, court without challenges and the ability to simply go read whenever he became bored. It wasn't enough anymore. He'd tasted more in Seibo Mura, and again this winter. A world where Sekken's actions *meant* something.

So what if his health was damaged, and Ryōtora's along with it? So what if they couldn't hope for a perfect life together, free of the obstacles that roughened their path? They were still *alive*. Sekken would take what they had, flaws and all, and count himself fortunate. Because he still had Ryōtora.

Whose gaze shot to him the moment the false image vanished. Sekken wanted to say something, but his courtly eloquence had deserted him; the newfound determination firing in his veins was too large to capture in words. Maybe he didn't need them: Ryōtora's eyes widened, and then he strode forward through the cluster of people to grip Sekken's arm in one strong, reassuring hand.

And because he was the real Ryōtora – the one who cared about other people first, himself a distant second – he didn't waste time on personal epiphanies that could be discussed later, assuming they all survived. The first words out of his mouth were, "Sekken. There's a baku–"

"I know," Sekken replied, and gestured at Hanemi. "She told me. Did you do something to it?"

Ryōtora staggered as the world swam once again. Through her teeth, Hanemi said, "I'm trying to keep us all together. It's difficult, with this many in one dream space. How the baku managed…"

"We exorcized it," Ryōtora said. "Miyuki and I did. Drove it out of the governor, or tried to."

"Out of the *governor*?" Sekken exclaimed – and then stopped.

Sodona Aimaku was still behaving like Shoun's dream. She gazed at a tree that twitched from flowering cherry to blazing maple to winter-clad pine as if she were about to compose a poem on the rapid shift of seasons. An inugami was frolicking at Chikayū's heels.

But Katahiro was trying to hide behind a niece a handspan shorter than he was. Seifū would never dream such behavior into being, Sekken knew. Nor imagine her uncle giving up his post to practice calligraphy.

Sekken lunged past Seifū and grabbed his provincial governor by the biwa. "What did you do?"

"I–" He'd never seen Katahiro look so off-balance, angry and ashamed all at once. "It wasn't supposed to go like this. And once it did, I- I–"

Katahiro. Who hadn't fallen asleep before Sekken, yet was here all the same.

Ryōtora said, "He's been possessed since the gathering. Lord governor, you must reclaim your body. You have to wake up."

Of course Ryōtora addressed a higher-ranking samurai courteously, even when accusing him of spiritual crimes. Katahiro's jaw clenched, but not in anger. "I can't. I've been trying, ever since I got here."

"We aren't here normally," Hanemi said, her voice thin with the effort of holding the world steady around them. "The barrier between the realms is too strong for any of you to pierce. I can wake up and then work from the other side… but if I do that, you'll all disperse into separate dreams. My clan and I will have to track you down one by one."

Mirumoto Kinmoku stepped up. "We can survive here, I imagine. If that's the only answer–"

"It isn't," Sekken said.

Everyone looked at him; he looked at Katahiro. "You did something at the Game of a Hundred Candles, didn't you?"

Shame-faced, Katahiro said, "It wasn't supposed to happen like this. The baku wanted to experience real life; I promised it would have the chance. I didn't know I would wind up here. Or that it would force others to follow, using your sleep to buy itself more time in the mortal realm."

Confessions like that were embarrassing at the best of times; here, where people's strongest desires were put on display, Sekken wished he hadn't heard it at all. "What I want to know is whether you can do it again."

"Summon the baku?" Ryōtora said, disbelieving.

"Thin the barrier between the realms." Sekken gestured at Hanemi. "She said it's too strong. But Ryōtora, you said it was thin, when you communed with the spirits at the pavilion. If what Katahiro did weakened it…"

Despite the strain she was under, Hanemi managed a laugh. "That will be one for my clan's annals. If you can make it work."

Katahiro straightened, looking more like the dutiful governor Sekken knew. "It relied on the stories you all told, and on the mirror. I- I wrote the character for *dream* on the back, to make sure the gathering called out to the right realm."

Ryōtora said, "So if we all told stories again–"

"But not kaidan," Sekken said, the shape of it solidifying in his mind. "We aren't trying to reach out to a Spirit Realm;

it's the mortal world we want. Write *that* on the mirror…
and tell stories of our ordinary lives."

The breath Hanemi drew and then expelled sounded like a
monk beginning one of the exercises that honed their bodies
and spirits into formidable weapons. And perhaps that wasn't
inapt, for as she pushed her hands forward and then spread
them wide, the shifting world around them solidified.

Into the Komoriyome Pavilion, as it had been when they
left it that night: shrouded in darkness, the screens that
divided the hall barely visible in the gloom. "I can hold
this," Hanemi told them all. "But not forever. Act quickly."

The dream people had vanished, leaving only the sleepers.
There were ten of them now, and Sekken hoped that didn't
mean they'd have to tell ten stories each. But someone had
to start, and since etiquette had flown out the window, he
supposed it might as well be him.

No kaidan. Nothing supernatural in nature. Ordinary
life, as human as he could make it.

"When I was in training at the Yōbokutei," he began, "my
friend Gorō and I used to sneak out of our shared room at
night."

It was a story only a Phoenix could love, about two boys
so determined to impress their teachers that they conducted
illicit late-night study sessions. Another boy, Kumawaka,
had wanted to join them – but Sekken and Gorō didn't
trust him to actually *study*, which led to an escalating war of
Kumawaka trying to rig traps that would wake him up when
they sneaked out, and the other boys thwarting those traps
so they could leave him behind.

Most importantly, it was completely mundane. Nothing

in it of spirits or strange occurrences; only boys whose notion of misbehavior was over-enthusiastic scholarship.

The tale was brief, and when it was done, Sekken passed behind the screen to the room full of lanterns, all sitting cold and dark. At the touch of his hand, the first one bloomed into light.

And there was a mirror on the table. He lifted it, as he had not lifted the mirror the night of the gathering, and found the characters for *human* written on the back. Sekken put it down, smiled ruefully at his reflection, and went back into the main room.

Following his lead, the others all told stories of the people they'd left in the mortal realm. For Chikayū it was Miyuki; for Katahiro, his former master, Asako Harunaga. Ryōtora related how his father had first begun to instruct him in the way of tea, and Sekken hoped his own expression didn't give anything away. That image of a courtly Ryōtora hosting a tea gathering in the garden lingered in his mind, half truth, half embarrassing fancy.

How many tales did they tell? In the manner of dreams, Sekken couldn't be sure. Time hardly seemed to pass, and yet the light grew stronger, more and more lanterns shining from behind the screens. Had he told the others about the time Ginshō tried to convince him, at the tender age of six, to become a warrior like her? Had Ryōtora mentioned the time he became lost in the forest, or was Sekken only remembering that from their days together at Ryōdō Temple?

It didn't matter. What mattered was the light, rising to kiss the gilded ceiling of the Komoriyome Pavilion...

...and the creature standing in their midst.

They hadn't only thinned the barrier between the Realm of Dreams and the mortal world.

They'd summoned the baku to join them.

CHAPTER TWENTY-SIX

Ryōtora shot to his feet – and then stopped.

Half his instincts told him to attack. To invoke the spirits – if he could even do that wherever they were now, Realm of Dreams or mortal world or some halfway point between – and strike at the creature that had hidden among them for days.

The other half hesitated. He'd never seen a baku in the flesh before; they looked every bit as strange as carvings depicted. The legs of its powerful, bear-like body ended in a tiger's claws, and its elephantine snout was flanked by sharp-looking tusks. But Ryōtora had faced countless varieties of yōkai when he fought the Night Parade, and from this one, he felt no aura of malevolence.

The baku's ox tail lashed, but it made no move to attack.

Whatever had led to this situation was a matter for them to address later. Ryōtora suspected Katahiro had a great deal to answer for. But in this moment...

He turned and bowed to the governor, as courteous as if they were in the palace. "My lord. You began this. I believe it is your place – and your duty – to end it."

The weight of that word, *duty*, settled visibly on Katahiro, making the man slump. Then, with a deep breath, he rose to his feet.

The baku stood braced as Katahiro approached. It truly was a peculiar creature, its mismatched components refusing to form an integrated whole. Some said that was because dreams could never truly cohere; there would always be strange discrepancies in them, gaps and odd juxtapositions. Others said it was because the baku was the last thing created by Lady Sun and Lord Moon, pieced together out of remnants left unused in the creation of the world. But not an unloved afterthought: no, they laughed in delight when they saw what they had made.

Katahiro reached out and laid one hand on the ruff of golden fur that covered the baku's withers. "It didn't work, my friend," he said softly. "Not for either of us. This is why we must deny our dreams: because they hurt other people. It is long past time for me to wake up."

Then he glanced over his shoulder at the rest of their group. "For all of us to wake."

Underneath Ryōtora's feet, the boards of the floor solidified, shifting from a dreamlike memory of wood to the substance itself. The warm glow of the lanterns died out, replaced by shreds of sunlight filtering through the shutters lining the walls.

Sekken rose and slid one open, letting brightness and the cold air of winter into the pavilion.

A trace of regret tinged his smile as he turned to face Ryōtora. "It seems we're back."

•••

It didn't take long for the guards to find them.

Then everything was chaos and shouting, half-articulated questions receiving less than complete answers. It might have gone on for quite some time, with the guards following their standing orders to forcibly detain anyone found at the pavilion, if Katahiro had not pulled himself together into the stern, authoritative demeanor of the provincial governor. "There is no need for alarm," he announced. "The threat has passed. Please escort my guests to the palace and see to it that they are given baths, food, drink – any hospitality they require."

Mirumoto Kinmoku's posture stiffened. "Are we not free to return to our own residences, lord governor?"

The authoritative tone softened into something more conciliatory. "It is not my intent to hold you prisoner, Lady Mirumoto. But I would like to speak with you all together, if I may. Once I have dealt with the difficulties caused by my... absence."

She held his gaze unblinking for a moment, then bowed. The Phoenix, of course, had little grounds for resisting their governor's orders, and Kaikoga Hanemi, leaning against a post, looked like she would agree to anything that allowed her to sit down. That left only Doji Suemaru with enough standing to object, and he was too flushed with embarrassment. His gaze carefully fixed on no one at all, he said, "I would be grateful for a bath. And for some fresh clothing."

It was disorienting for Ryōtora to walk across the palace grounds, with no memory of having arrived there. Had his body simply vanished from the embassy gateway, or had it walked off in the chaos resulting from Miyuki driving the baku out of the governor's body? Where was Miyuki now, and Yoichi? Still penned into the embassy by the guards, or here at the palace, demanding answers?

When Ryōtora tried to ask a guard, he got only a polite bow and an offer to take a message to the embassy. Which told him nothing at all.

But it was good to wash and change into a new kimono. It made him feel a little more rested, even though his body was quick to point out the utter falsity of that notion.

He'd tied his hair up out of the way while he scrubbed, but he dragged the ribbon out too hastily, producing a painful tangle. He was trying to extricate it when Sekken said, "Allow me."

Ryōtora went still as Sekken took over. They were both awake now; what would that mean for their health? He couldn't tell whether his current state of weariness owed more to the link between them or to what they'd been through.

But there was something soothing about the other man picking apart the knot the ribbon had formed, then gently combing the snarl from his hair.

"I'm sorry," Sekken murmured. This close, he could speak without anyone overhearing. "What you saw there…"

He'd seen himself – and yet not. A version of himself that he could never be.

He'd also seen that image vanish. Felt Sekken let it go. He wondered whether Sekken himself knew that his appearance had changed in that moment, his drab, ink-stained kimono shifting to the dark green Ryōtora so often favored in his own wardrobe. A color particularly associated with the Dragon Clan.

There was so much they needed to say to each other. "Sekken–"

"The lord governor will see you now," a guard announced, and they had no more time to talk.

For once they were not brought into the formal receiving chamber, with its gold-painted screens and step raising Katahiro above everyone else. Instead, they were in a detached portion of the palace, whose usual purpose Ryōtora didn't know. He suspected its virtue was its separation, away from ears that might overhear.

Rather than sitting cross-legged, Katahiro knelt with his back rigidly upright. He waited until the rest of them had settled onto the cushions provided, then said, "For what you have all suffered, I have no excuse. It was brought about through my own foolishness and weakness, the consequences of which I did not foresee. From my deepest heart, I apologize to you all." And he bent until his head touched the mat.

Silence greeted his words. When Katahiro straightened, he shifted slightly, turning to face where Ryōtora knelt with Kinmoku and Hanemi. "For the Dragon and the Moth, mere apologies cannot be enough. While you refreshed yourselves, I collected a report concerning what was done in my absence. It does no good to say that the one who threatened Lady Kaikoga and the Dragon embassy was the baku, not myself; those actions were taken with my voice, under my authority. Had they been done by one of my retainers, I would bear responsibility. So must it be in this instance."

Kinmoku, Ryōtora, and Hanemi had managed a swift conversation on their way to this meeting. Although Ryōtora had not remotely enjoyed his stint as temporary ambassador, he couldn't dispute Kinmoku's point that of the three of them, he was the only one who knew what had happened over the last few days. Therefore, he was the one most qualified to speak for them on the matter.

Ryōtora let his gaze drift over the small group, thinking of what he'd seen. Although he'd come in only at the end, it was enough to give him a sense of how nakedly these people's private dreams had been exposed. So much of courtesy was built on the foundation of politely ignoring things that should not be seen or heard.

And yet... to pretend none of that was relevant would be to fail to address what Katahiro had done.

"Lord governor," he said. "In your absence, I worked to uncover the cause of this affliction. Am I right in thinking the entire affair began with you reading the collected diaries of Isawa Minokichi?"

Katahiro's face settled into its well-worn lines. That expression could be mistaken for anger, but Ryōtora suspected it was simply a habitual mask. The expression he'd assumed for years on end, as he carried out the duty laid on him by his family and his clan. "Yes," he said. "I... permitted myself to be seduced by his ideas."

"Lady Kaikoga." Ryōtora turned to Hanemi, quiet and unreadable with her silk-covered eye. "You have been studying those diaries. What is your opinion of their contents?"

She took her time in answering. Finally, she said, "They are not hazardous in the way we usually speak of such things. They contain no instructions for attracting the attention of dangerous spirits, and nothing in them is blasphemous against the Heavens. But... they are not without their perils. As we have seen."

As the writer himself had seen. Ryōtora remembered the diaries ending abruptly, the tale that Minokichi had gone into his visions and never come out again. One could not live entirely in dreams.

But neither could one live without them.

Ryōtora said, "It would not be right to make a decision without first consulting Lady Asako Fumizuki, as she is the steward of the Kanjiro Library. I suggest, however, that it would be appropriate for all copies of Minokichi's diaries to be given to the Moth Clan for safekeeping. If the Phoenix wish to study them, they may negotiate with the Moth for access."

The Isawa would scream in outrage, he knew. But he had politely refrained from mentioning that one set of copies was in Katahiro's possession, and he trusted the governor to have noticed that omission. If Katahiro's actions became public knowledge – his involvement with a bakeneko masquerading as a geisha; his retreat from duty into fancy – the Phoenix would suffer significant embarrassment. If they wanted to avoid that, it should come with a cost.

Of which the diaries were only one part. "For the Moth, this is reasonable," Katahiro said. "But what of the Dragon?"

It had been within Ryōtora's reach several times over the last few days, and he'd never quite been able to understand why. In hindsight, he wondered how much the baku had even known about Seibo Mura. Had its interactions with Katahiro included any discussion of the debate? Had it bothered to read whatever documents the governor's clerks had on the matter? Or, reveling in the chance to make real decisions with real consequences, had it simply enjoyed the thought of bestowing victory on the Dragon?

Whatever the answer, Ryōtora's own mission remained unchanged. He drew a deep breath. "For over a year now, Phoenix negotiators have suggested that the Dragon are not capable of adequately protecting the village of Seibo Mura and the dangerous force it holds at bay. Lord governor, my answer is as it has always been: that Dragon wisdom can be trusted as much as that of the Phoenix."

At his side, he heard the barest snort from Kinmoku.

All right, so his wording wasn't the best. It could be read as a back-handed dig at his own clan, dragging them down to Katahiro's own level. But that, in its own way, was politeness, using humility rather than arrogance as a lever.

Katahiro had to have known it was coming, and he did not hesitate to bow in assent. "Lord Isao, before you came to my lands, I heard many tales of you – not only of your deeds in Seibo Mura, but of your own admirable nature. You have shown your quality, and it surpasses everything I have been told. With you as a model, I have no doubt that Seibo Mura is in excellent hands."

That wasn't the end of it, of course. Doji Suemaru also had to be placated, though he was happy to agree to silence about Katahiro's misdeeds in exchange for his own actions remaining unspoken. Ryōtora wondered what farm his sleeping body had shown up at – one all the way off in Crane lands? He pitied the peasants, wherever they were, going to tend their fields and discovering a samurai lord passed out in a paddy. And he wouldn't be surprised if Suemaru resigned his post in the near future to take vows instead. If he sought the simple life, a monastery could offer him that.

Ryōtora let his thoughts drift while Katahiro spoke with the affected Phoenix, knowing he probably ought to pay attention, but also wishing he could lie down. When Katahiro brought the audience to an end, he bowed gratefully, looking forward to retreating to the embassy.

But as he rose, Katahiro spoke. "Lord Isao, would you favor me with a few minutes more of your time?"

Ryōtora didn't need Kinmoku's prompting to know what his answer had to be. "Of course, lord governor."

The two of them stepped outside, going around the back of the building to where it overlooked a small pond. Although it wasn't the enchanted garden with the mulberry tree, Ryōtora couldn't help remembering his conversation with the baku. Would he need to apologize again to Katahiro for his rudeness at the Game of a Hundred Candles, since his first attempt had gone to the wrong listener?

No. "I wished to speak with you about Teishi," Katahiro said.

Ryōtora marshaled his thoughts. "Have you received news of what happened at the embassy? Is she safe?"

"She's at your embassy? I'm not surprised." Katahiro sighed and linked his hands behind his back. "My guards didn't arrest her, if that's what you're asking. Whether she's still there or not, I don't know. Did the baku hurt her?"

"Yes."

A curt nod greeted that news. "Please convey my apologies to her. She said in one of our early conversations that she was interested in learning about human nature, and I fear I have not presented her with a very worthy model."

The visit Ryōtora and Sekken had paid to the House of Infinite Petals felt as if it had taken place back at the dawn of the empire, but a leaf of memory floated to the surface: Sekken, talking about the benefits of having a community at one's side. A thing that Sayashi, having refused reincarnation as a human, did not have.

Ryōtora doubted such a life looked any more appealing to her now.

"You do not wish to tell her yourself, my lord?" he asked.

"I think it would be better if I did not see her again."

Was he attached to Sayashi? At one point Ryōtora had thought so, but when he heard about the experiments with Minokichi's diaries, he assumed that was the sole reason for Katahiro's favor. Now he wasn't so sure.

Which meant Katahiro was right not to associate with her anymore. Such weaknesses, such distractions from duty, were unfitting for a samurai.

"Lord governor... I would like to ask you an impertinent question."

Katahiro's breath huffed out. "Given what you have been through, that's a small boon to grant."

"If you dislike your position as governor so much, why do you remain in it?"

"You mean, why do I not retire?" Katahiro's gaze remained fixed on the pond, as if nothing else existed in all the world. "Regardless of how I feel about my responsibilities, I am *good* at them. I serve my clan well in this role."

Ryōtora hesitated, then pressed further. "But are you the only one who could serve?"

Another soft sound, not quite a laugh. "I am not so arrogant as that. No, there are others. Among my direct kin, though… one of my sons lacks the necessary patience. The other lacks the wit. My niece would be ideal, but the dissolution of her marriage offended the Isawa, and a governor with the enmity of that family will find this job very difficult." A grimace tightened the corner of his mouth. "As I will no doubt experience again in the near future. I was hoping I could resolve that issue for her, then pass the governorship into her hands. Otherwise, there is too high a risk that our clan will appoint someone else entirely to the position, and my lineage will lose its status."

Ryōtora hadn't expected such a candid unfolding of internal Phoenix politics, nor of Katahiro's mind. It wasn't just a matter of duty to the clan, but also to his province and his kin, their particular lineage within the broader Asako family. Multiple causes to be served, and they all pressed in the same direction: Katahiro as governor, regardless of his own wishes.

"A little while ago," Ryōtora said, "you praised me for an admirable nature. But I think you, my lord, embody the spirit we are all meant to aspire to, far better than I ever will."

Bit by bit, the discipline of years had reasserted itself. Katahiro showed no flicker of emotion at his words. "That has the sound of both a compliment and a curse," he said. "I hope for your sake, Lord Isao, that there is never cause in your life to mimic my achievement."

Then, before Ryōtora could find a response to that, Katahiro turned back toward the palace. "I will have my clerks draw up the formal agreement regarding Seibo Mura. You may return to your embassy; I will have it delivered to you there."

CHAPTER TWENTY-SEVEN

Their journey to the Realm of Dreams had not miraculously fixed anything.

Political problems, yes. Katahiro, Isawa Chikayū, and Mirumoto Kinmoku signed the Seibo Mura agreement in a public ceremony at the palace; it would go to the imperial court for approval, and that matter would be laid to rest at last. Spiritual problems, too: the baku was gone, everyone was awake, and both Miyuki and Ryōtora had been invited to participate in the ceremony that ensured the metaphysical fabric of the Komoriyome Pavilion was properly restored.

Sekken didn't attend. Not because he wasn't a priest, but because he suspected what would happen when Ryōtora invoked the spirits. And he was right.

In the dream, it had been so easy. Marry Ryōtora, and all became well. No more weakness. No more draining each other by doing too much. Sekken felt like he should have known he'd left reality behind the moment Ryōtora said that would solve everything. If it were performed in the theater, he'd have laughed the actors off the stage.

Ironically, it was in dreams that he'd found the real

answer. Stop hoping for perfection and mourning that it was out of reach. Potters had made an entire art form out of mending broken cups and bowls with gold- or silver-dusted lacquer; the resulting beauty was all the greater for having been marred. Sekken's life had been broken: so be it. What could he make from the shards?

Retiring to a monastery wouldn't be so bad. He was living like a monk anyway; he might as well do it in more suitable surroundings. He could devote himself to strengthening Ryōtora through his meditation, and meanwhile, they wouldn't be the first lovers to keep their relationship alive through letters. Or Ryōtora might retire alongside him, and then they could spend their remaining days in quiet study and contemplation. Sekken would rise early in the morning; Ryōtora could work late into the night, as his nature preferred. Like the sun and the moon, they would share the sky.

Or look for a way to sever the bond between them. Sir Naotsugu had said he didn't know for sure how that would work, or what the effects might be. There was no certainty that it would mean Sekken and Ryōtora had to part forever. Even if it did, they might both choose that, to save each other from their current pain.

Or something else. Medical treatments performed together, like they'd done in Ryōdō Temple; maybe that would be more effective. Some complex system of scheduling that let each of them know when to expect strength or weakness. A journey into one of the Spirit Realms, to beg for aid from some powerful servant of Heaven. All of these were possible.

The most important thing was that they do it together, in whatever form that might take. Their greatest problem wasn't the aftereffects of Seibo Mura; it was the fact that they'd each been trying to address those effects alone.

Sekken took his medicine, and meditated, and waited until the courtly furor subsided enough for him and Ryōtora to speak.

Before that moment arrived, though, a visitor came to his family's mansion. A young woman he didn't recognize – not until she gave him a look that somehow managed to imply ears flattening and whiskers twitching back. "Has your mind decayed that much?"

"Sayashi," Sekken said, standing at the base of the step to the front courtyard. "You look very different."

It was still the same face she'd worn as Teishi, but scrubbed of its cosmetics, her hair in a simple plait down her back. Her clothing was good but plain, a quilted cotton kimono shibori-dyed indigo with little roundels of white. A bundle rested on the flagstones next to her, small enough to be carried on her back. Eyeing it, Sekken said, "Are you going somewhere?"

"So your brain hasn't *completely* rotted away. Yes, I'm leaving."

"For where?"

Her shrug was still feline, lithe and uncaring. "Who knows? Anywhere that catches my interest. Crane lands, perhaps."

Peasants weren't allowed to roam at will; they needed travel papers. Sekken didn't bother asking how she intended to deal with that. "Not back to the Enchanted Country?"

"Pffft. I said somewhere that catches my interest."

Just in time, he bit back a pointed query about her experience of the mortal world thus far. It was a good sign that Sayashi wanted to wander; it meant she found human society worth paying attention to. Possibly for the purpose of trickery, but he didn't think so. If that were her intent, she would taunt him with it.

"I wish you luck and safe travels," he said. "And – if you don't find it too troublesome – write to me from time to time. I would love to hear about your experiences."

To his surprise, Sayashi said, "I can probably manage that. Some of the time, anyway."

Then she surprised him even further by stepping forward and putting her arms around him. "Marry that man," she whispered in his ear. "Keep the wolves from each other's heels."

It was the image she'd used before, describing Ryōtora's need to prove himself worthy of being a samurai. But this was the first time she'd spoken of Sekken having a wolf, too. *I suppose everyone has one,* he thought. *Or more than one.*

Sayashi didn't bother with farewells. She merely released him, shouldered her burden, and went out the gate, heading down the street without so much as a backward glance.

He was still there, standing in the courtyard, when Miyuki arrived. "Forgive me," Miyuki said, hesitating. "If you were about to go out…"

"I wasn't." Even though she knew about his weakness, Sekken still made an effort to pull himself together, for his own sense of dignity. "Come in. You can have tea, and I can have whatever's been prescribed for me today."

Tanshu had waited inside, which in hindsight should have been a clue to Sekken that his peasant visitor was a bakeneko in disguise. Now the inugami fell in alongside them as they went to a room overlooking the garden. The day was warm enough that one of the doors could be opened to give a view outside. A servant brought tea, Sekken's medicine, and a large cushion; Tanshu manifested and flopped on the latter, which protected the tatami against his claws.

This wasn't Miyuki's first visit to Sekken since he woke, but he could tell something was different this time. She held herself more formally, as if they were at court instead of at leisure in his house. He had enough Earth today to hold his tongue and sip his medicine, waiting for her to speak.

Finally, she said, "I come to offer you two gifts. One is from the governor; he would like to reward both you and Lord Isao for your efforts. But since it would place undue hardship on you to ask you to appear at court, he agreed to let me present it to you."

Sekken turned so he faced her rather than the garden and bowed as if to the governor. "I am humbled to receive it."

"In his personal library," Miyuki said, "he has the original scrolls of Asako Miaya's *Meditations on Unity*, written in her own hand. As she is your ancestor, he believes your family would be more fitting guardians for her work."

Enough Earth to sit in patience, not enough to hold back his instinctive response. "Is he giving away his *entire* library?"

Miyuki was kind enough not to point out that this wasn't the proper response to a gift. Sad-eyed, she said, "I think he may be. Though much of it is going to the Isawa, as reparations for the offenses he has given them."

Handing over all copies of Minokichi's diaries, and Seibo Mura to boot. Plus the old business with his niece. But Sekken was Phoenix enough, Asako enough, to feel the pain of surrendering one's library. "I shouldn't accept."

"If you don't take the *Meditations*, the Isawa will."

"Then I am grateful to the lord governor for his generosity." Sekken bowed again.

Miyuki had spoken of two gifts. Whatever the second was, it made her hesitate, formal grace stiffening into awkwardness. "My family would also like to thank you. After all, you and Lord Isao saved my mother; without you, she might still be in the baku's trap. But at the same time, we both know there's something my mother wants *from* you."

A tsukimono-suji heir. And now Miyuki knew the truth of his condition; Sekken couldn't hide behind that anymore. Like that condition, marriage was part of what he had to accept, as he journeyed in search of happiness with Ryōtora. It didn't have to be bad. "I am still willing, if you are."

"Yes," Miyuki said, "but no."

When he looked at her, confused, he found her cheeks reddening beneath the rice powder. She said, "I told my mother the greatest gift she could give you would be to set you free. You can have a child to inherit your lineage… without marrying the mother."

Sekken's mind was a little slow today. It took him several heartbeats to realize what she meant.

It wasn't unheard of. When like married like, some

adopted heirs, while others made discreet arrangements to bear or sire children with outside partners. Sometimes that meant an ongoing relationship, and sometimes it was purely a pragmatic trade.

"I wouldn't ask for much from you," Miyuki went on in a rush, as if embarrassment was pushing the words out of her mouth. "As I told you before, I like children. Or you could raise them, if you prefer. We'd have to see which ones, if any, inherit Tanshu, or bond with another inugami. But… I can't take you away from Lord Isao."

Her words staggered to a halt. Sekken had no words at all. An heir was only part of the reason to get married; there were others, like *who will support you if you're too unwell to serve your lord.* But marriage wasn't the only answer to that question. His family had cared for him this long. Or there was always the monastery option. Or a journey into the Spirit Realms. Or…

The day was a little overcast, and the clouds didn't actually part to let the sun through. It only felt like that as Sekken bowed and said, "I hope I may someday repay your gift five-fold, Lady Isawa."

Her smile held its own light. "Miyuki, please. I think we're past formality – don't you?"

Her words stayed with Sekken all that day. When he rose the next morning, there was a message from the Dragon, inviting Sekken to the embassy for a tea event.

The use of the word *event* instead of *gathering* meant this would be a full performance, the sort of thing that went on for hours, with a meal and different kinds of tea. Sekken thought reflexively about declining, unsure if his endurance would hold out. Or if it did, if that meant *Ryōtora's* would fail – for it was Ryōtora who had issued the invitation.

But those considerations would hardly have escaped the other man's attention. And truth be told, Sekken wanted to see him perform a tea ceremony.

He wanted to know whether it looked anything like his dream.

He arrived at the Dragon embassy at noon, on a bright day that pretended there would never be more snow or freezing rain. It wasn't yet spring, though, so instead of conducting the ceremony out in the fresh air, they would be in the small tearoom set amid the embassy gardens.

For an event like this, there were many formalities to follow. First Sekken went to the preparation room, where he changed into fresh tabi, drank hot barley tea, and studied the scroll in the alcove, depicting a famous mountain view from Dragon lands. Then he went outside to the garden, where he waited on a bench for his host to appear.

Ryōtora wasn't in the spring-themed lavender kimono of Sekken's dream, brocaded with a willow-branch pattern. His clothing was dark green, marked with a tiny pattern of white dots. *Less fashionable but more Ryōtora,* Sekken thought with a rueful smile.

Etiquette dictated they not speak yet. After bowing silently, Ryōtora gestured Sekken toward the fountain where he could purify himself. The water chilled his hands, making them stiff against the mat as he entered the tearoom, crawling through the low door.

With only a single guest, there was no need to wait.

Sekken took a moment to study the calligraphy scroll in the alcove, then shut the door loudly enough to signal that he was ready. Ryōtora entered from the back room and welcomed him.

Sekken nodded at the scroll. *"Different bodies, same heart.* Ordinarily that expresses a wish for harmony at court… but for us, it has a different meaning, does it not?"

"Indeed it does," Ryōtora said, his voice quiet but resonant.

There was so much more they could say about that – but not yet. Only certain topics were acceptable at this stage of the event. Sekken asked, "Who did the calligraphy?"

The conversation proceeded along ritualized lines, and then Ryōtora kindled a fire in the sunken hearth set into a cut-out corner of the central mat. The meal he laid out consisted of seven tiny, exquisite courses; afterward, Sekken left the tearoom to give him opportunity to re-set the scene. When Sekken returned, the shutters were open and the scroll had been replaced by an arrangement of a single curled bamboo stalk, and Ryōtora was ready to serve him tea.

Sekken recognized the bowl waiting on the mat. He'd seen it at the palace, when he was a guest for a tea event hosted by Katahiro. For him, the governor's gratitude had been expressed through the writings of his ancestor; for Ryōtora it was a prized tea bowl, handed down for generations through an Asako lineage.

A tea bowl once broken, now mended with delicate threads of golden lacquer.

The formality of this event, so deeply ingrained in

Sekken's bones, kept him from saying anything as Ryōtora began to work. The other man was not a master, but still, there was something beautiful in the single-minded focus with which he performed the gestures. The way of tea was not about flashy displays of dexterity; instead, one sought simplicity and harmony, living with pure intent in the moment. Ryōtora's style was not far different from the Five Elements school of tea Sekken and his family had all studied, drawing attention to the presence of each of those elements in the ceremony: Earth in the powdered green tea, Fire in the hearth, Water in the pot set above the coals, Air in the fan with which he encouraged the coals and in his steady breathing as he worked.

And Void. Philosophers said the way of tea allowed its celebrants to commune with the Void, the element that lacked any direct manifestation. It could only be felt through absence, through openness. Participating in this ritual dissolved the illusion of the separateness of things.

Different bodies, same heart.

Ryōtora finished whisking the thick tea, then offered the bowl to Sekken.

He rotated it in his hands, looking at the shining gold lines of its repair. Breakage was not the end of the bowl's use or its beauty; that became merely one part of its history. And this one's history was, so far as Sekken knew, unique.

Did Katahiro know what had happened to him and Ryōtora? Sekken couldn't remember what he'd said in that blissful dream; like a real dream, its details had faded from his mind. Or perhaps someone had told him afterward. The specifics didn't matter. Either way, Katahiro's gifts were not merely expressions of gratitude. They were messages, to him and Ryōtora alike.

Sekken lifted the bowl to his mouth, and he drank.

And something inside him shifted.

Not the unsteadiness he'd felt before. This was the shards of himself, of Ryōtora, coming together, fitting against one another like they'd always been made for that role.

Two bodies, sharing a single heart. This was the truth: at an elemental level, they were one.

After he learned the nature of his condition, Sekken had despaired, thinking that any pleasure in his life must come at the cost of pain in Ryōtora's. But that inevitability was an illusion. They could be balanced. They could be whole. As they were, here, in this moment.

For the first time in longer than he could recall, Sekken felt utterly at peace.

He set the bowl down for Ryōtora to take and rinse. At this stage it was permitted to compliment the tea and the utensils; instead, Sekken ventured a question. "Did the lord governor tell you the history of that bowl?"

Ryōtora did not comment on this diversion from etiquette. "He said it was originally made by Shiba Gen'an and gifted to his own grandmother out of respect for her learning."

"But not how it was made?" When Ryōtora shook his head, Sekken nodded at the bowl, whose colors shaded subtly from fragment to fragment. "That one is formed from *two* bowls, each broken so perfectly alike that their pieces could be joined together. There are various tales as to why Gen'an crafted it that way; some say the two originals breaking so precisely was an omen from the Heavens themselves, while others claim it was merely a drunken bet as to whether Gen'an could pull off such a feat." Either way, the result was a work of art, carrying with it all the history of both bowls.

The sunlight coming through the paper screen washed Ryōtora in a gentle glow. He drew in a breath, like a man rousing from deep and tranquil meditation. "When I saw the governor's gift, repaired in that fashion… I no longer see my own life as I did before. Both of our lives." He lifted his eyes, and Sekken saw his own inner peace reflected there. "The way of tea is meant to bring participants into harmony with each other. I hoped we might achieve that, but my hopes rose no higher than simple peace of mind. When you drank, though, I felt…"

He trailed off, trying to put into words what could not be said. Sekken found himself smiling. "Yes."

This serenity they shared now would inevitably prove fleeting. The peace brought by the way of tea was an ephemeral thing; one could strive to maintain it in one's ordinary life, but in time it would fade.

What faded could be renewed, though. They could bring themselves to wholeness, find this balance between them, again and again. For the rest of their lives, if need be.

So many things Sekken had done in pursuit of healing felt like a burden. This time, the prospect was an unalloyed delight.

Ryōtora shifted away from the hearth and bowed. Not out of formality, Sekken thought, but because for Ryōtora, courtesy was sometimes the truest expression of his feelings. "While you were asleep," he said, "your lady mother suggested marrying you into the Dragon, as a way of protecting you against the governor. I refused because it was not fair of me to make any such decision without you. But now – if you are willing – I would ask…"

In violation of all etiquette, tea-related and otherwise, Sekken reached across and lifted Ryōtora from his bow. With loving amusement, he nodded at the little hearth, the implements set in their precise places, the ritual not yet complete. "While I'm sure a proposal of marriage is far from the most improper thing that's ever happened in a tearoom, it would be a shame to leave your performance unfinished. We'll make a scandal of ourselves in the garden afterward. For now, Ryōtora, let us enjoy tea together."

ACKNOWLEDGMENTS

Two historical tidbits, and some gratitude!

The first tidbit is that "Asahina Jiyun" is my nod toward the Qing Dynasty Chinese writer Ji Yun. *The Shadow Book of Ji Yun*, edited and translated by Yi Izzy Yu and John Yu Branscum, inspired two of the stories told during the Game of a Hundred Candles, the one about the scroll and the one referred to here as "Youth and Age." The rest are drawn from the Japanese works collected by Lafcadio Hearn, except for the kobukaiba, which is a Rokugan-specific yōkai I invented for my *Legend of the Five Rings* novella *The Eternal Knot*.

The second tidbit comes from quite another part of the world: Sekken's tale of sneaking out at night with another boy to study, complete with having to thwart a boy who wanted to join them but was deemed insufficiently serious, came directly from the life of Charles Babbage, designer of what would have been a nineteenth-century computer if he'd ever managed to build it. (Unlike Babbage, however,

Sekken was never driven by the spirit of scientific inquiry to attempt to summon his setting's equivalent of Satan. This is probably for the best.)

As for gratitude, the poem Sekken and Ryōtora quote at each other in the dream is originally by the ninth-century priest Sosei; the translation is from Larry Hammer's collection *Ice Melts in the Wind*, used with permission. I am also grateful to Effie Seiberg and various other friends (names redacted to protect medical privacy) for discussing with me their experiences of the neuro-immune condition variously called "chronic fatigue syndrome," "myalgic encephalomyelitis," or "ME/CFS." I want to be very clear: what Sekken and Ryōtora suffer from is not meant to be a representation of this real-world condition. Theirs is a fictional ailment, embedded in the metaphysics of their world rather than the biology of ours. It was, however, very instructive to listen to the thoughts of those who deal with a similar disability every day. I also owe a broad debt to all the disability activists who have worked hard to communicate with the public about matters like the problem with "cure narratives," leading me to imagine what treatment and management for my characters might look like instead.

Finally, I would like to thank everyone without whom this novel would not be in your hands! At Aconyte Books that includes my editor, Charlotte Llewelyn-Wells; my copyeditor, Claire Rushbrook, and my proofreaders, Amanda Rutter and Andrew Cesario; Nick Tyler and Jack Doddy in production; Anjuli Smith and Joe Riley in marketing; and over at Fantasy Flight Games, Katrina

Ostrander for keeping me on the straight and narrow of L5R canon. And thanks as always to my indefatigable agent Eddie Schneider, my wonderfully supportive husband Kyle Niedzwiecki, and my sister Adrienne Lipoma, who saw to the care and feeding of authorial enthusiasm by reading chapters as I finished them.

ABOUT THE AUTHOR

MARIE BRENNAN is a former anthropologist and folklorist who shamelessly pillages her academic fields for inspiration. She recently misapplied her professors' hard work to *The Night Parade of 100 Demons* and the short novel *Driftwood*. She is the author of the Hugo Award-nominated Victorian adventure series The Memoirs of Lady Trent along with several other series, over seventy short stories, and the New Worlds series of worldbuilding guides; as half of M A Carrick, she has written the epic Rook and Rose trilogy, beginning with *The Mask of Mirrors*.

swantower.com
twitter.com/swan_tower

Adventures in Rokugan™

EXPERIENCE THRILLING ADVENTURES IN ROKUGAN LIKE NEVER BEFORE!

Adventures in Rokugan brings the famous setting of *Legend of the Five Rings* to the ever-popular ruleset of the 5th Edition SRD.

Alongside a new focus on vanquishing monsters, undertaking quests, and fighting for love or survival, *Adventures in Rokugan* promises to provide something for all fans of Rokugan.

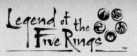

Legend of the Five Rings™

Brave warriors defend the empire from demonic threats, while battle and political intrigue divide the Great Clans.

Curse of Honor — DAVID ANNANDALE

the Night Parade of 100 Demons — MARIE BRENNAN

to Chart the Clouds — EVAN DICKEN

Follow dilettante detective, Daidoji Shin as he solves murders and mysteries amid the machinations of the Clans.

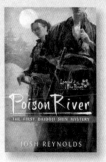

Poison River — THE FIRST DAIDOJI SHIN MYSTERY — JOSH REYNOLDS

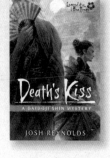

Death's Kiss — A DAIDOJI SHIN MYSTERY — JOSH REYNOLDS

The Flower Path — A DAIDOJI SHIN MYSTERY — JOSH REYNOLDS

The Great Clan novellas of Rokugan return, collected in omnibus editions for the first time, with brand new tales of the Lion and Crane Clans.

LEGEND OF THE FIVE RINGS

The realm of Rokugan is a land of samurai, courtiers, and mystics, dragons, magic, and divine beings – a world where honor is stronger than steel.

The Seven Great Clans have defended and served the Emperor of the Emerald Empire for a thousand years, in battle and at the imperial court. While conflict and political intrigue divide the clans, the true threat awaits in the darkness of the Shadowlands, behind the vast Kaiu Wall. There, in the twisted wastelands, an evil corruption endlessly seeks the downfall of the empire.

The rules of Rokugani society are strict. Uphold your honor, lest you lose everything in pursuit of glory.

ALSO AVAILABLE IN LEGEND OF THE FIVE RINGS

Curse of Honor by David Annandale
The Night Parade of 100 Demons by Marie Brennan
To Chart the Clouds by Evan Dicken
The Heart of Iuchiban by Evan Dicken

THE DAIDOJI SHIN MYSTERIES
Poison River by Josh Reynolds
Death's Kiss by Josh Reynolds
The Flower Path by Josh Reynolds

THE GREAT CLANS OF ROKUGAN
The Collected Novellas Vol 1
The Collected Novellas Vol 2